HELLFIRE PASS

LOOK FOR THESE EXCITING WESTERN SERIES FROM BESTSELLING AUTHORS WILLIAM W. JOHNSTONE AND J.A. JOHNSTONE

The Mountain Man

Luke Jensen: Bounty Hunter

Brannigan's Land

The Jensen Brand

Smoke Jensen: The Early Years

Preacher and MacCallister

Fort Misery

The Fighting O'Neils

Perley Gates

MacCoole and Boone

Guns of the Vigilantes

Shotgun Johnny

The Chuckwagon Trail

The Jackals

The Slash and Pecos Westerns

The Texas Moonshiners

Stoneface Finnegan Westerns

Ben Savage: Saloon Ranger

The Buck Trammel Westerns

The Death and Texas Westerns

The Hunter Buchanon Westerns

Will Tanner, Deputy US Marshal

Old Cowboys Never Die

Go West, Young Man

HELLFIRE PASS

WILLIAM W. JOHNSTONE
AND J.A. JOHNSTONE

PINNACLE BOOKS
Kensington Publishing Corporation
www.kensingtonbooks.com

PINNACLE BOOKS are published by

Kensington Publishing Corp.
900 Third Avenue
New York, NY 10022

PUBLISHER'S NOTE: Following the death of William J. Johnstone, the Johnstone family is working with a carefully selected writer to organize and complete Mr. Johnstone's outlines and many unfinished manuscripts to create additional novels in all of his series like The Last Gunfighter Mountain Man, and Eagles, among others. This novel was inspired by Mr. Johnstone's superb storytelling.

First Pinnacle Books mass market printing: June 2024

ISBN-13: 978-0-7860-5054-3

10 9 8 7 6 5 4 3 2 1

Printed in the United States of America

Chapter One

The first gunshot caused Marshal Shadrach Nelson to open an eye. The second convinced him to drop his feet off his desk. The third, fourth, and fifth brought him to his feet and reaching for the scattergun in the rack by the jailhouse office door.

"Early, Shannon!" He bellowed for his deputies. "Get over to Gold Dust City."

From the rear of the jailhouse came the sound of boots scrapping along the rough wooden plank floor. The bleary-eyed deputies pushed out from the cells where they had been sleeping.

"I'm comin' to hate Saturday night," Leroy Early said. He rubbed his bloodshot gray eyes, then yawned. He stretched mightily. Joints cracked almost as loud as the distant gunshots. He stood close to six-feet tall and still was two inches shorter than the rangy marshal.

"You used to like it," his partner, Ian Shannon said. He strapped on his gun belt and settled the weights on his hips. Two six-guns rested securely, one on either side in well-oiled hard leather holsters. Without breaking stride, he tied both holsters down to his legs as he left the jail.

"That was back when I was young and foolish."

"And not my deputy," Shad said. He broke open the shotgun and checked the load. He was ready for bear. And from the continued volleys of gunfire, he'd need both the scattergun and the Peacemaker hanging low on his right side.

With a shrug of his broad shoulders, he settled the bowler on his head, smoothed wrinkles in his coat, and took a quick swipe over the badge to be sure it was shiny. Sometimes, though not often enough, trouble evaporated when the malcontents and potential criminals spotted that badge. With shoulder-length blond hair, shot through now with increasing gray strands as the years slipped by, he put on his best "I'm marshal and you're gonna do what I say" expression. That worked more often than facing down someone awed by the sight of his badge.

The trio left the jailhouse and fell into unconscious step to the center of the crazy main street meandering through the middle of Utopia. Most streets were straight and truc. Arguments over the years raged whether the surveyor laying out Utopia had been drunk, one-eyed, or just plain blind. Shad was of the opinion the man got even with the town for not paying him for his work. Considering how hard it often was to get his own pay from the town treasurer, and that for his deputies, this carried the most verity.

The town had popped up as a railroad construction camp and had grown like a weed in the years following. When coal was discovered on the southern side of Hellfire Pass, there'd been a surge in population. The lead deposits to the north brought new citizens and new trouble.

The Gallagher family owned the Calcutta coal mine and jealously protected their property. The Morrisey clan was even more cantankerous and possessive of the lead mine, the roads on the north side of the pass and a noxious smelter that sent plumes of choking smoke down the west side of the pass.

Shad had tried to find what caused the blood feud between the two families, but nobody'd give him a straight answer. Mostly, the worst of each tribe avoided coming to town on the same night. The Gallaghers claimed Saturday for their night to whoop it up. The Morriseys made do with Friday, in spite of having to return to their property and hack out galena at their mountain mine all day Saturday.

There might have been trouble on Sundays if either side had been of a religious bent. Shad thanked his lucky stars that neither was since there were only two churches in town. It was bad enough that there were twelve saloons where the feuding families could run afoul of each other. Having Sunday go to meeting gunfights would have been intolerable.

"It's gettin' worse, Shad," Early said. The deputy cocked his head to one side. "That's more 'n two of 'em."

"I'm hearing at least three shooters," Shannon said. The dour deputy's flat tone might as well have pointed out the sun would rise in a few hours. He always saw the dark side of any matter. While his flame-red hair hinted at volatile Irish emotions, Shannon seldom showed more reaction to the vilest of crimes with more than a raised eyebrow and a sardonic comment.

Stopping in the street outside the Gold Dust City Saloon and Gambling Emporium, Shad looked at his deputies and then took a deep breath to settle his hammering heart.

"What do you want to do?" Early ran his hand up and down his thigh. His hand came to rest on the side of his holster, fingers tapping on the butt of his Smith & Wesson.

The marshal glanced over at Shannon. The redheaded Irishman looked as cool as if the raucous insults and steady gunfire from inside the Gold Dust were nothing more than wind through the pines. He wished Shannon was more keyed up, like Early. This wasn't going to be a cakewalk. In his gut, this felt like a fuse running to a keg of Giant Blasting Powder had been lit.

"Ian, go around back and cover the alley." He took in Early's nervous movements. "You stay out here and watch my back, Leroy."

Shannon silently went down the alley between the saloon and a gunsmithy. When he vanished, Shad made his play. With more confidence than he felt, he stepped up to the swinging doors and peered over them into the smoky interior. Oil lamps swung from ceiling chain holders every ten feet around the perimeter. The black fumes from the untrimmed wicks mingled with heavy cigar smoke.

And gunsmoke.

Through the choking fog, he scanned the scene out of Dante's *Inferno*. The faro table had been overturned. The saloon girl who ran thc tablc huddled down behind it, thin arms hugging herself tightly. The bartender was nowhere to be seen. That wasn't good. Shad knew Ralph Rockwell. He wasn't a man to avoid a fight, either with his bare knuckles or the room sweeper of a sawed-off shotgun he kept behind the bar. The waitresses had all lit a shuck. Shad didn't blame them one bit. If he had a lick of sense, he'd turn around and leave.

There wasn't much to be proved by interrupting the exchange of lead at the back of the saloon. Let the gunplay peter out. Men would be bleeding all over the sawdust-strewn floor, and maybe one or two would be dead, but this fight wasn't worth risking his life.

A bullet sang in his direction. He jerked a tad in reaction. Dust fell from the brim of the bowler. He glanced up at the brim and saw light coming through a hole that hadn't been there a second earlier. Death had come hunting for him and lost the scent.

"Awright, drop those smoke wagons!" His bull-throated order rumbled through the saloon. For a brief instant, he thought he'd cowed the gunmen. Then he found himself the target from at least three pistols.

With a quick move, he spun through the swinging doors. They flopped back and forth behind him. If luck finally rode with him, the movement would draw fire away from him—and his bowler.

Splinters exploded from the doors and gave him time to drop to the floor behind the faro table.

"Marshal Nelson," the girl said, her voice quavering. "You surely did take your time gettin' here."

"Missy, the jail's at the edge of town for a reason. Now tell me what's happening."

"They're shootin' up the place!" The pale, thin brunette's voice rose to a shrill screech.

"I got that," he said. "Who's doing the shooting? Gallagher? Morrisey?"

"Them knuckleheads? Naw, this is Billy Dixon and those two jackasses with him. They got liquored up over at the Drunk Dutchman's, then came in here." Missy's voice caught. "Th-they marched right in, arrogant as you please, demandin' that Ralph give 'em free drinks. He laughed at 'em, and they cut him down, just like that." She tried to snap her fingers and failed.

"They shot him?"

"They done kilt him!" Her voice screeched.

Shad understood her outrage. She and the barkeep had been sharing a room in the back for as long as he could remember.

"You keep low," Shad said. He'd been afraid someone would get put six feet under when he heard all the gunfire.

Of all the miscreants in Utopia, Ralph Rockwell was not one he'd ever wish that on. Ralph snuffed out trouble in the Gold Dust often enough that Shad could concentrate on other gin mills.

He duck walked to the end of the table and peered around. Billy Dixon crouched by the pool table. Shattered ivory balls littered the green-felt-covered table and the floor around.

"That you, Nelson?" Dixon thrust out his six-gun, waiting for Shad to show himself. "Come on over. Me and the boys was playin' a little bullet pool."

That explained the debris. Rather than using pool cues, Dixon and his gang had shot at the pool balls to drop them in the pockets. That explained a lot of the gunfire.

"Dixon, toss that piece out and stand up. Hands high. And the two with you? Herk and Squinty? All of you come on out, and I promise not to fill you full of holes like you did Ralph Rockwell."

"You mean the barkeep? He refused to serve us. Flat out insulted me. Herk, too. No self respectin' hombre's gonna put up with that. He should treat his customers better."

Shad drew a bead on Dixon. He relaxed the pressure on the trigger when Dixon ducked back around the pool table. Trying to figure out where Dixon's partners hid proved a puzzler. If he guessed wrong, he was a goner. Dixon and the other two were left over from the gangs that once used Utopia as a hideout. Some of the worst desperadoes in Colorado had made this their base of operations. No matter which side of the Rockies they robbed and killed, Utopia had proved a handy hideout. If the law came too hard after the outlaws, they'd keep on riding down the other side and disappear in Denver or Georgetown.

It had taken him close to two years to drive most of the worst out—the ones he didn't kill. But every now and then some of the outlaws that'd fled returned like bad pennies.

When Dixon had blown back into town, he'd hunted for a wanted poster with the man's scarred countenance on it. A hard case like Billy Dixon had to be wanted somewhere, but he hadn't found anything. The decision to let Dixon stay hadn't been an easy one, but it was the legal thing to do.

He wished he'd listened to Leroy and run them out of town on general principles and devil take legality. Hellfire Pass had trouble enough without the beginnings of a new outlaw gang setting up operations here.

"We can talk this out, Marshal," Dixon called. "Let's me and you get a shot of rotgut. Wet our whistles and palaver. That's what civilized men do."

The girl tried to bolt. Shad held Missy down and pressed a finger to his lips to keep her quiet. Moving slowly he worked to the end of the bar, chanced a quick look over the top, then slithered like a snake behind the long polished wood counter. Rockwell sprawled in the narrow space, his head resting in a pool of blood. Shad moved closer. The bartender stirred, moaned, and tried to sit up. Shad pushed him back down.

"They're shooting anything that moves. Missy thought they'd killed you." He tried to keep his voice low, but silence had fallen on the saloon. He worried that Dixon and his cronies might overhear anything he said.

Rockwell's eyes focused, just a little. He reached up and ran his fingers along a shallow gash across the top of his bald skull. Wincing, he jerked his hand away.

"My head feels like it's full of angry wasps."

"That's only a graze. Head wounds bleed like a son of a gun."

"I'm seeing two of you, Marshal."

"Good. To get them three into jail, I need to be twice what I am usually. Lie back down. If things go south, pretend you're dead."

"You mean if they kill you?"

Shad pushed Rockwell flat. He worked his way across the man and got to the far end of the bar. He knew better than to poke his head out here. Dixon had seen him creep behind the bar. He'd be waiting for him to come out.

It was an old trick, but it worked more often than not when dealing with trigger-happy gunmen. Balancing his bowler on the muzzle of his shotgun, he slowly raised it over the bar. Three quick shots sent the hat flying. Shad popped up, lowered the weapon, and discharged both barrels. Part of the pool table turned to dust in the blast. Dixon sprawled back, staring up at the ceiling. His six-gun was still in his hand, but from the weak twitches he made, he no longer posed a problem.

Another shot came Shad's way. He dropped the scatter-gun and went for his pistol. The .44 Peacemaker blared three times in Herk's direction. The dull click of a hammer falling on a spent chamber told Shad another of the trio was out of the fight.

"Drop it or I drop you, Herk. You know I mean it."

"You wouldn't kill an unarmed man," the rabble rouser said.

"That's true for tomorrow, but I got a couple hours til midnight to make my quota today." Shad cocked his Peace-maker. The sound echoed through the saloon like a peal of doom.

Herk threw his pistol onto the ruined pool table and lifted his hands.

"Where's your partner?"

Herk's quick glance toward the backroom caused Shad to swing his gun around, but Squinty was gone.

"Down on the floor," he ordered. Shad dashed into the backroom to see the third man flat on his back in the alley.

His deputy stood over the downed man who tried to adjust his eyeglasses.

"Shannon," Shad said sharply. "Ian, don't shoot him."

His deputy looked at him with a flash of anger at being denied. Then Shannon's usual composure returned.

"You take all the fun out of being a deputy," he said.

"Bring him inside. I've got the other two." Shad spun around, expecting either Herk or Dixon to be ready to cause more trouble. Both sat with their backs against the wall, hands folded on their heads.

Standing in the middle of the Gold Dust, Early had his Smith & Wesson cocked and aimed at the prisoners. He had been nervous out in the street. Not a trace of his uneasiness remained. Both Dixon and Herk read grim determination on Early's face.

"What're you going to do with 'em, Marshal?" Ralph Rockwell pulled himself up and leaned heavily against his bar. Missy rushed around and hugged him. She ended up supporting him more than the bar.

"For two cents I'd ventilate the three of them," Shad said. "But the town doesn't pay for my ammunition. I'd hate to be out the money replacing my bullets."

"The circuit judge won't get here for another couple weeks," Shannon said. He shoved Squinty toward his partners. "Keepin' them in jail means we'd have to feed 'em."

"I don't have the money for that, either," Shad said.

"I'd say you've got a problem then, Marshal," Dixon said. He picked splinters from his vest. Only a couple pieces of buckshot had hit him in the chest. Tiny red circles expanded slowly, but from the way the gunman moved and gestured, they weren't going to slow him down none.

"I'm letting you go," Shad said. Both his deputies protested. He held up his hand to quiet them. "That is, unless Mister Rockwell back there wants to press charges. He's the one who got his place all shot up."

"And his head," Early said. "They shot him in the head."

"I've done worse to myself back when I was a booze hound on a bender," Rockwell said. "Can you get them to pay for the damage, then run them out of town? I don't ever want to see their ugly faces in Gold Dust City again."

"Empty your pockets. Everything. Put it on the pool table." Shad saw that the pool table was beyond repair. The bullet tracks put there by the three owlhoots was nothing compared to him blowing off an entire corner of the table with a shotgun blast. He wished he'd aimed higher and saved the pool table. The buckshot would have reduced Dixon to a bloody mist instead of taking off the corner pocket.

Shannon pawed through the pile. His lips moved silently as he tallied the money.

"Close to eighteen dollars, Marshal," he reported.

"Each of their guns is worth five dollars," Shad said, "so that's another fifteen. Early. Are there horses and tack outside?"

"There are, Shad."

"That's another hundred, maybe," he said.

"One's got fancy silver conchas on the saddle."

Shad saw the way Dixon bristled. That was his tack.

"Call it two hundred more. Horses and all that money on the table might fetch two-fifty. Will that fix you up, Ralph?"

"It goes a ways toward it, Marshal."

"You can't steal a man's horse!" Dixon raged. He surged toward Shad. Shannon swung his pistol and laid the barrel alongside the owlhoot's head, driving him to his knees.

"I'm feeling mighty generous about now," Shad said. "If I think hard, I might take that fancy pair of Mexican boots as part of your fine."

Dixon's hot glare would have melted all the winter snow on Mt. Elbert. This reaction pleased Shad more than anything so far.

"Now, I'm still in a generous mood. I'm not making you gents walk out of Utopia. You'll get to ride on the train."

"You took all our money," Squinty said. "How're we s'pposed to pay for a ticket?"

"I'll see to that. Bring them along to the train station, men."

He felt as if he led a parade, the five trailing him as he made his way along the twisty streets to the depot. Another theory was that the streets of Utopia had been laid out by following a drunk cow, or so said his deputy, Ian Shannon. Shannon hailed from Boston and made that claim about his home town's streets, too. Shad had never been to Boston, but streets there couldn't be any more twisty than these.

He rounded a curve and walked directly to the railroad station. The train puffed and blew steam into the air. It had taken on water for its boiler. The last of the coal had been dropped down from a storage bin into the tender. The engineer worked in the cab while his stoker stood by, waiting to be told to get to work to build a head of steam. Shad waved to the engineer, who acknowledged him with a grunt. Highballin' Davey Fulbright didn't much like anyone, so Shad took this as the engineer being in a good mood.

The men behind him all grumbled about different things. He waved them to the back of the train. Just in front of the caboose a freight car stood with one door partially open.

"That one," the marshal ordered.

"What do you want us to do? Ride back here? There's a perfectly good passenger car up front." Billy Dixon started for it. Shad moved fast. A sweeping kick knocked the man's legs from under him.

"Tie 'em up and toss 'em in," Shad ordered.

"You can't do this. We got rights!" Dixon fought. Shannon's expression never changed as he drove his fist into the man's gut, doubling him over. It hardly mattered to the deputy whether he punched him or shot him. Dixon realized that and crawled into the freight car.

Shad watched as his men lashed the owlhoots together back to back. They glared at him.

"I know what you're thinking," Shad said cheerfully. "As soon as you get out of those ropes, no matter that they're tied real good, you'll jump off the train and come right on back to Utopia to bedevil me." He motioned for Ian Shannon to drop a noose around their collective necks and stretch it out to tie onto the far door.

A second loop secured them to the open door.

"We'll choke to death!"

"Better hope the ride's smooth all the way down to the west. You boys can shoot up those gold camps all you want. I've heard some towns don't bother with having a lawman. Vigilance committees take care of anyone so much as disturbing the peace."

"That's if you're lucky," Early said. "You've heard of Sheriff Glory Be Parsons? He likes to brag on never takin' prisoners."

The trio howled in protest until Shannon tightened the ropes.

"Them nooses on your necks will get you used to what's in store for you if ole Glory Be takes it into his head to run you out of Georgetown," Shannon said. He canted his head to one side, pretended to pull on an invisible rope and stuck his tongue out.

"I'll get you for this, Shadrach Nelson! I swear I will!"

Leroy Early put his back to closing the door on Dixon's protests.

"Stand back, men. Highballin' Davey's pulling out," Shad said. Three loud steam whistle blasts warned that the train built steam. The steel wheels dug into the rails. The screeching drowned out Dixon and his men as they protested inside the freight car.

"Think they'll choke to death 'fore they get to the end of the line?" Early asked.

"Don't know, don't care," Shad said. "Let's get back to work."

The three lawmen silently returned to the marshal's office. All the way, Shad thanked his lucky stars that the disturbance had only been three mangy misfits and not some new collision between the Gallaghers and the Morriseys.

Chapter Two

"Good morning, Pa." Abednego Nelson pushed the jailhouse door open and stood outlined by the rising sun, as if he was a lizard stretched out on a rock warming himself. He was a mirror image of his father, half his age at twenty-two years younger.

"It's about time you showed up," Shad said, standing. Every bone in his body ached. It had been a long night spent half-sleeping with his head resting on crossed arms. What dreams—nightmares—he had were of Dixon and his men shooting up Utopia while he watched helplessly.

"Don't you fuss like that, Pa. I'm on time. Early, even." Abe came in and looked around, taking in the empty cells at the rear of the office. "From what folks have been saying, I thought you'd have them cells filled to overflowing."

"With Billy Dixon and his cronies? I got rid of them. Why have the town pay to feed and shelter those worthless—?"

"No need to get specific," Abe said. He hung up his gun belt on a peg over the desk and idly leafed through wanted posters that had come in the day before.

"You can thank me. If I'd tossed those bottom feeders into cells, you'd have to listen to them squawk the livelong day." Shad detailed what had happened, his son nodding silently until he reached the end of his story.

"So Ian and Leroy took off already?"

"I let them go ahead of quitting time. That way you can call them back without feeling too guilty if any trouble boils up."

"It's Sunday. Nothing'll go wrong. You worry too much, Pa. I've been deputy here for two years. Who was it that helped you run off all the owlhoots roosting here in town? I'm not a greenhorn when it comes to being a lawman."

"I know, son, I know. I'm just tired. You look a mite peaked yourself. Aren't you sleeping?"

From Abe's grin he knew the reason for the dark circles under his son's eyes and an occasional suppressed yawn.

"Mary Beth has a way of bending my ear all night long."

"And all you want to do is listen." He snorted and shook his head. The long blond hair swirled about. He caught it and pushed it back out of his eyes. He doubted they did much talking, but that wasn't his place to remark. His son was twenty-two years old and a man. Twenty-two, the same age as he'd been when Ruth gave birth.

In fact, folks sometimes mistook them for brothers.

"How long have the two of you been sparking?"

"Close to four months," Abe said with a faraway look in his bright green eyes. "She's something real special, believe me. It's good that Dixon's gone. Mary Beth said he was annoying her the other day. If him and me crossed paths, he wouldn't be riding the train down to Georgetown. He'd be pushing up weeds out in the potter's field."

Shad didn't doubt his son for one second. What he doubted was that Mary Beth was worth the attention Abe showered on her.

"I'll come around ten tonight to take over. Like I said, you got a pair of deputies to call on."

"Get on back to ma. She'll want to hear all about how you ran off three more desperadoes."

Shad glared at his son. Ruth Nelson hated hearing about gunfights and the hard cases he dealt with. Things had quieted down a powerful lot recently, except for the feud between the Gallaghers and Morriseys. He had hopes of finding the cause and smoothing ruffled feathers to keep both families from shooting up his town.

He trudged along the winding main street and cut down a footpath leading into the foothills above Utopia. A small, neat house perched atop a low hill looking out over Hellfire Pass. At sunrise and sunset the entire town glowed as if it were made from gold. He enjoyed sitting on the porch, smoking a cigar, and enjoying the serenity. Sometimes, these days, he even had a snort or two of peach brandy. He preferred it to whiskey, but if offered rye or bourbon, he wouldn't turn it down.

Mostly he appreciated the quiet.

He opened the door and took a deep whiff. Eggs. Frying bacon. Maybe potatoes sliced up and mingled with onions and greens plucked from the hillside.

"We were getting ready to feed it to the pigs," his wife said. "What took you so long getting home?"

"We don't keep pigs, so that threat's not gonna work on me. You know why I'm so long getting here for your wonderful company—and breakfast. The climb gets a little harder every day. These old legs tire out fast." He settled his gun belt on a peg by the door. Moving around, he hid his bowler under his coat so Ruth wouldn't notice the new holes shot through the brim and crown. "And I wanted to talk with Abe some. I don't get to see him much now that we're splitting up duties."

"You don't see him much because he spends all his time with that Yarrow girl," Ruth said.

Shad sighed deeply.

"It's puppy love. Nothing more. He'll get tired of her soon enough." He dug into the plate put before him. In addition to the wonderful food he'd smelled cooking, Ruth had fixed a pan of biscuits. He speared one with his fork and looked around for butter or jam.

"Here, Papa." His younger child, Miriam, came into the kitchen carrying a box heavy with preserves put up the prior year.

"Strawberry. My favorite." He worked off the lid. The vacuum broke with a soft hiss.

"Your favorite's whatever is set in front of you," the eighteen-year-old said. "And you're wrong."

He looked at her. She was the spitting image of her mother with the same raven's wing dark hair and bright green eyes. That was something everyone in the Nelson family shared. Bright green eyes. Miriam was taller by an inch or two and had a fuller figure than her ma. But she shared more with her mother than looks. She'd never had any trouble disagreeing with him.

Abe had always been more roundabout when he disagreed. He thought things through rather than blurting out what he felt. Miriam might consider what she said, but the quick words and biting opinions were never far from her full, ruby lips.

He looked at his wife. Ruth nodded slowly in agreement. The two were ganging up against him.

"You're saying Abe is serious about her? This is something new. He hasn't gone with any other girl longer than a few weeks before moving on."

"It's the way he looks at her, Papa. His eyes sparkle."

"And, Shad, you just pointed out how Mary Beth is different. Other girls only kept Abe interested for a week or two."

"There was the Gonzalez girl. What was her name?"

"Teresa," his wife said, "and that flirtation lasted about a month. Not four months."

"He'll ask her to marry him," Miriam said. "Mark my words."

Shad ate slowly, concentrating on chewing to give himself time to think. His brain spun like a wagon wheel on a greased axle.

"She's a saloon girl," he said finally. "She came to town looking for a job dealing faro. Who knows what else?"

"She wanted a job as schoolmarm," Ruth said. "When she met Abe she stopped asking about the job. You know what that means."

"Yeah, Papa, you know what that means. She's as interested in Abe as he is in her. They'll get hitched. Do you have your fancy suit all patched up? I saw a hole or two where moths had chewed on the wool."

"You're joshing me, both of you. And maybe she worried about not being up to the chore of teaching a couple dozen kids."

He knew what Miriam meant but was hesitant to agree. Mary Beth had pulled back from asking about the teaching job because only single women could hold down the job. If she had her cap set for Abe from the start, that meant marriage would rule her out of the job after she'd barely begun. Such a short tenure would cause bad feelings all around. Better to never apply.

"What's she been doing all this time?" Ruth asked. "Not working in a saloon. Abe would have mentioned that."

"Odd jobs," said Miriam. "She clerks at Mister Sampson's store a day or two a week."

"That skinflint would never pay her a decent wage," Shad said.

"She gets paid in food he doesn't sell. Rather than let it go bad, Mister Sampson's willing to give it to her. She does cleaning at the hotel in exchange for a cot in the storeroom. And she shares the food she gets from Mister Sampson with Netty Michaelson."

Shad closed his eyes. His head began to ache from all the gossip. Netty ran the hotel, but rumor had it she wasn't the owner. Someone in Denver hired her and kept her on a tight budget. Making a deal like Miriam sketched out with Mary Beth benefitted everyone. Sampson wasn't tempted to sell tainted food, Netty got help keeping the hotel and Mary Beth got by with just enough so she could let Abe court her.

He shook his head, turned his attention to mopping up the last of the bacon grease and runny egg yolk with a biscuit and then popped it into his mouth.

"Abe can do better."

"You're right about that, dear," Ruth said, "but I think Miriam's right. He doesn't want to."

"What's wrong, Papa? You don't like the idea of being a grandpa?" Miriam laughed. She snatched the plate from in front of him and took it to the sink. She pumped water from the well into a bucket and set to work cleaning the plates and pans.

Being called grandpa irked him. He didn't know exactly why. Better gramps. Or nothing at all since there shouldn't be a new generation of Nelsons. Not yet, at any rate.

In a low voice, he asked Ruth, "Does she know something I don't?"

"I'd say she knows a lot more than you do about your own son and his druthers."

"I mean, about being a grandpa? Abe and Mary Beth aren't married."

"You know what they say, Shad. The first one can come at any time. The second takes nine months."

"That's not funny."

"Just wait until you dandle that grandson on your knee. I can see you setting on the porch after you've finished a smelly cigar. You'll take a nip of brandy, then scoop up the young'n and bounce him up and down and tell him all kinds of tall tales." Miriam dried her hands. "I've got to get to town. The bank'll open any time now, and Mister Reese wanted me to finish with the books as soon as I could."

"Have a good day, dear," Ruth said, giving her daughter a hug.

Miriam kissed her pa on his stubbled cheek, made a face, and hurried out. He didn't have anything to say to her. The image of him dealing with another small child intimidated him more than facing Billy Dixon and his gang. He had raised a family of good kids. Even if Abe seemed taken with the likes of Mary Beth Yarrow and Miriam worked for a banker as crooked as Wilson Reese.

"I know what's bothering you," Ruth said, sitting beside him at the table. "You're not afraid Abe will have a son. You're afraid it'll be a little girl and you'll be outnumbered."

"Very funny," he said. He stifled a yawn. "Time for a nap. I've been up all night."

"I heard gunshots," Ruth said tentatively.

"Cowboys whooping it up on Saturday night. Nothing unusual."

She scowled at him. The sharp look told him his lie had been detected, but she didn't ask for more of an explanation.

Shad fell into their bed and lay staring up at the fitted planks in the ceiling. As tired as he was, sleep was a stranger. Abe and Mary Beth Yarrow. He wasn't sure what bothered him about that. He expected Abe to get married sooner or later, but he'd always thought it would be someone he'd known for a long time.

"Four months he's known her," he repeated softly until he drifted off to a troubled sleep filled with dreams of Mary Beth complaining about Billy Dixon annoying her. How did *their* paths ever cross?

Chapter Three

"What do you mean you ain't seen nuthin'? Are you blind? There's got to be thievin' goin' on!" Winifred Gallagher thumped her son on the back of his head like she was testing a watermelon for ripeness.

"Aw, Ma, don't do that." Kenny Gallagher looked past his mother to where two cousins hid snickers behind their dirty hands. One of them made a rude gesture, then turned and looked innocent when the head of the Gallagher clan spun about.

"You two," Winifred snapped. "You're as worthless as Kenny. What have you seen? Or have you gone blind playin' with—"

"Ma, look there. Someone's sneakin' around the coal yard." Kenny Gallagher passed over the field glasses. His mother snatched them from his hands and peered through the smudged lenses. She lowered them and tried adjusting the eyepieces, then handed the binoculars back in frustration.

"Can't get 'em to work right." She rubbed her rheumy eyes. "Tell me what you see and be quick about it. That's our coal they're stealin'."

Kenny Gallagher shoved his eyes to the lenses and watched.

"Well, now, can't say he's stealin' anything. That's Mister Brushwell, and he's got a couple of his men with him."

"Keep watchin'. I know somebody's takin' our coal. The

numbers don't add up, what's dug from the mine and what's sold. We're bein' cheated, and I'm gonna find out who's responsible."

"Why not tell the marshal? If there's somethin' being stole, the law ought to stop it."

Winifred Gallagher snorted and kicked at a rock in her anger.

"That Shadrach Nelson is as likely to be the thief as any of them. I don't trust Brushwell. I don't trust any of them city slickers. They think they can swindle the likes of me 'cuz I ain't got a fancy eddy-ca-shun like them."

"You can read and write, Ma. And Beatrice can even cipher."

"She's the one what found the thievin'," Winifred said. "I'd trade the whole lot of you and your brothers for another one like her."

"But she's your niece and we're—" Kenny Gallagher ducked as his mother swung an arthritic hand at his head again, this time with the intent of doing more than whacking him.

"You're stupid, that's what you are. You've been watching that coal pile for two solid days and nights and haven't found who's makin' off with our property. Every last lump of that coal's ours 'til the railroad loads it into the locomotive tender."

"If—when—I spot the thief, what do you want me to do? Me and them?" Kenny Gallagher glared at his cousins. "We can stop just about anybody meanin' to do the Gallagher clan wrong."

"Tell me and I'll decide. You'd only get yourself kilt dead." Winifred Gallagher stomped off along the winding trail above Brushwell's freight yards. Beyond the ten-foot-high pile of coal scraped out of the Calcutta Mine high up on the mountain and a mile around to the south, gleamed the ponderous mountain of lead ingots ready to be shipped.

If lead burned, she'd set fire to each and every metal

brick. Those all belonged to the Morrisey family. She'd tried to stop Brushwell from dealing with those scoundrels, but the businessman claimed he had to remain neutral. The railroad didn't depend on lead the way it did Gallagher coal. The long climb up the tracks from east or west was easier if the train wasn't loaded down with a full coal tender. Start with just enough to reach the summit of Hellfire Pass, pour water into the boiler and take on a load of coal for the trip down the other side.

Denver to the east, Central City to the west after passing by the county seat of Georgetown. And smack in the middle was the indispensable Gallagher coal. Some of it graded out as anthracite but most of it bituminous. Good enough to burn in a steam engine, if you didn't mind the heavy black smoke. She wished that the new vein in the Calcutta had been quality met grade, but it wasn't.

She could sell metallurgical grade coal for three times what the railroad paid to fill their coal car.

There'd be time to bring another geologist out from Denver to poke around with his rock hammer and magnifying glass. But that'd be after she found who was cheating her on the coal down in Brushwell's yard.

The path took a steep turn uphill. She pushed back her ratty brown hair and fixed her eyes on the trail. Huffing and puffing, she climbed up to a twin-rutted road. This curled around the mountainside and ended down at Utopia. Once a week, sometimes twice, heavily laden wagons rattled down to dump fresh loads of coal in Brushwell's freight yard.

Winifred hiked along farther. Her dingy floral print dress was soaked with sweat by the time she came to a line shack. The door stood open, but nothing inside the small cabin was visible. She entered, took a lantern off a shelf in the bare room and lit it. The lucifer flared brightly. The wick in the lamp caught fire and spread a warm yellow glow all around.

A quick yank opened a door that seemingly led to bare rock behind the cabin. A long tunnel stretched deep into the rock. She took a deep breath, appreciating the damp smell and letting the cooling air evaporate the sweat she'd built climbing back uphill. Fifty yards into the hillside, the tunnel opened into a huge, yawning cavern. The dome stretching above was so high the lamplight failed to illuminate it.

All around the cavern hung canvas sheets, fastened into the rock to divide the space into private rooms. Furniture in the middle provided a common room for the entire family. Each of the canvas-enclosed rooms held one or more of the Gallaghers. Winifred had counted them once and decided thirty was close, but if they were all blood relatives, she couldn't name half of them. Beatrice claimed to know them by name and by sight and even where they fit into the family tree.

If her niece hadn't been so good at other things, Winifred would have called her a liar. As much as she looked down on the others in her family, she held a sneaking admiration for Beatrice. She didn't even hold the girl's good looks against her. At least, not too much. It never paid for a woman to be too pretty.

Winifred yanked back a canvas hanging. Beatrice Gallagher sat on a low three-legged stool, hunched over the table. She chewed her tongue as she worked down the columns of numbers on a sheet. The girl looked up. Her hazel eyes snapped with irritation at being interrupted, but not a hint of emotion played across her lovely face otherwise.

"Aunt Win," she said. "You want to know more about the missing coal." Beatrice tapped the sheet. "It's all here. What is dug out of the mine and what's sold? There's close to a ton difference."

"That's ten whole dollars," Winifred said, scowling. "Ain't as much as I thought, but it's still comin' outta my pocket."

"That's a week," Beatrice went on. "I can trace the losses

back a couple months. It might be more 'n a hundred dollars we been cheated out of."

"How's it bein' done?" Winifred asked.

Beatrice shook her head. A russet flow of hair moved around her head as if some hidden breeze sculpted it. In the cavern there was never a breeze. The motion came from the way she tossed her head like a frisky filly.

"It's got to be Brushwell doin' the stealin'," Beatrice said.

"If he records delivery from us as being a ton underweight, then sells it to the railroad at full weight, that'd do it," Winifred said.

"We need scales up here, at the mine," Beatrice said. "That'd let us match what we're shipping down to him and what he claims he's receiving."

"Scales," mused Winifred. "Can't do it. That'd cost too much. And who'd do all the recordin'? You?"

"I'm already—"

"Never you mind, lil darlin'," Winifred said. "You're worth your weight in gold for all you do." She snorted. "At least you're worth your weight in coal, not that you've got any flesh on those scrawny bones of yours."

"Has Kenny seen anything?"

"That lout? He wouldn't know it if a wagon ran over his foot. How that boy is my flesh and blood is a poser. He's even dumber than his pa, and that's sayin' something."

"Where is Uncle Luther? Nobody's seen hide nor hair of him in months and months."

"Knowin' him, he's off on a bender." Winifred squinted just a little as she studied the girl's guileless face. Beatrice tried to look innocent but she was needling her. "Why are you askin' after him?"

"Oh, nothing," Beatrice said innocently. "His birthday is coming up, and I thought it'd be good to have a party for him." She looked out of the corner of her eye at Winifred.

"He don't know how old he is. How can you?"

A disturbance brought her around. One of her nephews came running across the cavern, waving his arms like he was having a fit.

"Aunt Win, Aunt Win, we seen them stealin' the coal!"

"Who?" She grabbed her nephew by the front of his dirty shirt and shook. "Who're you talkin' about, Jer?" His teeth rattled as she shook harder. "Jeremiah Jones, you tell me. Who's makin' off with our coal?"

As if he was freezing and his teeth chattering, he got out, "Morriseys. A half dozen of them varmints is pokin' around our coal. Mister Brushwell ain't nowhere to be seen."

"Get your guns. We're gonna put a stop to their thievery right now." Winifred looked at Beatrice. The girl's expression showed confusion, then hardened into determination.

"I'm coming, too, Aunt Win. I can shoot better than any of them." She pointed to a half dozen of the Gallagher clan gathered in the middle of the cavern to see what the ruckus was about.

Winifred went to an open box at the side of the cavern and grabbed a goose gun. She wanted to be sure she got them scoundrels, and she wanted to do it from a distance beyond where any Morrisey could fire back at her accurately. Beatrice crowded behind her and grabbed a Winchester. It pleased her that the girl handled the rifle with confidence.

"Let's get 'em, boys," she said. Winifred marched down the tunnel like a general leading a charge into battle.

They reached the observation point where Kenny Gallagher watched through his field glasses. Seeing his ma, he held up the binoculars.

"You kin see 'em, Ma. They're scurryin' around like rats goin' after cheese."

Beatrice took the field glasses and slowly panned across Brushwell's yard. She handed the glasses back to her cousin.

"He's right, Auntie. Somebody's poking around down there and looking furtive about it."

"Furtive?" Kenny asked skeptically. "I didn't see no furry critters. Only them Morriseys."

Winifred Gallagher grunted and then motioned for her clan to follow her down. They had a fight to win.

Beatrice Gallagher trailed the others down the hillside. Her pa had been a drunkard and a dyed-in-the-wool liar about most everything, but she remembered one thing he said. "The early bird gets the worm but the second mouse gets the cheese."

Let her cousins get all shot up. If there was any glory to be bragged on, she wanted to be alive and the one doing it. More than this, she wanted to be sure who her family was shooting.

Kenny and Aunt Winifred plowed ahead, not bothering to sneak up on the trio in the coal yard. Before they reached the edge of the property, they opened fire. Beatrice cringed at the roar made by her aunt's goose gun. It sounded like a battle being fought all by itself.

Kenny's six-gun sounded pitifully inadequate when he opened fire. Beatrice ducked behind a low mound of coal and looked around when return fire sounded. She squinted and tried to make out who the Gallaghers had taken on. A curse escaped her lips. They were Morriseys, all right. She recognized two of them right away and knew who the third one was without seeing him. The trio was inseparable—except lately.

She rushed forward and knocked Kenny's gun hand just as he fired. His shot went high. The dark silhouette of his target sank out of sight behind another mound of coal.

"What'd you do that for, Bea? I had him dead to rights!"

"You'd've shot Nate, you fool. What'd your ma say if you gunned down your own brother?"

"Half-brother," Kenny muttered. "And that wasn't Nate. Nate's over yonder." He stood and pointed, using his pistol to pinpoint his half-brother's position. Kenny yelped in surprise when a shot from the target he'd missed took off his hat and sent it spinning into the night.

Beatrice smiled. This was enough to make Kenny frightened of every shadow for the rest of the fight—the rest of the night. She was glad that none of them was a better shot.

She crouched and waited. From the distance came loud, angry shouts. Two of Shadrach Nelson's deputies rushed forward to break up the fight. Her aunt boldly strode out, yelling and demanding the coal thieves be arrested. From the reply, the head of the Morrisey family, Leadbottom Morrisey himself, argued that Winifred had tried to murder him in cold blood. What had started as a gunfight turned into a hissing, spitting argument. Beatrice was sure her aunt had the advantage when it came to shouting the loudest.

Kenny ventured out, as timid as a marmot leaving its burrow. When no one took a potshot at him, he rushed to join his mother. The two of them stood inches away from a deputy to argue their right to gun down any Morrisey at anytime, anywhere.

"You lower that shotgun, Miz Gallagher," Leroy Early said. "I'll run you and your boys in, lock you up and throw away the key if you don't."

"It was them," Winifred Gallagher shouted. "Them Morriseys are stealin' my coal. Mine! I ain't called the Coal Queen of the Rockies for no reason."

"That should be cold queen, you old harridan," called a massive man as he lumbered up. "You're downright frigid!"

"Don't you go callin' me names, Leadbottom Morrisey! I know you and yours have been stealin' from me."

"We came to unload a pile of lead bricks. They're heading to Denver on the next train. If anyone was fixin' on stealin', it was you! Those lead ingots are worth more than all the coal you mine in a month!" The massive man stomped forward. His sheer bulk would intimidate a lesser man. Winifred stood her ground.

Beatrice stepped away, moving as quietly as she could. She skirted one hill of coal, and as she rounded it saw the man who had ambushed Kenny. He was listening to the argument between Leadbottom and Winifred and didn't hear her soft step. Beatrice came within reach of him and pressed the muzzle of her rifle into the middle of his back.

"You so much as twitch, I swear I'll drill you clean through, Patrick Morrisey."

He jumped, then turned slowly, hands raised. He stared at her hard, then grinned.

"That's what I'm supposed to do to you, Bea."

She lowered the rifle and stepped forward into the circle of his arms. They kissed. When they ran out of air, they broke off breathlessly.

"You almost let that fool Kenny shoot you."

"I didn't know who it was." He half turned and looked toward the spot where Deputy Early still held Leadbottom and Winifred apart as their argument got more personal. "My pa's right. We were unloading a couple dozen lead blocks and didn't expect to get shot at."

"Would you have shot me, if you knew I was here?"

"The only way I'd shoot you would be with Cupid's bow and arrow," Patrick said. "You know I love you."

"Love." Beatrice didn't quite reply in a mocking tone, but she came close.

"Let's get away from here," Patrick said. "It won't be long before the deputies chase everyone off. I don't want to go back up the mountain and set around the cabin listening to how we drove you off and made fools of all the Gallaghers."

"It'll be the same up in the cave."

"You promised me I'd get to see where you live. I can't imagine living underground like that, surrounded by rock all the time."

"You work in your family's lead mines. It's like that, only all the time." She clung to his arm. Patrick obviously worked the mines. There was nothing but rock-hard muscle under her fingers.

"I need to see the sky. I need sunshine. I need to see you. Smile so the sun will come out at night." He tried to kiss her again, but she ducked away. Holding his hand, she tugged him in the direction of a stand of trees at the edge of Brushwell's property. More than once they had used the spot as a rendezvous away from both their families.

They slipped into the woods and found their special clearing. Beatrice was glad to leave her aunt's strident haranguing behind. Patrick's pa was no better. After all the excitement, she was ready for a different kind offered by Patrick Morrisey.

He cringed with every gunshot. Moving around the mountains of coal was dangerous. The Gallaghers and Morriseys shot anything that moved. The pile of lead blocks looked like a good place to take cover, but he froze. Dashing across the open space to hide behind the wall of metal became more dangerous than simply hiding where he was.

Leroy Early and Ian Shannon double-timed it into the yard. Both had their six-shooters out, ready to shoot at anything they saw.

Edging away, he headed for the back of the yard. The shooting was tapering off and everyone yelled at everyone else now. When he heard Early try to keep the two families apart, he thought he was safe.

Then he rounded a pile of coal. Patrick Morrisey stood with his hands in the air. Beatrice Gallagher came into view, mostly hidden by dark shadows, but he recognized her by the way she walked. She had quite a sashay when she moved, and no one else in Utopia looked quite as pretty in figure. When he finally saw her face, he wondered what was going on. For a Gallagher woman holding a rifle on a

Morrisey man, Beatrice should have looked different. More like her aunt?

A slow smile crossed his face when the two kissed. He hunkered down and watched. He was too far to hear their whispered conversation, but he guessed what was said by the way the two moved back and forth, sometimes lightly brushing and other times parting. If this wasn't a mating dance, he'd never seen it before.

The two drifted toward the rear of the freight yard. He followed them into the wooded area. There wasn't any chance they'd see him once they'd found a comfortable spot among the trees. Watching them was better than getting his head shot off by carelessly fired bullets. After a while, he slipped away. Leadbottom Morrisey and Winifred Gallagher weren't the only two dealing with their family feud tonight.

Chapter Four

Leadbottom Morrisey shielded his eyes from the rising sun sneaking past the cracks in his cabin wall. He spun around and grabbed for the whiskey sitting forlornly in the middle of the table. When he had started drinking, five other bottles had kept this one company. He and his family had tied one on with a royal binge of drinking. His sausage-like fingers closed on the neck of the bottle. With a shaky hand he lifted the rotgut whiskey to his mouth and guzzled the last two fingers left.

"Aw, Pa, you didn't leave none for us," his son Anderson complained.

"I need it to think. It helps drown out your caterwaulin'," Leadbottom said. He closed his eyes and grimaced. "It don't do a thing to get rid of the other voices. They're gettin' louder all the time." He clamped his hands over his ears and screwed his eyes shut as tight as he could.

"Are you talkin' about the tommyknockers?" Patrick Morrisey lounged back on a pile of flour sacks. There was enough flour to make a thousand biscuits and have some left over, but Leadbottom refused to allow anyone cooking to bake biscuits. He claimed they were the devil's spoor.

"Naw, he don't mean them, Pat," Anderson said when he saw their pa wasn't inclined to answer. "The tommyknockers warn us if the mineshaft's gonna collapse or if some other trouble's waitin' to befall us."

"That's so," agreed Leadbottom's brother-in-law, Eric Sudderth. "Only last week one of them began hammering on the wall in the new stope where I was fixin' to blast. One, two, three, one, two, three, just like that. Some sort of code only they know. Bangin' on the wall to get my attention. It worked. I hightailed it."

"That's when the damp blew through the mine?" Patrick asked. Eric nodded solemnly. The noxious gases had ignited and taken out more than one newly added support. Shoring in fifty yards of tunnel had to be buttressed. "You were lucky to get out. The Calcutta had a white damp explosion that blinded one of them last month. It was one of Winifred's cousins."

Anderson looked at him.

"How'd you know anything about that? Them Gallaghers don't ever say a thing about their operation. They'd never tell nobody of losin' one of their blood kin."

Patrick swallowed hard. He tried to remember if Bea had told him or if somebody in town gossiped about it.

"One of the drunks at the Gold Dust said he'd heard a Gallagher had left town. Went back to Denver because his eyes were fried in an explosion."

"I pay close attention to gossip, and I ain't never heard a thing about that," Anderson said, looking more suspiciously at his brother.

"Pa's talking about the voices from underground?" Patrick looked down at the cabin floor.

"They're sent by Winifred Gallagher herself," Eric declared.

"They spy on us and try to confuse Pa." Anderson sounded confident in his condemnation.

Patrick stopped trying to find faces in the dirt and looked at his father. The man got crazier by the day, hearing voices and thinking somebody spied on him. The younger Morrisey stirred uneasily. He didn't know about the voices. They might exist, and he wasn't able to hear them. An explosion a year back had left him deaf in one ear. But one set of voices he was sure he could hear if he listened hard enough. Like Eric said, the tommyknockers sometimes warned miners of danger. They were souls trapped in the mines and only wanted to keep others from joining them in a dark and rocky limbo.

But the other voices Leadbottom heard? From what Patrick knew, they came and went. When his pa wasn't listening to them, he was as normal as could be. The voices were one thing. The only trouble was that Patrick knew they were being spied on. Beatrice had hinted at it several times, and he wasn't sure she realized it since they'd been talking idly after a tryst in the woods.

Winifred sent out her family all the time to find what they could of the lead miners and what the Morrisey family was up to. But what Beatrice hinted at was something else. Patrick looked around the crowded cabin. She had as much as admitted one of the Morriseys was spying for Winifred.

Everything Bea said warned him that her aunt was completely loco.

Matching her suspicions with ones whispered to Leadbottom Gallagher by people living underground seemed to balance things out.

"We need more men swingin' picks and movin' ore," Leadbottom said suddenly. His bloodshot eyes went wide, and he forced himself to his feet.

"About everyone in the family's here already, Pa," Patrick said. "You mean we should hire outsiders to help us?"

"I heard tell that some Cornish miners in Denver were lookin' for work," Anderson said. "They ain't been in the US very long. We can get them to work real cheap, and they're already trained."

"Cornish miners?" Leadbottom exploded. "They're *coal* miners. Winifred Gallagher is danglin' them in front of us.

She wants us to hire them so they can learn all our secrets and sabotage our mine."

"Reckon that might be true," Anderson said uneasily. "Who'd ever trust a man from a place called Cornwall?"

"Of course it's true!" Leadbottom stomped around the cabin. His girth was so ponderous he knocked over things on the table, and every time he turned something more fell from a shelf. He threw his hands over his head, hamlike fists banging into the roof.

Patrick cringed away when one punch knocked a hole in the ceiling. There were already plenty of leaks. This would create a mountain freshet in any decently sized rainstorm.

"Are you saying we should hire more miners, but not the Cornish miners over in Denver? I don't know if there are any in Utopia I'd trust in our mine," Patrick said.

"Let's go find ourselves some recruits," Leadbottom said. He banged from side to side and finally got through the door without creating too much more havoc.

"What's he up to, Andy?" Patrick watched their pa, wondering what devilment he'd get them into this time.

Anderson shook his head, then shrugged.

"We better git," Eric said uneasily. "When he gets in a mood like this, he don't much care who he whumps up on."

"He's been talking to himself ever since last night," Patrick said.

"We shoulda whumped up on the Gallaghers," Eric said. "Imagine them accusin' us of stealin' their coal. Why'd we want it?"

"It was the two deputies that burned me up," Anderson said. "We had things in hand and they stopped us." He rushed from the cabin.

Patrick trailed the others, grabbing his gun belt as he went. His pa and Anderson were already mounted and galloping off. Eric was slower to follow. Patrick wished he could avoid whatever lay ahead. There didn't seem to be any way. If he wasn't with the family, he was against them. That's what his pa always said.

He rode slower and still got to the outskirts of Utopia at the same time as the others. Anderson's horse was lathered from galloping too fast for too long. The poor animal was about ready to die under him. Leadbottom's horse always had a hard time supporting its rider's considerable bulk.

"What're we doing?" Patrick drew rein beside his father. Leadbottom's eyes were closed and he swiveled around as if trying to locate something lost. Patrick had seen diviners find water this way. They'd take a fork of a birch tree, hold the ends and somehow the end swung this way and that until it suddenly pointed straight down. Dig a bit and subterranean water sprung up into a pool.

"There. That way," he said. Leadbottom pointed. "We'll find ourselves what we want there."

"The hardware store?" Patrick tried to make sense of it. Then he realized there wasn't any.

"Them two comin' out. They're spies for the Gallaghers. We can find out what Winifred's learned about the mine from them."

Patrick kept a sharp lookout for the law. The two deputies worked all night long with Shadrach Nelson. By now they and the marshal had gone home to sleep, leaving Abe Nelson to handle trouble during the daylight.

He was a little scared of Abe Nelson. The deputy was the spitting image of his father, but he had a vicious streak a mile wide that Shad didn't have. Whether he wanted to look good in his pa's eyes or was just naturally mean hardly mattered. If Abednego Nelson arrested any of the Morriseys, they'd be lucky to survive the day in the town lockup. And this time of the morning, they weren't likely to get breakfast.

Patrick stopped a few yards away. His pa and the other two surrounded the men coming from the hardware store. He had seen the men around town but had never so much as said howdy to either. Most of the townspeople avoided the lead miners like they had the plague. Patrick didn't blame them, and, truth to tell, that suited him. There weren't many in Utopia he wanted to call acquaintances, much less friends.

Except Beatrice. And he considered her far more than a friend.

"Where are you goin'?" Leadbottom edged his horse closer to the pair standing on the steps leading up to Sampson's hardware store.

"We don't have a quarrel with you, Morrisey," one said.

"You're liars!" Leadbottom screamed at the top of his lungs.

Neither man was carrying iron. They backed up the steps, ready to seek refuge inside the store.

Eric was too quick for them. He spun a lariat around and dropped it over both of them. One tried to pull free. Eric backed his horse away, keeping the lariat tightly looped.

"Tell me or I swear you'll live to regret it!"

"Tell you what, you bloated—"

That was as far as the man got. Eric turned his horse's face and brought it to a quick walk. Both men were yanked off their feet, hit the creaking wood steps, bounced and then flopped around in the street.

"You're gonna tell me what you're tellin' her," Leadbottom promised. "If you don't, you'll learn every damned thing there is to know about my mine the hard way!"

He snapped orders to Eric and Anderson. They swarmed their prisoners and tied up the struggling men.

"Patrick, fetch their horses. Around the side of the store," Leadbottom ordered.

Patrick did as he was told. Both men were flopped belly down across their own saddles.

Eric led one horse and Anderson the other. Leadbottom whooped and hollered as he galloped from town. That drew the attention of people in the stores, not the prisoners being carted off.

Patrick rode slowly after them, wondering what his pa had in store for the two men. Whatever the voices told him, it wasn't going to be good for either man.

CHAPTER FIVE

"How long are you going to keep them, Pa? It's been all day. Somebody'll miss them if we keep them overnight." Patrick Morrisey looked at their two prisoners. A hard knot froze in his belly. He had no idea who they were. Other than being customers at the hardware store, they were strangers.

"Gotta find what they've found out spyin' on us," Leadbottom Morrisey grunted. He folded his hands on his ample belly. He leaned back in the rickety chair, staring hard at the two men trussed up and thrown into the corner of the cabin. A pudgy finger came up and stabbed toward the nearer of the prisoners. "Him. He's the one."

"What're you talking about?" The man tried to stand. Anderson Morrisey shoved him back down and made like he'd kick him if he tried to get up again. "Who are you people?"

"You're spyin' for her. I know," Leadbottom said. His head drooped down and his chin rested on his chest.

"Is he dead?" the prisoner asked.

"He's thinking," Anderson said.

"Don't let him hurt himself," spoke up the second prisoner. "Look, me and Jim here are mechanics. We work for the railroad. We repair stuff."

"All we did was buy some parts at that store. Neither of

us has been in town more 'n a couple weeks." Jim let out an exasperated sigh. "We don't know who you are. If you're one of them what's got a beef with the railroad, ask for Mister Sussman. He's the station master and—"

"Shut up," Leadbottom shouted. He balled his hands and pounded them on the table so hard the legs threatened to buckle under the onslaught. "You're spyin' on us for them coal diggers. What's Winifred Gallagher know about us?"

The men exchanged looks.

"She's the one selling the coal to the railroad," said Jim.

His partner laughed without humor.

"She calls herself the Coal Queen of the Rockies. That's a laugh. I know a half dozen other mines that dig out better quality coal."

Leadbottom canted his head to one side. His lips moved in silent conversation. His eyelids drooped, and he started to drift off to sleep again, only to snap awake.

"You want to know all about how we mine? Get 'em up to the new stope."

"It ain't safe, Uncle," Eric said. "The gas takes a spell to blow out."

"Now!"

"It is more 'n bad smellin'. Damp can blow up. These two ain't miners. If they cause a single spark, the whole tunnel will collapse."

Leadbottom Morrisey leaned forward. Spittle glittered in his unruly black beard. His ebony eyes peered out from deep, sunken pits. Under the filth on his face, his pasty white skin was stretched as taut as a drumhead.

"Get them, get them." His voice turned small. "I got such a headache. What was I sayin'?"

"You want them to work in the new tunnel," said Eric. "Is that smart, Uncle?"

Leadbottom started to erupt, then sank down in the chair.

"I got a headache and now my belly's actin' up. Do what

I said. Yeah, do that," he said. He made a sweeping motion with his hand.

Anderson and Eric pulled their prisoners upright and shoved them through the door. Patrick trailed behind. He closed the cabin door as he left so his pa couldn't hear what he said.

"There's no call to put them to work," he said. "Let 'em go."

"What?" Eric spun around and shoved out his gut to bang into his cousin. He knocked Patrick back a step. "You heard him. Uncle Leadbottom's the boss here, not you."

"I'm his oldest son. When he's not ordering you around, it's my job."

"Pat, it ain't your call to do any such thing. I'm only a year younger. There's no call to cross Pa." Anderson tugged on the rope around Jim's neck. His prisoner gagged as the hemp tightened into a noose.

"He doesn't mean it. You see how sick he's getting."

"He's workin' too hard, that's all. Ain't none of us can do the smeltin' the way he does. Him leanin' over the cauldron and pourin' off the molten lead into the molds. The sulfur fumes are enough to make anybody's head hurt." Anderson sucked in his breath. "I don't like bein' underground all day but that's better than turnin' the galena ore into bricks." He wrinkled his nose. "The smell's something awful."

"Makes everything taste like metal," Eric said. He spat.

Patrick watched as the two prisoners edged away, trying not to be too obvious. With their hands tied behind their backs, running would be nigh on impossible. A single yank on either of their leashes would bring them to their knees. That didn't stop them from entertaining just a tad of hope they might get away from their captors.

He considered letting them get away. Dealing with his brother and cousin wasn't that hard. Like his pa, they both had hair-trigger tempers. Get them arguing with one another and the world could come to an end around them and they'd never notice.

Patrick was too slow in deciding what to do. Eric spotted Jim bobbing and twisting his neck around to get free of the noose. A quick yank brought the man to his knees.

"You got some workin' to do. Then you can tell Winifred everything about our minin' techniques."

"Look, mister, I know Miz Gallagher. Who doesn't? Work for the railroad and you know her. That's where Sussman buys our coal. But I don't have any idea who you are."

"We try not to be too uppity," Patrick said. Any chance at letting the two men go was gone now. Both Anderson and Eric were alert again, their bloodshot eyes fixed on their respective prisoners.

"Come along. Step lively." Anderson jerked on the rope and started the long climb up the hillside. Eric followed with Jim trailing behind. Patrick brought up the rear, still thinking on ways of letting the two men go free.

Kidnapping was a crime. The two men were newcomers to Utopia, but they worked at the railroad depot. Somebody would miss them and ask questions. The last thing he—or his pa—needed was for the marshal and his deputies to come nosing around. If they started spying on the Morrisey family, the lawmen would find all about how he and Beatrice were sparking. From the start, Patrick knew the danger in giving in to the girl's wiles. But she was so pretty and the danger made it even more attractive to him.

If either family discovered them together, it was over. That added spice to every time they met. He held his breath as he remembered how they'd sneaked off after their families had started taking potshots at each other. The scent of pine needles and the soft whisper of wind through the treetops and—

"Pat, quit your woolgatherin'," Anderson said. "We need you to block the tunnel while we get 'em to work."

"Please," pleaded Jim. "I got a wife and a kid. They don't know what's happened to me. Let me go so I can—"

Eric shoved him hard. Jim stumbled and disappeared into the maw of the mine. His companion went more willingly, or so it looked. Anderson tightened the rope around his neck to guarantee him obeying. A lantern flared and cast a pale yellow glow that illuminated the depths of the mine.

Patrick heaved a sigh and entered. Every time he went in, he had the fear of never coming out. Eric talked about tommyknockers and gases threatening to either explode or poison anyone in the mine. Patrick shuddered at being closed in. Being afraid of tight, enclosed spaces wasn't a good thing for a miner. If he complained, though, his pa would pull him away from swinging a pick and put him to work smelting the ore. That was worse. He had seen what it did to his pa.

Stomach cramps and puking his guts out and the headaches were only part of it. Insane rages got worse every month and doing loco things like kidnapping the two men now stumbling along deeper in the mine became more frequent. Eventually Leadbottom Morrisey would cross the line. No amount of avoiding everyone in town would save them if enough got mad.

He had heard tales of vigilance committees. Mindless mobs that took an idea into their heads and hung whoever crossed them.

Patrick ran a finger around his collar. They'd string him up for sure. Then what would Beatrice think? Would she shed a tear when she saw her hanged lover swinging to and fro in the wind from the limb of that sturdy old oak tree just outside town?

"You watch after 'em, Pat. I'll go tell Pa we have them varmints workin'." Anderson pushed past him.

"Where's Eric?"

"He wants to catch a few winks. Been a long time since any of us slept. That dustup last night was enough to give anyone nightmares." Anderson tromped off.

Patrick listened until his brother's footfalls disappeared, hidden by the steady sound of a pickaxe digging into rock. He went deeper into the mine. Eric was already asleep in a drift that had played out fast. Patrick walked past, thinking he should kick his cousin awake. He wasn't the only one short on sleep, though Patrick grinned from ear to ear remembering why he'd lost sleep.

"Bea," he said softly, smiling. "You are such a wildcat."

"Mister, please, don't make us do this." Jim stopped his digging and blocked his way deeper into the mine. The way he held the pickaxe showed he was willing to use it on any of his captors to escape.

Patrick moved to put his hand on his holstered six-shooter.

"This isn't my idea. It's my pa's, but I do what he tells me." Patrick felt the need to explain the reason he had taken part in the kidnapping, in spite of what he wanted. He stepped forward and banged his head against the overhead shoring.

As he ducked, Jim acted. The man swung the pickaxe around and would have killed him except his aim was a few inches off. The metal head glanced off the rock wall. Sparks escaped like fat blue cockroaches skittering away from the light. The assault caused the handle to break. While the head bounced away, the wood handle smashed into Patrick's head. The world spun around him. Stunned, he sank down. Pain jabbed into his head.

He kept enough of his senses to clutch at his six-gun. Hands tried to pry it loose from him, but he clung on like a leech. Then the groping hands disappeared. Patrick sagged back. He tried to focus, but the world showed double everywhere he looked. In the back of his dazed mind, he knew he ought to call out for Eric to help him. Even deeper in his head came the thought that Eric would run to Leadbottom and blame everything on his cousin.

Patrick knew it *was* his fault, letting their captive miners escape. That made it worse. Pulling himself to his feet, he staggered along a few feet until the world stopped spinning. Only a throbbing ache remained in his head. He touched his temple. His fingers came away sticky and damp with his own blood. Gingerly, he pressed his fingers in and traced a large lump popping up on his skull.

He went after the escaping man. A quick glance showed that Eric still slept in the short drift. The other prisoner continued working deeper in the mine, unaware his friend had escaped. Patrick knew he had to do something about him or he'd have a second prisoner get away, but focusing was hard. When he burst from the mouth of the mine into the night air, he felt as if he'd been drenched with a bucket of frigid water. The freezing mountain air brought him around in a hurry.

His vision had returned to normal, for all the good that did. Nowhere did he catch sight of the escaping man. Patrick cursed. He knew what he'd do if their places were switched.

Half sliding downhill, he got to the cabin where Leadbottom and Anderson slept. Scattered around the hillside were a half dozen other cabins. Three or four Morriseys slept in each. His own cabin lay close to a mile away. Patrick almost went for it to recuperate. His head throbbed like a triphammer.

"Horses," he said. This was the way the prisoner got as far away as fast as possible.

He rounded the cabin and counted the horses tethered there. One was missing. Vaulting into the saddle of his mare, he sawed at the reins and headed the horse toward town. If luck was with him, he'd overtake the man before he found somebody in town to listen to his story.

Somebody like Abednego Nelson.

He put his head down and let his horse set its own pace. He hoped the old mare was up to the race. If he didn't stop the man, heads would roll.

And the first to go would be his.

CHAPTER SIX

Patrick Morrisey worried his horse would die under him. The mare stumbled more and more the closer they got to Utopia. He looked at the sky. Heavy clouds parted enough for him to get a clear view of the constellations and guess what time it was. He had owned a pocket watch but had given it to Beatrice as a gift the first time they spent the night together. She had been delighted to receive such a fine gift, especially since he'd stumbled through an explanation of how she could use the watch to count the hours until they were together again.

He missed that watch. It had been his granddad's. As the old man lay dying of consumption, only one of the family had stayed by his side. Patrick had earned that watch. None of the others had wanted to come too close for fear of catching the disease.

When his mare stumbled and almost threw him, he slowed to a walk. He worried more about stopping Jim than he did about his horse dying. A quick brush of his hand over the butt of his old Remington assured him he was ready to do what was necessary.

Necessary for him to keep on living.

His pa's sudden rages might doom him, but he worried more about the town's law dogs. Shadrach Nelson had run off some of the most vicious outlaws in all of Colorado. The town had been downright quiet since the last of them vanished—or died. But his son upset Patrick more. Abe Nelson had a hair trigger temper and wasn't above whaling away on anyone he arrested, if he took it into his head. Sitting around and gossiping convinced Patrick that Abednego Nelson was a cold-blooded killer. His pa said so, and so did most of his cousins and nephews. He wasn't sure he'd ever believe anything Anderson said since he exaggerated so much, but right now he wasn't inclined to find out if his brother's stories about the Utopia deputies were true.

He rode slowly down the meandering main street, keeping a sharp eye out for his quarry. The best guess was that Jim headed for the marshal to report his kidnapping. It was early enough that none of the stores were open yet. Most of the clerks hadn't even shown up for the day's work. That gave Patrick some hope of finding the escaped miner and capturing him without much fuss.

Miner? Slave.

He shuddered. His pa had made some terrible decisions lately. As the man's health declined, his erratic behavior became more worrisome. If he was honest, Patrick had to say his pa was downright dangerous now, both to himself and to the rest of the family.

His thoughts turned to leaving Utopia before life at the lead mine became unbearable. Leadbottom saw slights and downright insults where none existed. Before long, spurred on by Leadbottom's erratic hatreds, the Morrisey family would be gunning for any Gallagher on sight. That wouldn't do. His feelings for Bea were too strong, not that he saw everything from Winifred Gallagher's lofty perch. She was as crazy as Leadbottom.

Patrick had hinted that he and Beatrice might just get on a train one night and go somewhere else. Anywhere. It didn't matter to him as long as she rode beside him. Central City was a boomtown. There had to be opportunities for a man willing to work hard. He knew hard rock mining, even if he scrabbled out lead rather than gold or silver. And Bea was clever. The two of them had a better chance away from their families than sticking with them.

He understood blood ties. Leaving his relatives, brothers, cousins, even a couple nephews as young as they were, caused a hole to form in his heart. They supported him, and he depended on them. It had been that way all his life.

"How bad will it be if shooting starts and they get killed?" He spoke in a hoarse whisper, but his horse craned her head around and peered at him with a large brown, disapproving eye. A quick pat on the neck assured his mare that he wasn't going to start anything.

Except if Jim put up a fuss.

He had no reason to want the man to work as a slave, but his pa did. Something told Leadbottom Morrisey that Jim and his partner were conspiring against him. Patrick knew better than argue with his pa over something like this. His pa *knew*, no matter how loco it seemed.

More than that, if the escaped miner reached the marshal Patrick and the rest of his family would be locked up. He doubted Winifred would allow her niece to come see him then. As it was, they had to sneak around behind their families' backs.

Why hadn't she given him a straight answer when he hinted that they leave Utopia? Patrick came to the conclusion he hadn't been bold enough. Beatrice expected him to be forthright. More than this, she wanted him to be in command. He should have *told* her they were leaving.

In his gut, he realized that would have had the opposite result. She would have dug her heels in and told him she'd never leave Utopia. She was like a mountain trout. Hooking it was only part of the game. Beatrice had to be reeled in slowly, bit by bit, fighting as she came, even though she wanted to be landed. He knew she loved him as much as he loved her. All he had to do was be a man.

Voices caused him to jerk erect. Two deputies hurried

along a side street, arguing. He tried to overhear what they said, but their voices were low-pitched. What he did know was that they argued.

Patrick reached for his six-shooter when Abednego Nelson joined the other two. They turned and went down a cross street that led away from the jail. If Jim had stirred up a ruckus, it would draw three law dogs. And if Patrick tried to take on three armed and angry deputies, he hadn't a chance of recapturing the escaped miner.

Not knowing what to do, he rushed on to the jailhouse. The deputies would bring anyone back here who spouted a loud claim of being kidnapped off the streets of Utopia.

He let out a cry of relief when he saw his quarry hobbling along, leading his horse toward the calaboose. Somewhere in his wild escape, Jim had banged up his leg. Why he didn't stay in the saddle wasn't a question Patrick wanted to consider. This was his big chance. He galloped along the deserted street and hit the ground running.

As fast as he went, he stopped as abruptly. Coming from the marshal's office was his worst nightmare. Shadrach Nelson cinched up his gun belt as he hurried out. Jim called out to the marshal.

"I need help. I was taken up into—"

"Got a serious situation over at the Lucky Lady," the marshal said. He made shooing motions with his hand. "Wait here. We can talk when I get back."

"Marshal, please!"

"Two men have been in a knife fight. That's more important than anything you've got to tell me. Get inside or get lost. I don't care which." Shadrach Nelson pushed past Jim and jogged off. Hand resting on his holstered gun.

Patrick watched the marshal disappear down the street. He drew his six-gun and walked forward slowly. Jim had disappeared.

When the man's horse neighed loudly, Patrick saw that his escaped miner had taken the marshal's advice and gone inside to wait for someone to return. He took a deep breath and walked to the door. He heard Jim inside cursing up a blue streak. He looked around. He didn't want any of the lawmen to barge in on him now. The early morning streets were still empty.

He lifted the latch as quietly as he could. It still warned the man inside.

"Marshal, is that you?" Jim called.

Patrick kicked the door open and shoved out his six-shooter. He fired at the same instant Jim did. The man had found a pistol and leveled it at the doorway. Patrick staggered and fired again. The first two shots had missed. This one struck its target.

Jim grunted and clutched his side. His borrowed six-gun fell from his fingers as he slumped forward over the marshal's desk.

"Don't you go bleeding on the desk," Patrick warned. He stepped inside and looked around. The cells in back stood empty. Another glance outside let him release more pent-up breath. Nobody rushed back at the sound of gunfire.

"Get to your horse," he ordered.

"No. Won't. You shot me." Jim clutched his side.

"It's not bad. I'll patch you up when we get back to the mine."

"Don't make me. I don't want to be your slave."

Patrick grabbed the man by the collar and yanked him upright. Jim's face turned white from shock.

"I'll leave your dead body on the desk if you don't come with me. Now!"

Jim stumbled outside, leaving a trail of blood behind. After a quick examination, Patrick decided the wound wasn't too bad. He had probably run the bullet along a rib. Maybe the bone broke. The bleeding showed no sign of being fatal and was starting to clot over.

"Quit pretending you're hurt worse than you are." A hard shove got Jim moving to the side of the jailhouse where his horse nervously jerked about. The smell of fresh blood caused its nostrils to flare.

Patrick forced his prisoner to get into the saddle. He saw how the man favored his right leg. Somewhere during his escape he had banged it up. Taken with his bullet wound, he wasn't likely to put up much of a fight.

Just to be safe, Patrick held his six-gun in his right hand as he took the reins in his left. He got his prisoner's horse trotting along, heading out of town. It added a mile or two to the return trip, but heading west to the railroad tracks before turning north avoided the marshal and his deputies.

Patrick wondered what the lawman would think when he found all that blood on his desk and floor. He grinned at the confusion Nelson would experience. He grinned even more when he reached the outskirts of Utopia. With luck running his way, he'd get Jim back into the mine and hard at work again before his pa ever found out one of his miners had escaped.

Disaster had been avoided. How he wanted to share his triumph with Bea!

Chapter Seven

Winifred Gallagher cursed constantly as she picked her way through the rocky foothills that led up to the Morrisey lead mine. Her cane served her well. Her knees hurt like fire. Her feet were more swollen now than they'd been that morning. And the crick in her neck made twisting around hard. That bothered her most since she was sure she was being followed.

Stopping suddenly, she turned and tried to find who trailed her. The heavy shadows cast by the full moon defeated her. When something rustled in the ankle-high grass near her feet, she whacked at it with her cane. She missed a small, furry varmint and almost lost her balance. Winifred caught herself and leaned against a rock to recover.

The night was quiet enough that she heard someone trying to be sneaky coming from way upslope. She set her cane tip between two rocks to give a sturdy base to lean against. Her fingers closed around a small caliber pistol carried in her skirt pocket. Turning slowly, she homed in on the approaching footsteps. Her thumb rested on the hammer as she aimed for the spot between two boulders where her stalker had to show himself.

"That you?" came a hoarse whisper. "Miz Gallagher?"

"Shut your tater trap," she said. Her hand shook just a mite, but that wouldn't spoil her aim. "Get your carcass over here right now. And stop makin' so much infernal noise."

It took all her willpower not to cock the pistol and squeeze the trigger when a looming darkness filled the spot between the boulders. A single flash of moonlight off a snake-skin hatband told her this was the good-for-nothing she'd come all the way from the Calcutta Mine to meet.

"You'll want to hear what I got to say."

"Nothing a Morrisey says is worth spit," she said. Reluctantly, she lowered her gun and tucked it away in the folds of her skirt. Her finger remained on the trigger, but she took her thumb off the hammer.

"I don't think of myself as a Morrisey. You're right when you say they're all ne'er-do-wells."

"That's a two-bit word," Winifred said. "Nuthin' I'd ever say. What's it mean?"

"They're all lazy, the lot of 'em. Leadbottom hisself is the worst. That bucket of lard's not done a day's work hisself in years."

"You're not tellin' me nuthin' I don't already know. Spit it out or get lost." She moved to get circulation back into her legs. They tingled just a mite. As she turned, she caught movement behind her.

"You're gonna want to hear this." Eric Sudderth crowded closer. The eager look on his face put Winifred on guard. Leadbottom's nephew had told her how he hated his uncle for the way he treated his mother.

Ellen Sudderth might have been Leadbottom's sister, but he treated her like dirt. Winifred wasn't sure she believed Leadbottom let her die when he could have fetched a doctor to save her, Eric telling the tale and sounding like he was making it up as he poured out the story the first time she'd met with him all by his lonesome. Tales grew with every telling, and Eric Sudderth had spun this one many times in her hearing. Leadbottom's nephew had never revealed what malady had sent his ma to the Promised Land. Depending on how drunk he was during the telling, he had been either ten or fifteen. She suspected other tellings had him both younger and maybe older. Winifred had never been interested enough to find out from someone who might actually know.

She had approached him with the promise of money to spy on the Morriseys. So far, he hadn't earned his keep. But hope blossomed like spring flowers, always new and fresh and bright every time he told her he had something important.

So far, he hadn't delivered anything useful. One day he would. Then Winifred would have Leadbottom by his balls. She'd put them in a nutcracker and delight in applying pressure. For all he had done to her and her kin, she was going to squeeze real slow to make his agony last as long as possible.

Eric thought Leadbottom had done him wrong. Winifred's story of her dealings with the head of the Morrisey family would put that to shame.

"You come alone?" she asked.

"What? Of course, I did. If my uncle ever found out I was meetin' up with you, he'd skin me alive. Or worse."

"What's worse? That or makin' you listen to yourself ramblin' on and on?"

She pivoted around her cane. Looking downslope made her uneasy. Shadows moved that shouldn't. Someone had followed her. She believed Eric Sudderth that he had come alone. So who dogged her steps?

"He's got two new miners workin' the mines. They've been swingin' picks deep in the new stope for the past four days."

"So?"

"One of them escaped three nights back, but Patrick

chased him down and brought him back." Eric snickered. "That's 'cuz he let him escape. Uncle Leadbottom would slap shackles on him and put him to work beside the two if he knew."

"What are you goin' on about? Leadbottom is chainin' his miners? I didn't know he had hired anybody who warn't blood."

"He didn't hire nobody. We kidnapped them. The pair of 'em came out of the hardware store, and we snatched 'em and took 'em back to the mine."

"He's keepin' them at work as slave labor?" Winifred's eyes narrowed. There might be something useful to use against the Morriseys with this tidbit.

"That's what he's doin'. He claims they done him wrong somehow, but I never saw 'em before. I asked Patrick and the others. Not a one of 'em knows the two. It's like Uncle Leadbottom just picked 'em at random."

"Are you sure he's not payin' 'em?"

"Nary a cent."

Winifred chewed at her thumb as she turned over what she'd just heard, trying to find leverage against Leadbottom Morrisey.

"One of 'em escaped but your cousin fetched him back?"

"Pat claims he grabbed the fellow out of the marshal's office, from under the noses of all them lawmen. He won't say much more because he doesn't want his pa to know he was the one who let the slave escape."

"Slave," Winifred said. She smiled crookedly. "The two fellows are from town?"

"I never laid eyes on them before. Pat said they were mechanics for the railroad. How he knows that is beyond me. Maybe he ast them." Eric scowled, as if talking to the men was a new idea to him.

"So they'd be missed. They're upright citizens with responsible jobs."

"For the railroad," Eric added.

Winifred considered how much trouble Leadbottom would be in if the railroad officials demanded satisfaction for stealing away their workmen. Everyone working for the line was clannish. It made sense to her that the powers that be in Denver wouldn't take kindly to stealing away their hired help. Especially if they were mechanics. Trains broke down. They had to be fixed or money was lost.

"Can you let these two go free?" she asked.

"Why'd I do a fool thing like that? It'd make my uncle powerful mad. And after Pat had to track down the one he let slip away from right under his nose—"

She swung out her pistol and aimed into the rocks past Eric Sudderth. A single rock had been kicked free and came rolling downhill. Somebody spied on them.

"Show yourself!" she barked. "If you don't, I'll plug this one. He's your blood kin."

Eric recoiled and reached for his gun.

Winifred whispered, "You gotta go. Tell 'em you snuck away from me when I caught you. Make up some cockamamie story why you're out here at this time of night."

Eric's head bobbed up and down. He stepped away, looked around and took a step to his right. A shot tore through the night and sent rock fragments flying. He yelped and dived for cover. Winifred looked up the slope, then realized the bullet had come from behind her. Somebody downhill was taking shots. A second hunk of lead sang past, but it was farther from her. Whoever the hidden sniper was, they aimed at Eric.

She saw movement from the direction Eric had come. Winifred fired twice, uprooted her cane and began slipping and sliding away, back in the direction of who shot at Eric. Her feet skidded on a patch of loose gravel. She sat heavily and scooted along on her rump. With every bounce she let out a brand-new curse until she came to a halt at the foot of the hill.

Gunfire from higher on the mountain turned the still night into a battlefield. She raised her pistol to fire when a dim silhouette showed, limned by the silver moonlight.

"What are you doin' here, girl?" Winifred jerked her gun away from the new target.

"I wondered where you were sneaking off to and followed. It's a good thing I did, too," Beatrice said. She settled the rifle stock into her shoulder and fired. "There's a half dozen of those snakes crawling around up on the slope."

Winifred used her cane to lever herself erect. She turned and studied the area where she had met Eric Sudderth. At least two men moved around there now. A quick shot in their direction sent them scurrying for cover like rats.

"Let's get outta here," she said, hobbling along as fast as she could. Beatrice trailed, taking an occasional shot. They reached a road at the base of the mountain the Morriseys used to cart their lead ingots to the rail station.

Winifred made faster time now. In a few minutes they'd left Morrisey territory behind.

"Gotta rest. I'm all tuckered out," she said. Her legs gave way, and she collapsed onto a smooth rock beside the road.

"You went to meet him? He's one of *them,* Aunt Win."

"I've been payin' that sneak for months to tell me what goes on in Leadbottom's camp." She bent over and slowly caught her breath. Every time she exhaled it felt like fire burning her throat.

"Why didn't you tell me?"

Winifred looked hard at her niece. Her lip curled just a little.

"Because you didn't have no call to know."

"I only want to help."

"You coulda got me kilt dead tonight sneakin' 'round the way you were."

"Somebody followed him. Leadbottom now knows Eric is spying for you."

Winifred shook her head. It wasn't like that. Even if Leadbottom figured out he had a traitor in his family, losing Eric wasn't that big a loss.

"I found out Leadbottom's got a couple men in his mine."

"I heard. Are you going to tell the marshal? That'd get Leadbottom in a world of trouble with the law."

Winifred sat and thought about it. What difference did it make if Leadbottom "recruited" men by grabbing them off the streets of Utopia? It wasn't any skin off her nose. She'd always heard about how clipper ships headed for China from the San Francisco Bay shanghaied crewmen. Of course, that was different. Once the ship was out of sight of land, the men either worked or didn't get fed.

It'd be a long way to swim back. Trapped in a lead mine was a different kettle of fish. One of Leadbottom's slaves had gotten away, but Patrick Morrisey had caught him. Snatched him from under the marshal's nose, if Eric was to be believed. That had to make the man powerful angry at not only the Morrisey family for imprisoning him but Shadrach Nelson for not helping him.

A different thought came to her. Leadbottom wasn't paying the men he kidnapped to work as miners. She could always use a few more picks in the Calcutta Mine. Sending a few of her brood to town to kidnap some of the stronger specimens walking around fast and easy free made a certain amount of sense. Nobody'd miss a couple drunks in the dozen or so saloons scattered around the town.

"It'll be the end of us if you start kidnapping workers, Aunt Win."

She glared at Beatrice. In this case she was right. If trouble flared up, let it be Leadbottom that got burned.

"We got coal to mine, girl," she said. Using her cane, she struggled to her feet. When Bea tried to support her, she brushed off her hand. She didn't need any help. She was the head of the Gallagher family.

She was the Coal Queen of the Rockies.

Chapter Eight

"Things have been quiet enough lately," Shadrach Nelson said. "I want to take the days so I can get some sleep."

"That's not too bad, Pa," Abe Nelson said, "letting me take night patrol. Mary Beth's working all day. If I plan my time right, I can look in on her now and again."

"You neglect your job to see her and I'll fire you. It won't matter that you're my son."

"You know I won't do that," Abe said. The far-off look in his eyes told a different story. He intended to spend as much of the night with his lady friend as he could.

Shad needed to steel himself to firing his boy if it came to that. Right now things in Utopia were quiet enough. The feud between the Gallaghers and Morriseys simmered but hadn't boiled over in a spell. Getting rid of the last of the outlaws that had plagued Utopia for so long went a long way toward keeping the peace. All he needed to do was watch the depot to be sure some of the worst of the owlhoots didn't try sneaking back.

Prevention, he decided, was the watchword. Head off danger, and that kept all the townspeople safe and happy. Running the hard cases out of Utopia was easy enough, though, compared to dealing with Winifred Gallagher and Leadbottom Morrisey.

They had put down roots. Worse still, the town needed the money brought in by the families' mines.

"Have you ever heard what set off the feud?" he asked.

Abe looked up, puzzled. Then he got on the same track as his pa.

"More than one said Leadbottom jilted Winifred back in the day."

"Before they proved their respective mines?" Shad had some inkling of when that was, but the notion of Winifred and Leadbottom ever being together was as improbable as the sun rising in the west.

"You going to take the day shift?" Abe stood and hitched up his gun belt. "If you are, I've got fifteen-twenty minutes I can spend with Mary Beth before she gets to clerking for Mister Sampson."

Shad checked his watch.

"Better hurry, then. It's a quarter till seven. Sampson is a stickler for routine. If that door to his store's not open at exactly seven, he'll have a conniption fit."

Abe grinned and lit out running. Even if he made good time to the store, he wouldn't have more than a few minutes with his girlfriend. Shad settled into the chair and leaned back. He stifled a yawn. It'd be a long time before he got home. Ruth would appreciate him being around the house all night long. It'd be just the two of them again. Abe would be on patrol, and Miriam always seemed to be gone these days.

"Just the two of us," he said. A tiny smile crept to his lips. He felt the weight of the job, of family, and as much as he hated to admit it, of advancing years. He wasn't old. At least he told himself that, but keeping up with his children wasn't possible—or necessary—any longer. It was time to slow down a mite and appreciate other things in his life.

Like Ruth.

He jerked upright. His woolgathering would be the death

of him. A woman had entered the office, planted herself squarely in front of him and he hadn't noticed.

"Can I help you?" He cleared his throat. He tried to look more official, then gave up. The woman's expression told him she wasn't happy about something, and no matter what he did, he wasn't going to change her mind.

"You have to, Marshal. You don't know me, do you?"

He shook his head, not quite daring to tell her he had no idea who she was. She looked familiar, but Utopia was growing so fast that meant very little.

"I am Mrs. James Murton."

"What can I do for you, Mrs. Murton?" Shad scooted to the edge of his chair and leaned over his desk, attentive now.

"My husband is missing, sir. He's been gone for four days. That is not like him at all."

"And?" He heard more in her words.

"His best friend and coworker, Clarence Abbott, is also missing. They vanished at the same time."

"You think they're off together somewhere? On a bender?"

"My husband is a teetotaler, as I am," she said primly. "Mister Abbott is another matter, but James is not easily led astray."

"Even by a friend? His best friend?"

"They are friends and know each other through their work. They are employed as mechanics in the rail yard."

"I suppose you've asked their boss if he's seen the two."

Her sour expression told him that she'd likely asked immediately.

"Did their employer have any notion where they'd got off to?"

"Mister Sussman did not assign them a job elsewhere along the tracks, if that's what you're asking. I . . . I thought they might have, and James hadn't told me. Only this morning I went to find out. Mister Sussman was quite hostile."

"Is it usual for your husband to be gone for three days without letting you know?"

"I . . . it does happen. Since coming to Utopia he has been sent on work assignments like that more than once. He fixes switches along the route and sometimes even repairs the telegraph line strung beside the tracks."

He considered the situation. Mrs. Murton probably enjoyed her husband's absence, at least until it appeared he wasn't going to return. He had no proof but suspected a dalliance with a neighbor kept her occupied while Mister Murton—James—was gone.

"Is there a Mrs. Abbott?" He saw the small shake of her head. "You'd be the only one, other than their boss, to notice the men weren't in town?"

"Find James, Marshal. He is a good man and not inclined to run off. We have a daughter, and he'd never leave without talking to her." She stiffened and fixed him with a hot stare. "I assure you he did not run off with some floozy."

"And he's not sobering up from a three-day drunk," Shad finished. "Because he's not only faithful but is also a teetotaler."

"I am sure something terrible has happened to him."

"When's the last time you saw him?"

"He left for work four days ago. His superior said he sent James and Mister Abbott to buy some hardware."

"I'll ask Mister Sampson and—"

"He said they left the store with a significant amount of hardware, primarily nuts and bolts of various sizes. What they bought was piled up beside the store, untouched. Mister Sampson is the last one to see either of them. I have asked everyone I could find." She sniffed and looked down her nose at him. "People in this town can be quite inhospitable."

"You and your husband haven't been here long?"

"A few weeks. We should never have left Denver."

"The job paid too well for your husband to pass up," Shad guessed. He read the answer on her face. "I'll get right to it, Mrs. Murton." He stood, then asked, "Is his horse gone?"

She opened her mouth, then clamped it shut.

"You never thought to see? That's all right. It gives me a place to start."

"Thank you, Marshal." She folded her hands in front of her and said primly, "I expect James to be home for dinner." As if she were a soldier on the parade ground, she did an about-face and marched from the office.

Shad followed her outside, stretched his muscles and then headed for the depot. He enjoyed the warm late summer day. Storm clouds moved over the tallest mountain peaks, but he guessed that storm was an hour or more away. Probably more. When the storm came, he enjoyed watching the lightning as long as it didn't set fire to anything in town.

But he ran into a different kind of storm before he reached the railroad station. Anderson Morrisey stepped out into the street, blocking his way.

"Good morning, Andy. How're things in the lead mines?"

"You mockin' me, lawman?" Morrisey rested his hand on the butt of his six-shooter.

"When I decide to make fun of you, there won't be any question. Now get out of my way." Shad took a step forward. Morrisey moved to block him again.

"My pa says you're a coward, that you hide behind your deputies. They do all the dangerous work for you."

"Your pa's been sniffing those lead fumes from his smelter too long. It's gone to his head. I've heard tell that too much lead vapor can make a man loco in the head."

Anderson Morrisey curled his fingers around the butt of his pistol and lowered his shoulder, ready to throw down.

"Then again, there's a different kind of lead poisoning that's about to befall you."

"What?"

"Where do you want me to shoot you? In the leg? If I put a round in your belly, you might take a week to die. That's because I wouldn't fetch the doctor or let anyone else do that. He's a busy man and saving trash like you'd be a waste of time."

Shad drew and swung his pistol as Morrisey tensed to pull his iron. The Peacemaker's barrel collided with the side of the exposed head hard enough to knock Anderson a step away and send his hat flying. Morrisey dropped to one knee. His eyes glazed over.

"Let me relieve you of that hogleg," Shad said. "It'll get you into more trouble than a headache." He plucked Anderson Morrisey's gun from its holster and tucked it into his own gun belt. "You go set yourself down in the shade. I wouldn't want you to get sunstroke, not after you've guzzled more booze than you should this early in the morning." Shad pushed the top of the man's bare head, carefully avoiding getting blood on his fingers.

Morrisey toppled over and lay staring up at the bright blue Colorado sky.

"You can get your gun when you leave town."

Shad whistled tunelessly as he made his way to the depot. He'd felt down before putting Anderson Morrisey in his place. Still, he wondered why the man had tried to pick a fight. It was too early in the day for him to be drunk. He shrugged it off. What he'd said about Leadbottom being loco from breathing in lead fumes went double for someone like his son, who wasn't too bright to begin with. Long hours scraping lead from rock in a dark mine had to wear down any man's sanity.

"Howdy, Marshal. What can I do for you?" The station master balanced precariously on a chair as he painted the door lintel a different shade of green. The railroad changed its official colors once a month, or so it seemed.

"You can paint my house when you finish there, Mister Sussman," Shad said.

"Supply the paint and pay me more 'n the General does to run this depot, and I'm your man."

"You have two men working for you. Mechanics. They're—"

"Murton and Abbott. You got them locked up in your jailhouse?"

"Should I?"

"They stole horses that belong to the railroad and lit out."

"Four days back?"

The station master stepped down and put aside the paint bucket and brush. He rubbed his hands on his pants.

"Took more 'n the horses. I gave them danged near twenty dollars out of the cash drawer to buy more hardware. That was too much cash for them highwaymen, I reckon."

"You haven't laid eyes on them since?"

The station master shook his head, then looked at Shad more intently.

"What trouble are they in?"

"I'll ask when I find them. Mrs. Murton wants her husband sent home."

"Clarence don't have anyone to ask after him. He lives up on Pine Knob in an old line shack, him and a mangy mongrel."

"Have you been up there to see if he's around? Dead, maybe?"

"His dog'd have et him, if he died. No, sir, I keep real close to the station. That's the way the General likes it. Besides, I'm the only telegrapher in town worth his salt. Egan's not got the ear for the job. I get and send more traffic than you'd expect in a town like Utopia. Traffic. That's what we call the code dots and dashes."

"Who's been repairing the engines? There've been, what, eight through since Murton and Abbott disappeared."

"Nine and it's the same fool who's climbing up on a chair to paint the station. I don't know much about fixing busted locomotive parts, but I know enough to keep the train running. Me." He poked himself in the chest with his paint-covered index finger. "And besides being painter and mechanic, I'm a carpenter and even patched a hole in the water tower a day back. A goldarned woodpecker had banged a hole in the side."

"That must have been a chore," Shad said, looking around.

"Worst part was the bird hammering away all night long, kept me awake. From the soaked feathers, the leak it caused washed it to hell and gone." He made a face. "Chances are it just got a sudden bath, but a man can hope."

"That he can. If they turn up, let me know."

The station master turned back to his painting, mumbling about woodpeckers.

Shad went around the depot. Stables some distance away confirmed what the station master had said. Four stalls were ready for horses. Only two were there, munching at hay. No sign the other two had been occupied since the last time the livery had been mucked out.

Shad tried to put the pieces together. The pair had been on an errand, riding their company horses. They'd bought what the station master had sent them to purchase, set it down and then—?

"If those boys decided to hightail it, why buy nuts and bolts? Take the money and ride for the west." He turned over one idea after another until a sound behind him turned him cautious.

Someone dogged his footsteps.

Shad walked faster. The crunch of boots against the dirt and rock in the street came faster from behind him. He moved his hand around to secure the butt of the pistol he'd taken from Anderson Morrisey. With the grace of a dancer, he whipped out the pistol and spun about. The gun barrel sang through the air and collided with Anderson Morrisey's cheek.

Once more the man stumbled and went down.

Shad stared at him in disbelief.

"You are one stupid, mule-brained fool. You don't learn." He waved the man's gun around. "I took this off you so you wouldn't get into trouble. Now look. I have to clean your blood off my vest. And your barrel's all smeared now."

He reached down and grabbed Morrisey's greasy collar. With a hard yank, he dragged him to his feet.

"This time I'm throwing you in jail."

"I ain't done nuthin'!"

"You're disturbing the peace. *My* peace. That ought to be a hanging offense, but it's not. So all I can do is keep you locked up for a week."

He dragged Morrisey along.

"I'm bleedin'. You cut my face."

"For two cents, I'd empty your six-shooter into your foot to see how you liked that."

"My pa'll get you for this."

Shad shoved his prisoner into the back cell amid increasingly vile threats of what Leadbottom and the rest of the Morrisey clan would do. As he turned the key in the cell lock, he had to wonder why Anderson Morrisey was even in town, much less assaulting a peace officer.

He gave up trying to figure it out. The lead miners were loco. That was plenty good for an explanation.

And it still didn't give him a clue as to what happened to Murton and Abbott.

Chapter Nine

"I'll rip your lungs out," Anderson Morrisey screamed. He rattled the bars in the cell, then tried to kick open the door. He lost his balance and fell backward, nursing his injured leg.

Shadrach Nelson shook his head sadly. Keeping a feral animal in a cage was wrong, but he wasn't about to release Morrisey back into the wild.

"You keep that up and I'll send you to Denver for trial. The judges over there aren't too forgiving when a man's assaulted a lawman. You might get six months in the lockup down south in Cañon City."

This set off a new round of cursing and fist beating against the outer brick wall.

"I swear if you don't let me outta here, my pa's gonna do to you what we done to them Gallagher boys. You'll regret you ever saw me."

"That much is true," Shad said. "Every minute that passes makes me even sorrier I ever laid eyes on you." He moved his chair around to keep an eye on his prisoner.

Morrisey's outbursts died down and he sulked, sitting on the cot with his legs drawn up and his arms circling his knees.

Shad half turned toward the outer door when he heard someone working the latch. Leroy Early came in and immediately held up his hands.

"Whoa, Marshal. You got no call to gun me down."

"Sorry. My prisoner's making me edgy."

As if prodded with a stick, Morrisey began a new round of cursing.

"I can take care of that," Early said. "It'd bruise my knuckles some but you'd get some peace and quiet."

"Come on outside for a minute," Shad said. He pulled the door shut behind him as they stepped out to the street.

"What's on your mind, Shad? Or do you just want some peace and quiet?"

"That, too, but mostly it's something Andy said about Leadbottom doing to me what he did to some Gallagher boys."

Early shrugged.

"I don't know what he meant, either," Shad said. He explained how he'd spent his morning hunting for the two railroad workers.

"You reckon Leadbottom's got something to do with them, too? Them and the Gallaghers?"

"In my lofty station as marshal and you being a lowly deputy, I'm going up the mountainside to the Calcutta Mine and talk to Winifred."

"You mean I drew the short straw and get to nursemaid him?" Early jerked his thumb over his shoulder in the direction of the jail.

"I'll be back before sundown. I want to tell Abe about everything that's going on. Deep down I get the feeling of the town being a locomotive boiler with too much pressure. Things will blow soon, and I don't have any idea why or how."

"It's always that way in Utopia," said Early. He turned from the marshal's office and looked as far down the winding street as he could. "You mind if I find a chair and sit myself down somewhere yonder?"

"I only hire the smartest men as deputies," Shad said, laughing. He slapped Early on the back. "Just don't go taking a nap on city time."

"Just you get back here as quick as you can so I won't be tempted."

"I don't appreciate your boy putting me in his gun sights," Shad said. He sat his horse, one leg lifted up and curled around the pommel. "This is a friendly visit."

"Ain't no sich critter," Winifred Gallagher called down to him from behind a large boulder. "Whenever the law's nosin' around my mine, there's trouble."

"That's what I want to find out. Is there something I can help you with? Let's talk. Without you fixing to drill me if I so much as twitch an ear, that is."

Angry words echoed down the mountain. He waited. As shrill and abusive as Winifred was, she sounded like the only one in control. Whoever had tracked him with the rifle was close to pulling the trigger. The Gallaghers didn't much cotton to people riding on their road.

And they counted lawmen as less than mere "people."

He looked around for other trouble but didn't find it. The deeply rutted road was more rock than dirt. Heavily loaded wagons of coal rumbled along here several times a week. Their metal rimmed wheels chipped away at the stony roadbed.

Lumps the size of his fist glistened darkly on either side of the road and even trailed off downslope. If Winifred had bothered to pick up the spilled coal, the Calcutta Mine would deliver twice the tonnage that it actually did down in Utopia.

"Set your boots on the ground and advance slow-like," Winifred called to him.

Shad sighed and did as she ordered. This was her land, and her word was law here. Unless he wanted to insist that it wasn't. Legally, only the county sheriff had jurisdiction here, but that had long since been decided between him and Old "Glory Be" Parsons. Whoever wore the Utopia marshal's badge wouldn't find his authority contested over in Georgetown, no matter the uproar of local citizens. The only other law was the Clear Creek sheriff. He was content to never be called to Hellfire Pass for any reason since he had his own miners to fleece.

That suited Shad dealing with both sheriffs. He preferred doing things his own way, and sometimes he skirted the letter of the law.

More than one of the outlaw gangs he had driven out of Utopia should have been held for trial. Since that was too much of a bother and his jail only had three usable cells, he was happy to send them on their way to bedevil some other town.

Let Georgetown or Clear Creek or Central City or even Denver deal with the problem.

He walked close to a hundred yards before he came to a fork in the road. The main track continued around the mountain. A path, hardly more than a game trail, came straight down from higher up. Winifred stood there, leaning heavily on her cane.

"Good afternoon," he called.

"There's nuthin' good 'bout it, Marshal. What do you want?"

Winifred wasn't much for small talk. Seeing the muzzle of a rifle pointing at him from a clump of bushes irritated him. He thought they'd gotten past that.

"Tell your sniper to put down the rifle or I get on my horse and go on back to town. Utopia's a mite friendlier."

"You call that a threat, Marshal?" She laughed harshly.

"Did you have any of your boys up and disappear on you?"

"What's that? Ain't nobody in the Gallagher family gone missin'. Not recently. Not since my half-brother Rafe took a powder and run off with a red-haired saloon floozie. That was nigh on five years back."

"Maybe you added a couple men to your crew?"

Shad saw how defensive Winifred Gallagher turned. He'd struck a nerve.

"You have new miners named Murton and Abbott?" Again he was puzzled by her reaction. She had tensed up before, and now she almost sagged in relief. She used her cane to support herself more now as if her legs threatened to give way.

"Nobody named that up here."

He felt she wanted to say something more but held back.

"Might be you or some of your family's heard about them going missing?"

"Ain't my business. Ain't none of my kith and kin's business."

She sounded a mite too forceful. He looked past her. It took a few seconds for him to remember the name. Jeremiah Jones. He was one of Winifred's nephews. From the way he stroked the rifle trigger, he was as jumpy as she was over his questions.

"If you hear about them, let me know."

"Is there a reward?" Jones stepped from behind the bush. The rifle never wavered from the target in the middle of Shad's chest.

"Nothing like that. Nobody's accusing them of any lawbreaking."

"Missing," Winifred said. "That's all? Just that they've turned up missin'?"

"Sorry to have troubled you," Shad said. He pinched the

brim of his bowler. His finger dipped through the bullet hole shot there. This was his favorite hat, but a marshal had to show a stolid face when dealing with folks like the self-styled Coal Queen of the Rockies.

"Wait up," she called. Winifred hobbled down and stood an arm's length from him. He was always surprised at how tiny she was. Winifred Gallagher presented a big voice and confident face for a woman hardly five-foot-nothing.

He said nothing. The emotions playing across her wrinkled face ranged from outrage to something approaching uneasiness. The anger won.

"They're stealin' Gallagher coal," she blurted.

"Who's that?"

"It's gotta be them Morriseys. Nobody else has it in for me and my boys like they do."

Shad looked past Jeremiah Jones. Another of the Gallaghers edged closer, trying hard to hear what was being said. He wanted to see more of this one. He had to admit Beatrice was a handsome woman. Long auburn hair fluttered in the breeze whipping down from the higher elevations. Sharp hazel eyes fixed on him. If he'd been a bug pinned to a display board, all he lacked was a neat little card telling what he was. Shad wondered what description Beatrice would inscribe on that card.

"She's right, you know, Marshal. They're stealing our coal." Beatrice pushed past Jeremiah. He started to complain. Whatever she whispered angrily to him made him step back a pace and let her by.

Shad wondered if they were brother and sister. He wasn't sure he had any clear idea about the relationships in the Gallagher clan. Beatrice was everything Jeremiah wasn't. She was as pretty as he was homely. He had inherited Winifred's short stature while Beatrice stood a head taller and moved with easy grace.

More than this, if brains were dynamite, Jeremiah

couldn't blow his own nose. Every time Shad dealt with Beatrice, he felt as if she was running rings around him. She was as sharp as a whip while her aunt bulled her way through. The two of them together made for a force of nature.

"You give me proof, and I'll arrest them. You know I don't cotton much to the Morriseys."

"You don't cotton much to us Gallaghers," Beatrice shot back. "But you're a fair man and honest enough, for a law dog."

"I reckon that's a compliment," he said.

"We're gonna catch 'em when they try to steal our coal," Winifred said. She ignored her niece. Shad thought she did that at her own peril, but the leader of the family thought her position was permanent and for all time.

"I can't send a corpse to trial for theft," he warned. "You get proof, I'll arrest them. You try to gun them down, I'll come for you."

"Would you do that, Marshal?" Beatrice batted her eyes at him. Her ruby lips curled up in a smile he found just a trifle unsettling. "Is that a promise?"

"I can't abide by lawbreakers in Utopia," he said. He stepped up into the saddle and looked down at them. It wasn't his imagination that Beatrice tugged just a mite on her scoop neckline to give him a flash of white bosoms. As quickly as she revealed herself, she shrugged and covered up.

"You catch 'em, Shadrach Nelson, you catch 'em and hang the lot from that oak tree at the edge of town. If you need a rope, I'll make sure you got plenty." Winifred turned and herded her niece and nephew back up the steep path. She made her way doggedly, not wanting to show him any weakness, but he saw how hard it was for the woman to climb the hill.

He wheeled about and let his horse walk back down the

road. He'd found out a bunch. All he had to do was sift through everything he'd heard and try to make sense of it.

Shad was about ready to give up on this by the time he got back to town. Reading Winifred like a book was hard. Reading Beatrice? She might as well have been written in some foreign language.

Chapter Ten

"What do you think he really wanted, Aunt Win?" Beatrice watched her aunt like a hawk. She worried that the marshal had come for some reason he hadn't stated, but that Winifred knew. The two had danced around actually saying anything. That worried Bea, though she found it hard to believe her aunt and the marshal were in cahoots.

"He ain't the kind to pussyfoot around the truth. He said his piece."

Beatrice wasn't so sure. She saw how Shadrach Nelson looked at her. All she had to do was smile shyly and any man in town melted like winter snow in the spring. Some warmed up slower than others, but they all flowed away around her feet. All except Marshal Nelson. It bothered her that her charms were wasted on him. She had seen his wife. For the life of her, why he preferred Ruth Nelson over the prettiest girl in town—the prettiest within a hundred miles!—she couldn't say.

She ran her right forefinger around her ring finger. Whoever she convinced to give her a wedding band had to do more than look at her as if she were some kind of wild animal.

"Patrick," she said to herself. One day he'd inherit his pa's lead mine. Marry him and she'd be rich.

Beatrice looked around the mountain. A mile farther around the middle of this huge pile of rock dribbled the tailings from the Calcutta Mine. The Black Hole of Calcutta, she thought grimly, which was how it got its name. Aunt Win wasn't about to leave the ownership of the mine in the hands of her children. They were as dumb as the Morrisey boys.

Marry Patrick and combine the two fortunes. She'd be richer than Horace Tabor or any of the other silver or gold mine owners. The imaginative knew there was rock in the ground that was more valuable than precious metals. The railroad needed coal. There wasn't a cowboy or miner that didn't carry a six-gun at his hip, loaded with lead bullets.

"Coal Queen of the Rockies," she said, wondering if she'd be able to afford a house on Boulevard F in Denver's ritzy Highlands and another in Manitou Springs, maybe on the side of the canyon above the Palace Hotel. "Why not?"

"What's that? Speak up, girl. You known I'm a trifle deef in my left ear." Winifred Gallagher turned her good ear toward her niece.

"I was agreeing with you, Aunt Win."

"Of course you were. I'm danged near always right. The times I ain't don't matter."

"Who are the two men the marshal asked after?" She tried to appear ignorant. Listening to her aunt's conversation with Eric told her a lot. Patrick had told her everything she only guessed about Leadbottom kidnapping the two men and working them in the Morrisey lead mine.

"Don't worry your head over it, Bea. I got something more for you to do. I'd send Kenny, but I don't trust him to get it right."

Beatrice chewed her lower lip, waiting to hear what new scheme Winifred had cooked up. Then she smiled as her aunt poured out the scheme.

* * *

She got antsy sitting and doing nothing, yet that was what her Aunt Win asked of her. Beatrice stirred and yawned. Patrick wouldn't be able to come for another hour yet. Watching Marshal Nelson and his deputies come and go made her a trifle sleepy in the warm, sunny late afternoon. She had been at her assigned task for a full day and it bored her.

At first it gave her freedom. Winifred Gallagher had a knack for always being there, looking over her shoulder when she wanted privacy. Beatrice had no idea how her aunt was always everywhere all the time. Living in a cavern penned her up, but still, Winifred managed to hover. Even when she was scheming, she kept up her constant surveillance of every single family member.

Winifred had snooping down pat. Bea had long ago figured out which of the family snitched on the rest.

All of them. Each and every one eagerly told the family matriarch the most intimate details to curry favor. Being on her own felt . . . good.

Now she had spent a full day waiting for the marshal to do something she could report back on, and she wondered if boredom and freedom weren't the same thing.

"You, you there." A tousle-haired boy of eight or nine worked his way around the broken fence she used as a blind and stared at her boldly.

"Go away. Scat or I'll tell your ma."

"Ain't got one. You're Beatrice Gallagher, ain't ya?"

She picked up a rock to chunk at the boy. Her carefully chosen hiding spot was revealed now, and it had been a good one. The jailhouse was right across the street. If the door was left ajar, as it was now, she saw the marshal, his son and their deputies moving around inside. The squalls from the back cell came from Andy Morrisey. His misery kept Beatrice amused, just a little.

"Here." The boy held out an envelope. His grimy fingers

smeared dirt on the otherwise pristine white paper. “Go on, take it.” He thrust it toward her.

“What is it?”

“Dunno, don’t care.” He threw it toward her. “I get paid whether you take it or not.” He twisted through the broken fence and ran down the street. The meandering road aided him in disappearing from sight within a few yards.

She poked her head through the break in the fence and looked around. Nobody paid the least attention to the boy or her. Beatrice ducked back, not wanting to be spotted by the marshal who now sat at his desk, poring over a stack of wanted posters. She dropped the rock she’d meant to hurl at the kid, then picked up the envelope. Other than filthy fingerprints left by the young postman, there wasn’t anything on the outside. A quick tear opened the end. She blew, billowed out the envelope’s sides and looked inside.

A single piece of foolscap inside. Nothing else. She fished the yellow scrap out. It had been torn from a larger sheet. Turning it around she saw the terse message. Her heart skipped a beat, then she crumpled up the sheet and envelope. Her first reaction was to throw it away.

Beatrice stopped. If anyone else read the message, she’d be in a world of trouble. She sank to the ground, back against the rickety fence. Grinding her teeth together as she thought what to do only made her angrier. Somebody would pay for this. They’d pay big!

It was darker than the inside of a coal sack. Every small sound in the night made her jump. Beatrice forced herself to calm down. Since she had gotten the note that afternoon she had alternated between being furious and scared. Try as she might, she wasn’t able to come up with any idea what to do.

Footsteps crunched in the gravel. Coming toward her, the sounds keyed her up even more. Beatrice clutched the

.45 caliber derringer pistol she always carried. Then she tucked it away in her skirts and rushed forward. She threw her arms around Patrick Morrisey's neck and kissed him hard.

"I'm so glad you got here, Pat. Finally!" She smothered any answer with another passionate kiss. He pushed her away. This wasn't like him, not at all. "What's wrong?"

"I got a letter today."

Her heart skipped a beat, then she said, "Me, too."

"Somebody knows we, me and you, we—"

"They asked for fifty dollars."

Patrick slammed his right fist into the palm of his left hand. It sounded like a gunshot in the darkness. She reached out and clutched his upper arms to steady him—to steady herself.

"We can't panic. We don't dare. It means our lives if we do."

"Who'd send us this, Bea? What are we gonna do?"

Strangely, his anxiety calmed her. She was the one in charge and had to make the plans for both of them.

"Do you have any notion who's blackmailing us? Has anyone in your family hinted at this?"

"Nobody. You know everyone. If they saw us they'd shoot off their mouth the first chance they got and think it was funny." He pressed closer to her. She held him at arm's length as she thought.

"It can't be anyone in my family, either. They wouldn't ask for money. They'd use it to get in good with my aunt."

"Winifred'd kill you. And me." Patrick shivered. "I can't imagine what my pa'll do if he finds out."

"Is it worth fifty dollars to keep this skunk quiet?"

Patrick thought for a moment and shook his head. His eyes gleamed with what little light filtered past the trees from the distant coal yard. She felt the tension in his body. They knew the answer to that. Both of them.

"How do we find who did this? There won't be any end. He'll go to the well over and over until we don't have a penny between us. What then?" Patrick circled her waist and pulled her close. She let him.

Head resting against his chest, she heard the trip hammering of his heart.

"How do we know the blackmailer is a man?" she asked.

"It could be anyone," he admitted.

"We've been careful. You're probably right about it being a man. Someone from the coal yard who blundered into the woods and saw us?"

"There are a couple dozen men who shovel coal and load freight," he said. "The kid who gave me the letter wouldn't say who paid him to deliver it."

"He got away before I had a chance to ask, but you're right. If whoever's doing this is smart, they'd have someone else give the urchin the letter so we couldn't torture it out of him who was paying him."

"Not so it'd matter. By the time we got the name out of whoever paid the kid, well, word would be all over town."

Beatrice knew that was the hold the blackmailer had on them. If they tracked back to him, all he had to do was make their affair known to everyone in town. Netty Michaelson at the hotel was a big gossip. What if it ran in the newspaper? Or old man Sampson told every last customer passing through his store? Over the course of a week, those three talked to about every single soul in Utopia.

"We pay him off," she said with ice in her words.

"What? We can't! There'll never be an end to it." He calmed down. "You want to give us time to find who is responsible. Is that it?"

"If he's greedy enough, he'll pick up the money himself. We'll have him then."

Patrick grinned like a hungry wolf.

"They won't ever find the body. I'll see to that."

"*We'll* see to it," she said. This was too important to leave to her beau.

She kissed him hard, then slowly melted into his arms to seal the deal.

"There! Someone's out there!"

Beatrice Gallagher grabbed Patrick's arm and held him back. She pulled hard to force him to sink back behind the rubbish pile where they hid on the outskirts of the coal yard.

"He'll get the money. He'll find out we only put $37 in the sack!"

"Hush," Beatrice said. She tightened her hold on his arm. "This'll work for us. I put a note in saying it was all the money we could raise."

"It was all Pa had in the bread box. It's all *I* could find."

She ignored the implied accusation that she wasn't doing her part. What did Patrick expect her to do? Ask her Aunt Winifred?

"He won't give us away if he thinks there's a chance to get more from us."

"What if that's not him? He used a boy to give us the blackmail threats."

"He won't risk having that boy—or another—look into the sack. A hundred dollars would be worth double crossing him."

"But there's only—"

She clamped her hand over his mouth to prevent an outcry. A dark figure moved through the small mountains of coal. In the distance the locomotive took on water, causing huge pillars of white steam to rise in the night. The yard crew had already loaded the tender with a full supply of coal, letting it slide down the chute from the elevated bin they'd filled earlier. There wasn't any reason for the workers to be wandering around this part of the coal yard. Right about now, they'd want to finish servicing the locomotive and get on home to warm beds and willing wives.

The shadowy figure moved with too much assurance. The man had a destination in mind and wasn't going to be sidetracked.

Beatrice tried to make out details. The man strode along confidently. He suddenly stopped and reached for the iron hung at his hip. She caught her breath. Had Patrick given them away? She looked at her swain. He remained hidden. If anything, he was too scared to show himself. Alerted, the man in the yard moved farther away, to their right.

She strained to hear. The only sounds came from the train pulling out as it headed east toward Denver.

"He's not going to take the money. He's turning away!"

"Hush," she said. What she saw was different from Patrick's guesswork. The man wasn't turning away, he was making sure he was alone.

A slow grin curled her lips. The man made a complete turn, hand still resting on the butt of his holstered six-gun. When he completed the full circle, his hand moved from his side. Step by step, he neared the sack containing the money. To her surprise, he walked past it. She had to tug even harder to keep Patrick from surging up and rushing forward when he thought the pickup was going astray.

"Look, he's heading back for it," Patrick whispered.

Beatrice saw how the shadow-cloaked man turned around again, then retraced his steps to where they'd left the bag sitting atop a mound of coal. Unless you knew where to look, the dark burlap bag was invisible in the night.

The man knew.

He scrambled up the slope and grabbed the bag. He slid back to the base and felt the contents.

"I wish we'd put a rattler inside," Patrick grumbled.

Beatrice stood now to get a better view. The man shook the bag, listened, then untied the string they'd used to secure it. He peered in, then looked up.

It was as if he had spotted Beatrice and Patrick. He stared straight at them.

She felt a rising anger when she recognized the man. Her aunt had been smarter than she'd given her credit for when she sent her to town to spy on the marshal.

The man holding the bag was his son, Deputy Abe Nelson.

Chapter Eleven

"You can't keep me locked up forever!" Andy Morrisey rattled the cell bars and kicked at the floor. "What'd I do? You was the one what hit me. I was only defendin' myself!"

Shadrach Nelson swung around in his chair. He'd put up with the man's constant caterwauling long enough.

"You shut up or you don't get fed."

"You can't do that! That's . . . that's a'gin the law."

"Try me."

"Well, if it ain't, it ought to be."

Shad sighed. The man was right, but other than gagging him, there didn't seem to be any way to keep him quiet. He spun around when he heard someone huffing and puffing in an attempt to open the sticking outer jailhouse door. A quick move toward his holstered Peacemaker stopped when he saw that Leadbottom Morrisey wasn't coming into the office waving a gun around. Even better he left a couple of his boys outside. If they'd all crowded into the office, they'd have filled the place to overflowing.

"You can't bail him out, Leadbottom," Shad said straightaway. "He's standing trial and the judge won't be here for another couple days."

"Ain't why I'm here."

"Judge Zamora's due in on the afternoon train, whenever

it gets here. Mister Sussman said he'd received a telegram to that effect." Shad quieted when the man's words penetrated. He'd answered a protest that hadn't come. "Then why are you smelling up my office?"

The lead miner caused the single chair on the other side of the office to creak in protest as he settled down. Dust and less hygienic debris fell off the man's clothing like some poisonous rain.

"I been robbed. Somebody stole all my family's money from where I hid it."

"You should keep your money in the bank. It's not as likely to get stolen there."

Leadbottom snorted in contempt.

"You tellin' me that banker fellow's honest? He'd steal a penny from a widder woman, if he hadn't already stole her house by foreclosin' on her mortgage."

"Mister Reese cuts corners, nobody's disputing that, but nobody's ever accused him of outright theft."

"This ain't 'bout that low-down, no account snake. My money's gone. Somebody stole it."

From the back of the cell block, Anderson Morrisey called out, "Hey, Pa, you come to spring me? He's been mistreatin' me somethin' fierce."

Leadbottom ignored his son. He swallowed, causing his wattles to ripple. With a gusty sigh, he said, "They snuck in when me and my boys was workin' at the smelter. Stole the money from the bread box where I hid it."

"Under a rock is safer," Shad said sarcastically.

"Tried that. My boys turn over danged near every rock huntin' for new lead deposits. That mountain's filthy with galena, but not all the ore's high grade." The man shook his shaggy head. His lips thinned to a razor's slash as he got angrier by the instant. "I want him hung by the neck."

"Who?" Shad forced himself to pay attention again.

"Whoever took my money, that's who!"

"Your bread box was up on the side of the mountain? In your cabin?"

"Where else?"

"That's not in my jurisdiction. You've got to see the sheriff about that, and there's no telling where Parsons is right now. Not in his office, that's for sure. Maybe in Georgetown, probably not. He spends most of his time out riding the circuit, serving process."

Leadbottom grunted and rocked to his feet.

"You're danged quick to throw my boy in the clink, but when I got a real crime, you ignore it. You're gonna be in a heap of trouble over this, Marshal."

"Tell the mayor. Tell the town council. I might get lucky."

"What's that mean?"

"They might fire me, and I won't have to listen to you anymore."

Leadbottom started to spit on the marshal's desk, then stopped when he saw the look in Shad's cold green eyes. He grumbled, then huffed and puffed his way from the office. He left the door open. Shad didn't bother getting up to close it. The fresh air blowing in from the street helped clear the stench Leadbottom left behind.

"I hope he does go to the town council," Shad called to his prisoner. "Maybe then I can get them to pass a town health ordinance requiring every citizen to have a bath at least once a week."

"You don't need an ordinance to get me to dunk myself in some water." Abednego Nelson came in.

"You look like you've been out in the coal yard."

"Spent most of the night there chasing ghosts," Abe said. He settled down in the chair. It didn't protest his weight at all.

"You need to keep a sharp eye out. The Coal Queen of the Rockies is sure somebody's stealing her coal from under her nose. And the nose of Sussman and even Art Brushwell."

"Can't see anyone stealing so much as a pebble without Brushwell knowing. That man's got a ledger book for a heart."

"It keeps you out of the saloons," Shad joked.

"More likely to drive me to them. But Mary Beth wouldn't like me boozing it up."

"If she's the reason you want to take a bath, I have to say she's a good influence."

Abe stood and fumbled around in his coat pocket. He pulled out a small burlap bag and shook it.

"I found this out in the yard. Not sure what's going on but it's got—"

Both lawmen turned to Ian Shannon poking his head into the office.

"We got ourselves a problem over at the stage depot, Marshal."

"Robbery?" Shadrach Nelson was already halfway to the door.

"They lost a passenger somewhere back along the road. Dangest thing I ever heard, but they're all agitated, Mister Egan most of all. He sounds like a little girl, all squawking and running around waving his arms. If he did that any harder, he'd up and fly away."

"He should never have been put in charge of the stage company. The smallest thing causes him to run around like a chicken with its head lopped off." Shad turned and said to his son, "Look after the office till I get back, will you, Abe?"

"Don't be too long. I need some sleep and . . ."

"And Mary Beth's not likely to let you get much, I know. You brag on it all the time." Shad left the office. He heard his son calling something about money he'd found, but he was already jogging along to catch up with his deputy.

"I'd have taken care of it, Shad, but Egan looked like he was about to cry."

"You did fine, Ian." He knew asking for help in what seemed a minor thing irritated his deputy, but lately the deputy had been showing signs of wanderlust. From what Shad knew of Ian Shannon's background, he seldom stayed more than a few months anywhere before drifting on. He'd already been in Utopia longer than that. Going on a year might make Shannon antsy, thinking he was putting down roots.

He'd seen plenty of men like that. He hoped his deputy decided to stay a while longer. Good deputies were hard to find. Shannon usually proved completely unflappable. With a steady hand and sharp eye, he was the kind of deputy Shad wanted backing his play.

"There," Shannon said, pointing. The stagecoach had pulled up alongside the depot. Since the train had laid tracks through Utopia, the coach schedule had been sporadic and fewer people came into town this way. Mostly, those that couldn't afford the higher-priced ticket on the train still used the stage.

"How many passengers were riding on the roof?"

"Just the woman they lost. She must have bounced off and nobody noticed."

"There are some steep grades coming into town," Shad said. He hitched up his gun belt and went to calm down the depot master.

"What was her name?" he asked outright. By now Egan had built up an entire script in his head what to say and how to deny responsibility, both personally and as a stage company. Shad intended to cut through the denials and get to the facts.

"Marshal, I, uh, it's not—"

"Mister Egan, her name?"

"It was Melissa's sister," the driver called from his lofty seat up in the driver's box.

"Who?"

"The cute little faro dealer over at the Gold Dust Saloon."

"Missy," Shannon said softly. "Her real name's Melissa."

"Never knew that," Shad admitted. He motioned for the

driver to tell the story. It was about as he thought. Missy's sister couldn't afford a full ticket letting her ride inside the compartment. Two bits had let her cling to the roof, only she had been taking swigs from a flask the whole way.

"She got snockered and fell off," Shannon said in disgust. "You want me to ride back and find her?"

"No need," Shad said. He pointed. A disheveled woman the spitting image of Missy trudged along the street.

She never spoke a word. She stopped a few feet from the stage and pointed to a ratty carpetbag tied onto the roof. The driver crawled back, used his knife to cut the twine holding it and dropped the bag. Shad moved to catch it. Bag cradled in his arms like a baby, he turned to the woman.

"Yours, I believe."

She hiccuped, nodded and took the bag. With as much dignity as she could muster, she turned and walked off. Her gait was a trifle unsteady, but Shad allowed as to how it might have been the fall and hike into town as much as any liquor that caused it. Within a few seconds, she turned a corner and vanished.

"Seems to know where the Gold Dust is," Shannon observed.

"I'm glad somebody knows what they're doing," Shad said. "Go on back and relieve Abe. He's getting mighty anxious to take a bath long about now." He slapped his deputy on the back and marched past the still blubbering stage agent. Someday someone would put Egan out of his misery. It wasn't going to be today. Everything had worked out just fine for everyone involved.

For Shad, it was even better. Nobody had died and nothing was stolen. That was a good way to start the day.

He made his way across town, following the winding streets and occasionally slipping down an alley to take a different road. Eventually he reached Brushwell's freight yard.

Six men worked to move heavy crates away from the

railroad siding. Supplies that had come into Utopia. They stacked the crates and struggled with small crates, wrestling them onto a cart to move to the siding.

"Leadbottom's most recent shipment," Brushwell said.

Shad jumped in spite of himself. He had been concentrating too hard on the men working and not enough on someone sneaking up behind him.

"Six crates. What do they weigh?"

"Close to a ton. Whatever's he's doing up there at his mine, it's going great guns. He's increased the amount of lead being shipped by ten percent. If he keeps that up, he'll be supplying all the bullets for the entire Federal army."

Brushwell's words carried a tinge of hostility. Shad didn't know anything of the freight yard owner's background, but he suspected there wasn't much sympathy for the way the war had turned out fifteen years earlier.

"That's all going out on the midnight train?"

"No reason to sit on it. Nobody makes money letting the ingots collect dew."

"When they're done getting the metal to the loading docks, what do they do for the rest of the day?"

"Marshal Nelson, this is a freight yard. There's always something to move."

"Like Gallagher coal?"

Brushwell frowned but didn't reply.

"Winifred claims her coal's being swiped."

Brushwell heaved a deep sigh and shook his head.

"She's as delusional as Leadbottom, only she's not got an excuse. He works his own mine. Being a miner ten hours a day, six days a week will make anyone loco."

"Heard tell lead dust works against you, too," Shad said as he slowly studied the piles of coal some distance away. They'd have to be loaded onto wagons and moved to the depot to be shoveled into the coal tender.

"Coal dust's as bad. More 'n one of my workers has gotten sick and started coughing up blood. Only last week

I had to let one fellow go who'd worked for me since I opened the business."

"If a man, like the one you fired, took it into his head to steal the coal, how'd he go about doing it?"

"Was that you or one of your deputies poking around the yard all night?" Brushwell laughed harshly. "You're not gonna find a thing like that happening. Not here, no sir."

"But if he took it into his head, how'd he do it?"

"Even if you pulled a wagon up and filled it to overflowing every night, stealing enough to make a profit would be hard. Nobody around here'll buy coal from anyone but me."

"Even if they sold it for less than you do?"

"All I'd need to do would be to threaten to cut the railroad off. That's the thermal coal. A wagon loaded with met coal'd sell for more, but what smithy needs a ton to keep his forge hot?"

"Might be sold off a bucket at a time to local folks. The firewood all up and down the Rockies has about been burned up."

"Or cut down to use as shoring in mines. There are a lot of mines."

"You're saying that Winifred doesn't know what she's talking about, accusing you or someone of stealing her coal?"

"She thinks she has second sight." He tapped his forehead. "I've heard her say she has a third eye in the middle of her forehead. She's loco, too. Her and Leadbottom are both daft."

"You won't hear me arguing with you about that," Shad said. He hitched up his gun belt. "And if you repeat that to anyone, I'll deny it. Have a good day."

With that, he spun around and walked away slowly, memorizing the location of the coal piles and trying to estimate how tall each was. Winifred Gallagher saw bogeymen behind every bush, but Shad doubted Brushwell had been entirely honest about how little value was heaped up around the yard. That much coal had to be worth something.

Like the lead ingots and who knows what else in Brushwell's warehouse.

Chapter Twelve

"I wondered if you'd show up." Shad made a big deal of pulling out his pocket watch and staring at it. He didn't bother to open the case to see the actual time. He really didn't care what time it was. This was for show. "Mary Beth—"

"Yeah, Mary Beth," Abe Nelson said, nodding slowly. Then he grinned from ear to ear. "Seeing each other is a real chore. She finished with cleaning up the store and only had a half hour before Netty wanted her to work as desk clerk."

Shad wondered why he said it, but he did.

"For Pete's sake, go on and marry her."

Abe stared at him for a moment, eyes wide.

"I didn't think either you or Ma liked her."

"What we think doesn't amount to a hill of beans if you love her. Or is this just a summer fling?" Shad watched his son's reaction.

"I never thought on it that much. She has a way of getting my head all jumbled up when I'm with her, but . . . marry her?" Abe rubbed his chin. "It's something to ponder."

"Think on the matter. It'll give you something important to do that while you're out chasing ghosts."

"The coal yard?" Abe said. "There's something going on there, and I can't find what it is."

"I agree with that, son," Shad said. He started to say more, then stopped.

"Did you find something? I can't see how anyone is stealing Gallagher coal, not so it matters one whit." Abe hitched up his gun belt, ready to find someone to arrest.

Shad related his conversation with Arthur Brushwell and finished, saying, "If anyone's stealing even a lump of coal, it'd be the met coal."

"Metallurgical coal," Abe said, letting the words roll off his tongue as if they were some foreign language. "That's what the smithy uses. From what I hear, that's all that's used making steel rails. But it'd take a powerful lot of theft to amount to much."

"Swiping coal's not something you do without getting your hands dirty," Shad said. He liked it that Abe chuckled.

"More 'n that, where do you hide it? A wagonload of anything's not hidden easily. Stealing from the bank is better. A robber doesn't have to find a buyer for what's stolen." Abe mimicked leafing through a wad of greenbacks, counting them out.

"I better get home for dinner or your ma'll toss it to the hogs."

"We don't raise hogs," Abe said. "Wait a second. Did you find the bag in the desk drawer?"

"It had a few dollars stuffed into it."

"I counted $37. I found the bag sitting on a low pile of coal."

"Any idea who put it there?"

Abe shrugged and said, "It was dark, and I might be wrong, but I thought I spotted Patrick Morrisey sneaking around."

"I can't think of any reason for him to leave money in a bag out like that for just anyone to find."

"It beats me, too, Pa. You'd better get on home. And if Ma wants to throw out your food, tell her to save it for me. I hardly have time to eat these days."

"You are looking a mite scrawny." Shad laughed and left the jailhouse, heading for home.

Abe watched him go, then sat in the desk chair and opened the center drawer. The bag with the money rested inside. He counted the money again, then peeled off seven dollars and tucked it into his pocket.

"An advance," he said to himself. He replaced the rest of the money in the desk and went to check on their prisoner. Anderson Morrisey stretched out on his bunk, snoring loudly.

Abe returned to the main office as Leroy Early entered.

"Did you order dinner for him?" Abe jerked his thumb over his shoulder in the direction of Andy Gallagher's cell.

"I did. Since it's on the town bill, I ordered some for us, too. It'd be a shame if he slept through it and there warn't none left by the time we finish."

The food came, delivered by the fourteen-year-old daughter of the owner. Contrary to what Abe had suggested, they woke up their prisoner and let him eat. When they were all sated, Abe said, "I'll take the dishes back to the diner. Then I'll make a quick trip to the coal yard."

"The marshal's still sure that old lady Gallagher's right about her lumps being swiped?"

"I swear, Leroy, I don't know what my pa thinks," Abe admitted. "But the walk will give me a chance to clear my head. It's getting stuffy in here."

Early took a deep whiff and agreed.

"I'll leave the door open," Abe said, balancing the dishes as he twisted through the doorway.

Once outside the air was colder but hardly any fresher. At least one horse had died along the winding street. It was part of his job to remove it, but he'd leave that for his pa come morning. Such dead animal removal was always easier in the light of day. He looked up. Clouds, dark and forbidding, slid over the tallest mountain peaks and hid most of the diamond-hard stars. The moon was a brief occurrence in

Utopia, being nestled between such tall mountains in a deep pass. Sunrise and sunset were late, too, but Abe hardly noticed. He had lived here long enough to get used to it.

After leaving the dirty dishes, he walked past the hotel. He poked his head in, thinking to say hello to Mary Beth, but she wasn't behind the counter. Abe went to the desk and scribbled a quick note to her, wrote her name on it with a flourish, and propped it up where she'd be sure to see it.

Then he started the long walk across town to the railroad depot and the coal yard beyond. It was getting near ten o'-clock and the entire area was deserted. The station master was probably asleep somewhere, catching some shuteye before things turned hectic when the midnight train arrived.

He paused. The clack of the telegraph did nothing to rouse Sussman. But then Abe had never figured out how a telegrapher knew which messages were intended for him and which ones slid on down the wire to the next operator.

Abe kept walking until he reached the edge of the coal yard, then paused. Something moved between the small hills of coal. He touched his six-gun but saw no reason to draw. A worker might be readying the coal to be loaded in a couple hours. It got shoveled into a wagon, which was driven up an earthen ramp to a large bin. From there, gravity dropped the coal into the tender with only a little urging from workers.

Seeing no one in the darkened freight yard office, he turned and worked his way along narrow paths.

Sounds ahead turned him wary. Digging. Lumps of coal hitting metal. Someone shoveled coal. Stepping as carefully as he could to avoid the cinder crunching under his feet, he slipped his six-shooter from its holster and peered around a head-high pile. Two hunched figures bent low. One held a shovel and the other a large metal pail.

"Don't move or I'll drill you," he said loudly.

Childish shrieks cut through the still night air. Two little girls, seven or eight years old, dropped shovel and bucket and thrust their hands high over their heads.

"Don't shoot. Honest, we was gonna pay for it."

"Stop lyin', Bessie," the taller of the two said. "We don't have money. That's why we were takin' it."

"To stay warm," the smaller one, Bessie, said timidly. "It gets cold at night."

"We cook with it, too. Or Mama does."

Abe advanced slowly until he got a better look at them.

"You're the Jason girls, aren't you?"

"She's Bessie. I'm Amanda." The older girl curtsied. Then she held up her hands again. "Are you going to throw us in jail?"

"We're arrested?" The smaller girl began crying.

Abe slid his six-gun back into its holster.

"Your pa died a couple months back, didn't he?"

Bessie sniffed a little and said, "He got kicked in the head. He worked at the livery."

"Mister Watt wouldn't even pay for the funeral. Mama said he's an old skinflint."

Bernard Watt owned the livery stable. Abe wasn't about to argue over the way the man guarded his purse strings. More than one traveler passing through Utopia had complained about how Watt shortchanged them or didn't give proper feed to their horses. He was that kind of galoot.

"I bet that's not all your mama said about him," Abe declared. "Don't bother repeating it, if you did hear. You're too young to be saying words like that."

"Are you taking us to jail, Deputy Nelson?"

"You girls know you shouldn't be out this late at night. You should be home in bed. With a fire going in your stove." He turned away. The two whispered furiously. Louder, he said, "I think I hear something on the far side of the coal yard. It's not anyone filling a single pail with coal, either. Just this one time."

More whispers. Then sounded rapid scraping as they

loaded their bucket. He started to walk away when small arms grabbed him around his leg. It took all his skill to keep from losing his balance.

Bessie hugged him, then looked up. Her wide-spaced, guileless eyes met his. Then she was gone, she and her sister hurrying away with their stolen treasure.

"Coal Queen Winifred's not going to miss a single bucket." As Abe walked away, he wondered if he ought to see to leaving a bucket on the Jasons' doorstep every few days. It was late summer but nights in the high mountains always got mighty chilly.

The girls had gone, but he heard someone moving around in the yard. He glanced at the stars and tried to estimate the time. It was at least another hour, probably more, before the train pulled into the depot to take on water and fill its tender with coal.

More than this, the yard crew had no reason to be sneaking around. They worked here and even wanted to be seen to assure Brushwell they weren't malingering.

Abe cut past two tall hills of coal and saw furtive movement. Rather than calling out, he sprinted after the fleeing specter. In spite of the dark, he caught occasional flashes of starlight off skin. The rest of the man was hidden in shadow.

When he closed the distance between them to a dozen yards, Abe yelled for the man to stop.

Everything happened in a flash. The man did stop and turn. He held a bag in his hand. And something else. Abe went for his six-gun. He wasn't the fastest gunman in Utopia. He wasn't even as quick on the draw as his pa. But he was good enough. Weapon pointed at his quarry, he yelled, "Hands up or you'll regret it."

The man raised his hands as ordered. The bag remained clutched in his left hand and the six-shooter in his right. Abe slowly approached.

"What're you doing out here?" he asked.

The bullet tore through his left shoulder. When lead

glanced off his shoulder bone, the impact spun him around. Abe fell to his knees and almost lost his six-gun. Looking back toward his prisoner, he caught sight of the man starting to run. Abe fired. Again. And again. He wasn't sure he hit the dark, indistinct figure but it gave him a chance to climb to his feet.

His shoulder burned like the furies. Lightheaded, he tried to figure what to do. In his condition, he ought to let the man go. Blood ran down his arm and soaked his shirt and vest. It wouldn't be long before his coat was plastered to his body, too. Then anger fueled unexpected strength. He wasn't giving up after being ambushed like this!

He staggered along a few feet and regained his balance. His gait was ragged, but he advanced. Then the initial shock of being shot wore off and questions popped up to bedevil him.

"How'd you shoot me? Your hands were in the air." Abe wobbled when he took another step. A deep breath settled him and returned control of his feet.

He began walking with determination. Nobody shot him and got away with it.

"Come on, give up. I won't kill you, you ambushing son of a—"

Another report filled the silent night. His hat flew off into the night. Abe's head snapped up when the chin tie yanked against his throat. Trying not to gag, he pulled the hat down and then threw it away. It wasn't much good to him now with a bullet hole in the crown.

Pain dogged his steps as he pursued the man who'd run off. His shoulder burned, but strangely, where the chin tie had cut into his throat hurt more. He wiped at his eyes to clear his vision. Ahead he saw movement. Instinct caused him to jerk to the side just as a foot-long tongue of yellow and orange flame blinded him. This bullet tore past harmlessly.

Crawling on hands and knees, he sought refuge. There

were plenty of piles of coal, but peering around them wasn't possible if he wanted to bring his ambusher to justice.

The way he felt, all numb and with his head threatening to explode like a rotted melon, his justice would be deadlier and more permanent than anything the judge might mete out.

He flopped against a conical pile of coal and scooted around to see where his attacker had gone. Not ten yards away grew a sparse stand of trees. Small movement in undergrowth gave away his attacker's hiding spot. Abe rested his gun hand against the coal and squeezed off a round.

"He shot me!"

The exclamation gave Abe sudden strength. He rolled around, gathered strength and ran toward the spot where he had winged the ambusher. Halfway there his dazed mind finally urged caution. He should have realized immediately that he faced not one but two gunmen. The one he'd gotten the drop on had his hands in the air when the first bullet tore a chunk out of his shoulder.

Abe half reached for his left shoulder. Turning even a little again saved his life. He heard the hot lead whistle past his ear. If he hadn't turned, the slug would have bored through his head. He dropped to his knees and hunted for the spot at the edge of the forest where he had struck the first man.

Or was it the one who had shot him?

The world spun about in crazy circles. He rubbed his eyes and stared up at the sky. What had been sharp points of light before now expanded to blurry dinner plates. He tried to lift his six-gun up and shoot at one of them. He could hit a dinner plate.

"You missed him with every shot." The condemnation was hollow, distant. He wasn't sure who the speaker meant.

"He had the drop on me. It was easy for you. He never saw you!"

"You're under arrest," Abe croaked out. "Both of you."

He grunted when another round hit him. This one drove smack dab into the middle of his chest.

Shoulder, diaphragm. Dead center.

The thought made him laugh hysterically.

"You shot me dead center."

"He's a goner. Let's get out of here."

"I need to reload."

"Come on!"

Abe heard a small scuffle, then receding footsteps.

"Come back here. Y-you're under arrest," he grated out. Even in his own ears his voice sounded weak.

Footsteps approached from behind. He was all turned around. He faced the woods where the two would-be killers had vanished. Abe twisted about to see who came up on him.

The gunman approached with a steady stride, no hesitation. Abe tried to lift his gun. It was too heavy for him. Things felt liquid inside his chest. He choked and spat blood. He looked up and saw the muzzle aimed between his eyes. It was as big as a fire hose.

In a flash of clarity he focused on the hand holding the gun, the arm, the face of the gunman.

"You? What are you doing?" He reached out. His empty hand shook. "You can't—"

The roar of the discharging six-gun was the last thing Abednego Nelson heard. Ever.

Chapter Thirteen

"You gonna move him some time soon, Marshal? I don't want a body getting in the way of my crew. Besides, it's not . . . seemly. A body all smelling up the—" Arthur Brushwell took a half step back when Shadrach Nelson swung around to face him. His hands were balled into fists ready to lash out.

"That's a dead man on the ground, Brushwell. Show some respect." Shadrach Nelson tried to keep the tears from running down his leathery cheeks. He failed. "More 'n that, he's my son."

"He was your deputy," Brushwell muttered. "Never good when a lawman gets gunned down. I can understand that. From the look of it he was facing his killer."

"Get him out of here," Shad snapped. Both Early and Shannon closed in on the coal yard owner. He protested as they herded him from the body.

Shad went back and knelt beside Abe. He reached out and laid a hand on his son's forehead. The flesh was still warm, but the blood no longer oozed from the bullet wounds. That was a sure sign a man was dead. His heart had stopped pumping blood. It took all his willpower, but he had to examine the body.

Grim determination forced down his emotions so he

could logically think. Brushwell had been right. Whoever shot Abe had approached while the man was facing him. None of the bullet holes drilled through his back. From what he could tell, all three bullets were still embedded in the body.

"The ones in the chest show a big caliber. They weren't too close. The one in his forehead looks smaller. There's some gunpowder on the skin, so the final shot came from less than five feet. Who'd Abe let get close enough? How'd he let two of them get the drop on him?"

He checked his son's six-gun. It had been fired. None of the reports had given an accurate number of shots fired. Opening the gate, he spun the cylinder. Abe had fired five times.

"Here's his hat, Shad." Leroy Early carried Abe's hat in both hands, fingers running over the brim in a nervous gesture. "One shot went through the crown. That might have blown it off his head."

Shad saw the red line where the chin tie had cut into Abe's neck.

"Is the chin tie broken?"

"How'd you know?"

Shad tried to imagine what the gunfight looked like. Abe had advanced, maybe firing. A round had hit him in the shoulder. Blood on the bottom brim of the hat showed that wound had come first. A second round tore the hat from his head. After that, all Shad could do was guess at the sequence. However the fight had gone, it ended with his son getting cut down.

The round into his head had been the killing shot. The other two bullet holes showed considerable bleeding, meaning he was alive and kicking until *that* shot. He lightly touched the skin beside the head wound.

"He had one round left." Shad examined Abe's hands. The muscles were limp, but he thought that Abe had dropped his gun and then been killed. This was flat-out murder. It was one thing to shoot a man in a pitched battle. The give and take of hot lead let fate dictate. But Abe hadn't been holding his gun, the gun with a single round remaining, when the final round ended his life.

The shooter had taken Abe's life while he was unarmed.

"Doc Paisley's here, Shad." Early laid his hand on the marshal's shoulder. Shad pulled away angrily.

"Somebody beat you to it, Doc," Shad said. "He's dead."

"I can see that, Marshal. Sorry 'bout it. You got any notion who's responsible?" Paisley pulled back Abe's coat and vest, then peeled the blood-soaked shirt away from his shoulder. "That would have killed him, no matter if you got him to me in jig time."

"The one in the center of his chest would finally done him in."

"Yup, it would have, too. But the head shot's what took him away. He didn't stand a chance of making it, no matter what. You want me to see about telling the undertaker he's got a new customer?"

The doctor shook Shad gently to get his attention.

"You going to be all right, Shad? It's a terrible thing seeing someone killed. When it's your own boy . . ."

"I've got a killer to find. Do what you need to do, Doc."

Shad stalked off. Footsteps coming up fast behind made him spin around.

"What do you want?" He stared down Leroy Early.

"You've got an idea who done the deed. I can read it in your face. Let me come with you. Abe was my friend."

"Friend?"

"We had a beer or two on occasion. Not so much since him and Mary Beth took up."

"Keep watch here in town."

"Shad, what do you know you're not telling me?" Early's

tone spoke volumes. He wasn't letting the marshal run off on his own without an explanation.

"Abe found some money last night. He thought he saw Patrick Morrisey leave it but wasn't sure."

"You're going after another of the Morrisey boys? That's mighty flimsy evidence."

"It's all I've got." Shad settled his gunbelt and made sure the Peacemaker came easily into his hand. "It might not mean much, but tugging on this thread might unravel everything. I won't know until I do a little pulling."

Shad heard the steam whistle in the distance. The midnight train pulled into the depot to take on coal and water. Brushwell knew more than he was telling, but Shad wasn't convinced the yard owner knew anything about Abe's death. His reaction had been all wrong. Even the most cold-blooded killer would have shown some emotion other than irritation at having his schedule interrupted.

But the Morrisey clan? He could believe the worst of them all.

The sun sneaked above the mountains and warmed his back as he rode to the biggest cabin set high on the slope. A dozen or more smaller ramshackle buildings all spewed smoke from chimneys. The entire family was stirring. Shad had done his best hunting for any spoor on the road up from Utopia. It wasn't that he had found nothing. There had been too much. The Morriseys had delivered a couple of loads of lead ingots to be delivered to Denver the day before. Not only the wagon ruts but hoofprints from a dozen or more horses churned up the roadway.

He drew rein outside the largest cabin and waited to see if anyone noticed him. Shad wanted to avoid any gunplay. Surprising anyone at this time of day was a sure way to get shot at.

"Hello," he called. "Marshal Nelson. You in there, Leadbottom?"

Shad had once blundered onto a cave where a bear hibernated. The sounds from inside the cabin were the same, only louder. Leadbottom Morrisey appeared in the doorway, filling it with his bulk. He scratched himself and peered up at Shad with bleary eyes.

"What you want, Nelson? You found who stole my money?"

"I've got other business," Shad said. He swung his leg over and dropped to the ground.

More sounds of someone stirring in the cabin warned him of at least another occupant and possibly two. He rested his hand on the outside of his holster.

"Unless you're bringin' back my wayward boy, you ain't got no other business here, law dog," Leadbottom said. "You skedaddle and don't come back 'til you've found my money. Or let Andy go from that hoosegow of yours."

Shad hesitated. Leadbottom had said there'd been $37 stolen from his bread box hiding place. He tried to remember what Abe had found in the coal yard. How the money ended up in a sack down in Utopia was a poser, if he remembered everything properly. He hadn't paid his son much attention.

Now it was too late to ask him.

Memory of Abe shot to death welled up in him and caused him to see red for a moment.

"Were any of your boys in town last night?"

"You know there was."

Shad's heart jumped up into his throat. He croaked out, "Who?"

"You got Andy all penned up in that jail of yers." Leadbottom hitched up his drawers and shoved out his belly. "You ain't too good at listenin' to what I say, are you?"

Leadbottom lumbered from the cabin. Behind him crowded two more of his boys.

One of them was Patrick Morrisey.

Shad stood on tiptoe and peered past the Morrisey family patriarch.

"That's the one I want to talk to. Patrick."

Patrick Morrisey's reaction warned Shad something was wrong. The man reached around inside the cabin. It didn't come as a surprise when his hand reappeared, filled with an old black-powder Remington. Shad was middling fast and a better shot. He drew, cocked and aimed his Peacemaker straight at Patrick.

"Move a muscle and you'll have a new hole in your head," he said hotly.

"What's the meanin' of this, Nelson? You can't come on my property and point your smoke wagon at one of my boys for no reason." Leadbottom started to take a step.

Shad shifted his aim. From the way Leadbottom's eyes widened, he was staring straight down the .44's barrel. It had to look like a train tunnel this close up.

For a long second, they all froze. Morning breeze caught Shad's long blond hair and whipped it around into a banner behind him. His green eyes sparkled with anger, and the set to his jaw showed that he wasn't going to take any guff from a Morrisey, any Morrisey.

Then the frozen scene melted.

"I can plug him, Pa. I got a shot." Patrick Morrisey braced the Remington against the door jamb. His hand shook so badly he had to steady himself.

"If he tries, you're a dead man," Shad said. He met Leadbottom's now alert gaze.

"Don't go gettin' an itchy trigger finger, Pat. I ain't done with this one yet."

"Where were you last night, Patrick?" Shad saw the young man blanch. He might not have had anything to do with Abe's murder, but he'd been up to something powerful bad. No honest man reacted the way he did.

Shad got off a round as Patrick ducked back into the cabin. This set into motion too much for him to avoid. Leadbottom lurched forward, arms outthrust. His massive body collided with Shad. The marshal stood 6-2 and wasn't a lightweight, but the Morrisey patriarch outweighed him by fifty pounds. They crashed together. Shad fired twice, both rounds going into the sky.

Then he grunted as Morrisey's entire weight crushed down on him. With a feeble swing, he banged his six-shooter against Leadbottom's temple. This caused a loud roar of pain. Or was it indignation?

Shad wiggled a bit under the punishing weight and got off a better swing. This time he opened a cut over Leadbottom's ear. This made the man roll away and clutch his injured ear, giving Shad the chance to scramble around and get his feet under him.

"Don't!" He shoved his pistol in the direction of another Morrisey coming out of the cabin. This one carried a shotgun. "I'll drop you where you stand!"

The demonic laugh that escaped the young man's lips warned Shad what was coming. He fired twice more. Both rounds found bloody targets in the man's chest. The shotgun aimed at the marshal discharged with a roar like a clap of doom. Shad winced. One pellet tore across his left biceps. But the rest hit rock behind him and ricocheted. More than one cut Leadbottom and sent him hopping around, trying to stop the bleeding from his ear and two more minor wounds inflicted by his own kin.

Shad swung the gun around to cover Leadbottom.

"You call off your boys," he said. "Do it or you're gonna die on this very spot." He cocked the Peacemaker to emphasize how determined he was.

"You miserable . . ." Leadbottom's words trailed off

when he saw that Shad was taking careful aim, and he was the target.

"Get on back. Don't get no closer," he bellowed to Patrick and the others. "This so-called lawman's fixin' to leave. Ain't you, Nelson?"

"We're not done, Leadbottom. We've got business, you and me."

"If you come back, better have every danged soldier from Fort Crawford at your back. You'll need all of 'em and more! The Morrisey clan is hereby declarin' war on you and everyone in Utopia!"

Shad almost pulled the trigger. Instead, he backed away, snared the reins to his horse and mounted. By now every man in the Morrisey family had come out to see what the fuss was all about.

A quick look failed to locate Patrick Morrisey. He had hightailed it. That made him Shad's number one suspect in the murder of his son. Abe had seen him skulking around the freight yard the night before. It wasn't much of a stretch to believe he had returned and tangled with Abe.

He wheeled about and trotted away, the back of his neck all prickly with anticipation. There hadn't been any fewer than a dozen Morriseys with rifles who'd come to Leadbottom's rescue. Every last one of them had to be lining him up in their sights.

As he turned a bend in the road and blocked any ambusher, he opened the gate on his Peacemaker and checked the cylinder. Luck rode with him. He had fired every last round. If he had tried to shoot Leadbottom the hammer would have made a distinctive click as it fell on a spent cartridge. Shad shivered. That would have been the signal for every last one of the lead miners to open fire on him.

Taking this bit of luck to mean he was going to find Abe's killer, he rode another couple miles down the road until he reached a spot where he could spy on the Morriseys. Next time he wouldn't come up empty when he pointed a six-shooter at Leadbottom—and whoever had killed Abe.

Chapter Fourteen

He expected the Morriseys to come swarming after him. After an hour no one had charged down the hill. He settled down in a secure fortress made of rock. His horse grazed at a patch of grass hidden from the road while he sprawled belly-down over a large boulder. Field glasses pressed to his eyes, he watched as Leadbottom rounded up his family.

Shad tried to count how many there were in the camp. At least two dozen rough-and-tumble miners with a few women who looked harder than their men. After an hour of spying on the camp, he decided that Patrick Morrisey had made himself scarce. Not once did he see the man. That was downright suspicious.

Abe had claimed Patrick Morrisey left the money in the bag. At least, he had seen him scrounging around in the coal yard. Without a good reason for being there after dark, Patrick brought the heavy shroud of suspicion down around him.

Shad couldn't get the way Patrick looked when the stolen money was mentioned—and that Abe had been murdered.

"Ten minutes," Shad muttered to himself. "That's all I'd need to find out what he knows."

Patrick might not be the one responsible for Abe's death, but he knew enough to make interrogating him worth the effort. Somebody in the Morrisey encampment knew who had pulled the trigger. Shad was going to find out who that was.

He had plenty of time to debate with himself over the proper course of action. Find out who was responsible and string them up? As satisfying as that might be, aiming his trusty Peacemaker at them and emptying the cylinder would be more fulfilling. With every round he fired, he could make the killer squirm and feel some of the pain Abe must have.

Letting the no-account stand trial passed through his head, a thought as light as a spring breeze and as insubstantial. The judge wouldn't come to town for a while. Sussman had received a telegram from Judge Zamora telling of extra cases to be settled over in Blackhawk.

Shad wondered if Zamora was dragging his feet because he knew Anderson Morrisey was already on the Utopia docket. Still, Anderson Morrisey's crime was minor. Of all the Morrisey family, he was the only one Shad knew hadn't gunned down his son.

Daylight brough some warmth. . He stretched out like a lizard on a rock. Bit by bit, his eyelids drooped and exhaustion overtook him. Shad wasn't sure how long he'd slept when an explosion shook him awake. Turning his field glasses up the slope he saw a huge dragon's tongue of gray dust and white smoke lapping at the sky. They had blasted deep in the lead mine.

He pulled out his pocket watch and studied its face. Still groggy from his sleep, Shad finally figured out it was close to five o'clock. He had slept away the entire day. Somehow he didn't feel at all rested. His eyes were gummy, and no matter how he tried, he kept seeing a ghostly, ghastly image of his son sprawled out dead on the ground.

Shad slowly panned across the hillside. The blast had come from the main mineshaft. Several smaller ones also spewed smoke and debris, but one caught his attention. Standing in the mouth, hands on his hips, Patrick Morrisey peered deep into the mine.

Something set Patrick Morrisey off. He gestured wildly. Even at this distance Shad heard the muffled curses. When he disappeared back into the mine, Shad moved.

His field glasses went back into his saddlebags. With hurried moves, he pulled out all the spare ammo he always carried. His coat pockets bulged with the rounds. Holding off the entire Morrisey clan wasn't possible, even with a couple boxes of ammo, but he intended to arrest one, not kill them all.

A long drink from his canteen readied him for the climb up the steep mountainside. At first he worried someone might catch sight of him as he scrambled along, kicking rocks down the slope. Then he realized the Morriseys were all engaged in the mines. The blast had brought down a large section of rock requiring their attention.

It took the better part of a half hour for him to reach the mouth of the mine where his quarry had disappeared. Shad pressed back against the mine wall and listened. The sound of picks and shovels echoed out. While he wasn't able to tell how many men worked this smaller mine, he knew it was more than just Patrick Morrisey.

He slipped his Colt from its holster and entered the mine. It turned pitch black within a dozen paces. Shad reached up in the dark and felt for the ledge he knew had to be here somewhere. When his fingers found a slippery spot, he knew he had found where the miners kept their spare candles. A bit of fumbling brought down a pair of candles. He balanced one on the rocky floor and patted himself down, hunting for matches. A small box of lucifers filled out the bottom of his watch pocket.

The first match failed to light. The second flared and momentarily blinded him. The candle wick popped when he touched the flame to it. Using this light he found several more candles. He stuffed those into his pocket, then turned to go deeper into the mine.

Candle held high in his left hand and his Peacemaker in

his right, he made good progress. Dust hung in the air and choked him. He tried not to cough or sneeze and warn Morrisey that he was in the mineshaft.

He came to a split in the tunnel. One stope ran off at an angle, and the main shaft continued deeper into the mountain. He hesitated for a moment, then ducked down the side tunnel.

A candle bobbed along far ahead in the main shaft. Shad waited. Soon heavy footsteps marked the arrival of the miner carrying the candle.

The man passed. Shad studied his back. This wasn't the Morrisey he sought, but for some reason the departing man carried a sawed-off shotgun. The only reason to carry a shotgun in a mine was to salt the walls. But the Morriseys knew what they mined. Lead glance. Galena. Lead sulfide. Salting their own mine made no sense.

Shad edged back to the main tunnel. As he took a step, dust got up his nose. He sneezed loudly.

The man who had passed without noticing him before, stopped and spun around. The shotgun came up.

"That you, Pat?"

Shad had his six-shooter trained on the man, but shooting revealed his presence to anyone deeper in the mine. Two quick steps closed the distance between them. His body shoved forward and crushed the shotgun barrel between their bodies. If it discharged, both of them would be hobbling the rest of their lives.

He shoved the candle into the surprised face staring at him. Hot wax splashed into the miner's left eye. He flinched. This was all the opening Shad needed. He swung his Peacemaker in a short, savage arc. The power was robbed by the closed quarters, but he connected with a jutting jaw.

As the miner jerked back, Shad pressed his advantage. He shoved the pistol butt into a suddenly open mouth. Two front teeth shattered. Blood dribbled down the man's chin.

Eye burned and mouth damaged, he dropped his shotgun and reached to protect his face from further punishment.

Shad retreated to get a better swing with his pistol. This time he laid the barrel alongside the man's temple. The one good eye rolled up in his head. He let out a sigh and crumpled to the rocky floor.

Panting, Shad leveled the six-gun, finger on the trigger and ready to shoot. There wasn't any call to do that. The fight was over. He thrust his gun into his holster and picked up the shotgun. Breaking it open he plucked out the two shells.

Bird shot.

Why was the miner armed with a sawed-off shotgun loaded with bird shot? Hunting quail in the depths of a lead mine made no sense.

Shad hefted the shotgun and lifted the candle high again. Patrick Morrisey was still somewhere deeper in the mine. As he advanced the sound of digging increased.

Then a voice rang out, clear and strident.

"Dig, damn you, or you won't get any food tonight. Neither of you!"

Someone answered, but the voice was too weak for Shad to understand it. He walked faster and came out into a small cavern. His candle flared suddenly from having more air. The increased brightness drew Patrick Morrisey's attention at the far side of the hollow.

"Why'd you come back, Nate?" He squinted and held the smoky candle away from his face.

"I've got you covered, Morrisey. Make a move and I'll take you down."

"Marshal Nelson?"

"You're under arrest."

"What for?" Morrisey swiped at his eyes and moved forward. He wore a six-shooter and shifted the candle from his gun hand.

"You murdered my son."

"I never . . ." Morrisey dropped the candle as he grabbed for his six-gun.

In spite of being ready for resistance, Shad followed the sputtering candle when he should have watched the man. Patrick Morrisey dragged out his gun and got off a shot before the candle crashed into the mine floor. The bullet went wide, but Shad had to move to find a decent target in the man's chest.

He triggered the shotgun. It bucked and caused him to lose his balance. His reward was a grunt. The bird shot had found some flesh. Not much, and the small shot hardly damaged as much as it stung.

Morrisey scooted along and came up behind an ore cart. From the rocks poking over the top, it was almost fully loaded. Shooting through it unless he used a mountain howitzer was pointless. The lead ore stopped even the heaviest rifle fire.

"Save us. They kidnapped us!"

The cries distracted Shad. Two men rattled chains and yanked at their shackles. The brief instant he looked at them let Patrick Morrisey pop up and fire.

Shad fell backward, trying not to completely lose his balance. He was almost successful. But his six-gun went skittering from his holster. Grabbing frantically he tried to recover it. Morrisey fired steadily. If Shad kept trying to get back his pistol, he was going to be filled with lead.

He changed tactics. He picked up the sawed off shotgun and discharged the second barrel in Morrisey's direction. A loud shriek of pain followed by sulfurous curses rewarded him. The shotgun empty, he dropped it and flopped belly down to grab his six-gun. In his haste, he missed by a fraction of an inch. The butt slid through his fingers.

"Save us, mister. They're using us as slaves!"

Again distracted, Shad gave up on retrieving his six-gun to look at the two men chained at the far side of the cavern.

"Throw something at him. Try to get free." His advice

fell on deaf ears. The men continued to shout for him to do something while doing nothing to save themselves.

Shad rolled behind a pile of wood beams intended to replace roof supports. Splinters flew as Morrisey fired wildly. Although distracted, Shad had the gut feeling that Morrisey was running low on ammo. He popped up and exposed his head to fire. If he was wrong, he'd be dead, but anger powered him.

This was the man who had killed his son. Shad felt it. Abe had seen Patrick Morrisey the night before. There hadn't been any reason for him to prowl around the coal yard. Whatever the reason, Patrick Morrisey must have gunned down his son to cover whatever he'd been up to.

He ducked back, listened hard to hear Morrisey. The two men screamed and rattled their shackles, but the sound Shad wanted came loud and clear. A hammer fell on an empty chamber.

With a loud cry, he swarmed up over the pile of wood supports and ran hellbent for the ore cart where Morrisey hid. As he surged over the top of the loaded cart, he grabbed a hunk of rock. It almost pulled his arm out of its socket as he swung it around. Morrisey looked up from trying to reload his old black powder Remington.

The expression on his face added to Shad's satisfaction of driving the rock down hard. He felt bones break. Blood spurted from a busted nose. He fought to get over the ore cart. Shad landed on top of Morrisey. The rock came up and down again. Fury seized him. He wanted to beat the man to death for killing Abe.

Shad held back after three more blows. Patrick Morrisey's face was a bloody, wrecked mess. He made strange little animal noises unlike anything a human might utter.

"You're under arrest for murder." Shad looked up at the two men at the back of the cave. "And for kidnapping. There's got to be a law you broke about slavery, too. You're gonna swing, Morrisey. And I want to be the one putting the noose around your scrawny neck."

He grabbed a handful of shirt and yanked hard to get the man onto his feet. Patrick Morrisey's legs refused to hold him erect.

"Look out, Marshal. Look out!"

Again the two chained men distracted him. Shad looked at them. Then he heard boot soles grating against the gravel and debris on the mine floor. Straining hard, he whirled a limp Morrisey around to use as a shield.

He was too slow. A shovel rose above his head and came crashing down. The first blow mashed his bowler. The second drove him to his knees. The third made the world go away.

Chapter Fifteen

"You better be durned sure about this, girl," Winifred Gallagher said, fists on her hips. She spat toward a tin can in the corner of the room. She missed and never noticed.

"I am, Aunt Win." Beatrice Gallagher held up her accounting book. Neat rows of numbers marched from the top to the bottom where the final sum had been circled in red.

"We can't afford to lose a couple tons of coal a month."

Beatrice said nothing. She closed the ledger book and folded her hands in her lap. Her aunt bit off another hunk of chaw, worked on it a few seconds and then began pacing from one end of the canvas-walled enclosure to the other. Every second trip, she spit toward the crude cuspidor. More often than not she missed.

Winifred Gallagher threw her hands up over her head, as if surrendering.

"I'll skin him alive. It's got to be Brushwell what's doin' the stealin'. Who else could it be?"

"Nobody's seen wagons drive up empty and leave full," Beatrice said.

"That's right, Bea. That's right. That's gotta be proof he's swipin' our coal."

"What's he do with it?" Beatrice asked. "My numbers say he's stolen a powerful lot of coal. You don't just hide that under a blanket."

Winifred stared at her niece, wide-eyed. Then she understood what Beatrice meant.

"He's sellin' it to the railroad as his own coal. How else can he steal from us without bein' obvious?"

"Just accusing him's not good enough, Auntie. We have to prove it if we want the marshal to arrest him."

"It's my coal he's stealin'. Well, it belongs to the family, but I'm the head of the family so it's mine. Best way to prove it is to make the little vermin confess."

"Kidnapping him to torture the truth from him's not likely to hold up in court," Beatrice pointed out. "We have to get him to confess in front of somebody who'll look like they're unbiased."

"Ain't nobody like that."

"What about Mister Sussman? We can pay him if he peaches on Brushwell."

"That won't work too good," Winifred said, thinking. She spat mechanically. Without aiming, she hit the tin cup. Only when she tried to get the gob into the can did she miss.

"I see what you mean," Beatrice said. "What if Sussman is in cahoots with Brushwell? They'd lie to cover each other."

"My thought, exactly," Winifred said. "It's good to see your brain's workin' hard. But what are we gonna do? If I skin him alive, is that good enough for a judge and jury?"

Beatrice pointed out that this was too extreme for a judge to tolerate.

"Even if we let the jury help with the skinnin'? They'd like that." She threw up her hands in frustration and pushed through the hanging canvas to go into the middle of the cavern.

Beatrice followed her aunt down the tunnel and up the slope to the cabin on the side of the hill. Winifred went to the cabin door and opened it. She looked out into the late afternoon, spat without benefit of a cuspidor now and said over her shoulder, "We're goin' down to the coal yard. I want a word with Brushwell. You bring that fancy ledger book of yours. It's time we have it out."

"It'll be dark when we get there," Beatrice said, settling her accounting ledger under her arm.

"So much the better. You don't think he steals the coal in broad daylight, do you?"

"I would," Beatrice said softly. She checked the folds of her skirt. The derringer pistol tucked there gave a sense of security. The meeting with Brushwell wouldn't last long. Once she sent her aunt on her way, there'd be time to meet Patrick. Beatrice touched an envelope in her pocket. They had more important business than missing coal to deal with.

The coal yard was both dark and silent. Not even crickets sounded. The late evening wind off the mountain slopes had died. Without the soft rustle of leaves in the trees adjoining the yard or the whisper of pine needles being disturbed, the silence crushed in on Beatrice's ears until it felt painful.

"Quit fidgetin', girl," Winifred said. "You're makin' me nervous. It never pays to show your hand like that to a swindler."

Beatrice looked around. If Patrick had already come, she hoped he had the good sense to stay out of sight. Winifred carried a rifle. If she saw a Morrisey prowling around, she'd shoot first and ask questions later.

"You see anything suspicious?"

"Nothing, Aunt Win." She clutched the ledger book to her breast. The weight of her pistol tugged at her dress, but the letter in the same pocket felt like a lead ingot.

"I don't neither," she said crossly. "I'll have to get him to confess without givin' him evidence he can dispute."

"Somebody's coming from the direction of the warehouse," Beatrice said. She reached into her pocket and took the pistol in hand.

"It's Brushwell," Winifred said. "Let's get this over. I want a decent dinner at the hotel 'fore goin' back home."

"Ladies, what are you doing wandering around alone?" Arthur Brushwell strode up. He was dressed to the nines. The pale green paisley vest and silk cravat, the fine linen suit with black velvet tab lapels, the jaunty top hat and neatly creased trousers were all in keeping with a fancy night at the opera rather than knocking around in a coal yard.

"Checkin' up on how you're handlin' my coal."

Brushwell heaved a deep sigh.

"We've been over this before, Winifred. There's no way you're being cheated, by me or anyone else."

"My niece has proof we've bein' shorted. Show him, Beatrice."

Beatrice handed over her ledger book. She opened it to the last page.

"There. See? The amount sold to the railroad is less than we mine. The difference is quite substantial."

Brushwell ran his finger down the column. His lips moved. When he got to the bottom of the column, he said, "This means less than 5 percent isn't accounted for. If you weight it at the mine, all that jostling on the road as you bring it here might cause some of the dust to settle out. The rocks in the road bounce the driver around, right?"

"You're sayin' we lose that much to gettin' bounced out along the way?" Winifred folded her arms and looked fierce. "I sent Jeremiah out to see what he could pick up. There warn't much. Not this much." Her stubby finger stabbed down on the ledger.

"Jeremiah's an honest worker," Brushwell said slowly. "Why don't I get my foreman to go with him in the morning and see what can be found. I'm sure we can find what's happened during your transport to my coal yard."

"The other possibility is that the railroad's cheating you," Beatrice said.

"No," Brushwell said sharply. Then with more diplomacy,

"I doubt that's happening. They need to play fair. If they lose Utopia and your fine Gallagher coal, this route wouldn't be profitable for them anymore."

"They'd have to use bigger engines, which cost more," Beatrice said.

Brushwell looked at her.

"That's right. You've got a good head for business, missy."

"That's Miss Gallagher," she said coldly.

"Of course it is. As I said, I'll have my foreman ride up to the Calcutta. Send Jeremiah along if you will. Now you must excuse me. I am late for an appointment."

"The midnight train's taking on coal?" asked Beatrice.

"Of course it is," he said sharply. "Stay and watch as the coal's loaded. Or," Brushwell said, eyes fixed on Beatrice, "take your time and wander through the yard as long as you please. Now, if you'll excuse me." He touched the brim of his top hat and started to leave.

Winifred called after him.

"If I don't like the way you're handlin' affairs, I'll find another agent. The Coal Queen of the Rockies ain't gonna be denied!"

Arthur Brushwell kept walking and disappeared into the darkness without a look back at his accuser.

"What do you make of him, Aunt Win?" Beatrice chewed at her lower lip as she went over everything the coal yard owner had said. He had a haughty attitude at the best of times, but tonight he mocked them more openly.

Beatrice amended that. She had been the target for the man's words. And they burned in her head, as bright as the noonday sun.

"You keep an inventory of my coal," Winifred said. "If I don't get on over to the hotel 'fore Netty throws out dinner, I'll be danged near starved by the time I get home."

"I'll see you at the mine, Aunt Win."

Winifred Gallagher went off, muttering to herself about thieves and what she'd do when she caught them. Beatrice let her get out of sight, then dashed for the trees at the back of the coal yard.

The night remained still. She strained to hear anyone moving about in the copse, but not even small critters stirred tonight. Beatrice found her familiar spot, a stump hidden from sight by casual observers in the yard but one that gave her a view of anyone approaching. She and Patrick had met here more times than she could count.

Barely had she settled down on the stump than heavy footsteps echoed through the forest. Fingers resting on her twin-shot pistol, she waited quietly.

"Bea, are you here? It's so dark I can't see anything," Patrick said, blundering about. His words were slurred.

"Over here," she snapped. "Be quiet. You're making enough noise to raise the dead."

She stood to greet him. When he stepped close, she recoiled and pushed him away.

"What happened to you? It looks like you tangled with a wildcat."

He touched his face. He winced as he explored his bare head. Even in the dark she saw the lump there. But the cuts and gashes on his cheeks and forehead had barely scabbed over. Someone had beat him within an inch of his life. With a split lip, no wonder his words came out sounding funny.

"Don't mean a thing," he said. "I got into a scuffle, that's all."

"I hope you gave the other guy what for," she said. "I can't imagine you look this bad and that you won."

"He won't give us any more trouble."

Beatrice started to ask who had given Patrick such a beating, then realized more immediate problems faced them. She pulled out the letter and held it up.

"Another ransom demand?" Patrick asked.

"He wants two hundred dollars now. Tonight."

"Who can it be?" Patrick's voice turned shrill with strain.

"I don't have a dime more to give. That $37 was all Pa had in the family treasury."

"Some treasury," Beatrice said, her words dripping with sarcasm. "Aunt Win's got that much but she counts it every last night. If I took it, she'd know before I got halfway down the hill."

"Who coulda sent the demand?" Patrick asked. "Abe's dead, and he was the one what picked up the other blackmail money."

"The writing's the same. Since he's dead, no thanks to you, it means the deputy wasn't squeezing us for the money."

"I shot at him! Over and over!"

"You missed every last time." Beatrice sucked in her breath and then let it out slowly. "I was the one who killed him." She drew her derringer and held it up. "Two shots, smack in his body."

"You didn't miss," Patrick said. "But it wasn't my fault you killed him. I tried!"

Beatrice glared at him. He was a complete failure when it came to fighting. His face proved that. Patrick was an even worse gunman. He had fired repeatedly at Abednego Nelson and hadn't hit the deputy once. If she didn't still need him . . .

"Are you sure your family's all willing to lie for you? You don't dare tweak Shadrach Nelson's suspicion about where you were."

"They'll all say I was with them. But that doesn't matter too much. The marshal's not going to be nosing around none."

Beatrice started to snap at him for being such a fool. Once an honest man got a bee in his bonnet, he'd never stop until he found the truth. Patrick hadn't killed Abe Nelson, but the lawman would worm the story out of him. That led straight back to her. She hoped the Morrisey clan was solid and willing to lie for Patrick. She wasn't sure she'd trust any of her family to tell the truth, much less alibi her for a crime.

"We've got other problems, then, if your story is solid," she said.

"What are we going to do?" he asked. He ran his fingers around the edge of the new ransom note, then looked at her. One eye had swollen shut, giving him a grotesque expression.

"Get a sack. Find one out there in the yard and shred a newspaper to give it some heft. Or put a couple lumps of coal in it. Our blackmailing friend's going to have a very bad Christmas."

"It's months till—oh, I understand. The lumps of coal mean he's been bad."

"The lumps of coal mean he's going to be a couple ounces heavier with all thc bullcts I can pump into him." Beatrice drew her pistol and held it up for Patrick to see. She started to hand it to him. Let him do the dirty work this time. Then she drew it back. Patrick wasn't in any shape to pull the trigger. Whoever had beat him up had done a job on him. The lump on his head and one eye swollen shut meant his aim would be off.

Hers wouldn't be. Not tonight.

Chapter Sixteen

"Wake up, damn your eyes. They've doubled what we have to dig, thanks to you. You gotta dig your share or we'll starve."

Shadrach Nelson groaned as the sharp edge of a pickaxe poked into his gut. He swung wildly and missed. For his trouble he got another sharp poke. Forcing himself to sit up, he discovered his ankles were shackled.

"We don't get fed if we don't work. You gotta pull your weight."

"We're all in this together because of you," said a second man.

Shad rubbed a lump on his head where he'd been slugged. He winced when his fingers touched a sensitive spot. He saw two dark figures hovering above him. They held candles that flickered and cast a strange glow on their haggard faces.

"I know you," Shad said. "You came to my office."

"You shoved me aside. I tried to tell you me and Clarence'd been taken, but you wouldn't listen." Jim Murton held the candle up a little higher and looked around. "He found me 'fore you got back."

"Patrick Morrisey?"

"I escaped but you as good as turned me back over to him to die in this mine."

"You're responsible for us being here." The shorter of the two tried to poke him again with his pickaxe. "You might as well have shot us and put us out of our misery."

"The Morriseys are making you work their mine?" Shad focused better now. The dull ache remained behind his eyes, but he used the wall as support to stand. His chains rattled ominously. The links between his ankles were hardly enough for him to take a half step. There wasn't any way he was going to run off bound like this.

"We was mindin' our own business," the shorter one said. "Me and Clarence picked up some parts for Mister Sussman and the gang of 'em jumped us and drug us here to the mine."

"For no reason!"

"You're James Murton," Shad said. "And you're Clarence Abbott."

"Finally, the lawman knows who we are," Murton said sarcastically.

"And where we are."

"Your wife reported you missing. I hunted for you but didn't find a trace."

"We've been underground ever since they dragged us up the mountain," Murton said. "'Cept when I almost got free and you turned me back over to 'em."

"When you came in wavin' that scattergun around, I thought you'd set us free," Abbott said. "But you got yourself in the same pickle as us. Some lawman you are."

Jim Murton hobbled to the wall where Shad supported himself. The look of pure hatred on his face alerted Shad. He barely ducked when Murton swung his pick and tore off a hunk of rock where Shad's head had been an instant before.

"You're all bunged up," Shad said. "You limp and from the blood on your shirt, you've been shot."

"Being a detective sure is easy when you've got your victims starin' you in the face," Murton said. He took another swing. Shad avoided this blow. He turned to see the silvery vein where the prisoner chipped away.

"That's what we have to scrape out," Abbott said. "If we don't fill six ore carts a shift, they won't feed us."

"Nine," Murton said bitterly. "We got to dig nine, thanks to Mister Marshal here failin' to get us free."

"That's a powerful lot of ore for three men to dig," Shad said.

"You bashed in the one's skull," Murton said. "That won't set well with them. You're makin' it worse."

"Won't hurt him much. He's not got any brains," Abbott said. "That's Patrick."

"The other one looked like he'd been whupped on good. Did you do that?" Murton prodded Shad and pointed to the wall, silently ordering him to start digging.

"That was Nate, another of Leadbottom's boys. I've got Andy in a cell back in town."

"Nate's bad. Patrick's worse. But the one you got to watch out for is Eric. I swear he'll beat us to death and laugh while he's doin' it," Murton said.

"How'd you escape before?" Shad asked. "We've got to get out of here."

"Like you're the one who can do it, Mister High And Mighty." Abbott moved a few feet away on the other side of Murton and began chipping at the rock.

"We can't keep this up for long," Shad said. "You two are scarecrows."

"They don't feed us much. If Patrick thinks on it, they'll only keep givin' us food for two and force us to split it three ways. Leadbottom Morrisey is a devil. A big, fat devil who—"

He screamed and slammed forward into the wall. Behind him Nate hefted the sawed-off shotgun. He had rammed the stock into Murton's back.

"Don't you go badmouthin' my pa. You're danged lucky he's as generous as he is."

Shad turned, ready to use the pick on the shotgun-wielding man. He found himself staring at the double barrels. Both of the rabbit ear hammers were pulled back, and Nate's finger tapped the dual triggers.

"I'd catch a whuppin' from my pa if I kilt you, but it'd be worth it."

"The pick's broken," Shad said. "I need a new one."

Nate Morrisey poked him in the gut with the shotgun muzzle and looked.

"Yup, that prong's broke off. I guess that means you gotta work even harder." He laughed and shoved. The barrels about knocked the wind from Shad's lungs.

"Get them to work," came the order echoing across the large cavern.

Shad recognized Patrick Morrisey's voice, though it was slurred.

"He got his head bashed in real good, didn't he?" Shad goaded. "I gave you what for, too." In the flickering candle light he saw that Nate's eye was swollen shut and two front teeth were missing. His lower lip was puffed up to twice its size. The fierce fight back in the mineshaft had left Nate bruised and battered.

"Pat's real mad at you. Ain't no way he can explain the way he looks to Pa without telling what you done. Pa took a dislike to you way back, so it'd be twice as bad for my brother if he found you was responsible."

Shad grunted when Nate poked him again with the shotgun.

"Quit your lollygaggin. Get to work. You got ten carts to fill 'fore you get fed."

"Ten!" Murton turned on Nate, only to catch a hard punch to his ribs. He made a gasping noise and fell to his knees.

"Next time Pat won't miss when he shoots at you." Nate left, laughing. If Shad never heard such an ugly sound again, it'd be a day too soon.

"There's no way we can fill ten more carts. I can barely lift my pick now," Abbott moaned.

"He's in real bad shape, too," Shad said. "That means we escape as quick as we can or we'll die in this miserable pit."

"So how're you gonna get us free? You've done nothing but make things worse for us." Murton rubbed his side. "If you hadn't ignored me in town, you and your deputies could have flushed out this den of rattlers."

"My deputies," Shad said. A catch came to his throat. His deputies, when he had ignored James Murton, had included his son.

"Has Patrick bragged on killing any of my deputies?"

"Nary a peep from him 'bout that," Abbott said.

Shad wondered at that. Abe had seen Patrick Morrisey nosing around in the coal yard. That had been his only clue as to who had killed his son, but all the Morriseys were cut from the same cloth. If Patrick had murdered Abe he'd be shooting off his mouth about it to anyone who'd listen. Having two slaves under his thumb gave him a perfect—captive—audience.

But who else could it have been? Nate had said Leadbottom had a blood feud boiling against the law in Utopia. And the Gallagher family. And likely everyone else he came into contact with. Leadbottom Morrisey was nothing if not unvarying in his hatred of anybody not a blood relative.

Even then, Shad wondered if Leadbottom didn't harbor some animosity toward his family for reasons only he knew.

"The prong broke off my pick. If I put it against my shackles, you can hit it with the handle of your pick. The pin holding the iron cuffs together looks like the weak spot."

"They'll kill us for sure if they suspect we're tryin' to escape," Murton said.

"You'll die for sure if you don't escape *now*."

"Why should we get you free first?" Murton asked. "You'll leave us behind."

"Do Abbott, then," Shad said. "I'll hold the prong. I wish I had a chisel. Is there one here?"

"They made sure we didn't have anything we could use as a club or knife 'cept the pickaxes," Abbott said. "Here. Whack the cuff open."

Shad held the broken length of metal against the rivet holding the shackle. He looked up. The expression on Murton's face was one of pure hatred. Shad cringed when Murton slammed the butt end of his pick. He was sure the man would miss and crush his skull.

The blow drove the prong down hard. The rivet on Abbott's shackle popped free.

"Don't let on," Shad whispered. "We don't know where Nate and Patrick are."

"Probably gettin' knee walkin' drunk," Murton said. "They turn real mean when they're drunk."

Shad held the prong as the second shackle broke open.

"Do Jim next," Abbott said.

Shad hesitated. If both men were free, they might leave him behind. Murton's anger toward him knew no bounds. Abbott wasn't as caught up in fury against him, but he was Murton's friend. Back in Utopia they worked together, and their enslavement in Leadbottom's mine had gone even further toward creating a solid, unshakable bond. They had endured hell together.

Shad silently placed the prong against Murton's shackles. It took longer to free him, but he finally sat on the floor rubbing his chaffed ankles.

"Now," Shad said, positioning the metal spike against his own shackles.

Abbott worked over how betrayal would benefit them and feed Murton's vengeance. To his relief Murton said, "We gotta free him, too. There's no way we can get out on our own. I'm too weak."

"I'm not doin' so good, either," Abbott said.

Within a few minutes, Shad stood free of the iron cuffs

and connecting chain. He took a few tentative steps and stumbled until he braced himself against an ore cart.

"How're we supposed to get out now?" Murton held himself upright on the other side of the ore cart.

"Empty the cart," Shad said. "We'll ride it out."

"All three of us can't fit into it," Abbott said skeptically.

Shad considered making the escape by himself, but he had promised Murton's wife he'd find the man. Although she hadn't said, she was halfway convinced he had run off with another woman. Talking with Murton, Shad understood how that was believable.

He bent low and grabbed under the front of the cart. With a heave he rotated it on an axle and dumped the lead ore the other two had mined onto the floor in a knee-high pile. Stepping away, he let the cart rock back into level position.

"Get in. We're going for a ride. Be ready to run."

The two men exchanged whispered protests. Shad wasn't sure how fast or far they'd get in their condition. The only way to find out was to try.

With Murton and Abbott crouched inside the ore cart, he began pushing. Somewhere along the tracks he'd find Patrick or Nate. When he did, he'd have to deal with them.

Then he'd be free. If Lady Luck smiled on him, all three of them would be free of Leadbottom Morrisey's lead mine slavery.

Pushing the cart turned out to be harder than Shad expected. He bent low and put his back into it. Inch by inch the cart screeched along the tracks. When he hit a small down slope it gained speed, and he hopped onto the back. Faster and faster it rolled along.

"Light. There's light ahead!"

The ore cart careened out of the mine and into the starlit night. When it hit the barricade at the end of the tracks, they were hurled into the air and down the mountain side, screaming in fright.

CHAPTER SEVENTEEN

"This isn't going to work," Patrick Morrisey said. He sat with his back to a tree, legs drawn up. He rested his head on his knees.

"You're not going to cry, are you?" Beatrice Gallagher nudged him with the toe of her shoe. "We've got this far. We have to keep going."

Patrick looked up, his battered head turning him into a shadow monster.

"You killed his son, didn't you?"

"You let him beat you up. He clobbered you with a rock. Even if I did kill Abednego Nelson, why aren't you congratulating me?"

"We thought Abe was the one blackmailing us. Who sent that new blackmail note?" He pointed to the letter on the ground beside him.

"It might be another of the deputies. They're a tight bunch, always drinking and whoring together."

"We don't know."

"Look, Pat," she said, settling beside him and putting her arm around his shoulders. "Think this through. He might have given the letter to that kid to give me."

"Before he died?"

"Of course before he died," she said angrily. She took her

arm from around his shoulders. “Dead men don’t blackmail anyone.”

“It’s someone else. It’s got to be,” Patrick said.

“If it is, it ends tonight. Everything’s working in our favor. You said your pa’s got the marshal all chained up and digging in his mine.” She saw how he touched his head. Shadrach Nelson had beaten Patrick within an inch of his life. “Let him die in the dark swinging a pick. You should be glad about that. And his son’s death.”

“I never liked any of them,” he admitted, “but that letter!” He pointed to the extortion note.

“You can be such a baby. Maybe that’s what I like about you.” Beatrice bent over and kissed him lightly on the cheek, then grabbed the letter, stood, and tucked the paper into her pocket. She closed her hand around her pistol.

“What time is it?”

Beatrice shook her head.

“You lose that watch I gave you?”

“I . . . I keep it hid. Aunt Win or any of the others’d ask where I got it. I don’t want to answer questions. But it’s a nice watch. Keeps good time.” Beatrice couldn’t remember what she’d done with the watch. It mattered nothing to her.

“That was my granddad’s watch. It keeps good time.”

“It keeps good time,” she repeated, not trying to keep the sarcasm from her voice. Patrick either missed her tone or ignored it.

“Let’s find a place to spy. It’s got to be sometime soon he’ll come to pick up the money.”

Beatrice said nothing. She drew the pistol from her pocket and silently wended her way through the trees to the edge of the stand. From here she got a good view of the coal pile where they’d left a sack stuffed with newspapers. This demand had been for two hundred dollars. It never paid to deal with a blackmailer. They always wanted more.

Until they were dead.

She lifted her pistol, steadied it in both hands and took aim. The sound of distant but approaching footsteps keyed her up.

"Is it him?"

"Shut up," she snapped. "And don't crowd me. If you're not going to shoot him, I will."

"I've got my six-gun," Patrick said. He drew it. His hand shook, but he lifted the pistol and took aim beside Beatrice.

"Don't miss if you shoot," she warned.

Beatrice sucked in her breath, held it, then let it out slowly. Her finger came back on the trigger as a dark figure passed by the pile of coal.

"You got it all tallied?"

"Yes, sir. We're ready to begin movin' these here piles."

"Brushwell's got 'em all weighed and measured?"

"Sussman!" Patrick hissed the name of the railroad agent. He thrust his gun out on a stiff arm and put his thumb on the hammer.

"Put your gun down," Beatrice said. She relaxed her aim and made sure Patrick didn't do anything foolish. "It's not him. He's doing an inventory before getting the coal loaded on tonight's train from Denver."

"Who's that with him? Maybe he—"

"That's his assistant. I don't know what his name is."

"He's the one blackmailing us," Patrick said. He started to lift his gun again, but she pushed it down.

"Don't be a fool. Are you going to shoot both of them? They never so much as glanced toward the sack."

"But who'll pick it up?"

Beatrice considered the matter for a moment, then said, "Get on back to your mine. Nobody's coming to pick up the sack."

"They'll tell everyone about us!"

Beatrice said nothing. If the blackmailer wanted money, he'd let them know. As long as he didn't spread the word about her and Patrick, he had the upper hand and a chance to make a lot of money. Both the Calcutta Mine and the Morrisey's lead mine were flowing rivers of cash. Throwing away such money wasn't done easily.

Whoever it was trying to squeeze them, he was greedy.

"Should I take the sack or leave it?"

"I don't care. Nobody not extorting us who finds it will know why it's there," she said. Beatrice tucked her pistol away and turned to him. "Scat. Go on. Get back to your mine."

"What're you going to do?"

She gently shoved him. He started to come back to give her a kiss. Beatrice avoided that, turning her back and walking away. From over her shoulder she called, "Don't be seen leaving the coal yard."

Whatever he called to her was lost as she worked her way around a head-high mound of coal. She wished she had brought her ledger book to count what was here. Her aunt got crazy notions fixed in her head, but she agreed when confronted with the numbers showing that Gallagher coal was being stolen.

When Beatrice caught sight of Sussman and his assistant, she dropped back and let the depot manager hurry on, snapping out orders as he went. They vanished in the direction of the railroad depot. Beatrice started to backtrack and see if anyone had disturbed the bogus payment when she heard a steam whistle wail in the distance.

She followed the railroad agent and found a place just away from the tracks to watch as he directed a crew to prepare the water tower and then begin hauling coal in a freight wagon up the ramp to put into the bin.

The train pulled in and water gurgled into its boiler. Sussman supervised the loading of the coal into the tender. A long chute was moved around from the elevated bin and lowered to the mostly empty tender just behind the engine.

He yanked a rope to open the door. Coal tumbled out until the last lump was gone.

"All loaded," Sussman called to the engineer. They exchanged words. All she heard was Sussman's final, "It's not your concern. I say it's all loaded. Now pull out or you'll be behind schedule."

The engineer made an obscene gesture, which Sussman returned. The station master climbed steps to the depot platform and shifted metal signal flags to alert everyone that the train was no longer parked. Steam hissed and the whistle blew as the train picked up speed, heading west down the long slope.

Sussman dismissed his crew, yawned, and went inside the station. The lamp in the back room went out in a few minutes. The station master had turned in. The next train wasn't due until mid-day.

Beatrice started to leave, then curiosity got the better of her. She climbed the ladder on the side of the coal bin. Workmen brought wagon loads of coal from the yard and dumped it into the bin for loading into the train. Gripping the edge of the bin, she hoisted herself up to look in. A quick glance showed nothing but coal dust spotted walls and floor.

But something felt wrong.

With a heave, she flopped over the edge of the bin and dropped into the sooty box. Coal dust meant nothing to her. She lived next to a coal mine. She lived *in* a mine. All her relatives lived, breathed, and ate coal dust every day of the week. Beatrice paced back and forth, taking in the dimensions. A few taps showed the sides were solid.

When she stamped her foot down, though, a hollow ringing told her of a compartment underneath. She measured the depth of the bin, then swung around the loading door and measured the exterior height.

At least two feet at the bottom of the bin had been blocked off. If the railroad paid for an entire bin of coal, it only got about 90 percent. A full bin was lacking a complete allotment of coal by at least one part in ten.

She dropped from the bin, shook off what coal dust she could and began the walk up the mountain to the mine. Beatrice had plenty to think about every step of the way.

Chapter Eighteen

"Hang on!" Shadrach Nelson gripped the side of the ore cart as it barreled down the tracks. It gathered speed when it hit a steep hill. It was hard seeing where the cart headed in the dark, but Shad raised his head at the last minute.

He let out a cry of pure anguish. The heavy steel-ribbed ore cart hit a barrier that knocked it over as if it were made of cardboard. The cart sailed through the air. Rocks flew all around as the cart tipped over and sent the three passengers plunging down.

Shad kicked free and fell separately from the ore cart. He landed hard against rock and then scooted down, shredding his coat, vest, shirt, and back. For a moment he lay staring up at the night sky. The stars danced about, some of them doubled. When he sucked in a deep breath, he almost passed out. Pain drove into his chest like a railroad spike. The impact had knocked the air from his lungs.

Helpless, he laid back and let his body try to regain control of breathing and even rational thinking. In the distance he heard the ore cart crashing farther downhill. From the splintering sounds, it was completely destroyed. Then the cart crashed to a halt. No other sound came. Such an impact might have killed the two men he had tried to rescue.

Curses slipped from his lips. Every breath gave him

better control. He sat up. Blood oozed down his back from dozens of shallow cuts. Luck had been with him that he didn't drive a sharp rock into his spine. That would have left him paralyzed, maybe for the rest of his life.

His breathing returned to normal by the time he ran out of curses describing Leadbottom Morrisey and his outlaw offspring. Shad stood, lost his balance and went tumbling ass over teakettle all the way down the mountain slope.

He fetched up against a large rock not ten feet from the scattered debris left when the ore cart crashed.

Shad shook his head to clear it and got to his feet. His vision was blurred again, but his ears were in good shape. He heard moans. Using them to guide his footsteps, he made his way past the destroyed ore cart to find Abbott curled up in a ball, moaning piteously. He helped the man sit up.

"We've got to run for our lives. The sooner we get away from Morrisey land the safer we'll be."

Abbott nodded to show he understood. When he pulled away from Shad, the marshal went in search of Jim Murton. He found the man much farther down the hillside. Murton stared at him, then picked up a rock.

"I ought to bash out your brains. Why'd you do somethin' like that to us?"

"We're free of the mine. You're not wearing chains." Shad caught Abbott as the man slipped on loose rock. Together the two of them reached a deeply rutted road. Murton joined them a few seconds later.

"That way goes into town," Shad said.

"It curves around and comes down into the depot," Abbott said. "Me and Jim helped clear it off right after we got to town."

"Is that closer? To the depot? It's at least three miles into town. When Leadbottom finds we escaped, he'll have everyone in his camp hunting us down." Shad stared into the darkness. Going to town was what Leadbottom would expect. Reaching the railroad depot offered some refuge.

"Don't matter if it's farther or not. It's the way I'm goin'," Murton said. He silently motioned for Abbott to come with him.

"Which way are you headin', Marshal? You've done good so far." Abbott waited to hear what Shad said.

"The hell he has!" Murton erupted. "We wouldn't be in this pickle if it wasn't for him."

Shad wasn't in any condition to argue. His scraped up back turned into a single fiery pain. If he kept moving, the muscles weren't likely to seize up. Just the few minutes arguing warned him he was in worse condition than he wanted to believe. His leg, his side, his back. There wasn't any part of him that didn't hurt or ache or bleed. Too much of his body did all three at the same time.

He started walking away from town, hoping Abbott knew what he was talking about. Even if he didn't, the road took him away from the Morrisey mine.

The three trooped along in the dark, stumbling occasionally on rocks in the unimproved road. Ten minutes into the hike, Shad's toe caught something hard and sent him sprawling. He got to his knees and saw what had tripped him up.

"It's one of them lead bars," Abbott said. "Leadbottom ain't too good keepin' track of them when he's freighting them to the depot."

"He uses this road to move his lead?" Shad got to his feet and tried to walk faster. When Leadbottom found his slaves had escaped and that they weren't traveling the road into Utopia, he'd come this way. If he used the road all the time, he knew it better than Shad or the other two ever could.

Another ten minutes brought them to a fork in the road. The right path lead higher into Hellfire Pass. The left wended its way downhill. That had to go to the railroad depot.

"That way?" Shad asked. He didn't get a reply. Both men were frozen in place, staring at each other.

He cocked his head to one side and listened. The usual night sounds ahead told him that was safe terrain. But behind? Not a critter moved or howled or made even the tiniest sound. In seconds, he understood why. The clatter of ironclad wagon wheels came along at a good clip.

"They're after us," Shad said. "Hide out. Maybe they'll miss us in the dark."

"Here?" scoffed Murton. "There ain't anything to hide behind."

"A ravine. We can lay down, and they'll miss us," Abbott said. He looked around frantically. The only arroyos cut into the hillside ran from higher up toward the floor of the pass. They might not be seen if Leadbottom's boys were careless.

Shad knew the Morrisey boys'd be alert. The ones who hadn't let their prisoners escape would have bragging rights if they spotted the runaways. And those who had let them go would need to redeem themselves by spotting Shad and the other two. The only satisfaction Shad had was that he had bashed both of the Morrisey boys pretty good. He rubbed his hand against his coat. Some of the dried blood there had to be from both Nate and Patrick Morrisey.

He wished he had whaled away harder, longer, until only a dead carcass remained.

"Run," Abbott said.

"No, we can't outrun them," Shad said. "Hide."

"That'll get us killed," Murton said. He twisted around, torn between hiding and doing as his friend suggested. In better shape than the other two, Murton lit a shuck. His boots clopped hard and fast as he took the left fork and raced for the railroad depot.

Shad found himself a spot between two waist-high rocks. He wedged himself down. From here he had a narrow view of the road. Abbott dropped on the far side of the road and tried to burrow down in a shallow cut. Shad started to call to the man that he was still visible.

Then came the rolling and rattling heavy wagon. Three

Morriseys rode in it, arguing as they drove furiously along the rocky road.

". . . can't have got this far. They headed back to town in the other direction."

"Pa'll catch 'em if they did. That wrecked ore cart was all covered in blood. The trail comes this way," said another.

"That warn't blood, you fool. It was black as ink."

"That's the way it looks in starlight. How'd you ever get to be nineteen and not know that?"

Shad held his breath. The wagon creaked as it made its way up a short incline before reaching the fork.

"There's the split in the road," the driver said. "Joe, go hunt for any trace of blood."

"Why me? I—"

The driver and the man beside him in the box both went for their six-shooters at the same instant. They turned away from Shad and pointed their guns at Abbott.

"You crawl on up to the road, you slippery snake, you," the driver shouted. He stood to get a better aim.

"We got 'em!" crowed the man beside the driver. "Pa'll give us a bigger cut of the next shipment fer this."

Shad grunted as he pulled himself free of the crevice. His involuntary noise as he slid free caused the man with the rifle to half turn. Shad launched himself. He wasn't able to jump up to the driver's box, but he managed to spook the mule. The wagon lurched, sending the rifleman flailing about to land in the bed.

"Abbott," he called. "Get up here."

The driver and the other Morrisey were taken off guard by Shad's sudden attack, but they recovered fast. The driver waved his six-gun around wildly. The foot-long orange flame stabbed through the night.

Shad heard Abbott gasp. Then there was deathly silence.

Frantic now, Shad grabbed for a weapon, any weapon. His fingers closed on the third man's wrist as he tried to draw his six-shooter. A sudden twist sent the pistol flying.

The confusion now came in an earsplitting shriek as all three yelled at each other, trying to blame someone else for the attack.

Shad dropped down to the road and almost got run over. The mule had endured enough of the confusion and pulled hard to get away. The driver flopped around in the box, unable to fire. The other two fought in the wagon bed. Shad scrambled around on hands and knees, hunting for the dropped pistol. He lifted it to shoot, but the wagon turned uphill and took the right fork.

He didn't bother firing. Let them run off and concoct some lie to tell Leadbottom. As like as not, they'd claim they never found the runaway slaves.

Shad went to the far side of the road and looked down at Abbott's body. He'd been shot in the head. Other than the faint sound he'd made, the man had died instantly.

This wasn't a fight he could win by himself. Shad moved the body back to the shallow ravine where Abbott had tried to hide, then marked rocks on the other side of the road with broad V scratches to find the place again. He'd be back with his deputies to retrieve the body. Then he'd bring the full force of the law down on the entire Morrisey clan for what they'd done.

Grimly, Shadrach Nelson started hiking down toward the railroad depot. Just after midnight when the train loosed a long, loud whistle as it left, he banged on the depot door and ordered Sussman to go fetch his deputies.

Shad was exhausted both physically and mentally, but he felt justice within his grasp. The Morrisey family would pay for kidnapping and murdering Abbott. He'd make sure he found out if they'd also been responsible for killing Abe.

He curled up in the corner of the depot waiting room and drifted to sleep, the captured six-gun clutched in his hand as he dreamed of justice.

And vengeance.

Chapter Nineteen

"Wake me up if anything happens," Kenny Gallagher said.

"Aunt Win told us to both stay awake to see who's swipin' our coal," Jeremiah Jones said. "You know how she gets if you ignore her."

"The only way'd she find out is you snitch on me."

"Just 'cuz you're her son don't mean I'm any less a Gallagher," Jeremiah said.

"Your ma married a loser," Kenny said. "That means you ain't as much a Gallagher as me."

"Take that back! My pa was a good man. He married your aunt, didn't he?"

"Aunt Martha never had an ounce of sense. Ma said she was dropped on her head as a baby. And your pa was a drunk. Uncle Joseph wasn't sober a single day I ever saw him."

"That's 'cuz *you* was drunk! Now take it back that my pa was a loser."

"Where'd he get off to? He abandoned you and your ma." Kenny pulled himself up and thrust his fists in front of him, ready to have it out.

"Aunt Win drove him off. She was always callin' him—" Jeremiah caught a punch in the side of his rib cage as Kenny launched a haymaker. He stepped back, more surprised than hurt. "You're gonna pay for that sneaky attack!" With his hands balled tight, he stepped up.

"Stop it, you two. Stop it right this minute."

They turned to see Beatrice glaring at them. She stepped forward and pushed them apart.

"You're here to be lookouts, not get into fights. And you certainly don't fight each other. We're family. Save the fighting for the Morriseys."

"Ah, Sis, we was just passin' the time," Kenny said. "It's borin' out here. There's nothin' but rats runnin' around them piles of coal. And cats chasin' 'em."

"He's right," said Jeremiah. "After the train pulled out, even the railroad agent left."

"Winifred is right about someone stealing our coal," she said. "We need to find out how." Beatrice looked at each in turn. They had no idea what fraud was happening under their eyes. If she hadn't matched what the Calcutta Mine delivered to the railroad and how much the Gallagher family was paid, she'd never have known, either. Aunt Win had trusted both Brushwell and the railroad too long.

"We—" Kenny cut off his reply and held up his hand to silence the others.

Beatrice heard the sounds that her brother did. She pushed them toward the railroad depot and followed closely. Someone crashed about, not even attempting to keep quiet.

"There he is," Jeremiah said. He pulled out his six-shooter and started to shoot. Beatrice stropped him.

"That's one of the railroad mechanics," she said. "I recognize him."

"Even if he works here, what's he doin' prowlin' around this late at night?"

"That, brother dear, is something I need to find out." She led the way toward the depot. Beatrice worked to remember the man's name. She had only seen him working in the freight yard a couple times. When she did recall him, she called out. "Mister Murton, you look a fright."

Her fingers curled around the butt of her derringer, ready to fire if he proved belligerent. He turned toward her, reached out imploringly, then fell to his knees.

"Help me. I need help."

Beatrice motioned for her relatives to aid the mechanic. They pulled Murton to his feet. His knees refused to support him and he hung between them like a scarecrow on a crosspiece.

"Let's go to the repair shed," she told them. "It's out of sight and away from . . . trouble."

Murton did his best to walk under his own power, but Jeremiah and Kenny ended up dragging him most of the way. They dropped him onto a pile of burlap bags. A choking cloud of dust arose. Beatrice fanned it away and waited for Murton to speak. Her heart beat a little faster at the possibilities when he began spinning his story.

"They took me. They took me 'n Abbott and chained us up like animals."

"Who did that?" Beatrice hushed Kenny, who was all fired up to ask questions. She didn't want him confusing Murton.

"Leadbottom. He's plumb out of his mind. Loco. Him and his boys grabbed us outside the hardware store and put us to work in his mines. He used us as slaves!"

"Mister Murton, we'd never let a thing like that happen if we saw it. Me and the rest of the Gallaghers. We're all fine, upstanding, law-abiding citizens."

Murton rubbed his eyes and leaned forward.

"You're Winifred Gallagher's girl?"

"I'm her niece. I can speak for her because we share your outrage. Jeremiah, get Mister Murton some water to drink."

"Where?" he asked. "I don't know where there's water 'round these parts."

"The tower," she said impatiently. "They refill the locomotive's boiler. There's got to be water in the tower or however they fill it." She shooed him away, then dropped onto the pile of burlap bags next to Murton. She took his hand in hers.

"You need to help me get Abbott away from them. He . . . he won't help us."

"I don't understand," she said. "Who are you talking about?"

"The marshal. He was in the mine with us. He wants us both dead."

Beatrice had no idea what Murton meant, but she pushed the information aside to take a bucket from Jeremiah and give it to Murton so he could drink.

After gulping down close to half the bucket, he gagged. She patted him on the back like she would a colicky baby until he got his breath back.

"There, there. You're safe with us."

"Yeah, safe," said Kenny, trying to insert himself into the conversation. Beatrice put him in his place with a cold glare.

"You think Marshal Nelson is in cahoots with them? With Leadbottom and the Morriseys?"

Murton swallowed some more water. His head bobbed up and down.

"Bea, we got company," Jeremiah said. "It's the marshal."

Murton tried to stand. He legs weren't up to it. Beatrice put a hand on his shoulder and kept him down.

"We'll handle this, Mister Murton. Don't you fret none. The Gallaghers got your back."

She peered out of the shed and saw Shadrach Nelson slogging along, as if every step was uphill on Mt. Elbert. It didn't take any imagination to see that he had endured the same tribulations that Murton had. The difference was held in the marshal's hand. He carried a six-shooter.

"Don't do anything unless he tries to take me off to jail," she told her relatives. "Do you understand? Don't even show yourself unless I signal you."

"What signal?" Jeremiah asked.

Kenny poked him in the ribs to shut him up. Beatrice

grimly nodded to her brother. Kenny understood what was at stake. She slipped out and walked slowly toward the railroad depot. The marshal sat on the lowest step, head down and pistol beside him on the stair.

As she neared him, he jerked alert. He grabbed for the gun.

"Whoa, Marshal, don't go shooting me. It's only me, Beatrice Gallagher." She fingered her own gun hidden in the folds of her skirt. Whatever she did had to be on her own head. Depending on either Jeremiah or her brother was out of the question.

"What are you doing here?" he asked. He put the six-gun back on the step beside him.

"I can ask you the same thing." She stopped a few feet away. "You look rode hard and put away wet. Is there a problem?"

"Plenty of problems." He looked across Hellfire Pass toward the far mountain where the Morrisey lead mine clawed into the rock.

"Is there anything I can help with?"

"Have you seen anyone wandering around the rail yard?"

"Who do you have in mind? The train left close to an hour ago. Mister Sussman was here to supervise the loading of the coal and filling the boiler on the engine. There were a couple of the yard crew helping. I never saw any of the people on the train get off." She watched closely to see how her recitation was received. "I don't think I noticed if it was a freight train or a passenger train."

His head drooped until his chin bobbed on his chest. He snapped back erect, as if coming awake.

"Nobody came from the direction of the Morrisey claim?"

"Did you?"

"Never mind, Beatrice. I've got to find my deputies. There's plenty of trouble ahead of us, and its hours until dawn."

"God speed, Marshal," she said. He struggled to stand,

even using the railing on the stairs for support. He took a few wobbly steps, then strengthened and walked off with more assurance. The six-gun in his grip gave him whatever sense of security he had left.

Beatrice smiled as she watched him go. Things were happening to her benefit. All she needed to do was figure out exactly how to exploit them. She waved to Kenny to help Murton from the repair shed. Like the marshal, they had a ways to go before dawn.

"You just eat your fill, Jimmy." Winifred Gallagher stood to one side, letting Beatrice refill Murton's coffee and put more bacon on his tin plate. Sunlight slanted through the window and fell across the man, warming his hands and showing him the bounty offered by the Gallagher family. They tended him in the cabin rather than underground in the family's main residence. Winifred didn't trust anyone not of their blood down below. Letting anyone stay in the cabin, which led to one tunnel into the cavern was as much trust as she showed.

"Nobody ever calls me that. James, usually, sometimes Jim. My friends call me Jim."

"Like Clarence? He's your best friend, ain't he?" She sat in the chair beside him.

"Me and Abbott have been buddies since 'fore I got married. I need to tell my wife I'm alive. She must be worried sick."

Beatrice reached out and put her hand on his.

"Don't go worrying yourself on that account, Mister Murton," she said. "We'll let her know you're all right."

"She's right, Jimmy," Winifred said soothingly.

"Thanks for your hospitality, but I got to go." He tried to stand. Beatrice pushed him back down.

"We've got sad news for you, Mister Murton," Beatrice

said. She looked at her aunt, who nodded curtly. It was time to spring the trap.

"What do you mean?" He tried to push her hand off his shoulder, but she captured his hand and clutched it as she moved closer.

"Your friend, your partner. Mister Abbott. I don't know how to tell you this thing, but coming straight out with it seems best."

"What do you know?"

"Clarence Abbott is dead. His body was found along a road on the far side of the pass."

"On Morrisey land?"

Beatrice nodded solemnly.

"Clarence was shot dead," Winifred said. "We think it was the marshal who did the killing."

"Nelson!"

It took all of Beatrice's strength to keep him seated.

"It surely does look that way, Mister Murton. For now it might be safer for you to stay here. You're welcome to accept our hospitality. Gallagher charity is the best anywhere."

"The marshal killed him?"

"He might be a'gunnin' fer you, too," Winifred said. "You listen to Bea. When she says you're welcome to hide out here, she's speakin' fer us all."

Murton put his head in his hands and sobbed silently. Then he looked up, his face a mask of hatred.

"Nelson's not gonna get away with this. Him and Leadbottom are gonna pay."

"Count on it," Winifred said. She stood and waved Beatrice from the room to let Murton stew.

CHAPTER TWENTY

Shadrach Nelson leafed through the pile of wanted posters for the tenth time. His eyes turned watery and the already blurred pictures of ugly outlaws wavered even more. He slammed his fist down on the desk and started through the two dozen posters again.

When the jailhouse door creaked open, he grabbed for his gun laying on the desk in front of him. He had it cocked and aimed before he recognized his wife.

"Shad, really," Ruth Nelson said. "You put that thing down right this minute." She stepped into the office and kicked the door shut with her heel. A tray covered by a red-and-white checked napkin wavered in her hands as she moved. "I've brought you something to eat."

"Eat?" He closed his eyes and rubbed them. "I'm not hungry."

"You haven't been home in three days—and nights."

"Got to find him," he muttered.

"Running yourself into the ground by not sleeping or eating won't help you catch Abe's killer," Ruth said primly. She put the tray on his desk and pulled back the napkins.

Chicken and dumplings in a large bowl gave up steam and a mouth-watering aroma. Three buttermilk biscuits and a slice of peach pie crowded the rest of the tray.

"You've got something to drink here, I suppose?" She

went to the Franklin stove in the far corner of the office and peered into the coffee pot on top. Day-old coffee better used as varnish remover sloshed around inside. Ruth shook her head sadly.

"I thought it was Patrick Morrisey. He's got an alibi for when Abe was shot. Mister Egan claims the boy was at the stage depot waiting for a shipment."

"Whatever does Leadbottom have shipped in on the stagecoach?" Ruth asked. "Most everything comes into Utopia on the train now."

Shad shook his head.

"Egan was definite. Patrick waited inside all night long, from dusk till dawn."

"That's mighty peculiar," his wife said.

"I agree. It seems mighty convenient, giving the boy such a good alibi. If any of his kin had said they were together, I'd think they helped Patrick kill Abe. But Egan?" He shook his head sadly. "I don't much believe him, but he's not one of them. A jury'd have to think he was telling the truth. On the other hand—"

"Shad," she said, more sharply. "You haven't been home in days. There's more to life than trying to catch Patrick Morrisey in a lie."

"I have to find who killed Abe," he snapped.

"I want you to find his killer, too, but it's putting you into an early grave."

"An early grave, like the one Abe's in? You can't help, Ruth, you aren't helping at all."

Ruth sucked in a deep breath, held it, then let it out in a rush.

"I lost my son. I don't want to lose my husband."

"I have a job to do, woman. Let me do it."

"Come home when you can."

"Egan's not above being bribed," Shad said, rubbing his hands on his thighs. Panic rose inside. He had to find Abe's killer and everything worked against him. "Or threatened.

Egan is close to spineless. Even if he's telling the truth, that doesn't mean it wasn't another of the lead miners who cut Abe down."

"Wasn't me," came a loud call from the back cell. "You've had me locked up in here goin' on forever."

Ruth looked past her husband into the cell block.

"Andy Morrisey. What a reprobate," she said. She moved a chair around to face Shad across his desk. "What's keeping you from arresting Leadbottom and the rest for kidnapping and imprisonment? You said there were two others that got grabbed before you."

"I saw Abbott gunned down. And," Shad said, swallowing hard, "I was told yesterday that Jim Murton died, too."

"So the Morrisey clan killed both of them. Put their filthy necks in a noose."

"No bodies. I saw Abbott killed but when Shannon and I got to the spot—I marked it special—the body was gone. And there's no body to be found for Murton."

"Who told you he'd died?"

"Beatrice Gallagher. She complained about somebody poking around her cabin up near the Calcutta. She identified him as Murton. He ran off and fell into a crevice on the Gallagher side of the pass."

"You believe her?"

"Her word's as good—better—than the others."

"And your word's not good enough to see the lot of those owlhoots standing on the gallows?"

"No witnesses. No living ones other 'n me, and their lawyer'd say I was making it all up since I've got an established hatred of the whole danged family. I don't have a lick of proof," he mumbled under his breath.

"What's that, Shad?"

"I said I should have shot it out with them and put the lot of them into the ground."

"You did the right thing, escaping the way you did." She pushed the tray toward him, silently telling him to dig in.

"Mostly, not finding who gunned down Abe is eating me alive."

"Shad darling, you're like a dog running in a circle, chasing its own tail. Leadbottom's not too bright. None of them are. You'll catch them doing something else. Then you can throw them into cells next to him." She glanced toward Anderson Morrisey. The man hooted and hollered like a wild animal.

"I need to find the killer before the judge gets here. I have to."

"Warn't none of my kin what done it," Andy Morrisey called. "They'd be braggin' on it, if they'd done it. Mark my words, I'd've been tellin' the world if I'd killed that worthless son of yours!"

Shad reached back and slammed the door to the cells. This didn't stop the cursing and promises of death, but it muffled them.

"Thank you," Ruth said. Her lips pulled into a razor's slash. "Now I can say this without being overheard. You will come home for supper. You will sleep in your own bed, next to your wife, you will stop carrying the weight of the world on your shoulders. Do you understand me?"

"Leroy and Ian are working to find Abe's killer, but they're not getting anywhere. I need to find whoever shot him. He's somewhere in town. I feel it."

"Shad, you heard me. Home. By sundown." She stood and pushed the tray closer to him in silent command for him to eat. She turned so fast her skirts whirred. She left, closing the door behind her so softly it was almost silent. That was worse than if she'd slammed it in anger.

But he recognized how angry she was. He stared at the food, then picked it up and took it to his prisoner.

"It's your lucky day. You get good food." He left it on the floor and didn't open the locked door. Let Morrisey figure out how to get it into his cell.

Shad slammed the door into the cell block, then kept walking. Someone out in town knew who had killed Abednego. Someone out in town had killed his son.

He tipped his battered bowler down to shield his eyes from the setting sun. The day always ended too soon in Hellfire Pass because of the tall mountains all around. But Shad felt growing excitement as he walked along the meandering street beside Leroy Early. His deputy had finally come up with the news he'd wanted so desperately.

"He's just blowin' off steam, Shad. That's what I think." Early looked sideways at the marshal. "That doesn't mean he's not a nuisance, but he's drunk enough to say 'bout anything."

"He said he gunned down Abe? You're sure of that?" He ran his hand up and down over his holster. The weight of his Peacemaker gave him comfort. He was about to avenge his son's death.

"Not exactly."

Before Early said anything more, they stopped in front of the Gold Dust Saloon. The ruckus inside grew louder and louder until a regular donnybrook had to be destroying the saloon's innards.

Shad never hesitated stepping onto the boardwalk and pushing open the swinging doors. A quick look told the tale. Two tables had been pushed to the wall. The rest were upended. There wasn't a chair in sight that hadn't been broken to flinders. Ralph Rockwell stood behind the bar. His shiny pate glistened from sweat as he worked to bat down flying debris coming toward the liquor bottles along the back wall. Damage showed how ineffectual he was fielding the flying debris. The mirror behind him was shattered. So were half the liquor bottles.

The faro dealer, Missy, stood at the end of the bar working on a beer, as if nothing was happening.

Four men swung wildly at one another. They were so bloodied Shad couldn't put names to the faces.

"That one, in the tan duster. That's the one who started it. What do you want to do, Shad?" Early edged along the outside wall, hand resting on his gun butt.

Shad strode forward, feeling like some elemental force that could never be stopped. He pushed one man out of his way. That was Bernard Watt, the livery stable owner. He had one eye swollen shut and a busted nose. From the look of his puffy lips, he had at least one tooth knocked out.

The man in the duster reared back, ready to unload another punch at a clerk for Sampson over at the general store. Shad caught his cocked arm and twisted around hard. The man was smaller and lighter. Both boots lifted off the floor. Once Shad had him stretched across his back, it was easy enough to bend forward and keep turning. The man smashed face first onto the floor.

For a moment, he didn't stir. Then he shook himself like a wet dog and started to stand. Shad put a boot in the middle of his back and drove him flat.

"You stay down." He looked around the now silent saloon. "Anybody hurt bad enough to fetch Doc Paisley?" There weren't any takers. He shoved the man in the duster back down and moved around to grab a handful of cloth.

With a hard yank he got the man to his feet. He grabbed his collar and the seat of his britches. Lifting to keep the man on his toes, he steered him for the swinging doors out into the street. When they reached the boardwalk, Shad heaved. The man fell heavily into the street.

He rolled over, his hand going to his six-gun.

"Go on," Shad said, fury in his voice.

"It was just a friendly little scuffle. Didn't mean a thing."

Early eased from the saloon and stood beside the marshal. "Tell the marshal what you said about shooting a lawman."

The man fell silent, then sputtered.

"I was blowin' off steam. I never done anything like that. It was a lie meant to impress that cute little faro dealer. What's her name?"

"Missy," Shad said, "and that's not the way to impress her. Or anyone else. When did you kill the lawman? Out at the coal yard a few days back?"

"Is she your property? I didn't mean to intrude."

"The lawman you gunned down." Shad widened his stance. His hand hovered over his six-shooter.

"You're lookin' for a fight, ain't you? You found one. The Utah Kid don't back down, not for some tin star wearin' old coot."

"Shad, hold on. Don't do this." Early tried to take his arm. Shad jerked free.

"That was my son you killed."

"You're loco. I just got to town this morning, but if you want to call me out, I'm game."

"The Utah Kid," Shad scoffed. "That sounds dangerous, but you're nothing but a murdering swine."

The gunman got to his feet. He was shaky from the fight and all the booze he'd put away. Shad didn't care. The man had boasted on killing Abe. Justice was going to be served here and now.

"Marshal!" Early grabbed his arm again. "Listen to Missy. Do it!"

"Marshal," the faro dealer said from behind him. "He's a lout and a drunk, but he's right. He only got to town this morning. I was seeing my sister off to Denver on the noon train. He'd just got off the train from Central City."

"Shad. Don't do this. I don't want to arrest you."

The blood roared in his ears. His vision was blurred, but he knew he could take this upstart. Utah Kid! What a fool.

"Right about now, you got a world of trouble aimed at your back, mister." Ian Shannon came down the street, a Greener pointed at the Utah Kid. "Twitch a muscle and I'll blow you clean in half. I've got two barrels loaded with double-ought buckshot."

"Shannon, he's mine." Shad tried to pull free of his other deputy, but Early clung to him with more tenacity.

"Let's lock him overnight and see if he changes his tune," Shannon said. "Right about now, he's so drunk he'd say about anything."

The deputy advanced and poked the shotgun muzzle into the man's side just above his six-gun. The Utah Kid raised his hands and let Shannon pluck his iron from its holster.

"I'll see to it, Marshal. Go have yourself a drink, if this galoot left a bottle unbroken." Shannon steered his prisoner away.

At his side Early heaved a sigh.

"I'll stand you to a drink, Shad. You deserve it, breaking up a fight like you did."

Numb, Shad let his deputy steer him inside for a stiff drink. He felt cheated. That had to be the gunman who had killed Abednego. It had to be. But it wasn't.

He knocked back a shot of whiskey and felt even more panicked at not having found his son's killer. If justice wasn't dealt out soon, Abe's killer would slip away. Shad wasn't sure he could live with that.

CHAPTER TWENTY-ONE

"You must have seen something," Shadrach Nelson said, moving to pin the livery stables owner in a corner. "People come and go all the time. You feed their horses. Who was it?"

Bernard Watt reached up to put his hands on the marshal's chest to shove him back. Shad angrily batted the man down.

"I told you all I know, Marshal. I never saw anyone the night your son was gunned down. I was at home. Asleep. In bed." Watt licked his lips and looked around like a corner rat hunting for a way to escape. He was securely penned.

"There's something else. I'll get it out of you. I will!" Shad cocked his fist back, only to stop when his deputy came into the stables.

"There you are, Marshal. I've been hunting all over town for you." Leroy Early looked at Watt and shook his head.

"Are you coaching him, Early? Are the two of you hiding something about Abe from me?"

"Nothing of the sort, Shad. There's a gent down at the Two Bits Saloon who says his horse's been stole. You have to deal with it." Early moved closer. "Unless you want to get on home. You've been on duty going on two days now without a letup."

"He knows something," Shad said, turning back to Watt.

"I'll find out, Shad. You get on home, why don't you? I bet the missus has a fine dinner all set out for you."

"You know something," he said, his fist in the stable owner's face. He spun around and walked off, his gait unsteady. It had been a spell since he'd slept. But somebody in this town knew how Abe had died. He was going to find them.

Just outside the stables, he heard Early apologizing to Watt. He almost went back in to stop him, then kept walking. His deputy had a way of getting people to say things they wanted kept secret. Beating the damning confession from Bernard Watt might give him a moment's satisfaction, but a full confession on paper was better. Early deserved a raise if he got even a tiny lead about Abe's killer.

The sun sank fast at the western end of Hellfire Pass. The bright oranges and reds testified to how this pass in the Rockies had gotten its name. The sunsets turned the sky to fire. That and the blood feud between coal miners and lead miners threatened anyone on the valley floor. Gallaghers shot Morriseys ever since he'd come to town.

"One of them knows. Winifred knows everything. And Patrick Morrisey? He made himself mighty scarce. When I find him . . ." Shad's mind wandered. Early was right. It had been a long time since he'd had more than a catnap. When his belly rumbled, he tried to remember when he'd eaten. Both sleep and food had taken second place to finding Abe's killer.

Abe's killer. Abe's killer.

The taunting thought echoed in his head as he trudged up the side of the southern hill toward his house. Let Early deal with a stolen horse. That wasn't worth his time when he was on the trail of a killer. He pushed open the door, expecting the fragrance of cooking food. Ruth was a fine cook who enjoyed putting out a spread for her man.

"Ruth?" He went in. The place was in disorder. Such messiness wasn't like his wife. She kept a tidy house.

He smiled wanly when she came from the bedroom. She was always so inviting, so glad to see him. He dropped into a kitchen chair and leaned back. It felt as if all the strength had fled from his legs.

"Why'd you bother coming home?"

He blinked at the question. This sounded like some other woman. One who scolded.

"There was a chance to find out more about Abe's murder," he said. "I had to ask questions, find out . . . things."

His eyelids dipped. Exhaustion overtook him.

"Papa, wake up. You've been asleep at the table."

A hand shook him a little harder. He grumbled and leaned back in the chair. Every muscle in his body was stiff. A couple blinks let him focus on his daughter. Miriam stepped back from him.

"You need a bath. You need two baths you're so filthy," she said.

"Where have you been?"

"In town. I'm staying with . . . a friend."

"Why?" He looked around. Nothing cooked on the stove. And the mess had somehow grown while he slept. It looked as if someone had ransacked his house.

"You know why," Miriam said. "The last time you came home, you made things unbearable for Mama." Miriam circled the table and sat across from him. "And you weren't so good to me, either."

"I don't remember. Finding—"

"Abe's killer is all you care about," his daughter said. "I know. So does everyone in town. Ever since you almost killed that drifter, people are giving you a wide berth."

"Where's your ma?" He sat upright and looked around. A cold knot formed in his belly. Something wasn't right. "Did they kidnap her like they did me? Leadbottom and his boys?"

"No, Papa, she hasn't been kidnapped. Not unless that's

what you call her buying a ticket and taking the train to Denver."

"What's in Denver? She never told me."

"You were never here, and when you were, you were unbearable. You're completely obsessed with Abe's death."

"He's your brother. He's family," Shad snapped.

"He's dead and buried. Me and Mama aren't. She finally had enough of being ignored and treated like a stranger. You've shut us both out entirely."

"The train?" He felt as if someone hit him over the head.

"And I've moved on, too, Papa. You have the house all to yourself." Miriam stood and pushed the chair back under the table. The look she gave him was one of utter pity.

"Wait, Miriam. You can't just leave like this!"

"Papa, it's not that I can't just leave, I *have* left." She picked up a flour sack stuffed with the last of her belongings and closed the door behind her as she went out.

Shad stared at the closed door until tears blurred his vision. Then he went crazy and busted up the furniture throughout the house.

Out of breath and scared, he tried to figure out what had happened. He couldn't.

"Is that him?" Shad asked.

"You want me to talk to him?" Leroy Early wiped his palms against his pants' legs.

"I can do it."

"He ain't done a thing illegal, Shad. I can be wrong. He might be someone else."

"He's the one," Shad said. "He's the one annoying my daughter."

Early grabbed him by the arm and held on tight.

"That's goin' a ways beyond what I saw. He wasn't annoyin' her. They were hittin' it off pretty good." Early hesitated, then said, "Miriam was inviting him along. He wasn't forcing himself on her."

"Then there's no call for him to not talk to me. He might know something about Abe's killing."

"He got to town before then, but that don't mean he knows a thing. Shad, most of the town was here when Abe was gunned down, and there's not a single one you haven't questioned until they're fed up with you."

Shad spun angrily. He pushed Early's hand from his arm. "It's a good thing you're not marshal."

"Are you fixin' to fire me, Shad? If you're gonna do it, now's the time because I'm an inch away from quitting."

"Go make the rounds of the gin mills. There's always a fight or two to break up."

Shad ignored his deputy's exasperated sigh. He turned his attention to the man across the street, weighing him and his strengths. From the way he wore his holster slung low and tied down, he had the look of a gunman. He wasn't as tall as Shad, but he weighed as much. Although he wasn't far into his twenties, his brown hair was receding. He wore a big, bushy mustache that only made it more obvious he was losing his hair.

Shad crossed the street and stopped ten feet away.

"You're violating Utopia law wearing that gun inside the town limits," Shad said.

The man turned slowly. He kept his hands well away from his iron. Sharp brown eyes took Shad in and dismissed him right away.

"A lot of other folks have smoke wagons dangling on their hips. You wouldn't be going out of your way to harass me, would you, Marshal Nelson?"

"Why'd I go and do a thing like that?"

"You know I'm sparking your daughter."

"What's your business in Utopia?"

The young man's mustache bobbed as he smiled. "Reckon you could say it's pitching woo at Miss Miriam."

Shad went stiff.

"You got to town before you knew her. Why'd you come?"

"Let's say I got a case of itchy feet. I was in Denver and could go in about any direction, but the train over to Central City appealed. There might be work in a boomtown like that."

"This isn't Central City. You're not a miner," Shad said. "You're not a prospector, either. What are you?"

"Just a man passing through Utopia."

"The stagecoach will be here in an hour. Be on it."

"Hold on, Marshal Nelson. I didn't have any reason to do anything but pass through town. Until I met Miss Miriam. I'm not inclined to leave without telling her goodbye."

Shad took a couple steps closer and closed the distance between them until they were face to face. He was four inches taller and looked down at the drifter.

"I'll tell her you've gone."

"There's no need for that," he said.

"You got that kind of look to you," Shad said. "The kind that moves on without bothering folks too much with long goodbyes."

"Marshal, you've got it wrong. There's no need to tell her I've gone because I'm not going anywhere. I've met a lot of women but none so fine as Miss Miriam."

"You're refusing to obey an officer of the law?"

"You've got no right to—"

Shad didn't bother to wind up. He punched at the man's gut from a flat-footed stance. His blow lacked power but surprise made up for it. Caught off guard, the man stepped back, giving Shad a chance to wind up and take a more powerful swing. He followed the right hook with a powerful left jab.

The man staggered, dazed by the rapid punches. He made no move to fight back and stood with his arms at his side. Shad saw his chance and wound up. His haymaker lifted the man off his feet and dropped him to the ground, knocked out.

"What's the fuss all about?" The stagecoach company master came rushing out. Egan looked from the fallen man to Shad. "Reckon he's not gonna be on the next stage, is he?"

"Nope. He's going to jail for disobeying a lawman. Help me get him up onto his feet."

Egan shook his head and stepped back into the stagecoach office. From the safety of his lair, he said, "Tell him he's fired."

Shad frowned. Before he could ask Egan what he meant, the stage agent slammed the door.

Shad grabbed a handful of shirt and lifted the man to his feet. A quick move plucked his six-gun from the fancy tooled leather holster. Then he steered the groggy man toward the town lockup.

He wasn't going to get into any trouble bothering Miriam if he occupied the cell next to Andy Morrisey.

Chapter Twenty-two

"You gonna keep me locked up in here forever?" Anderson Morrisey hung on the bars and peered around to catch sight of Shadrach Nelson at his desk.

"Another telegram came in saying Judge Zamora was delayed again. We're not too important on his circuit compared to trials dealing with mineral rights and claim jumpers," Shad said. "The judge says he'll come to town sometime next week. You'll have your say in court then."

"What about me? Why'd you lock me up?" The other prisoner rattled the bars in his cell. "You never charged me with anything."

"Loitering," Shad said. "Mopery with intent to lurk. What's the difference?"

"You don't like my looks. That's why you threw me in here with that animal."

"I ain't no animal. Ask my pa," Morrisey said indignantly.

"Leadbottom's in no hurry to get you back, is he, Andy? He might not even notice you're not slaving away in his lead mine," Shad said. "He hasn't even sent a lawyer around to talk to you. That's how much you matter."

His anger built thinking of how Leadbottom had chained him, Murton, and Abbott and used them as slaves. Worst of all, Abbott and Murton were dead, and he had no proof that Leadbottom had committed any of those crimes.

Taking out his wrath on Leadbottom's son wasn't right, but Shad was past caring. Finding who killed Abe was proving as difficult as bringing Leadbottom to justice.

He ground his teeth together. For all he knew, Leadbottom was responsible for Abe's killing. The mine owner hadn't shown himself to be an upright citizen in any sense.

"Let me out of here. You're mad because Miriam is sweet on me." The man in the cell next to Andy Morrisey rattled the bars again.

This brought Shad out of his chair and into the back with the three cells. He stared the man down. Or tried to. Brown eyes refused to blink when his hard green eyes fixed on them.

"You have the look of a gunfighter bringing trouble to Utopia. I'm putting you on the next train out."

"I came from Denver. I've got no reason to go back there."

"Why were you hanging around the stage office? Egan seemed to know you. He said you were fired. What's that mean?"

"I had a job riding shotgun messenger."

"That ain't much of a job," Morrisey said. "Most everything's sent by rail now. Ain't cheaper, but it's faster."

"Except Egan said your brother was supposed to pick up a parcel sent from Denver," Shad said.

"That's just Patrick goofin' off. Pa'd never buy anything that had to be sent by stage."

"Shut up," Shad said. He frowned as he turned over in his head why Egan gave Patrick Morrisey an alibi if Leadbottom refused to ship using the stage line.

"You're leaving the stage open to being robbed by keeping me in jail," the other prisoner said.

"You can shut your big mouth, too," Shad said reflexively. "You want me to think you have a job?"

"Had. Mister Egan fired me. You heard why."

Shad shook his head. He didn't believe a word of it. This man was trouble. The sooner he hustled this pile of trouble on his way out of Utopia the better. The outer door slammed shut. Shad turned, hand going to his Peacemaker. He relaxed when he saw Miriam in the office.

He kicked shut the door between the cells and office when he went to greet her. He never got out a word.

"You're despicable! How could you, Papa? You locked up Rich for no good reason other than he's my beau!"

"Who's that?"

"Oh, you! Richard Williamson. You got him fired, not that Mister Egan isn't cowed by his own shadow. But you yelled at him. That's enough to make Egan hide in the stage office for the rest of the week."

"Richard Williamson?" Shad settled into his chair and leafed through wanted posters hunting for that name. Most of the drawings and photographs on the wanted posters were too blurred or inept to identify.

"Now you're looking to see if you have a reward on his head? Oh!" Miriam stamped her foot.

"He has the look of a gunman about him. I can tell by the way he wears his six-shooter."

"You don't know the first thing about him. I didn't leave with Mama. I thought she was overreacting, but I see her point now."

"What's that mean?" Shad looked up sharply at his daughter.

"She couldn't stand you having such a one-track mind. Find Abe's killer, but don't let that eat you up. There's more to life."

"She doesn't understand. He was my son."

"*You* don't understand. Mama feels his loss as much as you do. More. She was his mother. But she wanted to grieve and then get on with her life. You're stuck on avenging his death, and it's destroying you."

"What do you know about this Williamson?" He pushed the posters aside. The name didn't appear on any of the fliers.

"More than you do," Miriam said. Her anger matched his. "Let him out right now."

"The judge'll be passing through soon enough. He can decide what to do with this Richard Williamson fellow."

Miriam stamped her foot again, whirled around and stormed from the office.

Shad thought she'd cool down and come to her senses. She'd realize Williamson was no good for her. He went to the rack of rifles and shotguns on the wall and took out several. They needed oiling. When he found Abe's killer, he wanted every firearm to be ready for use.

"Shad, we got a problem over at Gold Dust City." Ian Shannon poked his head into the office.

"What is it?" Shad perked up.

"There's a drifter claiming to know something about Abednego's shooting. At least he makes it sound that way. He's cadging drinks. I thought you'd like to know."

Shad shot out of the chair, almost tipping it over. He grabbed his bowler and pulled it straight down on his head until the brim pressed into the tops of his ears.

"Show me the varmint," Shad said. Together the two of them dashed out.

The saloon stood mostly empty in the late afternoon. Shad slipped the leather thong off his six-gun hammer and pushed through the swinging doors. A quick look around failed to locate any stranger. Ralph stood behind the bar, wearing his leather apron and polishing glasses. He was too busy talking to Missy. Her faro spread stood forlorn and empty of chips, cards, or gamblers. Two men sat at a table halfway back, quietly talking. Shad knew both of them.

"Where is he?" He grabbed Shannon by the arm and pulled him around. "Where?"

"He's gone. I suspect he's ridden on." Shannon called out to the barkeep. "Ralph, the fellow who was in here earlier. Where'd he go?"

"He lit out of here like his tail was on fire. I don't know where he went." He put down one glass and went to work erasing water spots on the next.

"He said something about Central City," Missy said, looking at Shad. "Or maybe it was Georgetown."

"Naw, he wanted to meet up with a partner in Denver. He mentioned that a couple times." Ralph frowned. "I think he said Denver. Maybe it was Colorado Springs."

Ralph and Missy argued over what the man had said. Shad pressed them on a description and got two different men. Shannon added in yet another account. The marshal looked to the men drinking at the table. They both looked more frightened than interested.

One called out, "We never seen him, Marshal. He was gone before we got here."

Disgusted, Shad left. In the street he looked as far as he could see in either direction along the snake-spine curved street. The man might have ridden in either direction. In his gut, Shad felt asking anyone on the street wouldn't get him anywhere. From the three people who had seen him, all gave a different description.

He returned to the jailhouse, stewing in his own juices. He dropped into his chair and stared at the wall as if pictures would appear telling him what he wanted to know.

"Hey, is that you, Marshal? You gonna let me out, too?"

"Shut up, Morrisey. I've had enough of your lip."

"I want out!"

Shad boiled out of his chair and stomped back to the cell. He faced Anderson Morrisey, blood in his eye.

"I'm warning you. I—" Shad jerked around. The cell next to Morrisey's stood empty.

"You let him go. Let me go, too."

"What happened to him? Williamson? Where'd he go?"

"Your deputy came for him."

"Shannon was with me."

"The other one. Early. Came waltzin' back here pretty as you please, used the key to unlock the cell and ushered Williamson out like he was royalty. The pair of them left together. Now are you settin' me free?"

"How long ago did Early let him out?"

"Right after you and Shannon left. Now are you freein' me?" Anderson Morrisey hung from the bars, looking expectant.

Shad rushed back to the office, made sure the keys to the cell were secured in his desk drawer and then began to fume. Morrisey had no call to lie. Early had taken the keys and sprung Williamson. Nothing fit together right unless . . .

Shad left the office, certain that his deputy had some part in killing Abe. That was the only explanation. Williamson was a gunman and must have been the one pulling the trigger. It all fit together.

He ran to the livery where Bernard Watt carried a bale of straw into the stable to spread for the horses.

"Deputy Early. Have you seen him?"

"Leroy? He was here ten or fifteen minutes back. He wanted to make sure the yearling was ready. Fancy that, a deputy payin' for a horse like that when he's got a perfectly good one. Of course, like he said, his horse is getting old and slow, but that goes for all of us, doesn't it, Marshal? Of course, it was rarin' to go. I take good care of—"

"Did he ride out with anyone?"

"I didn't see. What's got you so riled, Marshal? You got this wild look in your eye. You're not fixin' on beatin' up on me again, are you? I told you I don't know nothing 'bout Abe's death."

Shad wasted no time explaining. He threw the saddle on his horse and led it outside. With a jump he was in the saddle and looking around. Watt had come to the door to stare at him.

"Which way'd they go?"

"Well, now, that's hard to say, but I think Early headed east down the pass. I'm not sure what he expected to find out there. Most of Utopia stretches from one side of Hellfire Pass to the other, and the Gallaghers and Morriseys got all the sides claimed for their mines. I—"

Shad left the stable owner talking to himself. He was in luck that not many riders went east. Any pilgrims passing through came from Denver and were intent on finding their fortunes on the far side of the Front Range, in Central City or Georgetown or even Blackhawk.

When he reached the town limits and slowed, he then dismounted, walking his horse to better see what spoor he could find. The dirt alongside the road was damper than usual after a few brief showers over the past couple days. He found two sets of hoofprints going east. He stepped off the depressions. The riders were galloping away.

This had to be Early and Williamson. He couldn't think of another pair of riders likely to come this way in the past few hours. The tracks were fresh. Fresh enough. The damp soil around the rims of the hoofprints had started to dry. The tracks might be older than a few minutes. As cracked and crumbling as the edges were, the hoofprints could be hours old.

He had no choice but to follow. This was all he had to go on.

Shad mounted and trotted along, doing his best to keep the tracks in view. Somewhere along the road, he lost the depressions. He backtracked and tried to will the tracks into being. The best he could determine was a trail of crushed grass and a few twigs broken on low-growing bushes. He looked up into the side of the pass. A flash of reflected silver caught his eye.

The path upward was hardly a decent game trail. He

passed through a stand of pines, curled around and found himself heading west along the southern side of the pass.

"Yes!" He let out a cry of triumph. Two sets of tracks appeared for a short stretch along the trail before it became too rocky. Some of the scratches on the rocks in the path might be new. He wasn't going to take time to figure out if they were caused by a shod horse kicking at the rock or something else.

The trail opened onto a mountain meadow nestled in the fastness of the steep hills rising sharply on three sides. He put his heels to his horse's flanks. He had plenty of territory to cover if he wanted to recapture his prisoner and find out what possessed Leroy Early into letting him out of his cell and then helping him hightail it from town.

He approached the trees lining the far side of the meadow when he saw another flash of silver from the corner of his eye. Shad jerked around just as the gunshot rang out. His boots slipped from the stirrups, and he sailed through the air as more bullets tore through the air in his direction.

He hit the ground hard and lay still.

CHAPTER TWENTY-THREE

Shad lay facedown without moving. After what seemed to be an eternity but what amounted to only a single gasp, he blinked dirt from his eyes. Part of the sparse forest was visible, but he saw movement there. Someone moved from tree to tree. The blued rifle barrel poked out, then swung around as the sniper steadied it against a tree trunk to make a killing shot.

This bullet would take his life. Shad dug his toes into the ground and flexed his muscles, getting ready to move. When the metallic click of a hammer coming back echoed like thunder across the meadow, he straightened his legs and shoved as hard as he could. From his prone position he wasn't able to move much, far, or fast.

It was good enough.

The bullet dug into the ground where his body had been an instant before. Scrambling now, he got his feet under him and fell full length forward. The next round that sailed his way also missed. Kicking up dirt, he regained his feet and ran for cover. Another bullet spanged off a rock just ahead of him. The sniper led him too much.

That made him think his would-be killer wasn't much of a hunter. If he had been a deer, he should have been an easy shot. Moving this way and that, jouking for his life, he reached the tree line. He pressed against the nearest pine tree trunk, ignoring the sap sticking to his clothing. Sucking in a few deep breaths calmed him a mite.

He slid his Peacemaker out and held it pointed up at the sky. When he fired, he had to make every round count. There wouldn't be time to reload in a pitched fight, and he faced a killer with a rifle's magazine that was probably loaded to capacity. Shad sucked in another deep breath, then acted. The smart thing was to run away.

Feet pounding, he ran straight for the sniper's sanctuary behind a larger tree. He heard a gasp. The would-be killer thought Shad would run from him.

Instead of firing, the rifleman turned and ran. Shad chased him.

"Stop. You're under arrest. I'm a lawman!"

The sniper kept running. Shad pulled up short and got off a round. It missed the man but made him drop his rifle. For an instant, the man froze, mentally torn over whether to keep running or try to recover his rifle. Shad got off another round. That settled the matter.

The sniper left his rifle behind and skedaddled.

If Shad had a lick of sense, he would have let the man go. Instead, he scooped up the fallen rifle, tucked his own six-gun away and pursued. Now and then he fired at the fleeing man. All he accomplished was to give wings to the man's feet.

Through the forest they ran, dodging trees, jumping over brambles. Shad had hoped to overtake his attacker, but he had put the fear into the man. The footrace slowly went to the assailant as Shad flagged. His leg muscles burned from effort, and his lungs worked hard to drag in enough of the thin, high altitude Colorado air to keep going.

Heart pounding, he stopped and lifted the captured rifle to his shoulder. He waited and waited and waited. His patience finally paid off. Through the trees a flash of a man's back showed.

Shad fired.

He let out a loud cheer of triumph. He brought down the sniper. In his gut he knew it wasn't a killing shot, but it had stopped him. Shad hotfooted it to a spot where he had a clean shot at the fallen man.

He drew a bead as the wounded man clutched his thigh. Blood soaked into his jeans. Shad took his finger off the trigger when he recognized the man trying to look so pitiful.

"Please, Marshal, don't you go killin' me. Ma wouldn't like it."

"Does Winifred know you're out shooting at riders along the road, Kenny?"

"You wasn't on the road. You trespassed. This is all Gallagher country. Every square inch of it."

"I'm taking you in," Shad said. He immediately regretted saying this. Kenny Gallagher wasn't the one who should be in jail. Richard Williamson was the one who had escaped the lockup.

And every minute he spent dealing with Kenny took away from finding his son's murderer.

"You ain't fixin' to throw me in the same cell as that Morrisey weasel, are you? You still got Andy Morrisey locked up?"

"That'd be like putting a terrier into a pit filled with rats, wouldn't it?"

"You can't do that to me, Marshal. I ain't guilty."

"Of what?"

"Whatever you intend incarceratin' me for."

"That's a mighty big word, Kenny. I suspect you know what it means. Get to your feet. I'm taking you back to Winifred."

Kenny's expression showed this was more punishment than anything the law could deliver.

Shad saw several guns pointed in his direction and felt several more he didn't see. The Gallagher camp was primed and ready for war. He tugged on the reins to Kenny's horse. He had the rider all trussed up. Kenny rode with his head down. In the distance Shad heard a few catcalls. They were as likely directed to his prisoner as to him.

He drew rein in front of the fanciest of the cabins. Even then, it wasn't much of a dwelling for a woman who owned a lucrative coal mine.

"Winifred Gallagher, I've got one of your worthless offspring out here. Come on out and claim him or I'll lock him up in a jail cell."

Scurrying sounds like rats in the walls came from the cabin, but nobody opened the door or even peered out the curtained window.

"I don't have all day, Winifred." He looked over his shoulder at Kenny. "It might be that she doesn't care if I throw you in the calaboose. What do you think?"

"Ma," Kenny bellowed. "Make him cut me loose!"

Another minute passed. Just as Shad was about to take his prisoner and return to Utopia, he heard her grumbling inside the cabin. Shad wondered what finally goaded Winifred into action. The cabin door opened a crack. He saw an eye peering out. More scuttling sounds from inside. It sounded as if she had a dozen men in there with her. When the sounds died, Winifred opened the door and stepped out. He wondered what the woman hid inside that she didn't want him to see.

"What do you want, Marshal?"

"You keep your boys in line. Kenny here took a shot at me." Shad lifted the rifle and then tossed it to the woman. She fumbled but caught it. "More than a shot. He tried to kill me."

"I didn't know who you was, Marshal!"

"That's what makes it so serious. Either keep him and the rest of your clan in line or there's going to be bloodshed, followed by a powerful lot of you being thrown in jail."

"Why are you taking Leadbottom's side, Marshal?"

Winifred clutched the rifle like it would pull her to safety before she drowned. "Why?"

"It's not my place to take sides. I've got no liking for Leadbottom and what he's doing over at his mine." Shad saw how Winifred perked up at that. She had to know that the Morriseys kidnapped men and used them as slaves. "I've got no liking for being shot at for no reason, either." He dropped the reins to Kenny's horse, touched the brim of his bowler and wheeled around.

The hair on the back of his neck rippled. He cast a quick glance back. Somebody pulled back the curtains and watched him, thinking he didn't notice. Shad shook it off. He had an escaped prisoner to find.

And whoever had killed his son.

"He's got me all trussed up like a Christmas goose, Ma. Cut me free." Kenny Morrisey wiggled around and almost fell from the saddle as his horse shied.

"Get yourself outta the mess you got into. Let this be a lesson. If you shoot at somebody, don't miss." Winifred Gallagher used the butt of Kenny's rifle to push open the cabin door.

Inside she looked around. Jim Murton pulled back the curtain and peered out as Shadrach Nelson rode away. She saw how his fists clenched and wrinkled the curtain. Four of her boys had come into the cabin from the cavern. She wondered what Murton thought of seeing so many men suddenly come up from what looked to be a cellar. If it made him curious, he didn't show it.

"Here," she said, tossing the rifle in his direction. "Take it."

He gripped the rifle and looked at her hard.

"What do you want me to do with it?"

"I reckon I want you to use it the same way you want to. He just rode off. He ain't my friend, and he's surely no friend of yours."

Winifred sank down at the table and looked up at Murton.

"Do a good enough job and I'll see about hirin' you on as mine supervisor. My lazy louts need someone to keep 'em in line."

"You'd put me on your payroll?"

"You'd get more 'n the railroad ever paid you."

Murton showed her a smile that would make a feral wolf back away. Without a word he left. Winifred wondered how long before word of the marshal's death reached her. And if it didn't, she had other ideas on how to deal with a meddling marshal.

Chapter Twenty-Four

"Where did he run?" Shad asked himself over and over as he rode away from the Gallagher cabin. Getting rid of Kenny was a chore he wished he hadn't needed to complete. Coming up the mountainside to turn him back over to his ma caused Richard Williamson's trail to go cold.

Even if he returned to the road heading toward Denver, he knew the escaped prisoner had too much of a head start on him. Then there was the chance that Early rode alongside the escapee. That rankled as much as Williamson being set free. Shad had lost prisoners before, but never had any of his deputies been responsible for the escape.

That betrayal burned in his gut like a volcano ready to erupt.

"If Williamson's got a lick of sense, he won't slow down until he reaches the Mississippi River," he grumbled. He hoped Leroy Early took that same trail.

The road down this side of Hellfire Pass was better kept than the one on the Morrisey side. That figured. Winifred Gallagher had more wagons to move with her coal than Leadbottom did with his metal ingots. The railroad required at least two wagon loads a day to keep running. The late noon and midnight trains would be stranded if Gallagher coal wasn't there to fill their tenders. Who cared if a freight car wasn't loaded regularly with lead being sent east to be molded into bullets and other products?

Shad made a sharp turn in the road and looked back up the mountainside. He sat a little straighter. Someone followed him down. And whoever it was tried to be invisible.

The furtive sounds inside Winifred's cabin became more important. Had she chained some kind of wild beast inside and released it when he left? She and a timber wolf had so much in common, he thought that was possible.

Shad had to laugh at that.

"Maybe Ruth was right. I am getting too tied up in just one thing. It's making me crazy."

He still took another look along the back trail and caught his breath. He wasn't imagining things. This time he caught the flash of a Stetson before it dropped behind the verge of the road. Kenny had been scared, but that wasn't anything new for him. Shad saw him as one of the more spineless among the Gallaghers. He certainly wasn't as hard as Winifred. Or, for that matter, Beatrice. Every time she spoke to him, Shad worried what she wanted. That girl always had something sneaky in whatever she said and did.

Shad rode faster, going downhill a damned sight faster than his sure-footed horse preferred. Despite equine protests, they reached the base of the road without breaking any legs. He tried not to be too obvious as he reached the main road into Utopia and stopped, took off his bowler to swipe at sweat and turn just enough to see who trailed him.

Whoever was there did a poor job of it. Shad decided they weren't skilled in even ordinary frontier crafts. Stalking a deer with such poor habits would mean going hungry for a long time—until the deer died of old age.

That thought barely crossed his mind when a flurry of movement caused Shad to bend forward over his horse's neck and rake its flanks with his heels. The horse leaped forward at the same instant the rifle report echoed down the mountainside.

He had no idea how far off target the sniper was. Keeping away from lead intending to end his life was always a good idea. But Shad had reached the end of his patience. He veered off the road and headed for a tumble of rocks where he could make a stand. Whoever had followed him wasn't likely to give up after missing with a single shot.

Shad counted on his attacker having more determination than Kenny Gallagher.

He hit the ground running and ducked behind waist-high rocks. Pulling himself around, he cautiously peered out to see who was after him. He swore when he caught sight of James Murton. The man rode along, looking for a sign that his quarry had left the road. When he found it, he perked up like a prairie dog over its burrow.

"Why are you shooting at me, Murton? I saved your life!"

"You killed my best friend!"

"The Morriseys killed Abbott. I tried to save him. And what are you doing alive? Winifred Gallagher said she found your body."

"And you wanted to believe her because you wanted to kill me, too." Murton swung his rifle around and got off a shot. It went high over Shad's head and ricocheted off a rock a few yards more distant.

"I should have left you to die in that lead mine," Shad said. He measured the distance to the road against how well he knew his Peacemaker fired. It paid him to wait. Let Murton come closer. And he would.

He did.

Murton turned his horse's face directly toward Shad's sanctuary. He raised the rifle to his shoulder and kicked hard to get the horse into a gallop.

He fired as he charged forward. Shad had to give the man credit. For someone with no obvious skill in tracking or doing anything more that fixing railroad machinery, Murton shot well. Every round hit the rock in front of Shad. One or two sneaked past, making it dangerous to sidle around to get a clear field of fire at the galloping horseman.

As Murton came within a dozen yards, Shad tossed his bowler out. Murton was decoyed. He tracked it with his rifle. Shad stood and got off three quick rounds. From the way the rider jerked about, at least one round struck its target.

Then Murton galloped past. Shad turned, but Murton leaned forward to present as small a target as possible. Shooting his horse from under him was a consideration, but Shad thought more of the horse than he did of its rider. There wasn't any call to harm an animal only doing what it was told.

He retrieved his bowler. It had a brand-new hole in it. In a rainstorm it'd leak on both sides of the narrow brim. He didn't bother counting the holes in the crown. It was starting to look like moths had a picnic.

With the brown hat once more settled on his head, he ejected the three spent rounds and reloaded. He balanced the reloaded weapon in his hand. It was time to end this firefight.

Loosing a cry of frustration and anger, he went after Murton.

The man's horse had thrown him and ran a few yards. Without more gunfire to spook it, the horse nibbled at a patch of grass. It turned a big brown, accusing eye toward Shad as he came up. He secured the reins with a large rock and then went hunting. Just beyond boulders stretched a steep-banked ravine. He didn't have to hunt to find Murton's trail. The man took a couple more shots at him from down in the gully.

Shad cursed when his bowler flew off his head. It had taken another bullet hole in the brim. Then he gave thanks that it was the bowler and not his head on the receiving end of so much lead. He bent low and reached the lip of the ravine.

Murton crawled toward the far side, sloshing through a quick flowing ankle-deep stream hardly two feet wide.

"Throw down your rifle, Murton. Do it or I swear I'll shoot you!" Shad took careful aim at the man as he crept along the rocky bottom.

"You killer. You murdering swine!" Murton rolled onto his back and pulled his rifle around, bracing it on the ground to get off another shot.

Shad fired first. His aim was deadly. Murton jerked up, his back arching. The rifle fell to the ravine floor beside him.

Slipping and sliding, Shad descended to the bottom of the gully and approached cautiously. Murton's chest heaved. He wasn't dead, but from the liquid sounds coming from his mouth, it wouldn't be long. He had taken a slug through a lung.

"You're a goner, Murton." Shad saw the man's dying eyes focus on him. "Why'd you try to kill me? I got you and Abbott out of the mine."

"You—" Murton gurgled now. Pink foam dotted his lips.

"You got any last words? I can pass them along to your wife, though what she'd think is beyond me. She's already accepted that you're dead."

"Son," Murton spat out. "Your son dead by—"

Shad dropped to his knees and raised the man's head to keep him from choking on his own blood.

"Who killed Abe? Do you know? How do you know?"

Hate-filled eyes fixed on Shad.

". . . killed him. Sorry I . . ." Murton convulsively twisted about, then died, his open eyes still fixed on Shad.

If the marshal had to put words to it, he'd say Murton died hating him. For no good reason, his fury had brought about his own death.

Shad lowered the man's head to the hard rock. This would be about the last time Murton was on the topside of the ground. Backing away, he stared at the body and wondered.

What had Murton meant? It sounded as if he had gunned

down Abe. Or maybe he was trying to say he was sorry he hadn't been the one to pull the trigger. Did that mean he knew who had?

Shaking his head, Shad went to get the man's horse. He'd be damned if he was going to drag a body up the side of the ravine. It was hard enough killing him. And worse not knowing what Murton knew before he died.

CHAPTER TWENTY-FIVE

"Shad?" Leroy Early didn't get the marshal's attention. He slammed the jailhouse door hard enough to wake the dead.

This brought Shad out of his funk. He jerked around, hand going to the six-gun laying on the desk beside him.

"What is it?"

"You were staring at the wall. Just staring."

"You want something. What is it?" His tone carried nothing but derision.

Before Early answered, a call from the back room with the cells reverberated.

"Hey, Marshal. You up there?"

"What do you want? I'm not letting you go." Shad was no more pleased with his prisoner than he was with his deputy.

"No, I don't want outta here," Anderson Morrisey bellowed. "I've changed my mind. Tell my pa he ain't takin' me out. I like it here. I got three meals and don't have to swing a pick. I danged near ruptured myself movin' ore."

"Calm down, Morrisey," Shad said in disgust. "You're not going anywhere until the judge arrives."

"Next week," Early said, sighing. "I just talked with Mister Sussman. He got another telegram. Judge Zamora's tied up with two more murder trials over in Georgetown. If it's not a miner killing another over claim jumping, it's them shootin' each other over high grading."

"Hear that, Morrisey? It's going to be a week before you have to face a jury."

"Only a week? Can I have more of that venison stew fer supper? That hit the spot. I—"

Shad rocked back in the chair, reached out and slammed the door. His prisoner's demands were muffled and indistinct now. That suited him, just as staring at a blank wall had occupied him before his deputy showed up.

"I know things have been strained between us, Shad, and I want to clear the air." Early cleared his throat, preparing to launch into a full-blown speech.

Shad didn't want to hear it.

"You let a prisoner go free. Worse, you escorted him out of town. I should have fired you. I should have thrown you in the cell you emptied!"

"And I intended to quit. I've about had all I can take of you moping around, accusing people of killing Abe and not getting a single lead."

"Murton," he muttered. "He had something to do with it."

"He had nothing to do with Abe's death," Early said. "That's why I'm about fed up with you, Shad."

"Just because his wife said he was at home with her doesn't mean she's not lying."

"Murton didn't have a grudge against Abe. Why'd he want to kill him?"

"Maybe Abe caught him stealing."

"Listen to yourself, Shad. Murton wasn't at the coal yard. He never even passed through going to work in the rail yard."

"He said he killed him."

Early said nothing, letting Shad stew.

"He had a grudge against me for no reason," Shad said. "Maybe it started with Abe and worked on up to me."

"I don't have an explanation for why a man you saved from being a slave in Leadbottom's mine wanted to kill you."

"We've been over that. Are you quitting? That why you came by rather than patrolling up and down Main Street?"

"If you want my badge, you can have it. Either way, I'm going to tell you where to find Williamson."

"You're turning on him?"

"Nothing of the sort. After I let him out, I had no idea where he got off to."

Shad jumped from his chair, hand going for his six-gun. He glared at his deputy, ready to put a round in him.

"Where is he?"

"Miriam told me where he was. She said he wants to square things with you because he's not used to be wanted by the law."

"He had the look of a running gun."

"Do you want to know? I promised Miriam that I wouldn't give out a peep unless you went in to only palaver."

"He had the look of someone who'd ambush me."

"He's had plenty of chances the past couple days. He's been around town."

"With my daughter?" Shad took another step toward leaving.

"She's why I let him out. You aren't listening to reason. Miriam's got that and plenty to offer."

"You sided with her on letting her beau go scot free?"

"The charges you levied against Williamson were you talkin' through your hat, Shad. He didn't do a danged thing to warrant ending up in a cell. If anything, me letting him out meant I was following the law you chose to ignore."

"You say he's been hiding out?"

Early nodded.

"Miriam's not going to get in the way, is she?" He saw how Early tensed at that.

"No guns blazing. Talk to him, Shad. He's a decent fellow."

"Like you'd know, you who let him out of jail and consorted with him. You even bought him a horse."

"What?" Early's expression was one of complete surprise. "What's that nincompoop Bernie Watt been tellin' you?"

"You bought a horse and gave it to Williamson so he could escape town, that's what."

"Do tell." Early snorted. "My old mare's about done in. I've ridden her for twelve hard years. I bought *me* a new mount. You can go around back and see, if you'd ever get your behind out of your chair. My old swayback mare's being put out to pasture. I'm thinkin' on naming my new horse Shadrach."

"What?"

"He's a horse's ass," Early said. "Just like you."

Shad fumed a mite, then settled down. Exchanging insults wasn't going to settle anything.

"Williamson broke out of jail. That's a crime. And you aided and abetted. That's a crime, too."

"Your daughter's gonna be in the cell next to mine, if you believe all that." Early took a deep breath, then told the marshal where Richard Williamson hid out.

The abandoned line shack was halfway around the southern side of the pass, maybe on Gallagher territory. If it wasn't, Shad was certain Winifred would claim that it was. There'd been extensive prospecting in the area before the railroad came through Utopia. Where Blackhawk and so many other places on the western slope produced boomtowns because of precious metals, Hellfire Pass was lacking in big strikes and blue dirt.

Only coal. Only lead sulfates. Only products needed long after gold and silver mines played out.

He sat astride his mount, studying the cabin. Leroy Early had been a decent deputy for years. It galled him to think the man had turned on him. It was even more infuriating to think that Early aided and abetted a man who was Abe's likely killer.

The rocky slope above the shack showed no place for a sniper to hide. It was sheer rock for close to fifty feet up to a ledge. Anyone shooting almost straight down from there had to be more than a good marksman with a rabbit's foot in every pocket. The nearest tree to the cabin stood twenty feet off. Signs showed where trees had been chopped down years ago for firewood and to build the shack. Two horses were tied to a rope at the edge of the forest.

This put Shad on edge.

Getting caught in a crossfire was dangerous, if not downright deadly. He should have brought along Ian Shannon. He trusted Shannon, in spite of his dour outlook and occasional jibes.

"Hello, in the cabin." He kept his hands on the pommel and not on the butt of his six-gun.

The door opened. Richard Williamson stepped out, showing not a shred of fear he'd be cut down.

"Come on over, Marshal. I'm glad you came. We've got things to discuss."

Shad rode slowly, wary of who else was here. The sudden appearance of a gun barrel in the small window wouldn't have surprised him.

"You thirsty after the ride?"

"Is that your plan? Get me knee-walking drunk?"

"I don't have any hard liquor in the larder, but I just started boiling a pot of coffee. Some folks tell me my coffee's more potent than brandy." Williamson acted as if he hadn't heard Shad's objection.

"Brandy?" A knot formed in Shad's belly at the mention. "Why'd you say that?"

"Rumor has it that's your choice of poison." Williamson turned back into the cabin.

Shad stepped down and looped his horse's reins around a post at the side of the ramshackle building. He studied every nook and cranny for a possible ambush. By the time he came back around to the door, the odor of coffee wafting from inside made his mouth water.

He stepped in. He went stiff when he saw Miriam at the stove, lifting the ceramic coffee pot up using a corner of her apron as potholder. If he hadn't known better, Shad would have thought he'd come on some married settlers in the middle of the day. Everything seemed easy and open.

"Papa, I'm glad you listened to Leroy."

"I should have fired him. I should have thrown him in the cell where *he* was." He glared at Williamson.

Williamson carried three tin cups to the rickety table and put them down for Miriam to fill. Again the easy domesticity irked Shad.

His daughter pointed to a chair. He pointedly took a different one. The way her lips thinned in irritation made her look like her ma. Shad sank down, lost in conflicting emotions.

Williamson took a sip of the hot coffee, made a face, then put the cup down carefully on the table. He aligned the bottom of the cup with a ring stain already there. With words as precise, he said, "I had nothing to do with Abednego's shooting. I've got nothing but sympathy for you. My own brother was shot in Laramie five years back and nobody was ever caught who fessed up to the crime."

"That's when Rich moved to Denver."

"There's a lot about you that tells me to look out for you," Shad said, ignoring Miriam. "Like the way you tie down your holster. That's how a gunfighter carries his piece."

Williamson looked down, as if noticing this for the first time. He locked eyes with Shad.

"You do the same."

"I'm a lawman."

"Rich was, too, over in Denver. For three years he was a Deputy Federal Marshal," Miriam said. She clutched her coffee cup but made no move to drink. When the metal got too hot, she pulled her hands back and folded them in her lap.

"Old habits die hard," Williamson said. "When I'm riding along, it helps keep the holster from flopping around."

"What were you doing at the stage office? That was mighty suspicious."

"Yes, it was, Papa. What's most odd is that Mister Egan finally decided to hire Rich as a shotgun messenger because of the outlaws along the trail from Denver."

"It's occurred to some of the brighter owlhoots that men on their way to the gold fields on the far side of the mountain are more likely to have cash with them."

"And equipment. The smarter ones know prices in Georgetown are outrageous. Some even bring along a dozen or two pick axe heads and sell them to other miners and prospectors to pay for their own hunt."

"Blue dirt is quite a lure. Not all the men hunting it are paupers," Williamson said. He locked eyes with Shad again. "Egan hired me because I was a deputy. He telegraphed the Marshal's office in Denver and verified that I'd worked there."

"He arrested the Platte River Gang. All six of them." Miriam looked at Williamson with glowing admiration.

"I didn't do it singlehanded," Williamson said, showing a trace of irritation. "The Marshal and a couple from a posse helped out."

"But Rich found their hideout. He had already clamped the shackles on Cross-eyed Bill Keene."

"I saw the poster on him," Shad said. "He was a real desperado."

"He claimed to have killed seven men. We only had proof of one, but that was enough to —send him to the gallows." Williamson sipped again at his coffee.

"There're other matters," Shad said. "Maybe you didn't shoot Abe, but—"

"But Miss Miriam and I are pledged, sir. I need to find a ring and a minister."

Williamson looked at Miriam, whose radiant smile lit up the room. It only made Shad feel as if he had stepped off a cliff and fell endlessly.

"You never thought to ask my permission?"

"Papa, the way you've acted since Abe was shot makes even saying 'good morning' to you like poking a grizzly."

"What if I say no?"

"That'd be a real shame, Marshal. It's not my way to go against a bride's pa."

"But you would?"

"For Miriam, I'd walk barefoot across the Rockies. Both ways."

"So going against my wishes wouldn't bother you none?" Shad gulped at his coffee. It burned his tongue and throat.

"No, sir, it'd bother me greatly. It just wouldn't stop me." Williamson spoke with such calm assurance that Shad felt as if all the air in his body had leaked out. He wasn't sure what to say.

"We're going to Denver, Papa. On the train. To be with Mama." Miriam made a simple statement into a challenge.

Shad wasn't up to meeting that challenge. Everything in his life slipped through his fingers. His son was brutally murdered. His wife left him. Now his daughter and her beau intended to go to Denver to be with her.

Words failed him. Head hanging, he stood, turned, and walked slowly from the line shack. Miriam called out something to him. The words were muffled. Williamson's words came through to him more clearly. He wasn't relenting. He was saying he was sorry that Shad couldn't accept what he and Miriam had already decided.

Shad rode slowly back to Utopia, his thoughts jumbled up and incoherent.

Chapter Twenty-six

"You miss her, don't you?" Leroy Early sat in a chair across the desk from Shadrach Nelson.

Shad looked at him, eyes dull.

"Who're you talking about?"

Early shrugged.

"Miriam. Your wife. Both of them. Toss Abe into that. If I didn't know better, I'd think you missed Williamson, too."

"He's not family," Shad said sharply.

"From gossip I hear around town, he will be. Folks are saying that's why he and Miriam went to Denver, to get hitched."

"Too good to do it in Utopia," Shad said. He pushed to his feet. "Sitting around here lollygagging's not keeping the peace."

Early stood, too. He stretched. He had been up half the night, splitting that shift with Ian Shannon.

"I've got another three-four hours before I call it a day. Where do you want me to go?"

"Up and down Main Street. At this time of day there's not likely to be much trouble, but it is Saturday. Some of the boys start their celebrating before the sun goes down."

"Missy told me she's a mite worried," Early said. "One of Leadbottom's kin was in last night, shootin' off his mouth 'bout cleanin' the town of Gallaghers."

"Nothing that's not been said before." Shad tied down his holster and made sure the six-gun slid smoothly against the hard leather.

"Missy's not one to get all flighty. Something 'bout this spooked her. It worries her so much she asked Ralph if she could skip dealin' faro tonight."

This caught Shad's attention. Missy would keep dealing in the middle of an earthquake or a tornado. Something worse than those natural disasters nudged her to walk away from a night's gambling take.

"The coal yard seems to be a sore spot for both sides of the pass," Shad said.

As he stepped out, he heard Early say, "Watch your back."

He took a leisurely walk getting to the railroad depot. The sun was already behind the distant peak, and kerosene lamps were winking on all over town. Sussman had not only lit up the depot interior but had put out lanterns to signal the train. Shad checked his watch. The train wasn't scheduled for another six hours.

Weary but determined, Step climbed to the railroad platform. From behind his ticket window Sussman looked up. His expression changed to a scowl when he recognized Shad.

"Good to see you, too," Shad said.

"Whenever you show up, Marshal, there's trouble. What's the problem now? Still listening to that crazy lady up in the hills rant on about how everyone's stealin' her coal?"

"I hear gossip that both families might take it into their knuckleheads to dispute that matter. No timetable's been attached, but folks who know think it'll be soon. Maybe tonight."

Sussman shook his head.

"I haven't seen hide nor hair of either Gallagher or Morrisey for hours and hours. That suits me just fine. Winifred's boys dumped three loads of coal around noon. I got no idea when Leadbottom intends to ship more ingots.

Seems he's been workin' his miners overtime. They're bringin' down half again the number of lead bricks they used to."

Shad wondered if Leadbottom had nabbed others to use as slaves. There hadn't been any new complaints of men going missing. That didn't mean the Morriseys weren't preying on solitary travelers or even passengers intending to board the stage. Men like that weren't expected to arrive on any decent schedule and wouldn't be listed as missing for days or even a week or more.

They could pickaxe out a lot of lead ore in a week or two.

"I'll take a look in the coal yard to chase out any kids there."

"Whatever butters your biscuit, Marshal. I already got all the coal loaded into the hopper for the midnight train so my crew's done gone home." Whatever he did with his ledger occupied him again. Sussman ignored Shad.

The marshal prowled around the empty depot as much to kill time as to check for any urchins hiding there. The town's kids had a way of getting into trouble. The novelty of the powerful locomotive chugging up the mountain never grew old. All he found were clumps of dust in the corners and the occasional chatter of a telegram coming in over the wires.

He refrained from asking Sussman which way the traffic flowed, from Denver to Georgetown or the other way. The telegrapher didn't bother writing any of it down so the 'grams weren't intended for anyone in Utopia.

He descended the steps and checked the water tower, then the nearby elevated coal bin. He leaned against one support. It was rickety but strong enough to support a large box of coal. He nodded in approval at how the railroad had dealt with the chore of loading the dark lumps. The box was built to hold just enough coal to fill a tender. A chute dropped down and gravity did the work loading the fuel onto the train. On the far side of the bin was a road tamped into a dirt mound. Load a wagon in the coal yard, let the mules drag the wagon to the top and then shovel it into the bin.

Or, depending on the wagon, back it up and have it dump the coal without need of shoveling. This way the only time any workman had to use a shovel was getting the piles of coal loaded into the wagon.

"Sure beats loading the coal shovel by shovel," he said to himself. In answer, a rat skittered away.

He followed the rat toward the coal yard, then slowed. The rodent's scurry-scurry had faded away, but the crunch of boots against the coal-covered ground warned him of more than one man moving around. A curse came. Then a heated exchange. He didn't need to hear the names to know the Morriseys were prowling around where they didn't have any business.

Moving steadily toward the disturbance, he squinted when a lucifer flared. In the brief flash he saw one of the Morrisey cousins' face lit up as plain as day.

He rested his hand on his Peacemaker and quietly went toward the bright red glow of a coal at the end of a cigarette.

"You got business here, Sudderth?" Shad got a tad of satisfaction watching Eric Sudderth jump like he'd gotten a hot foot.

"Who's there?"

"Marshal Nelson, that's who. Who're the reprobates with you?" Shad made out two dim shapes moving to get away like the rats they were. He snapped at them to halt. To his surprise they did.

The trio moved closer until he got a better look. He went cold inside when he saw Patrick Morrisey. The man had an alibi when Abe was cut down, but having Egan claim Patrick never left the stagecoach depot seemed like a flimsy excuse. Any Morrisey would lie like a trouper to protect a blood relative. There was no telling what lengths they'd go to forcing a citizen like Egan to lie. Money? Possible. Threats? More likely.

The third one was Patrick's half-brother Nathaniel.

"You got no call stoppin' us," Patrick said.

"You Morriseys got no call kidnapping men and using them as slaves in your mine."

"Can't prove it, can you, Marshal?" taunted Patrick.

"You heard that Murton died, too. I haven't found Abbott's body, but some of your kin did him in. Where'd you move his body?"

"Might be a giant thunderbird swooped down and carried it off," Eric Sudderth said arrogantly. "I heard tell them Injun birds get real hungry for dead human flesh."

"They really like law dog brisket," Nathaniel added, jutting out his chin. Shad did his best not to clip him, just out of spite.

"If you don't tell me why you're out here, that thunderbird'll have a real feast off your carcass," Shad said. He stepped to within a few inches of Sudderth. The man tried to back away to put distance between them, but he ran into a pile of coal and fell back.

"You're gettin' your clothes all dirty, Eric," Nathaniel said. He stepped past Shad to give his relative a hand up. He wiped the sooty hand on his shirt. The two of them faced Shad. Patrick joined them.

"You get on back home and don't go prowling around where you don't belong," Shad said.

"You got no call tellin' us what to do," Eric Sudderth said.

"You're going to jail in ten seconds if you and your kin don't clear out." Shad decided Patrick was the closest they had to a leader. He stepped over to him and gave him a cold stare. "You know the way home. Take it." He rested his hand on the butt of his Peacemaker, then drummed his fingers to emphasize his order.

"Come on, boys. We got places to go," Patrick said.

"And things to do," Nathaniel added. "Real important things." He pushed past Shad. When he did he shoved the marshal.

Shad reacted instinctively. His fist filled with his Colt. Off balance he fired into the ground.

The Morrisey clan let out a collective yelp. They slapped leather and began firing wildly. Shad scrambled away, only to find that the trio was shooting off into the dark, past him. Shad made his way on hands and knees until he came up behind a low pile of coal and chanced a look around.

At least four men behind him fired at the Morriseys. Two used rifles and the other two fired pistols.

"Stop shooting!" Shad yelled. "Stop!"

His command disappeared in the echoes as a new volley from both directions erupted. Getting to his knees, he peered out to see Eric Sudderth standing exposed, shooting at any shadow. Shad had an easy shot at the man but didn't take it. He didn't have to.

Sudderth jerked when one of the riflemen took advantage of the exposed position. Patrick Morrisey scuttled out and dragged the wounded man back to safety behind a tower of coal.

"You chose the right side, Marshal," came a voice he knew all too well.

"You put down that rifle, Kenny Gallagher," he said.

"Why? Because you missed the shot at that thievin' owl-hoot? I took him down for you."

The other three in the ambush moved forward. One by one, he identified them as Gallaghers.

"What're you doing out here?" he asked.

"Protectin' our property. Ma thought they'd try to steal our coal. We got a big shipment comin' up in a week."

"That's right," chimed in Jeremiah Jones. He crouched beside Shad, holding a still smoking six-shooter. "The twice daily coal delivery to them railroaders makes a few dollars but when she ships tons down to Denver for the main lines, that's where the big bucks are."

"They're not stealing your coal," Shad said. "There're only three of them."

"Hear that?" Kenny said. "We got 'em outnumbered. And I done plugged one. Let's go!"

Shad shouted for them to stop, but the Gallaghers launched a full-out attack. Screaming and firing as they rushed their enemies, they closed the distance between them in a few seconds.

Heaving a sigh of resignation, Shad joined the assault. He hadn't stopped Sudderth from being shot, but he might keep the others from ending up a pound or two heavier from lead puncturing their worthless hides. Even more ironic, the bullets fired by the Gallaghers had probably come from the Morriseys' own mine.

He rounded the mountain of coal to see Kenny Gallagher standing over the fallen Eric Sudderth. Kenny stood with one boot pressing down into the middle of the fallen man's chest. He made a big deal of jacking in a fresh round and pointing his rifle at a spot between the eyes.

Shad wasn't sure if Kenny would have fired. He never gave him a chance. Head down, he ran full tilt into Gallagher. His shoulder caught a hip. He dug in his toes and lifted Kenny Gallagher off his feet, sending him crashing into the side of his coal pile. When Kenny landed, his finger tightened. A round sang off into the night.

The response was immediate. Patrick and Nathaniel opened fire. The racket made Shad wonder if it had sounded like this at Gettysburg. Worse, the Morriseys returned bullet for bullet. Standing in the midst of so much flying death was suicidal.

Shad grabbed Kenny's ankles and hugged tight. The man threw up his arms in a vain attempt to maintain his balance. His rifle went flying. Then he crashed to the ground, struggling to get free.

"Stay down, you yahoo," Shad snarled. "You'll get ventilated in a second if you stand up."

As reward for his warning he got a boot in the face. Growling, he swarmed up, drew his pistol back and unloaded. He smashed the butt into the side of Kenny's head. A soft sigh filled the silence between gunshots as Gallagher collapsed.

"You stay down, too," Shad snapped at Eric Sudderth.

"He was gonna murder me. Arrest him, Marshal. Unless you're takin' *their* side."

Disgusted, Shad left Eric Sudderth spouting his conspiracy theories. He scrambled up to where Jeremiah Jones fumbled in the dark to reload. Shad knocked the gun from his hands and pointed his Peacemaker in as menacing a fashion as he could.

"Stay put. Stop shooting," he ordered.

Without thinking what he did, he stood and stepped out. He fired his pistol a couple times and yelled, "Drop your guns. Take your fingers off them triggers and drop your guns!"

He fired again.

His heart almost exploded when all he heard was silence.

"Patrick, come get your cousin. He's in a bad way." He spun and aimed his gun at Nathaniel Morrisey. "Go help him. Stuff that hogleg back into your holster and help your brother."

"Half-brother," Patrick mumbled. Shad silenced any further complaint with a cold stare.

"And you Gallaghers," he shouted, "go fetch Kenny and drag him back to Winifred. Tell her she's lucky all he's got will be a sore skull. Clear out, all of you! I don't want to see so much as a whisker in the coal yard unless you're here on business."

He pointed his six-shooter at Patrick when he started to protest.

"You've got no business here right now. Is that clear?"

"Is Eric dead?"

"He will be if you don't get him out of here. Take him to Doc Paisley. Right now. Go. Go!"

"You took them Gallaghers' side, Marshal. I'm gonna tell Leadbottom about this," Nathaniel threatened. "You're gonna be sorry."

Shad launched a kick at the man's rear. He missed but accomplished his intent. The two Morriseys hoisted Eric between them and dragged him away.

"You busted Kenny's head," protested Jeremiah Jones.

"He won't notice. He doesn't use his brains for anything important," Shad said. He herded the Gallaghers off in the direction of their side of Hellfire Pass. In less than a minute, they vanished into the night.

Only then did Shad drop his six-gun into his holster and stand in the darkness. The silent dark. It was still hours until the midnight train pulled into the depot. He looked around, shivered although it wasn't that cold, then went to find a spot to sit and wait for the next eruption.

After the dustup he'd just ended, it was only a matter of time before the Gallagher-Morrisey feud erupted again. It wasn't likely to be tamped down when it did, any more than a case of exploding dynamite could be.

CHAPTER TWENTY-SEVEN

"An army, Marshal, you got to bring in an entire company of soldiers," the station master demanded. Sussman slammed his fist down on the counter, causing a pen, a bottle of ink and several unsold tickets to jump.

"I'm not sending for any bluecoats," Shad said sourly. "It wouldn't do any good, not at the last minute."

"The train's coming in at noon," Sussman said. His eyes were squinty with anger. "There's gonna be three carloads of passengers, too. Mine owners from all along the western slope are headin' to Denver for some big confab about mineral rights."

"I heard about that," Shad said. "There's been a rich strike at Blackhawk, and the owners are all angling to get the Denver financiers to pony up money to pay for a dozen more mines."

"A dozen? I heard a hundred. The greedy ba—" Sussman spun when a gunshot rang out.

"Stay here," Shad ordered. He cleared leather and reached the depot platform overlooking the tracks in three long strides.

High on the side of the pass—the Morrisey side—he saw a half dozen riders. All of them carried rifles across their saddles. That was a bad sign. It took only seconds for a deadly volley to come tearing down on anyone in the depot or the rail yard beyond. Leadbottom's entire family was armed and ready to shoot something.

Something . . . more.

There'd been the shot that frightened Sussman and put Shad on edge. He tried to find the target for their lead. The riders kept coming, rifles at the ready. Behind them along the poorly kept road up to the galena mines rattled a heavily laden wagon. It swayed precariously and more than once threatened to plunge over the edge of the road. As bulky as its load was, it'd roll over a dozen times before it came to rest across the railroad tracks.

"What's going on, Sussman?"

The railroad agent crowded close, using Shad as a shield should any of the guards on the shipment take it into their heads to shoot at him.

"Leadbottom's got a monthly cargo to ship. Along with the lead ingots already in the yard, he's shipping a couple more tons today."

"He's guarding it like it's gold instead of lead," Shad said.

"He's a suspicious cuss. Who'd steal a lead brick? Who'd want to? They're only valuable to the foundries down in Denver."

"I suppose one of those bricks'd give a fellow a lot of bullets," Shad said.

"They got shot towers and ways of forming bullets nobody in Utopia can imagine. The ammunition is what's valuable. Wouldn't surprise me one little bit if the brass cartridges cost more than the lead slugs once they're all put together. Or the gunpowder." Sussman edged out from behind the marshal when no further shots were fired.

"If you'd wanted more protection, you should have told me weeks ago. The army'd never send even a patrol to guard lead bricks, but I could have made sure both my deputies were in town."

"Where are those lazy—?" Sussman bit off his denunciation.

"Shannon is out serving process. The judge in Georgetown telegraphed a stack. It was his turn to find them." Shad sucked at his teeth. Each paper served brought a fee, sometimes as much as two dollars. Shannon needed the money, so Shad had sent him.

"What about Early?"

"He's in town. If he's got any sense, he's sound asleep. He worked all night."

"There was one hellacious fight at the Prancing Pony, I hear," Sussman said.

"He took care of it himself."

"Where were you?"

"I have to sleep sometime. Early did just fine breaking up the fight. And the Morrisey boys look like they've settled down after getting run out of town then."

He watched the four leading riders like a hawk. They fanned out to let the wagon drive to the far side of the tracks. The freight yard was on this side, but there wasn't much point unloading the lead ingots, then heaving them into a freight car. Let them remain in the wagon where it was easier to heave them straight into the freight car.

"There's a second wagon," Shad said. "How much lead are they shipping?"

"That's not got any metal in it. Unless you think Leadbottom is well named. He rides in his own wagon, and it weighs purty near as much because of his bulk." Sussman snorted in contempt and made his way down the steps and across the tracks to talk with the leading rider.

Shad identified Patrick Morrisey right away. He followed the railroad agent to where the guards fanned out even more to make way for the creaking freight wagon burdened with their patriarch.

"You fixing to stay and watch over your cargo?" Shad rested his hand on his pistol to emphasize the question.

"We're not going to cause any trouble, Marshal," Patrick Morrisey said, "unless the Gallaghers start it."

"I meant, are you and your family intending on getting a drink or two in town once all that's aboard the train?"

"Not now. We got to get paid for the ingots."

Shad nodded, relieved. That was good. Having a dozen Morriseys running around Utopia all liquored up and looking for trouble would cause more mischief than he and Early could handle. Even if Shannon made it back before sundown, a dozen drunks intent on finding trouble filled his jail to overflowing.

And maybe added a grave or two out in the cemetery.

"You and your pa figure on guarding your cargo?" Shad asked. He watched the rickety wagon bringing Leadbottom down the last steep decline toward the railroad station. The driver stood hard on the brake. Even this barely slowed the wagon until the two mules found themselves being hurried along by pressure on their rumps from the harness and balked.

If the wagon had overturned and sent the Morrisey patriarch rolling, Shad wanted to be able to jump out of the way. That would have been worse than an avalanche from high up in the pass.

"He's signing the manifest," Patrick Morrisey said.

"I'll go talk to him."

Shad stepped across the railroad tracks and started walking. Patrick Morrisey put his heels to his horse and bolted for the freight yard. He zigzagged through the stacked crates and disappeared in a few seconds in the direction of the Gallagher coal. Shad was a trifle uneasy about one of Leadbottom's boys vanishing like that, but stirring the pot by complaining got him nowhere.

"Good morning," Shad called. He took off his bowler and brushed away soot from the brim as Leadbottom's wagon came to a creaking halt. The other wagon had pulled alongside the tracks. He guessed they knew where the train stopped and how to make the transfer of ingots to a boxcar as quick and easy as possible. These weren't men inclined to put out more effort than necessary.

Even thinking about kidnapping slaves to dig ore from their mines showed that.

"You come to watch over my property?" Leadbottom grumbled as he forced himself to stand in the rear of the wagon. He'd ridden this far stretched out on a mattress and heavy blankets put in the wagon bed to cushion the ride.

"I—" Shad never got any more words out of his mouth.

The shot passed over his head and dug into the side of Leadbottom's wagon. For a man as heavy as Leadbottom Morrisey to move like he did was a thing to behold. Flat-footed, he jumped a good three feet straight into the air. When he crashed down, the wagon's back axle broke, spilling him onto the ground at Shad's feet.

The marshal stared at the struggling mine owner. He was as stunned by the potshot as all of Leadbottom's family.

"Somebody tried to kill me!" From his spot on the ground, Leadbottom began screeching like a hooty owl.

The men arrayed down the tracks all lifted their rifles and began shooting at random. Some filled the railroad depot with holes. Others fired into the coal yard. Still others turned and began shooting back in the direction of their own mine.

"Stop firing! Stop it!" Shad whipped out his six-shooter and intended to knock the Morriseys out of their saddles one by one.

"It was them Gallaghers. They tried to murder me! Arrest them, Marshal. You take their part, but you got to arrest them now. They're all consarned ambushers!"

Shad lined up the bullet hole in the side of the wagon and tried to backtrack it. Whoever had taken the shot did so from the top of a towering pile of coal. Leadbottom's son Patrick had ridden that way.

"Who's missing? Where's Eric Sudderth?" He tried to identify the Morrisey contingent.

"He's all laid up from gettin' shot," Leadbottom said, rolling onto his belly and pulling himself erect.

"Patrick . . ." Shad threw out the name to see what Leadbottom said.

"He's done rid off. He must be huntin' for that sniper. Good boy, Patrick. Go get 'im!" Leadbottom roared like a lion now. He shouted conflicting orders to the rest of his guard.

They finally got it into their heads to hunt for the sniper among the coal.

Shad saw the station agent cowering behind a stack of trunks on the platform. Sussman wasn't hurt. In the back of his mind, Shad had wondered if Sussman might not be the one taking a potshot at Leadbottom. The man's blanched complexion told how scared he was.

"You just gonna stand 'round or you gonna find the Gallagher what tried to kill me?" Leadbottom waddled over and tried to bump Shad with his bulging belly. The marshal stepped away and avoided the impact.

"It might have been me they were shooting at," he said.

Leadbottom sputtered incoherently.

"You've got a point, though. If the varmint is going to get caught, I'll have to do it. Your boys are making too much of a racket and will scare him off." Shad turned to fetch his horse.

"Wait!" Leadbottom grabbed him by the arm. The man's grip was immensely strong. Shad wasn't able to jerk free.

"What is it? You see who shot at you?"

"It had to be a Gallagher. Who else? But you can't traipse off and just leave me!"

"Go sit under your other wagon," Shad advised. "The lead blocks will be more effective stopping another shot than anything I can do."

Leadbottom's grip weakened for an instant. Shad yanked

free and left. He had a good idea where the shot had come from, and it wasn't anywhere near where the Morrisey clan had lit out to hunt for their patriarch's possible killer.

He crossed the tracks and made his way toward the water tower. Next to it loomed the sooty black box used to load coal into the locomotive tender. From the lumps of coal scattered around the base, it had already been filled. All that remained was for the engine to pull up. The chute would be lowered and the coal would tumble out.

The marshal circled to the ramp leading to the top of the box. Two mules were all it took to pull a load of coal up the earthen slope. He dropped to his knees and tried to make sense of the tracks. More than one trip by the loaded wagon had cut up the ground too much for him to find any boot prints. Even if he had, there wasn't anything to tell him that they were left by the sniper. If they weren't able to just dump the coal directly, it had to take a half dozen men to shovel the coal from the wagon into the loading bin.

Shad trooped to the top. As he expected, the box was filled to the brim, waiting for the train to be loaded. Not far off, the water spout on the tower slowly dripped down to form a deep mud puddle. Shad edged forward and found the spot looking down at the depot.

"Perfect," he said. He imagined sighting along a rifle barrel and then squeezing the trigger. It wasn't that Leadbottom hadn't been hit. It took a powerful bad shot to miss such an easy target.

He scuffed at the dirt on the top of the ramp. A shiny brass cartridge caught his eye. Holding it high, he studied it in the bright morning sun. It hadn't been on the ramp very long. Letting his imagination run wild, he felt the hot brass as it had been ejected from the rifle. He tucked the spent cartridge into his vest pocket.

Slowly turning in a full circle, he scouted for whomever had fired the round. Again, he wondered how the marksman had ever missed. Moving on from where Leadbottom had tumbled to the ground, he saw that Sussman was busying himself with work inside the depot. The Morrisey family chased their own tails throughout the coal yard. Trying to identify them proved impossible.

Patrick had headed out first, but he was nowhere to be seen. The others he put names to. Leadbottom had said Eric Sudderth was laid up. Shad wasn't able to see him anywhere.

He turned a bit more to see if the woods at the rear of the coal yard hid any clues. His eyes swept past, then returned to deep in the stand of trees when he saw movement. He pulled down his bowler so the brim shielded his eyes. He finally cupped his hands to block out more sunlight.

Definite movement.

Shad caught his breath when he saw Patrick come from the woods leading his horse. Close by him rode Beatrice Gallagher. She leaned over until she almost fell from the saddle to kiss Patrick. He returned the kiss, then pulled away. Shad wasn't able to hear the words they exchanged. There wasn't much need. The way they touched each other, then exchanged a parting kiss told the story.

Beatrice galloped off toward the road leading up to the Calcutta Mine. Patrick watched her for a moment, settled his shirt as if it had been twisted around, then slowly walked a ways into the coal yard. When he was sure Beatrice was out of sight he yelled for his relatives.

They gathered around him, then trailed him as he returned to where his pa hid under the wagon creaking under the weight of the lead ingots.

"Bea and Patrick," he said, shaking his head as he walked down the ramp.

Shad wasn't sure what to make of everything he had seen, but it spelled even more trouble for Utopia—and him—in the future.

It'd be a toss-up whether Winifred or Leadbottom would be more outraged.

Chapter Twenty-Eight

"You gave up too easy," Patrick Morrisey said. He tried to stare down the marshal and ended up looking away.

Shad knew the man's secret and somehow that guilty knowledge warned Patrick Morrisey not to press his complaint too hard.

"Who'd think a brick of lead was worth anything compared to the same amount of gold," Shad said. He tried to pick up one of the lead ingots and couldn't. He shifted his weight and got his feet under him. Even then it was hard to lift the brick.

"It's makin' me rich," Leadbottom said.

"All you need to do is stay alive to spend it," Shad said.

"Hellfire Pass is Morrisey country. Ain't no Gallagher gonna drive me out. Not me or any of my kin." Leadbottom's wattles bounced as his anger mounted. Shad was sorry to have poked the bear in his den.

"Feels like the train's coming," he said. He pressed his foot down on a track. The distant engine strained to make it up the grade. Vibrations sent along the steel rail warned the train wasn't more than a few minutes distant.

"I see it," Patrick said. "The smoke from the engine."

Shad stood on the rail and took a hard look down toward the west. A tall column of smoke rose as the locomotive strained to reach Utopia.

"Them!" Leadbottom cried out. His family all cocked their rifles and swung around, aiming high.

"Put those down," Shad snapped. "They've got every right to be up there."

He saw two Gallaghers at the top of the ramp where he'd found the spent brass. They worked to get the chute swung around prior to dumping the coal into the train's tender.

"They got every right to be *dead*," snapped Leadbottom.

"Make a move on them and I swear I'll pump some lead into your carcass, Leadbottom."

"You got no right."

Shad said nothing. Without the coal mine, Utopia would dry up and blow away. The climb in either direction into Hellfire Pass burned a powerful lot of coal. Loading the tender for the trip down the slope on the other side of the pass made this a profitable route for the narrow-gauge railroad. Riding on such closely spaced rails limited the size of the engine that could be used in the mountain passes.

No Gallagher coal, no Utopia.

In spite of everything that had happened to him in the past week or two, Shad liked the town and wanted to live here.

If only Abe was here—and Ruth and Miriam.

He looked around at the Morrisey boys. One of them might have murdered his son. In his gut he thought Patrick was the guilty party, if only he could get Egan to back away from his alibi, but he *did* have an alibi. How long it'd take him to convince Egan to tell the truth wore down on him. He had so little time keeping the two feuding families from killing one another and any Utopia citizen who happened to get between them.

The memory of shackles on his ankles and how Patrick had lorded it over him would never go away, not until he breathed his last.

If only he had Murton or Abbott to back up his claim. His word was good. A lawman against Leadbottom Morrisey in court carried considerable weight, but it was his word against the entire family. If only Murton hadn't gone loco and Abbott's body hadn't been spirited away, he'd have evidence to back up his claims.

They were capable of anything, those offspring of Leadbottom Morrisey. He kept looking hard at Patrick. The man was uneasy under such scrutiny. And for good reason. He had a guilty conscience sneaking off to see Beatrice Gallagher the way he did. How far Patrick Morrisey would go to prevent anyone from finding out was something Shad needed to figure out. Leadbottom would disown him. Winifred Gallagher would go even further. She'd scalp him for certain.

"You're the one," he said softly, his eyes following Patrick as he went to the heavily laden wagon to prepare for transferring the lead bricks right away into a freight car. How or why he had cut down Abe was something that had to be proven.

Shad would do it. Patrick Morrisey was lying through his teeth, and so was Egan and any of the family members who backed up his story.

"There she comes!" Sussman came out onto the platform and began switching signal flags around. The post holding the metal flags wobbled but he steadied it to give the proper information to the engineer.

Shad had no idea what message the signals relayed.

He looked away from the wagon to the Gallaghers up at the coal bin. They tugged on ropes to move the chute out of the way until the train came to a halt. From the way the engine screeched, metal wheels digging into the rails, it wouldn't be long.

Shad watched Highballin' Davey Fulbright draw up with a few inches of what looked like the perfect position. The engineer gave the signal. The water spout opened and dropped hundreds of gallons of water into the heated boiler amid rising clouds of steam. The two Gallagher men positioned the coal chute, cursing each other to move this way and that. Finally satisfied the chute was properly aligned, Kenny Gallagher yanked on ropes attached to a pulley. The crash and crunch of coal tumbling into the engine tender rivaled the sound of the water hitting the hot boiler.

Not to be outdone in showing how industrious they were, the Morriseys moved the lead ingots into a boxcar amid great grunting and inventive cursing. Sussman came over and counted the bars. When Leadbottom and the station agent agreed on the number loaded, Sussman heaved a tarp over the pile and fastened it down with a wire. He used special crimps to mash a lead slug around the wire, sealing the cargo until it was opened again down in Denver.

Paper changed hands. Shad reckoned these were receipts for the freight. He was more interested in watching Kenny Gallagher and another of the fecund clan finishing off loading the coal. Kenny and what was likely a cousin stood close together atop the ramp, arguing over something.

"All loaded," Sussman told Shad. "You got any call to hold up the train? Davey's anxious to get down the mountain. There's a storm brewing around Colorado Springs, and he wants to avoid the weather."

"I've got no objection," Shad said, surprised that the agent bothered to ask. The railroad and its timetable were matters always left to the engineer and company, but mostly to the engineer. In his way, he was the captain of a ship at sea.

"Good." Sussman moved closer and lowered his voice. "Weather's a concern but more 'n a storm, he's a bit on edge bein' caught betwixt them." Sussman jerked his thumb over his shoulders in Leadbottom's direction, then turned enough to indicate the Gallaghers atop the loading bin.

"I don't blame him one little bit," Shad said. "I'm worrying about them getting into a fight once the train leaves."

"Don't you go nowhere, then, Marshal Nelson." Sussman sounded uneasy. "Neither of them's making a move to go back where they belong."

"I'll shoo them off." Shad's assurance disappeared in the raucous steam whistle signaling that the train was pulling out.

The boiler hissed and the wheels screeched. Inch by inch, the locomotive pulled on the now heavier load. The engineer waved to Sussman as the cab passed. Sussman changed the signal flags again, as if this had anything to do with the train's progress. Then the locomotive's speed was enough for the train to pull away more rapidly. The cars flashed past, all the three filled passenger cars and then the freight cars. One by one they sent cinders Shad's way, and then came the caboose.

Shad was left standing near the Morriseys, staring up at Kenny Gallagher and his kin. Both of Winifred's clan stared down at their enemies. Kenny leaned on a rifle. His cousin crowded close and nervously fingered his six-gun. If Shad had called "Boo!" he would have started a new war between Gallagher and Morrisey.

"Go on, boys. Stake out our claim."

Shad jerked around and stared at Leadbottom. The grin splitting the man's face was downright obscene it was so big.

"What's going on?" Shad demanded.

"We decided to put down markers and claim that part of the yard." Leadbottom pointed at the Gallaghers' mounds of coal. "That'll 'bout be good enough to repay me for them yellow bellies shootin' at me."

"Brushwell owns the yard. It's not Gallagher property," Shad said.

"What's settin' on Brushwell's land is theirs, and we's takin' it as our due." Leadbottom raised his arm, made a fist and then dropped it fast like a hammer into an anvil, pointing at the coal.

Shad cringed in spite of knowing what was going to happen. The entire Morrisey family opened fire and charged into the yard, shooting at anything that moved.

He heard Kenny Gallagher screech. For a moment a deathly

silence fell, then came volley after volley. The Gallagher side gave as good as they got.

"Stop them. Tell them to put down their guns," Shad ordered. Leadbottom smirked and shook his head.

For two cents, he would have drilled the lead mine owner then and there for not only starting this battle but for everything he'd been doing over the past few months. Both Murton and Abbott were dead thanks to him. Kidnapping, killing, forcing men to work as slaves in his mine—Shad had plenty to hate Leadbottom for.

There was no call for him to detail more crimes and misdemeanors. The Morriseys piled them up like dirty laundry.

But he was a lawman. Keeping the peace was his job.

He reloaded and then went after Patrick and the others amid the mounds of coal. There wasn't any way Leadbottom could steal the coal. There was too much of it, and it was heavy, dirty, impossible to hide. Then he saw how wrong he could be.

One soot-covered figure struggled to light a torch. If the coal ever caught fire, it'd burn down the railroad terminal and probably take most of Utopia with it.

"Stop!" Shad's order didn't prevent the man from striking one dud match after another. His bullet did.

The man gasped, staggered a step, then fell facedown. The lit torch rolled away from the coal, but so much coal dust lay around that the fire began gnawing away at it.

Shad rushed forward, stamping out what he could. The fire spread too fast for him. He grabbed the shoulders of the man he'd just gunned down and began rolling him over the smouldering ground. The man was half burnt by the time Shad extinguished all the smoking spots.

"What's going on?" Brushwell rushed up, a pistol in his hand.

"Get over to the depot and don't get mixed up in this scuffle. The Gallaghers and Morriseys took it into their heads to kill each other."

"This is my property! What're they doing trying to set fire to it? If the coal dust catches fire—"

"I know what'll happen." Shad cringed at a new round of ferocious gunfire. "Fetch Leroy Early. I don't know where he is, but I need help." When Brushwell hesitated, Shad shoved him. "Go!"

Brushwell moved slowly, hesitantly, then walked more briskly away. That was the best Shad could hope for. Remove the combatants one by one. Brushwell likely would have added to the confusion, shooting anything moving about in his freight yard.

Shad stared at the smoking body on the ground. At least killing him had some benefit. His corpse had smothered the fire he had tried to start.

Shad ran forward and found himself being targeted from all sides. Reluctantly, he retreated and skirted a hill of jet black coal. If he rounded it in either direction, he'd be a goner. Gritting his teeth, he dug in his toes and started climbing the pile. It was hard going, but he reached the top. From here he got a better idea what was going on.

To his right the Morriseys had spread out and fired across an open area to where they had at least four of the Gallagher family pinned down. Those weren't the only ones prowling around. Shad hadn't seen them before. Kenny Gallagher and the other man who had loaded the coal into the engine tender were still on the earthen ramp, defending the high ground.

But Leadbottom's attack had taken not only Kenny but the rest by surprise. If they tried to escape, they'd be killed in seconds.

Shad saw that. The Gallaghers knew that, but they weren't patient to wait out the assault. Eventually the Morriseys had to run out of ammo, but holding back for that required more than patience. They needed common sense. That wasn't something in abundance on either side.

Shouting at them accomplished nothing. Shad had to do something fast or the Gallaghers would try a frontal assault that'd end with all of them being slaughtered. Shad braced his gun hand and began squeezing off rounds at the nearest Morrisey. His second shot hit one in the arm. The momentary confusion this caused when he loudly squawked about his injury to his kin gave Shad the chance to fire three more times. A second Morrisey was hit.

They looked around in confusion, not sure where the deadly fire came from. His final shot caused one of them to grab his belly, fold forward, and sit down.

Shad dropped down and reloaded. By the time he got off another round, the attack was over. The Morriseys retreated, shooting over their shoulders as they went. They half dragged their wounded with them.

A cheer went up from the other side. The Gallagher faction thought they had run off their hated enemies.

Shad slid down the far side of the heap and landed hard. He tried to brush off the coal dust. It smeared. Worse, the dust rose and made him sneeze. For a fleeting instant he was glad it had been Leadbottom and not Winifred who had chained him to work in their mine. He'd still be snorting black if he'd spent any time at all in the Calcutta Mine.

"What's going on, Shad?" Leroy Early came running up. He carried a scattergun. "It sounded like the Injun wars had started all over again."

"Keep the Gallaghers from going after the Morriseys," he said. "I'll deal with Leadbottom."

"If you arrest him, you'll need a bigger lockup. He's too big to fit into a single cell."

"I'll stake him out back," Shad promised. He had to smile at that. It'd be fitting. Leadbottom Morrisey in shackles just like he'd kept the marshal and the two railroad mechanics.

Shad ran after the retreating gunmen. He caught up with them clustered around the family patriarch. Leadbottom sputtered and cursed when he heard how they'd been routed.

"You!" Leadbottom cried, pointing a sausage-sized finger at Shad. "You took their side. You shot my boys!"

"I don't take sides," Shad said. "I keep idiots from killing each other."

"They got shot," Leadbottom said, glancing at two of his clan being doctored by the others. "You done it. I know you did!"

Shad hesitated, then said, "And one more's dead. He tried to set fire to the coal."

"Who? Who's dead?" Leadbottom looked around.

"Pa, Ernest ain't here."

"Go fetch the body," Shad ordered. "You can see to burying him."

"You shot him?" Leadbottom squinted as he watched Shad closely. His eyes went wide when realization hit him. "You *did*! You're gonna pay for this, Nelson. It warn't enough that your boy was killed. I see it now. You got to die, too."

Shad started to raise his pistol. It sounded as if Leadbottom confessed to killing Abe.

"Let's clear out, Pa," Patrick said. "They got us outgunned."

From the corner of his eye Shad saw his deputy raise the shotgun to his shoulder. Early had overheard everything Leadbottom said about Abe.

"Yeah, clear out, all of you. Get off my property." Arthur Brushwell had found a rifle and shifted it from one man to another. He finally came to sight in on Leadbottom. The patriarch was the easiest, largest target.

"See if we use your freight yard anymore, Brushwell." Leadbottom harumphed and let Patrick help him to the remaining intact wagon that had delivered the lead ingots.

"You're banned from ever storing anything here again, Morrisey. Go on, skedaddle!" Brushwell lifted his rifle. He lowered it when Shad aimed his six-gun at the freight yard owner.

The Morriseys retreated in disorder, their dead and

wounded rattling around in the back of the single freight wagon containing Leadbottom.

"I'll burn that broke-down wagon of theirs to cinders," Brushwell said. He shook his fist at Leadbottom. "I swear it. They're not getting it back or repairing it on my property." He turned and stormed off.

Shad dropped his hands to his sides. His Peacemaker banged against his right thigh. Drained of energy, it took some doing to return the weapon to its holster.

"I ran the Gallagher boys off. They're hightailin' it back up their hillside," Early said. "Hell of a day," he said, shaking his head. "One hell of a day." The deputy walked away.

Shadrach Nelson wanted to agree, but he wouldn't form the words. He was too drained. The gut feeling that things were only going to get worse refused to go away as he returned to his office.

Chapter Twenty-nine

"We've got to find a way of getting together other than meeting here," Patrick Morrisey said. He rolled over and stared up through the canopy of leaves above them. He swatted Beatrice's hand away when she began exploring his nakedness again.

"This place is safe enough. Anywhere else we'd have to sneak through town or ride a long way."

"But it's right next to the danged coal yard. I swear Brushwell saw me more 'n once. He's a suspicious cuss. He must guess why I'm sneakin' around."

"He's never noticed me," Bea said. She rolled over and laid her cheek on his chest. His heart hammered away as if he'd run a mile.

"If he had, he'd surely have mentioned it. Nobody sees you and doesn't say, 'that's one beautiful gal.'"

"You're so sweet, Pat," she said.

"And I'm serious about sneakin' around. What if my pa found out?" He shivered. "Or your aunt? I think I'm more a' feared of her than I am of my pa."

"There's no reason to be scared. I've got her wrapped around my little finger."

"Like you do me?" Patrick laughed now. "And every guy who comes within ten feet of you. I swear, you could also make that stick-in-the-mud marshal do whatever you wanted just by battin' those long eyelashes and givin' one of those come-hither smiles."

"Come hither smile," she said. It was her turn to laugh. "You make me sound like some fancy woman from the big city."

Patrick was quiet for almost a minute. This worried her. He always suggested something really dumb after he thought on it a spell. This time wasn't any different.

"Let's run off. Get on our horses and start riding. It don't matter where we go. Denver. Central City. Maybe we can go even farther. Laramie."

"And do what, Patrick?"

"I can find a job. I know mining."

"What about me?"

"We'll get hitched. You can take care of our house."

"While you grub away in a black hole in the ground for pennies a day. You know how much your family's lead mine makes. The Calcutta brings in a profit of nigh on a thousand dollars a month. Are you really telling me to give all that up?"

"But you got to pay folks and buy things," he protested.

She sighed. He had no idea about money. When she said "profit" she meant what her aunt hid away in a Ball jar behind their cabin. All expenses were met, and at least a thousand dollars was left over. At least. Usually more. Winifred got rich. The rest of the family jumped whenever she said frog and lived on pennies.

"Our families need us," she said. "Both of us."

"If anybody finds out what we're up to . . ." Patrick's words trailed off.

"Nobody will," she assured him. "And if they do, I'll bat my eyes and smile all cute and they'll forget all about it. Just like you said."

"You're makin' fun of me," Patrick said. He sat up. She swung around and began pulling on her blouse. Sometimes he irritated her. Of course she made fun of him. He deserved it.

"What's that?" He grabbed for his six-shooter.

She wrapped her long fingers around his wrist and pushed the muzzle down so he wouldn't fire.

"You're hearing things," she said.

"I'm not. Somebody's out there spyin' on us."

Beatrice's eyes narrowed as she studied the undergrowth that hid them from prying eyes. She caught her breath when she saw movement.

"There," he said, jumping to his feet. He struggled to pull up his jeans with one hand and aim the gun with the other.

"It's only a fox," she said. "Or a rabbit." She smoothed her skirts. The lump in a pocket assured her she carried her derringer.

"When will I see you again?" He tried to kiss her. She dodged the attempt and put her hands on his bare chest to hold him away.

Softly, she said, "Make yourself scarce for a while. An hour or two. Then go into town and have a drink. Be where everyone can see you."

"To create an alibi?" Patrick sounded skeptical. "For what?"

"You just do it, my love. Things will be just fine." She pushed him away after giving him a quick peck on the cheek. He started away, stopped and looked longingly at her. Beatrice blew him a kiss. This was enough to satisfy him. For the moment.

She finished straightening her clothing and brushed off twigs and dirt. There wasn't any way to get rid of the coal dust that worked its way into the land all around the coal yard, but she wasn't worried about anyone noticing and asking about it. The dust from the Calcutta made every Gallagher a walking lump of coal.

Rather than go directly to the spot where someone had spied on them, she took a narrow path away from the freight yard. When she came out at the edge of the hill leading up to Gallagher land, she circled the woods and found a spot near the ramp leading up to the bin used to load the locomotive tenders. She only had a few minutes to wait.

Her cousin limped along, going to where he'd tethered his horse.

"Hello, Kenny," she said.

He jumped a foot. He spun, fear etching every line in his face. When he tried to step back, his injured leg gave way. He sat heavily, looking up as his cousin approached.

"Bea," he said. He tried to stand. She kicked his hand out from under him and sent him sprawling. "What're you doin' here?"

"Did Aunt Win send you?"

"No, yes. She sent me to watch you. I seen what you and that Morrisey was doin'!"

"What was it you saw?"

Beatrice watched as he turned over and over all the things he might say. Most were lies. Then Kenny decided on blackmail.

"You and him was actin' like you was married. You shouldn't be seen with a Morrisey, much less doin' what you two was doin'. Ma's gonna have a conniption fit. She just might throw you out. What'd you do then?"

"I'd get by just fine, Kenny. Just fine." She slipped her hand into the folds of her skirt and found the double-barreled pistol. "What do you expect to get out of threatening to tell Aunt Win about me and Patrick?"

"So it's you and Patrick," he mocked. He scuttled back and got to his feet. Moving a foot or two along the ramp put him higher than her. He obviously thought taking the high ground gave him the upper hand.

"He's useful," she said. "I can find out what's going on in Leadbottom's camp."

"There ain't no call for you to do that. Ma's already got a spy up there."

"Do tell," Beatrice said, interested in what Kenny had to say now but trying not to show it.

"It's Eric. Eric Sudderth."

"How come you know that Leadbottom's nephew is spying for Auntie?"

"He got all shot up the other night. He thinks they are on to him and tried to kill him. His own kin or the marshal. He wants her to pay him off so he can go down to Georgetown."

"And work the gold mines there," Beatrice guessed. She knew nothing good could ever come of trusting a Morrisey to do anything honestly. Kenny's head bobbed up and down.

"See? I know lots of secrets. I can keep my yap shut." Kenny's grin was malicious. "For a price."

"What might that price be?"

"I seen what you do with Morrisey. Some of that'd be real good." Kenny saw her reaction and hastily added, "Or money. You keep the books for Ma. How hard is it to move some of it from one pocket to mine?"

"Are you the one stealing our coal?" Bea saw the confusion on his face.

"Nobody's stealin' our coal. I watch real careful. They get a full bin every time the train fills up and never one lump more."

"How often do you repair the bin?"

He blinked in confusion. His mouth opened, then snapped shut. He shook his head.

"So you don't swing a hammer or measure the boards to repair it?"

"That's Brushwell's concern. He built it, and I just see the bin's filled and the coal's dumped into the tender. I don't spill a single lump. I'm that good."

"But you want me to steal from Aunt Win. How good is that?"

"How terrible would it be if she finds out what you're doin'? Payin' me not to sorta *mention* it is worth it. You can't tell me you ain't stealin' hand over fist from her already. You and *Mister* Morrisey." The smirk returned to his face.

"I don't want her to find out anything about me and Patrick," she said. "That would upset her something fierce."

"Five dollars a week sounds like a decent amount." Kenny rubbed his filthy hands together.

"I can think of an even better amount," she said.

"More?"

"How does two ounces of lead sound?" Beatrice pulled out her derringer. Her cousin stood less than five feet away when she pulled the trigger twice. Both rounds slammed into his chest, knocking him backward. He sprawled on the ramp, arms outstretched.

Beatrice stepped closer. Kenny's eyes were open and staring into the bright blue Colorado sky. He might have seen her and Patrick together, but the sky was the last thing he'd ever see. She nudged him in the ribs to make sure. He was dead.

Kenny already drew flies.

She tucked her derringer away and rummaged through his pockets. She found his lucky rabbit's foot and took the cheap timepiece from the watch pocket in his filthy jeans. Clutching her take, she fetched Kenny's horse. It was a better mount than hers, but she had a better use for it than taking it for her own. Beatrice stepped up and rode away slowly, heading across town, taking back streets to avoid being seen by many of the citizens bustling about. Mostly they kept to Main Street and never paid her any attention.

When she finished her chore behind the Gold Dust Saloon, she started the hike up the side of Hellfire Pass toward the Gallagher claim.

"At least he wasn't shot in the back," Leroy Early said, staring at the body. He shooed away flies.

Shadrach Nelson walked a full circle around Kenny Gallagher. He tried to figure out what had happened from footprints and tracks, but the jumble was too great. The wagons going up and down the ramp to the coal bin obliterated any chance of finding footprints.

"He was shot from close up. He never went for his six-gun, so he was either taken by surprise or knew his killer."

"Could have been either," Early said. "Could have been both. He stood uphill a couple paces. Somebody strolled over and *bang*." He made his index finger and thumb into a gun and pretended to shoot Kenny. "No way to tell how tall his killer was or anything about him."

"He wasn't shot with a rifle. If he was, the killer picked up the spent cartridges."

"Not a rifle, not this close. The slugs didn't go all the way through him. A rifle's powerful enough to send the slugs skittering all the way up this slope."

The sounds of someone approaching alerted them. Early turned and waved to the undertaker.

"I'm not looking forward to telling Winifred her son's been gunned down. I don't reckon you've got a hankering to do it, do you, Leroy?" Shad would gleefully report Kenny's death for an obituary but facing Winifred Gallagher with the news was a different matter. She wasn't a woman to take news like this easily.

And she already blamed him for a powerful lot that wasn't any of his doing.

The deputy shook his head.

"You ain't paying me enough for that. And if you don't have somebody locked up for the killing, it'll make it even worse. Winnie Gallagher's got one fearsome temper. She won't take kindly to one of her boys being killed like this."

"Not when Leadbottom is doing his level best to stir up trouble between the Gallaghers and Morriseys."

"You're keeping me in business," the undertaker said. He adjusted his eyeglasses and studied the corpse. "You need to find a better class of dead body, though. Collecting from that skinflint Winifred Gallagher is hard work."

Shad wasn't arguing with Martin Donovan. The black-dressed, solemn man had a point.

"Maybe the mayor will give you a few bucks out of his bribe money to bury him in the potter's field," Early suggested.

"The last time he did that was when Hector was a pup. If anyone's tighter with a nickel than Winifred, it's our dear mayor." Donovan gestured for his assistant to move the handcart closer to the body. Together they hoisted Kenny Gallagher onto it. "Did he leave behind a horse? Tack? I can sell his gun for a few dollars." The undertaker lifted and dropped Kenny's feet. "Nobody in their right mind would pay a dollar for those boots. Both soles have holes the size of a silver dollar in them."

"If you can collect, sell whatever you can," Shad said. He stepped away and let Donovan and his assistant wheel the cart away.

"There was a horse tethered yonder," Early said, walking back. "Fresh flop. Whoever killed him might have stolen his horse."

Shad and his deputy began the long walk back to the jailhouse. Ian Shannon met up with them halfway. Shad closed his eyes for a moment. He didn't need more aggravation, and his deputy looked agitated.

"Shad, we got problems," Shannon said.

"The canyon walls haven't cracked and dumped rock on Utopia, and there hasn't been a flood here in years. That means it's a problem of lead against coal."

"You guessed right," Shannon said. "Down at the Gold Dust. One of the Gallaghers accused Patrick Morrisey of killing one of his kin."

Shad and Early exchanged glances. They lit a shuck. Shannon was hard-pressed to keep up. They heard the ruckus in the saloon before they rounded the curve in Main Street so they could see the boardwalk.

Shad grabbed for his six-shooter when a body came flying through the large plate glass window beside the swinging doors. He didn't recognize the man who landed in the street. A couple moans and feeble thrashing told him this wasn't a killing. But from inside he heard the hoots and catcalls and knew the crowd egged on two men with six-guns.

He never slowed as he pushed through the double doors. Facing off was Patrick Morrisey and one of Winifred's nephews.

"You cut him down, then stole his horse."

"You've been breathin' too much of that coal dust," Patrick Morrisey said. He widened his stance and rested his hand on his holster, ready to throw down on Jeremiah Jones.

"And them lead fumes destroyed your brain if you think you can get away with killing Kenny."

"Whoa, back away," Shad said. He shrugged off Early's hand when his deputy tried to keep him from stepping between the two.

A hush fell over the crowd. They expected some entertainment, and the marshal added to the chance gunplay would happen.

"He murdered Kenny. He's got to pay for it."

Shad looked at Patrick Morrisey. The man's expression told him nothing.

"Why do you think he killed him?"

"Kenny's horse is outside. It's got the Gallagher brand on it."

"Maybe your cousin was here before he got shot."

The crowd began a low murmur. They hadn't known of the killing for sure. Their marshal now confirmed the death. This added spice to the showdown. Having one Gallagher accuse a Morrisey of a crime was old hat. Fresh blood meant a bigger show to drive away boredom.

"His saddlebags are slung over Kenny's horse."

Shad glanced back at the saloon door. Shannon already stepped out to check.

"What do you have to say about that, Morrisey?"

"I don't have anything to say since every word out of his mouth is a big fat lie."

"Don't get twitchy. Keep your iron in its place." Shad saw the muscles in Morrisey's face, around his eyes and on either side of his mouth tense.

"He's right, Shad," came Shannon's appraisal. The deputy threw a set of saddlebags onto the bar. "Those are Morrisey's. They've got his belongings in them, and I took them from Kenny's horse."

Jeremiah Jones went for his gun. Shad saw him jerk around, reaching for his Colt. Rather than shoot, the marshal lowered his shoulder and charged. He caught Jones in the biceps. With a roar he lifted and jerked around, like a bull throwing a matador off its horns. Jeremiah Jones flew through the air and crashed into a table.

Shad spun and went for his gun now. He had it out, cocked and aimed at Patrick Morrisey's heart before the miner cleared leather.

"I *will* shoot you," Shad promised.

"If you don't, Marshal, one of us will," Early called out. Both he and Shannon had their pistols out.

Morrisey let his gun slip back down into the holster and slowly raised his hands.

"I didn't do anything."

"Shoot him, Marshal. Go on, shoot him!" Jones slipped and slid in the sawdust on the floor as he tried to stand.

"You stay down." Shad looked around the crowd. They were turning surly. Robbed of their show, they were easily pushed into violence right now. To the barkeep, he called, "See that all these gents have something to wet their whistles. Will you, Ralph?"

"Yes, sir," Ralph Rockwell said. His bald pate shimmered with sweat beading on it. He was willing to pay the price of a round of drinks to keep his place from being busted up any more than it already had been. The plate glass window alone was small enough damage compared to what the two dozen men intended because they'd been denied the pleasure of seeing either Gallagher or Morrisey—or both—bleeding into the sawdust spread on the floor.

Shad plucked Morrisey's gun from its resting place and shoved him from the saloon. It had been a rough hour or two, but things went better than he expected when he found Kenny Gallagher's body.

He already had the man's killer in custody, even if it would stir up a tornado of trouble in Utopia.

Chapter Thirty

Beatrice tried not to smile when her cousin rushed into Winifred's cabin, bursting at the seams with the news.

"He—he's done been kilt, Aunt Win." Tommy bent forward, hands on his knees to regain his breath. He looked up. His long, dark, lank hair was matted to his forehead with sweat from the hard climb up the mountainside from Utopia.

"Quit pantin' like a dog. Next I know you'll have your tongue all floppin' out. That'd be disgustin'." Winifred Gallagher pushed back from the table where she had been going over the mine's ledger with Beatrice. "What are you tryin' to say, boy? Go on. Spit it out."

"It—it's Kenny. He's dead."

"Between the ears, you mean. He's never been the brightest light in any room." Winifred got to her feet when she saw the wild look on the messenger's face.

"He's not joshing you, Aunt Win," Beatrice said, unable to keep quiet any longer. Watching her aunt convinced her that the Gallagher family matriarch was truly shocked at the idea Kenny had been cut down. He wasn't the smartest one working the Calcutta Mine, but that didn't stop Winifred from taking a shine to him.

That was another point against her aunt. Beatrice always took second place to Kenny, for no good reason. She was smarter, she was better looking—but she wasn't a man.

Kenny might have been Winifred's son but that shouldn't matter when it came to running the family business.

The Calcutta Mine belonged to the entire Gallagher family. Winifred ran it like her own personal property.

"How'd you know about Kenny?" Winifred demanded of her niece.

Beatrice opened her mouth, then closed it. She had spoken out of turn. There wasn't any way she could have known. Her hand pressed into the derringer hidden in her skirts.

"It's the way Tommy looks, Aunt Win. He didn't run all the way to play a joke on you." She stared hard at her cousin. "You'd never do a danged fool thing like that, would you, Tommy?"

"No, Bea, you know I wouldn't. The marshal found the body. In the coal yard." He controlled his breathing better and didn't gasp like a smithy's bellows any longer. Sweat glistened on his face. The wild look lingered in his eyes.

"The marshal!" Winifred exploded. She slammed both fists down on the table, hammering it so hard the ledger bounced off to the floor.

Beatrice picked up the book, closed it, and tucked it under her arm where it'd be safe. From what she had seen looking over the numbers, her aunt was stealing from the family, just as Kenny had said. This had to be where the glass jars stuffed with greenbacks buried behind the cabin came from—the jars Winifred didn't think anyone else knew about. Winifred had discounted how observant her niece was.

"He can't be dead." Shock turned Winifred pale now. She settled back in her chair and looked at a blank wall, as if seeing her son there with a silly grin on his face.

Things fell into place for Beatrice, just as she had suspected. Her aunt used Kenny to do the dirty work. He collected the money and doled out the bribes. With him gone, her aunt would either take over the sneaky dealings personally or chose someone else close to her.

Beatrice clutched the ledger book a little harder. Her aunt had to pick her. Who else knew the business better?

And being the one to pass out the bribes meant she could deal herself into the illicit money. It was only fair. Aunt Win treated her like a second-class family member so far, just because of her no-account pa.

"Marshal Nelson already arrested Patrick Morrisey," Tommy finally got out after catching his breath. "Morrisey had done stole Kenny's horse. The marshal searched the saddlebags and found Kenny's lucky rabbit's foot. That didn't mean nuthin' to him, but I saw it and knew."

"That smelly old thing," Beatrice said. She rubbed her hand against her skirt, remembering how the fur had come loose when she plucked it from her cousin's pocket.

"I'm sure it was Kenny's. I seen it on the marshal's desk after he emptied the saddlebags. And his watch was there, too, the one his pa gave him on his fifteen birthday."

"The one stolen off a body of some miner who died coming into Utopia," Beatrice said under her breath. She had heard the story too many times not to believe it.

"Morrisey took Kenny's horse?" Winifred looked up. Her face was strained, and she gritted her teeth together.

"He musta stole it and then went right on over to a saloon to drink and brag on it. That's where the marshal caught him."

"I want him strung up," Winifred said. "And the marshal musta had a part in the killing. That's the kind of man he is."

Beatrice slid her hand from the folds of her skirt, letting the derringer weigh down her pocket. She made sure the ledger was secure before going around the table to put her hand on Winifred's shoulder.

"There, there, Aunt Win. The marshal might be a scoundrel, but he did the right thing arresting Patrick . . . Patrick Morrisey." She looked hard at Tommy. He hadn't noticed how she started to call her lover familiarly by only his first name.

"We've got to retrench now that Kenny's gone." Winifred pushed Beatrice's hand from her. She looked up. "Tommy, you and Kenny were close."

Tommy's head bobbed up and down. He licked his lips as if he wanted to speak, but no words came out. Beatrice tensed. She stepped away to stare at her aunt. Reading the woman's intent was easy. Too easy.

"You and Kenny, you shared things?"

"Like women?" Tommy went pale under his dirty face. "I mean, me and him, when we went to Lady Sarah's, we—"

"I meant you and him worked in the coal yard, loading the bin, collecting the money."

"Sure, me and him did that. Kenny made sure he always had the money, though. I never touched a dime of it. Honest!"

"The family needs you to take over what Kenny was doin'," Winifred said. "I want you to dicker with Brushwell and handle those railroaders."

"I can do that," Tommy said. "That'd kinda make me the family agent, wouldn't it?"

"Aunt Win, there's no need to get Tommy involved in that . . . business. I know all the details. Let me," Beatrice said. Her voice turned shrill. She hated herself for showing such panic.

"Quiet, girl. This is business."

Beatrice threw the ledger down so hard onto the table it sounded like a gunshot. Both Winifred and Tommy jumped. But they paid no attention when she stormed from the cabin. They already began discussing how Tommy would represent the Gallaghers.

Beatrice stood outside, arms crossed, fuming mad.

She looked around. The men were working in the mine at this time of day, and the women were at home tending children and cooking or cleaning. Every last one of them owed her for keeping the books and not letting Winifred steal too much of the revenue from the mine. And not a one of them knew or would appreciate her efforts.

Beatrice rounded the cabin and squatted down. She began turning over rocks. Winifred had developed a system of hiding the Ball jars stuffed with money. Not every rock hid a jar, and some jars were mostly empty.

"The future," Beatrice said, her fury rising.

By the time she had unearthed a dozen jars containing several thousand dollars, she had cooled down and thought more rationally. Her aunt and Tommy still talked over the details of skimming money from what Brushwell paid. She wondered how badly Tommy would endanger the house of cards Winifred had built to defraud the family.

Beatrice stuffed the greenbacks into a new hole and covered it with dirt and rocks, then used a bit of sage to sweep away any sign where she had moved the money. It wasn't much, a few thousand, but it was a start. Before long, she'd make sure Tommy met the same fate as Kenny. Her aunt had to see who the best one to run the family finances was then.

"You sure of that, Tommy?" Winifred Gallagher stood with her fists on her flaring hips.

"I am for certain sure. Leadbottom and half his family's in town, all hollerin' and screamin' for the marshal to let Patrick and Andy out of the hoosegow."

Beatrice felt as if she walked on a tight wire strung between the peaks on either side of Hellfire Pass. The slightest slip and she'd fall a long ways. This was the minute she'd wanted to happen for years.

"Get the boys to a spot behind the Morriseys," Winifred told Tommy. "When you got them varmints all penned up, open fire. Kill Leadbottom and as many of them Morriseys as you can."

"The marshal won't like it none," Tommy said.

"When he and his deputies come out from the jailhouse, you gun them down, too. Make it look like Leadbottom done the deed. When the shootin's over, you claim you kilt all the Morriseys 'cuz they shot the lawmen."

"Sort of an ambush only we're all out in plain sight. What if somebody in town sees what we done?"

"They won't let out even a tiny squeak. They know what side of the bread's buttered," Winifred said.

"And who's buttering it," Beatrice chimed in. "Without Gallagher coal, the railroad wouldn't bother coming to Utopia."

"The railroad don't need lead," Tommy said, nodding. "They surely do need our coal."

"Get yourself and the rest of the boys down into town. Do me proud, Tommy." Winifred hugged him and got a black patch on her dress from coal dust off his overalls.

"Do it for Kenny," Beatrice added, trying to keep from laughing.

A loud cheer went up. Tommy did his best to get to his horse, mount it, and work his way to the front of the small army rushing down the mountainside.

"He'll get himself killed," Beatrice said. "Tommy's worse than Kenny."

"Don't matter. This is the night we bust Leadbottom and send him to the boneyard." Winifred peered across the darkness of Hellfire Pass at the far side. Lanterns dotted the entire hillside, showing the Morrisey family was on the move down to town. "We got to be ready to move in and take over his lead mine. It ain't as profitable as the Calcutta, not by a country mile, but it'll do us proud."

"Not all the Morriseys will be killed," Beatrice pointed out. "What of the ones that're left?"

"We'll have them varmints outnumbered. If they got the guts of their pappy, they'll hightail it so fast all we'll see is the dust cloud they leave behind."

"If Tommy's shot, do I get to take over from him?"

Winifred made a shooing motion with her hand, as if flies bothered her.

"Ain't reason to worry your head none on that account, girl. If Tommy's gunned down, I reckon Jeremiah can take over. His last name's not Gallagher, but my sister's was, curse her black soul."

"She's dead, Aunt Win. Jeremiah's a mite young to lead the family."

Winifred snorted like a pig, laughing.

"Ain't nobody runnin' this family 'cept for me. The Gallaghers are *my* family and nothing's gonna change that." She walked forward and stood on the brink of a steep cliff. Fifty feet below, the road curved back as it wound down into Utopia.

"When Leadbottom's killed, that'll set off the feud like nothing before. There're plenty of Morriseys who'll take his place."

"Like Patrick? You thinkin' on him?"

"I got him out of the way, or I thought I had," Beatrice said. "I expected the marshal to shoot him down. Patrick's always disappointed me."

"What are you sayin', girl?" Winifred turned and stared hard at her. The frown deepened. "You and that no good lead miner? You and him were—"

"Oh, yes, Aunt Win. Quite a lot," Beatrice said, feeling powerful with the revelation. She had done something her aunt never suspected.

Understanding lit Winifred's face.

"You framed him for Kenny's killin'?"

"Of course I did. I didn't want to go to jail for shooting Kenny."

Profound silence descended. Then came a small whistle of wind through pines higher up, almost at the tree line.

"Why'd you kill a blood relative? That's, that's—"

"Something you'd do?" Beatrice laughed now.

"I'd never hurt any of my family. Why?"

"He saw Patrick and me together. He was going to tell you. What would you have done?"

"Disown you! Whip you like a dog and lock you up naked in a shed 'til you got some sense back into your head!"

"I saw a chance to do to him what I'd already done to Abednego Nelson. He saw Patrick and me, too."

"You shot the marshal's boy? Well, that's not as bad as killin' your own cousin," Winifred said, pursing her lips and rubbing her chin as she thought on the matter. "But it riled the marshal up. That wasn't good for us."

"You can see how Patrick was becoming a noose around my neck." She reached into her skirts and found her pistol.

"You can teach Tommy a thing or two, that's the Gospel truth." Winifred looked more sour. "And Jeremiah if Tommy don't come back."

"There won't be any need to do that, Auntie. I'll be the head of the family. They can do what I tell them."

"Girl, you don't know what you're sayin'. *I'm* head of the Gallagher clan."

"Not if you just disappear. Do you think any of the others know you've got all that money stashed behind the cabin?"

"I—" Winifred swallowed hard. "Is that what you want, Bea? I'll show you where it is. We can split it. Then you—"

"I already found it all. I've already figured out everything about how you are cheating all of us. You skim money off—or you had Kenny do it so your hands'd be clean. There's no way I'll pass up that opportunity. From the books, you make danged near as much off thievery as you do selling the coal."

"You stop this crazy talk, Beatrice. There's no way I'll let you do any of those things. I run this family. Always have, always will."

"You *ran* the family," Beatrice said in a cold, level voice. The derringer slipped from her pocket. "The Gallaghers will be in good hands, Aunt Win. My hands."

Winifred let out a screech of pure hate and lunged forward.

Beatrice fired once, twice. The bullets hit the elder Gallagher and stopped her forward rush. Winifred looked down at the growing red splotches on her breast. She reached up and touched the damp spots, then stared at her niece, surprise on her face.

"Time for you to leave, Auntie." Beatrice shoved hard. Her aunt stumbled back, came to the brink. Her arms flew out and flapped like a flightless bird. She toppled back and hit the side of the cliff twice before crashing into the road a hundred feet below.

Beatrice stared at the unmoving body so far below. She slipped her derringer back into her pocket. Her aim had been as good as with Abe and Kenny. Turning, she went to saddle a horse and ride out. She wanted to be far away so that Tommy or whoever returned from the massacre found Winifred's body.

That'd give her a chance to sob and weep and protest and figure out who to blame the killing on. Whichever Morrisey escaped from Utopia would be good, credible. They'd evaded the Gallaghers and had come seeking revenge and found the Gallagher matriarch. They fought. A fight that Winifred lost. That was a believable story.

Or one of the law dogs might have done the dirty deed. It hardly mattered to her now who was blamed for Winifred's death, as long as it wasn't her.

As Beatrice rode off, she made plans for how she'd run things. Winifred had done a good job. She'd be even better as head of the Gallagher family.

Chapter Thirty-one

"We got a town overflowin' with Morriseys tonight," Ian Shannon said. "All day long they've been comin' into town. Right now they're over at the Gold Dust gettin' all liquored up. The ones that ain't there are down at the Prancing Pony."

"Dutch courage," Leroy Early said. "They need to get knee-walkin' drunk before they try to spring those two." He glanced toward the rear of the jailhouse where Patrick and Andy Morrisey were caged. The two prisoners sat close together in adjoining cells, whispering their plans. Somehow they knew Leadbottom had decided to send the family to spring them.

"How many are there?" Shad asked.

"Well now, Marshal," said Shannon, "they don't need more 'n Leadbottom himself. He amounts to half a dozen burly men all by himself. But he's got a couple dozen of his kin with him."

"Most all of his family," Shad said thoughtfully. "There's no way the three of us can hold them off."

"It galls me to let the likes of Leadbottom Morrisey just take our prisoners," Early said. "It makes a mockery of bein' a lawman."

Shad started to say that Early had done that by letting

Richard Williamson go free but held back his criticism. He needed Early's support. Provoking him now wouldn't be right.

"We don't owe the town a plugged nickel," Shannon argued. "Turn them two miscreants out. Or maybe just shoot them in their cells. Nobody but Leadbottom'd care."

"I'd care!" Patrick Morrisey shouted from the back of the jailhouse. "You can't shoot us like caged animals."

"Shut up," Shad said. He swung around in his desk chair and used his heel to kick shut the door between the office and cellblock. It did nothing to stop Patrick Morrisey from shouting, but it muffled the noise. He needed some quiet to think on the matter.

He jerked around, hand flashing to his Peacemaker when the outer door slammed open. The livery stable owner stood in the doorway, eyes wide and face flushed from exertion.

"What's got you so het up, Mister Watt?" Shad asked.

Bernard Watt stepped into the office and pointed back into the street.

"They're coming. They're on the way here."

"They? You got to be more specific. You mean Leadbottom and his thugs?"

"Marshal, it's the entire Gallagher family. They're pouring down off the mountain like ants going to a picnic."

Shad swung around and leaned on his desk. His mind raced.

"How many would you say, Bernie? How many Gallaghers?"

"Twenty-thirty. My stable boy saw 'em. He's not one prone to exaggerating."

"I know him," Early said. "Roger's not one to tell a fib just to hear his own tongue flapping."

"That'll mean we got fifty men intendin' to kill each other in town," Shannon said. He took out his six-shooter, checked each chamber before snapping shut the gate and sliding the gun back into his holster. A quick look at the rack on the wall showed a pair of shotguns and a half dozen rifles. Drawers underneath were crammed with spare ammunition. He took down a shotgun.

"We can't hold them all off," Shad decided. "What we have to do is decoy them away. Leroy, get back there and tie up and gag our prisoners. I don't want them to make any sound louder than a baby snoring."

"What're you thinking on doing, Marshal?" Bernard Watt was an imposing man. Not quite as tall as Shad's rangy 6 foot 2, he outweighed the marshal by thirty pounds, not a speck of it fat. There wasn't a man in Utopia who'd not think twice about arguing with the stable owner.

"You want to wear a badge, Bernie?"

Watt stared at Shad in disbelief.

"The answer's not no, it's hell no! I'm not dying for either of them." His finger stabbed out in the direction of the cellblock.

Early returned and went to the gun rack.

"They're all trussed up like a New Year's pig with an apple in its mouth. They're not gonna utter a peep." Early took down a rifle and levered it open to check the magazine before rummaging in the drawers for a couple boxes of cartridges.

"You've got an honest face, Bernie. How're you at telling a whopper of a lie and making folks believe you?"

"He's real good, Shad," Shannon said. "Ask him what his rates are to board a horse and see how he explains what he actually charges."

"You listen up, Ian Shannon. My business is—"

"Quiet!" Shad shouted to silence them. "You won't have to wear a badge. I just want you to tell anybody and everyone asking that we've taken the prisoners to the railroad depot."

"Why?" Watt looked confused.

"To get the crowds way away from where the prisoners

actually are, that's why." Early sounded peeved. "That's a good idea, Shad. Divide them up, get them scattered all over town. Send both sides on a wild goose chase."

"If we're not here, they'll think we are putting the prisoners on a train to Denver. The depot's easier to defend than the jail."

"Leastways, if they burn it down, we've still got a desk where we can hike up our boots," Shannon said glumly.

Shad watched as Bernard Watt shifted weight from one foot to the other. He wanted to bolt and find a place to hide. Then something firmed inside him, and he stood straighter.

"All I have to do is get them to chase you to the railroad terminal?" the livery owner asked.

"Don't let 'em see we've still got the prisoners in a cell," Shad said. Heading off the next question, he said, "If anyone finds out, don't shoot it out. Let 'em have the prisoners. You're not being paid to defend the law."

"We barely are," Shannon said, looking even more dour. He hefted the shotgun and took four boxes of shells. He looked expectantly toward the door.

Shad grabbed the second shotgun and enough ammo for it and his Peacemaker to hold off a small army. The problem was that they faced a large army. Anyone in the street was going to shoot at them. The best he hoped for was one side of the blood feud seeing the other and opening fire. The lawmen might get caught in a crossfire, but they wouldn't be the targets.

"Don't matter if you get shot by accident or because someone's aimin'," Shannon said, as if reading his mind. The deputy slid past Watt and headed for the railroad depot.

Shad shook the livery owner's hand and left, Leroy Early trailing behind.

"We might reduce the odds a mite if we went to the saloon and talked it over with Leadbottom," Early said.

"He's building up a head of steam to tangle with us. There's no way to talk sense into him now."

"He'd lose face if he did," Early agreed. He slowed and then walked over to a pair of cowboys sauntering toward the saloon. He exchanged quick words with them, then returned.

"What'd you say to them?"

"They're good boys off the Triple W. They owe me a favor since I didn't run them in for hurrahing Sampson's store."

"You convinced them to tell Leadbottom we've already got his boys at the depot," Shad guessed.

"Something like that." As Early walked, he loaded his rifle's magazine. "It's not like I think Watt'll fail, but he was so scared might be no one believes a word he'll say.

The rest of the way to the railroad station was done in silence. Shad knew he ought to say something inspirational. He'd heard enough Fourth of July speeches and enough politicians on the stump to have the words. Nothing came to him. Besides, his deputies knew the stakes.

He trudged up the steps. Shannon already stacked luggage to make a small fort at the end of the platform. Inside, Sussman worked on the telegraph key, clicking madly. Shad pointed to the roof. Early walked around to find a ladder to climb up. If the depot was on a hill, getting even better high ground couldn't hurt.

Shad went inside. Sussman looked up, then frantically keyed even faster. The clicks turned into a fierce chatter.

"Who're you telegraphing?" Shad asked.

"I asked Denver for a company of railroad bulls. Nobody's burning my station down around my ears."

For a moment, Shad dared hope. A dozen of the railroad dicks was enough to turn the tide, even against fifty angry rioters. He pulled out his pocket watch and did some quick calculating.

"The train's already left Denver," he said. "There's no way to stop it for the bulls to get on, even if the powers that be wanted to get involved."

"They want to protect the station. This is one of the most

profitable routes. Supplies to the gold fields, gold from Georgetown and Central City. Blackhawk's starting to produce." Sussman shook his head. "The railroad officials would hate to lose Hellfire Pass and Utopia."

"Especially the coal mine," Shad guessed. He stared Sussman down. The depot master averted his eyes and moved away from the telegraph key. Amid the heavy odor of sulfuric acid and lead, Shad detected fear.

Sussman was scared out of his wits.

"How long have you been shorting the railroad?" he asked.

"What're you talking about?" Sussman stepped back another pace. He looked like a trapped rat.

"Brushwell doesn't give the full allotment of coal when he fills up the tender, does he? The engineer gets paid to look the other way. So do you."

"The engineer's got to make the coal last. It's a good thing we're at the top of the pass so Davey can coast down, no matter which direction he heads."

"What do you do with the coal not being loaded? It's not like there's another train that'll buy it . . ." Shad's words trailed off. Then he said, "There is, though. Once a week an extra train's scheduled. It loads up to take coal down to Denver for other engines."

"Sometimes we're three entire coal cars to the good. That's a lot of money to pocket," Sussman said.

Shad heaved a deep breath. Such a scheme required men all along the line to get a cut. Brushwell and Sussman and the engineers and now he understood the men working the yard in Denver were in on it.

And Winifred Gallagher? Did she know? Or were they cutting her out and pocketing the money stolen from the railroad thinking they received a full tender twice a day? Knowing the woman as he did, Shad found it hard to believe she wasn't dipping her beak into this lucrative trough.

Stealing from her would be hard since she was so suspicious of everyone and everything.

Or maybe not. The easiest people to cheat were swindlers. They always thought they were smarter than everyone else and that no one could work a nobble on them.

"What's that?" Sussman jerked upright, turning around like a jack rabbit using its ears to track a coyote.

"You have a gun? You might want to get it ready," Shad said. He recognized gunfire when he heard it, no matter how muffled by distance.

He rushed back to the platform and looked out. An undulating black sea moved toward the railroad depot. Here and there men carried torches. Whether they intended to light the way for Leadbottom's men or if burning down the depot was more in line with their intentions hardly mattered. Shad and his men now faced a street filled with a mob intent on bloodshed.

"I can pick 'em off one by one, Shad." Early called down from the roof.

"Hold your fire. It's a long shot, but I might talk Leadbottom out of turning his men loose."

Shannon snorted in contempt at such a fantastic notion. He scooted around and opened a box of shells by his knee. He braced his shotgun atop a trunk. Shad heard the metallic click of the hammer cocking. Shannon was ready for a fight. It was probably a good idea.

Shad walked to the edge of the platform, ready to call out to the crowd. He never got a chance. It looked like the Fourth of July fireworks display as dozens of pistols and rifles fired from positions among the piles of coal. The fusillade scattered the Morrisey gang. After they took cover, the battle began in earnest.

Shad stepped back and crouched down, watching in amazement at the way the night lit up from muzzle flashes. One volley followed another until his ears rang.

He caught his breath when the Morrisey faction rose as

one and launched a full assault on the gunmen hidden in the coal yard. Keeping track of the progress proved impossible. Neither side had an advantage, and both had more ammo than he thought possible for anyone to carry.

Shad spun around when boards creaked behind him. His Peacemaker was out and in his hand. He lowered the gun when Sussman motioned to him.

"What do you want? Did you reach Denver in time for them to send reinforcements?"

"Nothing of the sort," Sussman said, dejected. "You've got to stop them, Marshal. Look at them! They're carrying torches into the coal yard. If they set off even one pile, it'll burn for a week. There won't be any way to put it out."

Shad shouted over the loud reports from dozens of rifles and pistols. "You have an idea how I should go about doing that?"

He ducked as a stray bullet sang above his head. Glass shattered, sending Sussman to find shelter inside the station. Shad turned back to the fight, trying to sort out where each side's strongest redoubt lay.

Reaching the Gallagher side was impossible. They were scattered all around the coal yard. The best he could do was talk to Leadbottom and get him to back off. The Morrisey faction had concentrated in a short line using crates in the freight yard for protection. Somewhere in that concentration Leadbottom was bellowing orders.

Shadrach Nelson knew his chance of getting close to Leadbottom was close to zero, but he had to try. He dropped from the railroad platform and made his way into the night, heading toward Leadbottom Morrisey's firing line.

Chapter Thirty-two

"Don't be a fool, Shad." Ian Shannon duck-walked from the pile of trunks and crouched beside the marshal. "They won't listen to you." Shannon cursed under his breath. "Hell, I won't listen to you. I shouldn't have. None of us are gonna get away from this alive."

"Maybe I'll just get a body part or two shot off," Shad said.

"With luck running your way, that's the best you can expect. Them two families hate each other with a flaming passion. Anybody poppin' up between them's not gonna be listened to."

"I'll let them run out of ammunition."

"Or kill each other. That's my choice," Shannon said sourly.

Shad slapped his deputy on the back.

"You might get your wish yet." He took a deep breath, sat on the edge of the platform and then dropped to the ground five feet below. Landing with bent legs, he stayed low and looked around. Above him on the platform Shannon loosed the double-barreled roar from his shotgun every now and then to cover him. From the roof, Early opened fire with his rifle, punctuating the report with the gentler sound of his six-gun to make it seem more than the three of them defended the station.

Shad kept low as long as he could. He came to an open area he had to cross. Standing, but staying bent over, he ran as fast as he could. An occasional bullet kicked up dirt around him. From the sporadic firing, he guessed he wasn't a target and those were random shots. He reached crates intended to be shipped on to Georgetown. Whatever was inside had grown a few ounces heavier from bullets crashing through the sides.

He ducked around. A quick peek showed that one of Leadbottom's men hid not ten feet away.

"Hey, cover me!" He yelled to the man, who jumped in surprise. The Morrisey lifted his gun but saw Shad waving frantically and yelling. "I got to talk to Leadbottom."

In the dark, with a pall of gunsmoke hanging low in a choking cloud now, the man wasn't able to identify Shad.

"Get down. They got a sniper on top of yonder coal pile." The man pointed with his pistol toward a towering black heap. Even as he warned Shad, a tongue of yellow-orange flame leaped from the summit. Where the bullet went didn't matter to Shad. It wasn't aimed in his direction.

Four long strides brought him to the man's side.

"Thanks," he said. "Where's Leadbottom?"

"He's—" The man turned and recognized Shad. He raised his six-gun halfway. That was all the marshal allowed. He swung his Peacemaker in a short, vicious arc that ended against the man's cheek.

He unbalanced the man who tumbled back, clutching his bleeding cheek. Shad stood, stepped over and swung again. This time he put out the gunman's lights. To be sure he wasn't shot in the back, Shad threw the man's six-shooter into the dark. Panting hard, he edged farther along behind the row of crates.

The next stack of crates protected four men. From the size of one of them, he had found Leadbottom in a hurry. He had gotten this far by being as bold as brass. Shad saw no reason to change his tactics now.

"Cover me!" He waved his pistol around as he dashed from where the man he had buffaloed began moaning as he regained consciousness. Again in the confusion of the skirmish, any confident command carried the day.

He reached the man to Leadbottom's right. A quick, short thrust with the pistol butt knocked the man to the ground. Shad cocked his Colt and shoved it into Leadbottom's ear.

"Listen up and listen fast, Leadbottom," he ordered. "Keep these owlhoots off me. I want to parley."

"Nelson! The only thing we got to talk over is when you're gonna let my boys go free. You got them in the railroad depot. I'm fixin' to burn it down if you don't release them."

"It's not your bottom that's made of lead," Shad said. "It's your brain. Burn the depot down while Anderson and Patrick are inside? They'll cook real fast."

"We're gonna shoot our way in, then." Leadbottom flinched when the sniper atop the distant mound of coal sent a round singing an inch from his ear. Leadbottom pointed and yelled at his family to stop the marksman. The ones nearest him all turned their guns toward the coal pile.

As far as Shad could tell, they only drove their bullets into the side of the mound. The sniper had slipped down the far side and was protected from the new barrage—filthy from the coal, but protected by it at the same time. He doubted a Gallagher cared much about getting dirty. Mining the black mineral and breathing the dust took its toll day in and day out. For them this was a holiday.

"Go home. I'll see about letting Andy go free."

"What about Pat? You got no call to keep him locked up."

"He killed Kenny Gallagher. He had Gallagher's horse and belongings."

"Pat don't know nuthin' 'bout that. You got the wrong man. I ain't sayin' he wouldn't kill that worthless lump of coal, but he didn't. Why'd he stay around town if he had shot him down the way you say?"

"To brag on it."

Leadbottom made a rude sound.

"Did anyone hear him *say* he'd shot Gallagher?"

Shad hesitated now. If a Morrisey had gunned down a Gallagher, he'd be boasting on it. Everyone in the saloon would have had an earful.

"You've got a point. I think he still shot my boy."

"You got a burr under your saddle 'bout us Morriseys. We're hard-workin' miners, and we don't take guff off nobody. Especially them Gallaghers."

"Call off your attack, and I promise we'll talk this out."

"You let my boys go first. Have them sashay right on out onto the railroad platform, and we'll leave you be."

Shad couldn't do that. Both Anderson and Patrick Morrisey were still locked up in the town jail. He hoped they were. They were the only bargaining chips he had in this deadly game.

"If the Gallaghers stop shooting, will you stop, too?"

Leadbottom pondered that. Shad saw the three with him begin to get uneasy. One of them would do something stupid at any instant. That meant Shad either put a bullet through Leadbottom's head or he got himself ventilated. Even if he killed Leadbottom, that did nothing to call off the attack. If anything, it might give the Morrisey boys even more determination.

"Settle down now, Leadbottom," he said. "I'll take care of what I can." Shad backed away, turned, and ran back toward the depot. As he passed by the first Morrisey he had cold-cocked, he took another swing and sent him back to the ground.

That gave him enough time to dive belly down and slide the remaining few feet to the base of the depot platform. He pulled himself up and waited to see if Leadbottom ordered his men to fire.

He dared hope when no more bullets came from that

direction. The few whistling through the air all came from the Gallagher camp.

He edged around, climbed the stairs and dropped beside Shannon.

"They're still shooting," his deputy pointed out.

"Not as fast as they were before. And Leadbottom's declared a cease fire. For the time being. That means I've got one last chance to stop this."

Shannon looked at him in disbelief. Then he laughed harshly.

"You're 'bout the stupidest man I ever met." He reloaded his six-gun. "You're headin' over to the Gallaghers to tell them to stop, aren't you?" He heaved a deep breath, then asked, "You want company?"

"You and Early stay here and keep the depot from getting burned to the ground. I'll be back." Shad paused to consider how stupid this was. "I hope I'll be back."

He made his way through the station and out onto the tracks. It took a while, but he found a horse. The best he could tell, this was one of Brushwell's mounts. He'd make a point of thanking the freight yard owner. Later.

Shad had been right that Winifred Gallagher wasn't taking part in the fight. She stayed high up in Hellfire Pass, looking down on the gunfire. But she had set the fight in motion. She had ordered her entire family into Utopia to tangle with the Morriseys.

He grudgingly admired Leadbottom. The patriarch miner joined in the fight and risked his life. Maybe there wasn't much danger surrounded by four or five men to keep him safe, but he was there to spring his sons from jail. Winifred stayed aloof. He cursed her for realizing this was the perfect time to begin the battle that'd decide which family prevailed.

He rode the winding trail with as much speed as he could.

The horse preferred to make its way slowly in the dark. The gunshots spooked it, too. But the farther up the road to the Calcutta Mine they rode, the quicker the horse moved. Shad leaned out and craned his neck around. Only a few hundred more feet of mountain to scale before he reached Winifred's cabin.

Both she and Leadbottom lived near their claims. They had more than enough money to buy decent houses in Utopia, but they stayed close to their source of wealth. Shad wondered if they both feared claim jumpers or thieves swooping in. Gold miners had more to dread. A pocketful of nuggets made thieving profitable. Stealing a lump of coal or a heavy lead ingot was hardly a draw for a robber. A good road agent taking down a stagecoach made far more than either the coal or lead was worth, even by the wagonload.

A hairpin turn brought him to a stretch of road directly under Winifred's cabin. For the first time since getting a ways up the mountainside, the horse balked. It tried to rear and throw him. He worked to control it.

"What's wrong? A snake in the road?" Shad peered ahead. He saw a dark lump, but it wasn't moving. He swung down and walked forward, one hand on the reins and the other hovering over his Peacemaker. When he got close enough to identify the shape in the road a cold lump formed in his gut. This wasn't a giant snake or a fallen boulder.

He secured the reins under a rock and crept forward.

"You hurt?" No answer. Shad stopped a few feet away and made out arms and broken legs. The face had mashed down in the rock. Blood had seeped into the dry roadbed.

He stepped closer and dropped to his knees to roll the body over. The face was a bloody mess, but he recognized Winifred Gallagher. He rocked back and stood, staring at her.

Leadbottom and his boys weren't responsible for the two bullet holes in her chest. Not even the best marksman ever produced could have reached the woman from the coal yard.

Winifred had been shot and then took the long fall from above. He craned his neck upward, hoping to catch sight of who had shot the matriarch of the Gallagher family.

Seeing nothing outlined against the night sky, he returned to his horse and coaxed it around the bloody body. He put his heels to the horse's flanks to reach the cabin as quickly as possible.

"Hello!" he called out, not expecting an answer. Winifred's killer wasn't likely to stay around the scene of the crime.

Shad looked over the verge. In the dark he wasn't able to make out the woman's body, but he knew where to look and imagined he saw arms and legs outstretched on the rocky road.

He poked around in the cabin and saw nothing to give a clue as to her murderer. Shad mounted and started back down the trail when he heard another horse approaching from around the mountain. The area was festooned with double-rutted roads showing where the Gallaghers had dug out coal and had once transported it from played-out mines. The entire hill was hollowed out by their extensive burrowing.

Hand on his six-shooter, he sat his horse and waited for the rider to come to him. Beatrice Gallagher rode slowly and stopped some distance away.

"What are you doing here, Marshal? Aunt Win said she won't talk to you."

"You got that right," he said. "She's dead."

For the span of a heartbeat, Beatrice remained silent. She finally said in a choked tone, "What happened? Did you kill her?"

"She's in the road below us."

"You killed her and came up to the cabin to rob her. You . . . you're a lowdown thief. You wear a badge, but you're worse than any of them." She wildly gestured toward Utopia where the fight was quieting. "You're worse than Leadbottom or any of his pudding-head family!"

"Who else is up here on the mountain?" Shad began piecing together the facts as he knew them. No one had ridden past him as he came up to the cabin. Beatrice was the only one he'd run into unless the killer hid somewhere on the Gallagher claim. He saw no reason for that.

"You, Marshal, you're trespassing on our land. You killed Aunt Win. You're in cahoots with Leadbottom!"

Shad said nothing about believing the killer was still around. Beatrice dragged a rifle from a saddle sheath and brought it to her shoulder.

"You killed her! I'll set every Gallagher to get you, Marshal. I will! I'm head of the clan now!"

Shad considered riding into the rifle's muzzle, then turned his horse's face and began the descent back to Utopia. The hairs on the back of his neck rose at the thought of Beatrice pointing the rifle in his direction. She had nothing to lose and everything to gain if she shot him.

Somehow he reached the floor of the pass. The gunsmoke lingered, but the flashing of fired rifles and pistols and the whine of hot lead filling the air was gone. Leadbottom had retreated. Shad could only guess that the Gallaghers had filtered into town and found a saloon to serve them. Both sides probably declared victory.

He was content to still be among the living and able to go to the still-standing railroad depot to wait for the midnight train to pull in.

Chapter Thirty-three

"They ought to do this themselves." Ian Shannon shifted restlessly from foot to foot as he watched the midnight train roll to a halt. He flinched when the whistle let out a long, loud shriek.

"You mean the railroad should send out their army of bulls?" Shadrach Nelson considered this. He wanted to be free of the war raging between the two families. It'd only get worse when all the Gallaghers found that their matriarch was dead.

He pictured Winifred in the middle of the road, her body growing cold. Two bullet holes in her chest and her face all mashed to pulp when she tumbled off the cliff. Another image came to him. Beatrice riding up. When he told her how her aunt lay dead down the mountainside she had reacted, but was it the way a loving niece should? Or was Beatrice pleased?

Was everything he told her old news?

Kenny had been killed by two shots to the chest, just like Winifred. But Abe had taken three rounds. Two in the chest and one to the head. That gnawed away at him even worse now than it had when he first saw his son's body. Too many possible killers and no evidence against any of them.

"Patrick," he said. Patrick Morrisey remained his top suspect, no matter his alibi. The same was true of Kenny

Gallagher's murder. Patrick could have done it, but even a Morrisey had better sense than to steal a dead man's horse, go drinking, and—what?

Nobody had heard him boasting of gunning down Kenny. Shad himself wasn't much of a braggart, but if he'd just killed a dedicated enemy of his kith and kin, he'd mention it. Maybe he wouldn't get drunk and shout out his evil deed, but surrounded by so many in a saloon he'd have said something. Someone would have peached on him if he had so much even hinted at killing Kenny Gallagher.

Patrick hadn't uttered a single word. And Shad found that peculiar.

"So we stand around and watch? Or can we get back into town and do our jobs?" Shannon took out a plug of tinfoil-wrapped chaw and bit off part of it. He worked aggressively, then spat. The brown gob arced high in the air and cleared the edge of the platform to vanish down onto the steel rails. If his words didn't tell Shad what the deputy thought, the action did.

"The feud's cooled off for a spell," Shad said. "Get on back to the jail and let Watt go home. I suspect that he's about beside himself by now with worry."

Shannon nodded once, spat again, and walked off. His boot heels clacked angrily as he left.

"That man's got quite a chip on his shoulder, don't he?" Leroy Early sat on a bench intended for waiting passengers. He broke open the shotgun left behind by Shannon and dropped in two shells. The sound of him closing the breach made Shad uneasy. Things were too quiet now, in spite of the noise made by the chuffing steam engine and the shouts to add water and get the train positioned for loading the coal.

"I'm going to talk to Sussman," the marshal said. He went into the depot. The agent was nowhere to be seen. In spite of the late hour, the telegraph key chattered out a message. Whatever it said was lost, or maybe it wasn't intended for the Utopia station.

He made his way down to the tracks and saw Sussman in the cab, talking with the engineer. As he approached, Sussman jumped to the ground.

"Glad you run off them danged fools shooting at one another," Sussman said.

Shad looked up at the engineer. The man adjusted his black and white striped cap and pointedly looked away.

"Paying off the crew?"

"You know what's going on, Marshal. It don't concern you none. This is what it takes to keep the train running and the good people of Utopia employed."

"Yeah," he said. "Most everyone in town depends on the railroad in one way or the other for a living." The ranches and few farms scattered on the slopes on either side of Hellfire Pass struggled because of the altitude to grow more than ankle-high grass. The heavy snows and long winters made most farming difficult compared to catering to the railroad passengers and crews.

"Glad we got that squared away," the agent said, relieved. He stepped back and yelled, "Finish getting that water dumped into the boiler. The coal's awaitin' and so's the train!"

Sussman walked away to talk with the crew riding in the caboose. Shad hiked around, found the ramp to the coal bin and made his way up. He was winded by the time he reached the fully loaded coal container. Arthur Brushwell snapped orders to a pair of men struggling to swing the chute around and align it with the rear of the tender car.

Brushwell glanced over his shoulder. "What do you want, Marshal? You're in the way."

Shad stood to the rear of the bin. Brushwell was acting peevish for no good reason.

"Those aren't Gallaghers, are they?" Shad asked.

"I had to hire 'em out of my own pocket. And you can tell they don't know the job." Brushwell shouted at the men to better align the chute with the back of the coal tender.

"But the Gallaghers loaded the bin?"

Brushwell glared at him and nodded sullenly. He turned back to the men he'd hired and gave more specific instructions. The workers swung the chute around and finally positioned it to satisfy the train's stoker. He half turned and motioned as if ordering a cavalry charge.

"The train crew's satisfied you dolts finally got it right. Let 'er slide," Brushwell ordered.

The workman pulled a rope attached to a pulley and opened the chute door, The coal grated against itself and the chute before tumbling downward. Bit by bit the tender was filled. The man grappling with the chute moved it to keep from dumping the coal onto the ground. When the bin came up empty, the coal tender was close to three-quarters full.

"Good work, men. Get on home. Take some time off. Don't bother coming in until nine." Brushwell stepped back to let the pair pass. They were covered in coal dust from head to toe. He avoided most of the soot, as befit the owner of the freight yard.

"Looks like there should be more coal in the tender," Shad said.

"They got what they always do," Brushwell said. "The stoker and the engineer are happy."

"Not disputing that," Shad said. He dropped into the bin. The top plank on the side about matched his height.

He climbed out and ignored Brushwell's attempt to get him away from the bin. Shad dropped outside and had to look up. There was a good foot, maybe more additional height. Measure on the outside, get a different volume than what was loaded inside.

"It's been a long and tiring night, Marshal. I'm glad the Gallaghers and Morriseys finally stopped killing each other in my yard, no thanks to you. I don't even mind having to oversee the loading myself."

"I talked with Leadbottom. Then I went to talk to Winifred

about the feud." He watched Brushwell closely for any reaction when he mentioned Winifred.

"You need them talking to each other." Brushwell shook his head. "Shouting at each other's still better than shooting it out. How're you fixing to get them together for a peace talk?"

"There might be something else to take care of before that happens."

"What?" Brushwell asked suspiciously. He moved his coattail back.

"Cheating the railroad might not be a crime under my jurisdiction," Shad said, "but the owners of the line might find it worrisome how you're cheating them."

"You can't prove a thing, Marshal." Brushwell pulled back his coat even more. He wore a Colt in a shoulder rig like some tinhorn gambler.

Shad tapped the side of the bin.

"I'm not much of a carpenter but whoever built this was a lot worse at measuring than I am."

"Now, now, Marshal, you spoke the truth when you said this was out of your jurisdiction. What you should worry about is keeping the peace in Utopia and not letting a ferocious blood feud spin out of control."

"How do you suggest I do that, Mister Brushwell?"

"Your salary, Marshal. If I recollect, it's only a dollar a day or thereabouts."

"Thereabouts," Shad agreed.

"That's hardly enough for a man with a family to support."

Shad sucked in his breath and held it. His anger rose at mention of his family. Brushwell knew that Ruth and Miriam had gone to Denver. Everyone in Utopia did. And he certainly knew Abe had been killed. The crime had happened in the man's own freight yard.

The train whistle drowned out any possible reply Shad might have made. The metal screech of steel grinding against steel signaled that the train was pulling out. By the time the peaceful night had been restored, Shad had cooled down.

Brushwell turned and made his way down the earthen ramp. Shad followed to the bottom. Brushwell turned and faced him. The man's face was cloaked in shadow so Shad wasn't able to see his expression.

"A few dollars might come your way if you don't mention the coal bin to anyone working for the railroad."

"A few?"

"Ten dollars a month goes a long way toward getting back into the good graces of a truant wife, I suspect."

Chapter Thirty-Four

Shadrach Nelson plodded along, feet as heavy as any of the lead bricks Leadbottom Morrisey shipped to Denver. He slowed, then stopped to look at his jailhouse. *His* jail. He locked prisoners up inside, and he was as surely a prisoner as they were.

He pushed open the door. Ian Shannon sat at the desk, his arms folded and his head using them as a pillow. When the door closed, the deputy came awake, hand going to his six-gun. He blinked a couple times, then growled.

"Oh, it's only you."

"Yup, only me," Shad said. "The one who's relieving you. Clear out. Get some sleep in a real bed, and I don't mean on a cot in the back."

Shannon stretched. His day-old stubble looked like rusty wires. Bloodshot eyes and a paleness unusual even for the Irishman completed the picture of someone ready to up and die.

"Watt did a good job guarding the two weasels in the back," Shannon said. "You ought to give him a dollar or two for his service in the name of law and order." The sentiment was right but the way he said it turned bitter. It fit with Shannon's usual demeanor.

"I'll see what the mayor says. Maybe I can wrangle a bonus for you and Leroy, too."

"When hell freezes over," Shannon said. "But don't you dare not try." He settled his Stetson squarely on his head and left without another word.

Shad felt the need to argue with his deputy that things weren't so bad. Only they were. Rather than ask the mayor for a bonus, he needed another deputy. Two more would be better with the way the feud between one side of the pass and the other was building. The exchange of lead last night had been all sound and fury with nothing happening.

Nothing except for Winifred Gallagher being shot down. Shad sat and rocked back. He yawned. He needed sleep, too, but he might as well stay in the jail as wrangle someone to watch over things while he slept. There wasn't any reason for him to go home. It was cold and empty.

For two cents, he'd quit and go to Denver to convince Ruth she'd walked out on him for no reason. But he knew that wasn't true. She had good reasons. He tapped the badge pinned on his vest. That was the real reason. The way things boiled over in the cooking pot that was Utopia meant he had to put in long hours. If he didn't, citizens died.

"Like Winifred Gallagher," he said to himself.

A quick look into the cellblock assured him his prisoners were still secure. Both snored softly. Anderson Morrisey was a wastrel and would come to a bad end eventually. But Patrick Morrisey? Rage built inside as he stared at the sleeping prisoner. He was sure he had shot Abednego, but evidence kept mounting that he was innocent.

"Not innocent, no, not that," he said, shaking his head. It felt as if nuts and bolts came loose inside. A headache grew and his vision blurred. Somewhere behind his eyeballs a cowpoke rode them like a bronco, using his Spanish rowel spurs to create wild bucking.

Shad closed the door between the cells and his office. He turned and jumped when he faced a pair of masked owlhoots with levelled pistols.

"We've come for 'em," one said, the bandanna over his mouth muffling his voice.

"You boys ought to know it's a crime to bust prisoners out of the calaboose," he said. "But then you two think wearing masks hides your identity."

They exchanged quick looks. He saw their eyes go wide in fear.

"Tell Leadbottom to come talk to me himself. You'll only get yourself in hot water waving your pieces around like this."

"We've come for 'em. Open their cells," demanded one.

"Nathaniel—that is you, isn't it, Nate?—will only get your half-brothers into more trouble. They'll be fugitives from justice rather than suspects."

"There's the keys, Nate," said the other one. He gulped when he realized he had verified the marshal's guess as to their identities.

"The way it stands, I couldn't round up a posse if I offered ten dollars a day and all the whiskey they could swill. Not for what Andy and Pat are charged with. But breaking out of jail? I'd have my pick of posse then."

"You got Patrick for killin' that cross-eyed fool Kenny Gallagher. That's a big charge."

"It is, Nate, it is. But half the town sides with your pa. Some folks think Kenny had it coming, and I don't blame them. I'm of that persuasion myself."

"Then why won't you let Patrick go?"

"Evidence against him has to be presented in a court. A judge and jury'll say whether he done the deed. Now, just put away your six-guns and get yourself some breakfast. If you were trading lead last night with the Gallagher boys over at the freight yard, you've worked up a powerful hunger."

"I am kinda peckish, Nate."

They half turned and whispered furiously. Shad took no pleasure in convincing them to leave. Neither man seemed right in the head. For all that hardly any of the Morrisey family did much more than react when faced with a problem. Only Leadbottom was a thinker and a planner. Him and maybe his son, Patrick, and Shad wasn't too sure about Patrick.

"We gotta get 'em out of jail."

"If I had to guess, you came up with this on your own. Leadbottom doesn't know a thing about it."

"How'd you—?" He grunted when Nathaniel poked him in the ribs with his elbow.

"We're clearin' out. You don't try to follow us. You hear?" Nathaniel Morrisey waved his six-shooter around.

"I hear you as loud and clear as a mountain lark," he said. Shad watched the two crowd through the door at the same time and run off. He shook his head. Crooks and thieves and scoundrels in Utopia weren't as good as in other towns.

Here they needed the head of their family to tell them what to do. Either Leadbottom hadn't had time to think about breaking his boys out of jail or he had enough sense left to let the court do it for him. Andy had even asked to stay in jail since he got fed, had a better bed and wasn't in the galena mine twelve hours a day swinging a pick.

The circuit judge had to arrive sooner or later. Until then, the town fed and sheltered two of Leadbottom's offspring.

Shad's belly growled at the thought of breakfast. Feeding the prisoners was a necessary evil, too. He made sure the door leading to the cells was locked, then left. It'd only take a few minutes to grab enough grub for himself and his two prisoners. Barely twenty yards away, he paused, then stopped, turned, and went for his six-gun. The two masked men he had chased out a few minutes ago had returned.

"Don't you think about it, Nate!" he bellowed. Eyes fixed on the two Morriseys, he didn't see three more men coming at him.

Bullets flew and broke a plate-glass window in Sampson's store. Shad spun, going into a crouch. He fanned off three quick shots at the trio who thought to ambush him. His rounds went wide, just as theirs had. The lead tore up a wall behind them.

In the confusion, Nate Morrisey swung his gun around and fired wildly. The three who had attacked Shad turned their fire on Nate.

The street filled with death as bullets flew all over. The storekeepers slammed their doors and tried to stay out of the fight, but one or two ventured out.

"Back!" Shad shouted. "Get under cover!"

His warning drew fire from both the three gunmen and Nate. He took better aim and got off a round. The smallest of the trio yelped. Shad recognized him then. Not only did he have to deal with Nate Morrisey and his partner trying to spring Andy and Patrick, he had three wild-eyed Gallagher gunmen trying to put holes in him.

"I got 'em, Marshal. Keep yer ever lovin' head down!"

"Don't, Mister Sampson. Don't!" The warning came too late. The general store owner opened up with both barrels on his sawed-off shotgun.

Shad flinched when one pellet grazed him. The rest tore through the air in the direction of the Gallagher boys. He emptied his Peacemaker and, as he reloaded, Sampson cut loose with more buckshot. This routed the Gallaghers. They turned tail and ran for their lives.

He was distracted but only for an instant. Riders galloped away in a cloud of dust that obscured the front of the calaboose.

"There's a jailbreak," Shad called to Sampson. "Watch the street, but be careful who you're shooting."

The storekeeper growled a reply, obviously mad that he wasn't praised for his civic duty. Shad ran to the jail and kicked open the door. A quick glance told him he was too late. Nate and his relative had sprung the prisoners.

Shad sagged in defeat. It had been one of those nights. Now it was turning into one of those days. He left the jail to find his two deputies. Early wouldn't complain, but he expected as much of a fight out of Shannon as he'd already faced.

He couldn't blame him. For a plugged nickel he'd throw his badge on the desk and walk away. But later. After he recaptured Patrick and Anderson Morrisey.

Chapter Thirty-five

"I oughta quit. I've been thinkin' on it." Ian Shannon slumped in the saddle. "There's no end to this feud."

"The town needs you, for a while longer," Shad said. Seeing this had no effect on his dog-tired deputy, he added, "I need you." He said nothing more. His eyes met Shannon's. The anger there faded into resignation. That was good enough.

For now.

"I'll keep folks all tamped down in town," Shannon said. "Later, we gotta talk." He rode away slowly, looking left and right, forcing himself to be alert. With both the Gallagher clan and the Morriseys shooting at anything that moved, he was a likely target because he wore a badge.

"He won't quit. He likes to hear you say nice things about him too much." Leroy Early snapped the reins on his horse and took off at a trot. Shad hurried after him.

"He's talked about it enough times that I have to believe him. Since Abe was killed, we've all been working more 'n we should."

"That's part of it, Shad. Only three of us to keep the peace is pushing us to the end of our rope, but Shannon's gettin' itchy feet. This is longer 'n he's been any one place in years."

"Do you think he wants to try his hand at being a

prospector? There's always a new strike on the western slopes. He sounds kinda wistful when he talks about being a prospector."

"Blackhawk, Central City, I've heard tell that Leadville and Cripple Creek might have even bigger strikes." Early shrugged. "Shannon might fancy bein' all alone, him and a mule, the chance of becomin' filthy rich just around the next bend. More likely, he just wants to drift on."

Shad thought on that. Shannon was smart enough to know that prospectors seldom struck it rich. It was a lonely existence, out poking around the hills hunting for just the right kind of rock. Blue clay was hard to find. Gold nuggets in that blue dirt were even rarer.

If Shannon left, it'd put even more weight on his shoulders. As long as Early remained, there wasn't any way he could take a powder and leave, even to go to Denver to get Ruth to come back to home and hearth. Dumping the weight of all his responsibility on the man's shoulders was cruel. Early was a good deputy. There wasn't a snowball's chance in hell he'd work out well as a marshal because he lacked the temperament.

They came to the edge of town. The road leading up the northern side of the pass toward the Morrisey lead mine stretched away, empty as a whore's heart. Seeing nothing made Shad uneasy. He'd ridden this road often enough to know every turn gave a perfect spot for an ambush.

"Unless your eyes are better 'n mine, Shad, I don't see signs anyone's come this way. Not in the last day or two."

"The road's so rocky, it's hard to tell unless you find fresh horse flop. There's no dust to leave tracks."

"I don't cotton much to ridin' further. This skin of mine is old and wrinkled, but it's not got any extra holes in it." Early glanced at him and touched his hat, reminding Shad how many holes he had in his brown bowler. It was reaching the point where it was more bullet hole than cloth.

"After last night's fight, that counts as a miracle." Shad

saw a tiny dust devil swirl around, blowing a coffee-colored column ten feet into the air. It died as quickly as it formed. A lizard scooted across the road just in front of his horse's hooves. And the road seemed to stretch miles and miles farther. Reaching Leadbottom's cabin without getting shot out of the saddle seemed a pipe dream.

"You find yourself a spot to watch. No need to go after Andy and Patrick. If they've already gotten to their mine, ferreting them out isn't going to be easy."

"And if they ride up, there's a chance we can nab 'em."

Early nodded slowly. "I like this plan of yours, Shad. It makes sense."

"It makes sense in that it'll keep us both alive awhile longer." He settled the bowler on his head, then said, "I'm going to hunt for them somewhere else, if they haven't run back to papa."

"There's a lot of Leadbottom to run to," Early said. "Where are you going?"

Shad looked toward the rail yard.

"Don't waste too much time here, Leroy. If they haven't come by noon, go on back to the jailhouse and see how Shannon's doing."

"The noon train whistle'll give me a good signal. My watch got broke."

"It never kept good time," Shad said. "I'll see if the mayor will foot the bill to get it repaired."

"Replaced is more likely. It stopped a bullet meant for my belly."

Shad laughed and made a comment about it not being Early's time but was his timepiece's. He turned his horse toward the railroad depot and worked down the incline to the main road that ran alongside the tracks. Since the train had come through, there wasn't much traffic along that road. Egan only handled one or two stagecoaches a week now. He had handled all the telegraphy traffic until the railroad strung wire alongside the tracks and took even this small business away. For all Shad knew, the telegraph in the stage office wasn't connected to anything now.

With progress, some things prospered and some things died. He had the feeling he was numbered among the latter and had been ever since he found his son in the freight yard.

He reached the railroad depot with fifteen minutes to spare before the train arrived. Shad circled the building, keeping a sharp eye out for any hint that Patrick Morrisey intended to jump the train and get away. Nothing about Patrick struck him as courageous. He had lived under Leadbottom's thumb all his life and had any gumption squashed out like a bug under a boot heel, but the threat of going on trial and maybe being sentenced to getting your neck stretched changed a man.

Patrick Morrisey might chose to do something bold. That made him all the more dangerous.

Satisfied that Morrisey wasn't hiding out anywhere close, Shad dismounted and climbed the steps. Sussman hunkered down over the telegraph key, sending as fast as he received. When the clacking stopped suddenly, Sussman leaned back and wiped sweat from his forehead.

"You come here to greet 'em, Marshal?"

Shad had no idea what the agent meant and said so.

"The boss in Denver answered my call for help. There's a company of bulls on the train. Yes, sir. A whole danged company of 'em come to protect railroad property."

"I hadn't heard," Shad said.

"You're fessing up to not knowing what's going on in your own town, eh? Figures." Sussman stood and rounded the counter to stand near the marshal. "You should give up that badge and let the railroad coppers keep the peace."

"I do the job I'm paid to do."

Sussman snorted in contempt and went back around the counter when the telegraph began chattering away.

Shad stepped out onto the platform, then froze. Movement across the rail yard caught his eye. He made sure his gun slid easily from his holster, then took the steps down to ground level two at a time in his hurry to narrow the distance between him and Patrick Morrisey.

The fugitive twisted in and out between the tall mountains of coal, then disappeared. Shad looked around, desperation growing when he failed to see Morrisey. Sussman's accusations rang in his ears. Maybe he wasn't cut out for the job any longer. If the railroad brought in their army of armed agents, they could do a better job of enforcing the law than he ever could. The blood feud between the two mountain families was something that needed an army to extinguish.

Shadrach Nelson and two disheartened deputies hardly counted.

Cursing, he climbed up a hill of coal and reached the top. From this vantage point, he had a better look at not only the coal yard but the rest of the freight being readied for shipment. Some of that was Morrisey lead bricks. Other crates had been marked for shipment. Shad had no idea what those were—still more evidence that he wasn't aware of important things in Utopia.

Turning slowly, he scanned the rail yard. Nothing. He retraced the areas already scouted and then caught his breath.

"Morrisey!" He almost shouted out the name. If he had, he would never have caught the fugitive. Shad slid down the coal and landed hard. He tried to keep Morrisey in sight but lost him when he ducked into a wooded area beyond the coal yard.

This was all Brushwell's land. He had fought to keep the small stand of trees when everyone in town needed wood for heating and cooking. Letting the urchins steal lumps of coal for their families had preserved the pines. The next stand of any size grew much higher on the sides of Hellfire Pass. The railroad had used up plenty of wood for ties. Both the Gallagher and Morrisey clans had taken all the trees they needed for support beams in their mines. The Morriseys used wood to heat and cook but the Gallaghers chiseled the lumps of coal from their own Calcutta Mine.

He put down his head and ran for all he was worth. Shad reached the edge of the wooded area and slowed. Crashing through the undergrowth like a raging bull only made it possible for an ambush to take him out. Shad slipped from tree to tree, trying not to make any sound as he moved.

Voices reached him. Angry voices. The argument silenced the usual sounds of small animals and even wind moving through the upper tree branches. Shad moved more confidently now. If the two were occupied arguing, they weren't paying attention to see if anyone sneaked up on them.

In a small clearing he saw Patrick Morrisey waving his arms around. The broad-shouldered man blocked the identity of whomever he argued with. Then he stepped to one side.

"Beatrice Gallagher!" Shad wasn't surprised. He slipped his gun from his holster and stepped out.

The twenty-yard distance made for a hard shot, so he wanted to edge closer to make it more likely he hit Morrisey and not Beatrice. His luck ran out fast.

"Pat!" Beatrice shoved Morrisey to the side. "Run!"

"Give up, Patrick! We've got you surrounded!" Shad fired into the air, then leveled his Peacemaker. Beatrice grabbed her lover's shirt and pulled him toward the far side of the clearing.

A second shot whined toward Morrisey and missed as he dodged. Then he vanished into the woods at the far side of the clearing.

"Where'd he go?" Shad demanded of Beatrice. But the woman lit out in a different direction. He started to take a shot at her, then lowered his pistol. Beatrice claiming he had killed her aunt was bad enough. There'd never be peace in Utopia if he shot Beatrice.

Cursing, he crossed the clearing, intent on finding Patrick Morrisey. He plunged into the copse and stopped dead in his tracks when he came across a game trail. There might be a boot heel print in the dirt. Or there might not. He looked the other direction along the winding trail and thought he saw another footprint. Then he realized he had no idea where the tracks led—if they even were boot prints.

He had lost his escaped prisoner again.

Dejected, he returned to the clearing. Tracking Beatrice was similarly impossible. Before he decided to do something stupid like continuing after Beatrice, the train whistle let out three quick hoots. Above the treetops he saw a huge pillar of black smoke, warning that the train had arrived.

He slammed his six-gun into his holster and stomped back through the rail yard and climbed the steps once more to the depot. The train screeched to a halt. Two passenger cars suggested several dozen railroad bulls had been sent to protect railroad interests in Utopia.

The rush of men exiting the cars never happened. Shad frowned. Sussman must have been wrong about this being the train carrying the railroad detectives. Then he went cold inside. One man stepped from the train, hitched up his gun belt and looked straight at Shad.

He touched the brim of his hat in acknowledgment and then slowly came toward Shad.

Richard Williamson had returned to Utopia.

CHAPTER THIRTY-SIX

"You're the railroad detective," Shad said in a wooden voice.

"Yes, sir, I am. They asked me to be a Deputy Federal Marshal again but that job'd take me away from home for too long."

"Home?"

"Miriam hasn't told you?" Williamson scowled. "I reckon it's up to her to let you know."

"Riding shotgun messenger with the stage company wasn't a way to rob them, was it?"

"No, sir. It wasn't much of a job but was all I had offered since nobody in Utopia knew me then."

"You think they will now?"

Williamson looked past Shad. Both Sussman and Brushwell came over. They walked in step, soldiers marching to a drumbeat only they heard. Both whispered at the same time until they got closer.

Brushwell pushed past Shad and thrust out his hand. Williamson shook it. Shad was amused that the boy's powerful grip was almost too much for Brushwell. When he retrieved his hand, he rubbed it against his leg, not to get dirt off but to regain circulation.

"The troubles we're having here are beyond the marshal's

ability to deal with. I'm glad the railroad's sent a real troubleshooter."

"Well, sir, I'm sure Marshal Nelson can handle whatever comes his way. The boss in Denver wanted me to be sure that the weekly coal shipments weren't disrupted. From reports, pitched gunfights in the coal yard make folks a trifle uneasy."

"He was supposed to send a company of bulls. You're scoutin' for the rest, right?" Sussman tentatively offered his hand and received the same bone-crushing grip. He wasn't able to hide the discomfort as well as the freight yard owner.

"No call to roust out so many detectives, Mister Sussman. I must say, though, that your description of all the woe piled onto this station produced a chuckle or two. Nobody in the home office has heard such language before. You're a regular Frank Reade, yes sir, you are."

"It's not made up. It all happened."

Williamson laughed and looked around.

"I see a bullet hole or two that needs repairing. I can do that in my spare time. I'm handy that way."

"That's not why you're here," Brushwell snapped. "We've got two families feuding and the town's caught in the middle."

"This *depot* is caught betwixt the Gallaghers and Morriseys," Sussman cut in. "That's all that should interest you."

"It does, Mister Sussman." Williamson turned when a carpetbag dropped onto the platform. Next to it was a round box all tied up with brown string. He waved to the conductor. "Looks as if the train is ready to pull out. You do load the coal and water in a timely fashion. Why, we've only been here talking a minute or two it seems."

"I got a passenger to sell a ticket to," Sussman said. He turned and stopped. At the other end of the platform Jeremiah Jones took his time drawing his six-shooter.

"Down!" Shad collided with Sussman and Brushwell, knocking them off the platform. They fell near the tracks, narrowly avoiding the slowly turning steel wheels as the train pulled out on its way westward.

Shad cleared leather and took a shot at Jeremiah. It went wide. Jones fanned off three fast shots and then dropped to one knee, taking careful aim.

"You done kilt Winifred. You're gonna die, Nelson." He loosed two more rounds.

Williamson turned sideways, put his left fist on his hip, drew his piece and took careful aim as if he engaged in some affair of honor duel. Jeremiah Jones yelped and dropped his six-gun. Shad got off another shot but missed. Williamson took another shot, but Jones flopped face down and mysteriously slid backwards on his belly off the platform.

Shad rushed to the end of the platform, Williamson beside him. Two other Gallagher boys had grabbed Jones by the ankles and yanked him to safety. All three hightailed it away, screaming curses and how they intended to bring Shad to justice for murdering Winifred.

"Things around here are certainly . . . unsettled," Williamson said. He returned his pistol to his holster. "What'd they mean that you killed Winifred?"

"They're mistaken," Shad said.

"That's certainly not the first time those boys have been wrong, I reckon."

"And it won't be the last." Shad took time to reload. By the time he finished both Sussman and Brushwell had returned to the platform looking the worse for their adventure.

"This is the last straw that broke the camel's back, Nelson. Resign. Turn in your badge," Brushwell demanded. He plucked a cinder from his cheek. The fiery crescent-shaped wound began to ooze blood.

"Yes, he's right. Arthur's right. Quit. You being marshal makes the violence worse," Sussman added. "You're not stopping it, you're causing it!"

"There's no call for the marshal to turn in his badge," Williamson cut in. "Instead of reducing the number of law dogs in Utopia, you ought to be adding to them. That's why you asked the home office for a detective to come here, isn't it, Mister Sussman?"

"You butt out, boy," Brushwell said angrily. He immediately regretted it. Williamson stepped so close their chests bumped. Brushwell's anger flared. "You can't take his part just because you and his whore daughter—"

Williamson hardly moved. He arched his back slightly, bumped chests and sent Brushwell staggering. The man barely regained his balance before he tumbled off onto the tracks again. Glaring, he climbed to his feet, whirled around and stormed off.

"He didn't mean anything by that," Sussman said uneasily. He faced two stony faced men with steady hands resting on their revolvers.

"I'm not quitting," Shad said.

"And you won't have anything to worry about when the train comes for a full load of coal. I'm told the Denver yard wants five full coal cars this time. The line's expanding north to Laramie, doubling the schedule in that direction. The extra coal will be necessary until mines at Powder River start producing."

"I, uh, I'll be sure Arthur's got the coal ready. And that the Gallaghers mine plenty for the railroad. You won't be disappointed, Williamson. Not at all." Sussman hurried away, muttering to himself. A minute later the clack-clack of the telegraph key sounded.

"I don't know what he's sending, but I'd bet it's a message to the Denver office about you." Shad looked as if he had bitten into a bitter persimmon.

Williamson cocked his head to one side. His lips moved just a little. They stopped when the telegraph message ended.

"I heard what he sent, and it's not just about me, sir." Williamson touched the brim of his hat and strode off.

Shad wasn't sure if he appreciated the help Richard

Williamson offered. What was certain, he didn't have any say-so about it.

"They'll shoot your fool head off, Shad." Leroy Early scratched his chin and shook his head slowly. "I can't see any way it won't end up like that."

"The town's on tenterhooks. Nobody wants to go on living like this, jumping at every sound and always looking over your shoulder waiting for someone to shoot you in the back."

"Which of the preachers do you want to say words at your funeral? Father Ignacio's got a good sermon about sin and guilt, but then he's Catholic so you'd expect that. You might ask Reverend Jakes for his damnation special. It's a barnburner, so to speak. I've heard it a couple times."

"You're getting to be as ornery as Shannon."

"I might be as melancholy, but I sure am a lot more handsome."

Shad smiled. It was the first time in days since he had anything to be lighthearted about. The Morriseys had pulled back to their lead mines in the hills, but only because Beatrice had taken over from her aunt and had declared Shad to be their worst enemy. Leadbottom was happy enough to let Beatrice remove the marshal for him. When Shad was dead and buried, the town would be free for the taking.

Or so they thought.

Shad had watched as Williamson went about his job at the rail station. Never straying far from the tracks, the young man managed to find out more of what happened in Utopia than Shad and both his deputies.

The only way Shad saw to break free was to catch Patrick Morrisey and lock him up again for killing Kenny Gallagher. And somehow, some way, he'd find how Abe had taken three bullets while prowling around Brushwell's freight yard.

"Patrick Morrisey is the key to this," he said.

"You're back to that, are you? I swear, Shad, you've got a one track mind. Not that I mind, you understand," Early said quickly. "Abe's dead and all and that's an unsolved crime."

"Patrick Morrisey," Shad repeated. "He and Beatrice are sneaking around to be together."

"You're still sure she killed her aunt?"

"There're enough bodies to hang the lot of them. The longer they get away with it, the worse it'll be for Utopia."

"And you. You've heard the gossip, same as me. Folks are coming around to thinkin' like Brushwell and Sussman. Get rid of you and all their troubles go away. That's what they think."

"It's time to prove the gossipmongers wrong." He headed out the door.

"Don't get yourself killed, Shad. The mayor'd want me to pin on your badge. There's no way I want to be marshal in this town."

Shad smiled again and felt better than before. But when he stepped out, he didn't expose himself by walking into the middle of the snaking, sinuous Main Street. He pressed his back against the jailhouse wall and hunted for sign of an ambush. It wasn't hard to find. He caught the glint of sunlight off a rifle barrel from across the street.

He edged around the building, then dashed to circle it so he came up on the far side in time to spot one of the younger Gallagher boys crouched behind a water barrel, rifle resting on top to steady his aim. Stepping carefully, he sneaked up behind the boy.

He let out a loud, "Boo!" Gallagher jumped a foot, fumbled and dropped his rifle, then saw the marshal had caught him. Before the youngster had a chance to run, he found himself lifted off the ground. His boots kicked at the dust as

Shad hauled him up and dropped him over the water barrel where the rifle had rested seconds earlier.

"You tell Beatrice that I want to talk to her. You find out when and where, let me know and I'll be there."

"She don't want to talk to you. She wants you dead!" The boy squirmed. Shad pressed down and held him across the top of the barrel. With a little pressure he might break the boy's back. That was better than drowning the rat in perfectly good rainwater.

"A powwow. That's all. You go tell her that right now."

Shad released his captive. The boy dropped to hands and knees. He reached for his rifle, but Shad stepped down on the stock to prevent him from retrieving it. A feral growl escaped the boy's lips, then he scrambled to his feet and took off running.

Beatrice was sending them out younger and younger to kill him.

His horse stood beside the jailhouse. Shad vaulted into the saddle and trotted after the fleeing boy. Since he didn't go directly for the road from Utopia leading up to the Calcutta Mine, he knew where Beatrice was in town. In a flash, so did Shad. The boy ran pell-mell for the rail yard.

Beatrice was nothing if not consistent. Shad suspected she was hiding out near the clearing where he had seen her last with Patrick. If luck finally stood at his shoulder, he had a chance of catching Patrick with her.

The Gallagher snoop headed straight into the woods. Shad circled and came up on the back where Beatrice would try to escape up the mountain to the Gallagher claim. He hit the ground, ran a few steps, then let the reins drop. There wasn't time to secure the tether. He wanted to catch Patrick with Beatrice, if the Morrisey scion was here with her.

Angry voice made him walk faster through the trees. He hid behind a pine tree leaking sap from a spot where a woodpecker had hammered away at the bark. In the clearing where he had seen them before, Beatrice and Patrick stood close, arguing again. He wondered how they ever got any loving done since all he had seen was the pair of them shouting at one another.

The Gallagher boy stood a few feet away, staring at the two, his eyes wide with surprise. That the two supposed enemies were so familiar with one another startled him.

"What if he didn't kill Winifred?" Patrick Morrisey tried to take Beatrice in his arms. She pushed him away angrily.

"The marshal's got to pay. He shot her down like a rabid dog."

"I couldn't get a good shot at him or I'd've done it, Bea. Honest," the boy said. He lied through his teeth. He had chickened out but wasn't able to tell the new matriarch of the Gallagher family.

"He'll get what's coming to him soon enough," Beatrice said. She turned to Patrick. She poked him in the chest with her index finger and forced him back a pace. "You're a disgrace. You should have done it by now."

"Done what?" the boy asked, looking from Beatrice to Patrick.

"He's my pa. I can't just walk up and plug him."

"You were gonna kill your own pa?" The boy's eyes went wide. "That's even nervier than gunnin' down the marshal. Why'd you want to do that? I mean, I'd do it 'cuz I'm a Gallagher and we hate all you Morriseys, but you'd kill your own pa?"

"You get on back home," Beatrice said to the boy, never taking her eyes off Patrick. "Skedaddle!"

"But, Bea, I wanna—" His shoulders sagged, and he turned when he saw how determined she was.

Shad waited to hear more between the two illicit lovers now that a witness had been sent away. Beatrice wanted Patrick to kill Leadbottom. That'd make the two of them head of their respective families. From the way Patrick deferred to Beatrice, that'd make Beatrice Gallagher the head of both families.

That notion chilled Shad. If Patrick killed his own pa and Beatrice married him, she'd control everything on both sides of Hellfire Pass. The families'd own the high ground and the only sources of income. The railroad needed the coal. Beatrice could dictate to the line as well as run both lead and coal mines. Patrick might seem to be the head of the merged family, but he wasn't man enough to stand up to Beatrice.

Shad began to wonder if any man was. She was a force of nature, sweeping through the pass and creating nothing but chaos as she went.

"There's been too much killing," Patrick said.

"The marshal's responsible for it all. He murdered Aunt Win and Kenny. For all I know he shot his own son."

"You know that's not so, Bea. *You* shot Abe. I was there. I saw you."

"Abe saw us. He'd blab it all over town that a Gallagher was sweet on a Morrisey. Our families would never allow us to stay together."

"If we'd left, we'd be married by now."

"Married," she said sarcastically. "Doing what? This way we own both mines. We're rich, Pat, rich! We wouldn't be on the run and disgraced in the eyes of our own families."

"You think the marshal killed Winifred because you shot Abe?"

"I wouldn't put it past him," Beatrice said.

Shad slipped his six-shooter from its holster. He'd need a touch of luck to arrest them both. He had thought Patrick had gunned down Abednego, but with his own ears he had heard Beatrice confess. It had been a while since a woman got hanged for murder or anything else. He'd see to it that justice was done. Abe might not rest easier in his grave, but Shad would at night.

He stepped forward, lifting his pistol. Things went loco in a flash.

"You're never going to kill Leadbottom, are you?" Beatrice accused.

"I can't, my love. I can't turn on my own flesh and blood!"

"It's real easy. I know it is," she said.

Shad took aim at Patrick, then shifted his sights to Beatrice. She was the one he wanted to bring to trial for killing his son. As he did, a wild cry from across the clearing echoed as a half dozen of the Gallaghers rushed out, brandishing pistols and rifles.

"You're under arrest!" Shad cried. His words vanished in the roar of six-shooters discharging as the Gallaghers ran toward Beatrice and Patrick.

She pushed Patrick back. A derringer came into her fist.

"No!" Shad cried. Too late.

Beatrice fired both barrels into Patrick's chest. The man staggered away from her, clutching at two red, wet spots on his shirt.

The sight slowed Shad. He stared at Patrick, then reacted. Gun twisting around, he tried to get a shot at Beatrice. Her family surrounded her. For a moment, they milled like a confused crowd, then all retreated as if they had rehearsed the move. He never had a shot at her. Shad started to mow down as many of the Gallaghers as he could, but again his confusion slowed his trigger finger.

The woods swallowed them up.

Shad stood numb and then recovered. If the coal miners had spotted him, they'd have attacked. He was lucky in that respect. They outnumbered him and certainly outgunned him. The one who had tried to shoot him back in Utopia had fetched them to come to Beatrice's aid. Seeing her with the son of the Morrisey family's patriarch had to be a shock.

Steps slow, he went to the center of the clearing. He slipped his six-gun back into its holster and knelt beside Patrick Morrisey. The man's eyelids fluttered.

"I feel all wet inside. Things aren't right in my chest."

"She shot you," Shad said, taking no pleasure in tormenting Patrick.

"Her family came rushin' out. They'd've killed me if they found us together. I love her. She made it look like she'd killed me so they wouldn't. So they wouldn't . . ."

"She shot you," Shad repeated. "Let's get you to Doc Paisley. If you don't get those slugs yanked out quick, she'll have done more than shoot you. She'll have killed you."

"I love her," Patrick Morrisey said in a husky voice. He shuddered when Shad wrapped an arm around his shoulders and pulled him to his feet. Morrisey walked with surprising strength until they got to Shad's horse. He weakened then.

By the time they got to the doctor's surgery, Patrick Morrisey had passed out and wasn't in any condition to incriminate his lover in Abe's death.

Chapter Thirty-seven

"So that's how they're cheating the railroad out of money," Richard Williamson said, lips pursed and eyelids half closed in thought. "Can't say I'd ever have figured that out."

"You would have," Shad insisted. "If it wasn't the coal swindle that brought you, what did?"

"The railroad doesn't cotton to losing good mechanics. Two of them were killed."

"Murton and Abbott," Shad said.

"Them's the ones."

Shad told Williamson what he knew of their deaths. The railroad detective's eyes widened when he told how he had been one of the men enslaved and made to work in Leadbottom's mine.

"You got every right to plug him," Williamson said. "There's laws against that."

"It's my word against Leadbottom and his entire family. Without the bodies, there's no proof that Murton and Abbott didn't up and leave."

"From what I hear, Murton was a devoted family man."

Shad said nothing. Murton had been seduced by Beatrice Gallagher into believing things that weren't true. How much of that depended on her feminine wiles. How persuasive she was at inciting hatred was a poser. She had filled Murton with enough hate—increased his feelings toward

Shad—that he had willingly abandoned his family to commit murder.

Williamson let the silence drag on before continuing. "This feud isn't good for the town or the railroad."

"Which bothers you more?"

Williamson sucked his teeth as he considered. He finally came to a decision.

"The railroad pays my salary, but it's not right for the folks in Utopia to fear for their lives. What caused the feud?"

"Don't know, doesn't matter," Shad said. "What keeps it going is Beatrice Gallagher's need to run everything. It wasn't enough for her to put the entire Gallagher family under her heel. She wants to control the Morrisey lead mines and . . ."

". . . and Utopia. That's a mighty ambitious woman."

Shad fell silent, lost in thought. Beatrice was more than ambitious. She was smart. He'd never heard her actually say she'd murdered anyone, but Abe had ended up with two of her slugs in his chest.

"She shot my son," Shad said, "but Patrick Morrisey says she only used her derringer and didn't reload. The third shot is what killed Abe." He tapped the middle of his forehead to show where the deadly bullet struck Abednego.

"It could have been her putting two rounds into your son and Morrisey adding the killing shot."

"Only a man without a spine would do that. An evil son of a gun. Beatrice was powerful mad at him for being spineless. That makes me think his wasn't that third bullet."

"From what I've heard, that describes Patrick Morrisey. He's got a spine of oatmeal. A mushy man easily led astray."

"She might have told him to fire that third bullet, but I doubt it hit. I've seen him in gunfights. He gets so nervous his lead flies all over the place and never at what he's aiming at."

"That presents us with a question begging for an answer.

Who did fire that third bullet?" Williamson asked. "You got a suspect?"

"Doesn't matter what I think. There's no way to prove it." Shad drummed his fingers on his pistol butt.

"That sounds like most of the killings happening in these parts. I can't arrest Leadbottom or any of his men for killing Abbott and Murton. No witnesses that can't be impeached, no bodies, no proof. You think Beatrice Gallagher's responsible for shooting her aunt, and on Patrick Morrisey's shaky testimony, she shot Abe."

"But didn't kill him," Shad said in disgust. "According to Patrick Morrisey." His thoughts tumbled over and over and never came up with an answer.

"The way to solve this pile of crimes is to grab a thread and pull. As things unravel, maybe we'll get lucky and find out more about other crimes," Williamson said.

"We? You don't have any authority to arrest anyone. You work for the railroad."

"Sorry, sometimes I forget I'm not a federal deputy anymore. But the one thread you've been teasing that I can help on is the coal. That's [illegible] the railroad wants to stop."

"Sussman already told me his part in the scheme."

"Using him, we can find out what Brushwell knows and that's got to lead back to the Gallagher family."

Shad thought for a moment, then said, "Brushwell tried to buy me off. A nice little bribe if I looked the other way. That means he knows exactly what's happening with the coal."

"It makes sense that he's the one who thought it up. He's in position to cheat both the Gallaghers and the railroad." Williamson half drew his pistol, then let it drop back into his holster. It looked like an unconscious action on his part.

"Brushwell knows about the swindle, but does Beatrice? Winifred might not have twigged to what was happening, but Beatrice is a world smarter than her aunt," Shad said softly.

They sat in silence for a spell, each lost in his own thoughts. Shad finally pushed himself to his feet.

"Time's a' wasting." Shad paused, considering that he let Richard Williamson accompany him. He wasn't comfortable with the man as much because he had taken Miriam away as anything else. He felt Williamson was slowly pushing him out of his job as marshal.

Shad took a deep breath. Deeper, he resented Williamson still being in touch with Ruth when she wouldn't even acknowledge him.

They walked in silence to the railroad depot. Shad heard the click-click of the telegraph key before he mounted the steps and peered inside. Sussman hunched over the key, then picked up a pencil, wetted the tip and began scribbling when a new telegram rattled through.

"You can't tell what he sends," Shad said to himself. He had sent several telegrams to Ruth and never gotten a reply. Or had he? Sussman could ignore a reply. Or had he even sent Shad's begging to get back with his wife?

"I know Morse code," Williamson said quietly. He looked sheepish. "I've had a lot of jobs."

"Before the railroad hired you." Shad didn't conceal his contempt too well. Williamson sucked in his breath and held it as he tamped down his irritation at the implied criticism. Shad didn't care.

"You two bringing good news?" Sussman came over and looked from one to the other.

Shad thought the question carried a tone of anxiety, as if they had discovered something. Something more than the fraud going on with the coal shipments?

"Good news for us, not for others," Williamson said. Shad grudgingly appreciated how the railroad bull had picked up on Sussman's uneasiness. This fed the man's fear.

"You mean good news for the railroad," Sussman said. He licked his lips and looked around like a trapped rat. Shad moved to box him in. The railroad agent was caught between him and Williamson. He stepped closer to increase the dread.

"You already spilled the beans how you and Brushwell defraud the line," Shad said. "Wait!" He grabbed Sussman's arm and held him firmly. "Don't go running off like a scared rabbit."

"I know what he knows," Williamson said. "All I want is to stop the theft." He cleared his throat and added, "Or to keep it from getting worse. You take money from Brushwell. He looks like the middleman in this nobble."

Sussman nodded vigorously.

"I'm just looking the other way. It's Brushwell who's responsible. He collects the money and passes it out."

"What about the Gallaghers?" Shad wondered at the agent's reaction. The question confused him. "Was Winifred taking a cut of the money?"

"I never asked. It wasn't healthy for me to ask about things like that."

"Brushwell is the scoundrel I want," Williamson said.

"Let's arrest him," Shad said. He pressed the railroad agent against a wall. "We can rely on testimony against him, can't we?"

"Mister Sussman, as a loyal employee, will testify," Williamson said. "And he'll name all the engineers taking a bribe to ignore the empty coal tenders."

"They all had to know," Shad said. "Without a full tender, they needed to coast downhill in both directions to keep from running out of coal before they reached Denver or Georgetown, depending on which way they drove."

Sussman bolted when Shad released him. The marshal called out to Williamson, who had gone to the end of the platform. Williamson snared the running depot agent.

"You don't have anywhere to run," Williamson said softly. The words carried more menace than if he'd shouted them.

"What're you gonna do with me?"

"That depends on how useful you are," Shad said, coming

up behind. He laid his hand on Sussman's shoulder. The man flinched.

"I was sent to find what happened to Murton and Abbott," Williamson said. "Looks like I kicked over a rock and found a den of rattlers."

"The Morriseys killed them two." Sussman looked wild. "You know that, Marshal. Tell him."

"Brushwell," Shad said, imitating Williamson's soft tone. "You will testify against him?"

Sussman's head bobbed. Shad had pried the agreement from him before, but now he read determination not to lay down on the tracks and let the engine run over him—a locomotive run by Arthur Brushwell.

"He's out in the freight yard. He'll be getting the coal ready to ship to Denver, whenever that train shows up."

Williamson and Shad left the quaking station master behind quickly.

"He won't try to warn Brushwell, will he?"

Shad shook his head. Sussman was too scared now. It pained him to admit that he hadn't been able to put the fear into the man as well as Williamson had. The power of the railroad backed the detective. All Shad could do was throw Sussman in jail. The reins of power through Hellfire Pass were more obvious than ever to him.

They were all held by the railroad.

"There. He's got three men with him." Williamson reached for his six-shooter. Shad stopped him.

"Let me decoy them away. You can take Brushwell then. All I have to do is show my face."

"Those men are all Gallaghers?"

"And up there on the hill. That's Beatrice Gallagher. She's watching Brushwell like a hawk. That says they're all mixed up in the swindle. She's figured out what he's doing and has dealt herself into the game."

"I need Leadbottom and the Morrisey boys who killed my railroad mechanics."

"Tug on this thread and see what else unravels," Shad said, smiling grimly. He pointed out a route around a small mountain of coal where Williamson had a chance of getting the drop on Brushwell. The instant the railroad bull stepped out of sight, Shad rushed forward, pistol out.

"Grab a cloud," he bellowed. A quick glance toward the nearby hill convinced him that Beatrice had disappeared the instant he had come forward. She wanted no part in this.

"It's him. The marshal!"

Shad recognized the three Gallaghers but couldn't put names to their faces. The two closest went for their irons. He blazed away. Both sagged and sat heavily, clutching wounds in belly and shoulder. The third Gallagher dropped his six-gun and ran.

"Don't be stupid, Brushwell. We know everything." Shad turned his gun on the freight yard owner.

Brushwell turned white, then he went for the six-shooter in his shoulder rig. Shad fired and missed. He fired again, and once more his bullet went wide of its target.

By then Brushwell had his smoke wagon out and rolling along. Huge puffs of white smoke rose from the muzzle as he fanned off a quick series of rounds. Shad felt as if a horse kicked him in the chest. He took a step back, caught his heel, and fell.

"You're a dead man, Brushwell. I'm putting you under arrest for all you've done to the railroad."

Brushwell swung around and fanned off the rest of the rounds in the pistol's cylinder. Shad fired. The next time he pulled the trigger the hammer landed on a spent cartridge.

"You killed him!" Shad yelled, thinking Brushwell had mowed down Williamson.

"He found out," Brushwell cried. "He should never have turned down my bribe to keep quiet."

Shad fumbled at his gun belt to draw out six more rounds. His hands shook and his fingers felt like bloated sausages. When he sucked in a deep breath, the pain that shot through him almost made him pass out. Brushwell's bullet had smashed into the badge pinned on his vest, robbing the round of a kill. But a bit of lead and badge got embedded in Shad's flesh directly above his heart.

"Neither of you'd take a bribe. I had to kill him or he'd've arrested me. I have to kill you!"

More lead flew in Shad's direction. He rolled over and over, picking up cinders in his elbows and knees that hurt as badly as the bullet and torn metal badge in his chest. Somehow his bowler stayed squarely on his head.

He sat up and braced his hands on his upraised knees. The pall of gunsmoke made finding Brushwell hard.

Movement. He fired. And cursed. He wanted to hear a gasp as his bullet tore through Brushwell's putrid heart. Instead the echoes of pounding boots came to him. Brushwell was getting away.

He pulled himself to his feet and staggered along. A quick glance in the direction where Williamson should have stood to get the men in a crossfire failed to show a body. Finding whatever happened to the railroad bull had to wait. He had to run Brushwell to ground.

Rather than play hide and seek among the mounds of coal, Brushwell had run into the freight yard where the stacks of crates waiting to be shipped gave better cover. Panting harshly, Shad pressed against a pile at the edge of the yard. Blood pounded in his temples, making it hard to hear movement. Slow, deep breaths slowed the heartbeat thundering in his ears.

Quick looks on either side of the crates failed to show where his quarry had run. Going after him on the ground put him at risk for an ambush. Brushwell knew where all the freight was stacked and the best places to wait to take out his pursuer. Shad looked above him. The top of the pile was eight feet up. He took a step back, then jumped for all he was worth.

He caught the upper edge and almost released his hold

when his body crashed into the wood crate. The impact drove his badge deeper into his chest. The world spun wildly, but he held on, determined to catch Brushwell.

Catch him? Arrest him? Kill him?

Toes kicking at the side of the crates, he got a foothold and then pulled himself up. He flopped on the crates and had a better view across the freight yard. Again luck worked against him. Even from this elevation he couldn't find Arthur Brushwell. Gun gripped in his sweating hand, he walked slowly to the far end of the pile.

The aerial view wasn't good enough. Shad stepped back a couple paces, then ran for all he was worth, kicking hard to launch himself to the next pile. He crashed down, making such a clatter a deaf man couldn't miss it.

"I'm coming for you, Brushwell!"

"He would have died anyway. She shot him twice. I put him out of his misery."

Shad tried to make heads or tails of what Brushwell meant. All he knew was the direction of the man's confession. Brushwell's words acted as good as any compass needle. Trying to walk softly was a fool's errand. Speed mattered more now. Shad put his head down and thundered along the top of the crates, sending himself flying to the next stack.

In midair, he saw Brushwell on the ground. The man looked up in surprise. He swung his pistol up and fired. Shad was moving too fast. He got off a couple shots before he landed on the next crate. Taking the impact and rolling, Shad fell off the side and plunged downward. The ground came up fast, and he hit hard.

Blind determination kept him in the fight. He pressed into the stack and steadied his hand against the rough wood. The instant he spotted movement, he fired. The bullet ripped a deep groove in the wood before finding a target in Brushwell's leg. The cry of pure pain gave Shad newfound strength.

He used the crate as a support and got to his feet. A quick intake of breath and he spun around the edge of the box.

He fired without seeing a target.

He missed. And it didn't matter. Arthur Brushwell sprawled flat on his back, trying to stanch the blood spurting from his leg. Shad had cut an artery with his shot.

"Don't let me die. I had to do it. Don't let me bleed to death."

Shad kicked away the gun that fell from Brushwell's hand. It was soaked in the man's blood and would have jammed if the freight yard owner tried to fire it. He wanted to be sure he never got a chance.

"You killed my son?"

Anguished eyes looked up. Brushwell turned pale from shock and loss of blood.

"She shot him. She musta thought he was blackmailing them. That was me. Me." Brushwell flopped back.

"Her? Beatrice Gallagher? She and Patrick were being blackmailed?" Shad nodded. Beatrice would kill anyone threatening to reveal her affair with a Morrisey.

"I tried to collect from them. Nothing went right. Abednego shoulda taken my bribe. Got to their money 'fore me."

"Beatrice shot my son?"

"D-derringer. Hit here and here." He took his hands away from his leg wound and touched bloody fingers to his chest. "He shoulda taken my bribe. Don't know how he found out about the coal."

When Brushwell moved his hands from his leg to show where Beatrice had plugged Abe, the leg wound became a geyser.

"Simple plan. Nothing worked right. Nothing . . ." Brushwell's voice faded as the gushing blood from his leg became a trickle and then stopped. The freight yard owner lay staring up sightlessly at the blue sky.

Footsteps behind Shad made him whirl around and go

into a gunfighter's crouch. He had the hammer back and his finger on the trigger, ready to shoot when he saw Richard Williamson.

The railroad detective held up his hands in silent surrender. He looked past Shad at Brushwell on the ground.

For what seemed an eternity, they stood there, frozen like marble statues. Then Williamson lowered his hands slowly and came forward. He gently pushed Shad's six-shooter to one side. This broke the tension. Shad fell to his knees and lurched forward. Williamson caught him and kept him from collapsing onto his face in the dirt.

They remained in that mute pose until Early and Shannon came running up, guns drawn.

Chapter Thirty-eight

"Why so glum, Shad?" Leroy Early pulled up a chair and faced the marshal across his desk. "You found out who killed Abe."

"He's planted six feet under, too." Shadrach Nelson stared out the open jailhouse door into Utopia's twisty main street. Nothing seemed different now from four days earlier when he and Richard Williamson had shot it out with Brushwell and the Gallagher men who'd been working with him in the freight yard.

"And?"

"And I don't feel any better. There's still something missing."

"It might be that Abe was shot down by Bea Gallagher, and she's getting away with it because Brushwell fired the killing shot."

"I don't have any proof what she did now that Brushwell is gone."

"It was a real mess," Early said. "Brushwell was blackmailing her and Patrick, Abe picked up their money by mistake, Bea and Patrick shot Abe thinking he was onto them when it was really Brushwell they wanted to kill." He shook his head. "She's gonna get away with a powerful lot of crimes. Is that what's eating at you?"

"That might be it," he said. "Or maybe nothing brings

my son back. Brushwell paid for his crime as surely as if a noose had been dropped over his head. But Abe's still dead. Nothing changes that, even if Beatrice confessed and I sent her off to prison."

"Other things remain unresolved," Early said. He picked at his teeth with a splinter, then spat when a piece of lunch came free from between his front teeth. "The townsfolk ignore how the Gallagher and Morrisey boys take potshots at each other. Keeping them apart is a full-time job."

"She killed Winifred," Shad said. "I know it. She just about confessed, and there's nothing I can do about it."

"And Leadbottom and his kin done in them two railroad mechanics." Early tossed the toothpick out the door. "You learned something useful then, though."

"What?" Shad looked hard at his deputy. "What'd I learn?"

"You don't need to be a marshal. You can always go to work in a lead mine." Early chuckled, then stood. "I got to make the rounds."

"You wouldn't want that drink Missy sets at the end of the bar to evaporate, now would you?"

"She's a cute one, Missy is. Too bad she's taken. Anybody who so much as looks twice at her brings down the wrath of Ralph Rockwell on their heads."

"Settle for the free drink," Shad said, smiling in spite of his sour mood. "Maybe she'll take a liking to you and let you win a hand or two of faro."

"Free drinks is one thing, but cheating at faro?" Early shook her head. "Some folks in this town got scruples. Missy'd never cheat at gambling either for or against the house. It's not in her soul."

Early left. Shad glanced over his shoulder back into the cellblock. Three empty cages. He tried not to go down the list of people who ought to be locked up. Beatrice and Leadbottom and—

"You got a minute, Marshal?"

"Only a minute. You can see how busy I am." Shad pointed to the chair Early had just vacated. "Take a load off."

Richard Williamson settled down and said nothing for the span of several heartbeats, then, "I got 'em to agree to come to the depot. Both sides. At the same time."

Shad started to ask the railroad bull what he meant. Then he figured it out.

"How'd you get a Gallagher to talk to a Morrisey, ever? The only communication recently has been along the barrel of a gun."

"It took some doing," Williamson said. He smiled, just a little. "I told a whopper of a tale. Both of them bought it, hook, line, and sinker."

Shad waited to hear more. The youngster was good looking and personable. He had to give him that. It was easy to see why Miriam had fallen for him, but Shad had never figured out whether his daughter followed Williamson to Denver or if it was the other way around. It shouldn't matter, but it did.

At least he knew Williamson wasn't after Miriam for her money. There wasn't any.

Williamson cleared his throat and smiled a little more broadly.

"Yes, sir, it was a big tale. I told them if they didn't get together to talk with me at noon, that'd be the last train to ever come to Utopia."

"Do you have that authority?"

"I'm the low man on the totem pole, as a Nez Perce friend once told me. There's not much I can say to anyone in Denver that'd get listened to for longer than five seconds."

"Even after you cleaned up the fraud in the coal sales?"

"You got the credit for that."

"What do you mean?"

"I told the home office it was all your doing. Me, I was sent to find what happened to Murton and Abbott. I did that, even if the bodies aren't in graves I can find."

"So you arranged this powwow?"

"It'd be too easy for me to step onto the train and return to Denver. I don't want to leave them two families feuding. That's a headache you don't need, sir."

"I reckon I should thank you for the chance to settle the bad blood, but as you said, that's my problem. Not yours."

"I feel obliged. The chance presented itself, and I took it."

"Neither Beatrice nor Leadbottom would listen to you."

"I used Sussman as a middleman. He'll jump through hoops to keep his job. And," Williamson said, grinning crookedly, "I told him what the railroad does to employees who steal."

"Another whopper?"

"Just a tiny white lie. Hardly a fib."

"Your soul's going to get as tarnished as my badge." Shad pulled his vest away from his body. The wound under his shirt still hurt like the devil, though the doc had plucked out four or five pieces of the badge and a partially buried bullet. The blacksmith had done what he could to repair the badge, but it still had a tiny, ragged hole smack in the middle where the bullet had torn out the most metal.

"For a good cause," Williamson said. He looked at Shad. "You don't have any objections?"

"Why should I?"

"I don't want to step on your toes, sir."

"This isn't a square dance."

"Glad you feel that way." Williamson took out his pocket watch and peered at the face, then held it up so Shad could get a better look at the fancy watch. "It comes with the job. An engineer's timepiece. We need to get over to the depot."

"For the powwow," Shad said, heaving to his feet. "There hasn't been a palaver this important since Ouray broke off the fighting."

"I hope it turns out with as good a result." Williamson tucked the watch back into his vest pocket, took out his railroad detective's badge and pinned it on his coat lapel. "Adds some authority to whatever new lies I have to tell."

"Let me do the lying," Shad said. "I'm used to it. I haven't spent the past few years being a marshal without learning what it takes to soothe ruffled feathers."

The two walked to the railroad station side by side, not saying anything. As Shad began climbing the steps to the platform, a steam whistle sounded.

"Right on time. Noon," Williamson said. "And we're late to the meeting. Everyone else is here already." He touched the butt of his six-gun.

Shad doubted Williamson realized he had signaled how prepared he was if things went south. He checked his own Peacemaker. Just in case.

The lobby didn't have a line drawn down the middle dividing the two sides, but it may as well have. Beatrice Gallagher and three of her family pressed against the far wall. Leadbottom, Patrick, and another of the Morrisey clan leaned against the wall opposite. Straddling the invisible line in the middle of the lobby, Sussman shifted nervously from one foot to the other, as if changing loyalties repeatedly.

"Gentlemen," Williamson said to get their attention. He paused and touched the brim of his hat in Beatrice's direction. "That is to say, ladies and gentlemen, Mister Sussman has told you the railroad's position in your feud. Put bluntly, we will not let the train be caught in the middle of it."

"Then git them to leave Hellfire Pass," Leadbottom said. "They're the ones causin' all the trouble."

Shad watched Beatrice's reaction. She wasn't going to budge an inch. When he looked back at the Morriseys, he saw that Patrick's look of panic told how worried he was that Beatrice might be run off. How he could still love her after she'd shot him was beyond Shad's reckoning. But it gave a wedge between the Morriseys. Leadbottom and Patrick weren't united in the fight against the Gallaghers.

"The railroad will close this line. We've got Mosquito Pass and other ways to reach Central City from Denver."

"Them's longer routes," Leadbottom said. "And you'd need to reload coal somewhere along the way. The grades are steeper."

"All true, Mister Morrisey," said Williamson. "And if we shut down this depot, you'd have to go back to shipping your lead to Denver in wagons. How many mules does it take to pull just one of those wagons?"

"It's downhill. Not like we'd have to drag the dead weight upslope."

"Why not?" Beatrice said. "You got nothing but dead weight between your ears to drag around all day."

This provoked angry responses. Both sides moved toward the center until Williamson drew his pistol and fired it into the ceiling. Sussman protested such damage to railroad property. Williamson ignored him.

Shad listened to the ebb and flow of arguments. Williamson handled both sides fairly enough, though he showed bias against Leadbottom. The Morriseys had killed the railroad employees. He was less interested in what Beatrice did to her aunt than how Murton and Abbott's killers were brought to justice.

As Shad thought, Leadbottom denied any knowledge. He glanced somewhat fearfully in the marshal's direction, then looked away.

They were all guilty as sin. And Shad wasn't likely to be able to do anything about the killings. But Arthur Brushwell had met his Maker. Shad took some consolation in watching Brushwell die from the single shot to the leg. He had avenged his son. That had to be good enough.

For fifteen minutes, the debate rattled around inside the lobby until both sides ran out of steam.

"It's settled. No more feuding, at least not in Utopia. Not near railroad right of way. Kill each other all you want elsewhere in Hellfire Pass, but the town and tracks are off limits." Williamson spelled out other conditions Shad hardly listened to.

"Shake hands on the deal." Williamson motioned Leadbottom and Beatrice forward.

She held out her hand. Leadbottom vented a belly laugh, took her hand and kissed it. She yanked it back and wiped it off on her skirt. Shad tensed when her hand slipped into the folds of her skirt. He had seen how her derringer weighed down part of the cloth. Beatrice glanced at him, lips pulled back in a thin line. Then she relaxed and yanked her hand back into plain sight.

"The Gallagher family'll honor the agreement—until they break it."

"Oh, no, darlin', if anyone goes back on their word it'll be one of you Gallaghers."

Williamson headed off a new argument.

"Done. As God is my witness this day, your feud is a thing of the past," he said.

"In town," Beatrice said.

"And along the tracks," Leadbottom added. He grabbed Patrick by the shoulders and spun him around. They left the depot lobby.

Beatrice and her family members weren't far behind, leaving from the other end of the lobby.

"Whew," Williamson said, taking off his Stetson and wiping his forehead. "I don't want to go through that again."

"You should run for office," Sussman said. "Yes, that'd be good. Senator or something."

"Something to get you out of Colorado," Shad said.

"There's the whistle. The train's ready to head back to Denver. I have to give my report to the superintendent tomorrow."

Williamson and Shad walked to the train. Not many passengers rode down to Denver. Williamson would have a Pullman car almost to himself.

"It's up to you to hold both sides to the agreement."

Williamson settled his hat on his head. "I don't envy you that, sir."

"Utopia will be mighty quiet, for a while, at least. I can use the peace."

"I talked to Sussman about the telegraph," Williamson said unexpectedly. "Your telegrams to Mrs. Nelson will go through now or I'll know the reason."

"Thanks," Shad said. "I don't know if that'll do much good, but thank you."

Shad started to go, but Williamson stopped him.

"I've got something here for you, sir." He picked up the round box tied with string, bounced it up and down a couple times then thrust it out for Shad to take.

"What is it?"

Williamson indicated he should open it to find out. Shad broke the string and took off the top. He carefully pulled out a brand new brown bowler. He held it up and stared at it in admiration.

"It's a beauty."

"Try it on, sir." Williamson reached out and knocked the bullet-holed, filthy old bowler from Shad's head.

Shad lowered it slowly, then smiled.

"It's a perfect fit. How'd you know what size I wear?"

"Someone who knows such things told me when I asked."

"Someone?" Shad said hesitantly.

"Mrs. Nelson picked it out. You ought to send a telegram now and thank her for it."

"Will she . . ."

"She will," Williamson said. He gripped Shad's hand in his vise-grip and shook hard.

Williamson stepped onto the metal grate platform between cars. He turned.

"I don't reckon you got any of the telegrams Miriam sent, so I suppose I should tell you."

"Tell me what?"

"You've got a son-in-law now. Miriam and I are hitched."

Shad opened his mouth, but nothing came out. The steam whistle sounded, and the train began gathering speed.

"And there's one more thing, sir."

Shad croaked out, "What's that?"

"You have another name to get used to—Grandpa!"

Shad shouted after Richard Williamson, but the train was already beyond the station and building speed for the downhill trip to Denver.

He stepped back and shook his head. The bowler stayed firmly in place, as it should.

"Grandpa? No, not that. Never that." He turned and headed back to his office, mumbling to himself. He ran his fingers around the slick brim of the new brown bowler. "Gramps? Granddaddy? Maybe Gramps." He nodded. "That's better, Gramps."

TURN THE PAGE
FOR A RIP-ROARING PREVIEW!

JOHNSTONE COUNTRY.

WHERE BOOT HILL IS FULL OF MEN
WHO PULLED THEIR TRIGGERS
WITHOUT AIMING.

As hardworking families and ambitious dreamers
set down roots across the American West,
others swooped down to prey upon them.
And after the smoke cleared,
those who lived by the gun found themselves
facing justice—and vengeance . . .

CHAPTER ONE

The bare prison courtyard deep in Coahuila, Mexico, was hot as Hell's foyer, and Hack Long would have given anything to be somewhere cooler. Dirt and rocks packed by decades of hooves and human feet reflected the desert sun's rays back against the brick, rock, and adobe buildings, making the enclosure feel like a massive oven.

He sat on the ground in a sliver of shade with his back to the rough exterior wall, chewing at a tough piece of meat that could have come from a cow, bear, horse, donkey, or wolf. Dog, for all he and the others knew. He'd eaten plenty of dog in Two-Horses' village over the past few years, when they were in the Indian Nations.

It didn't matter. The plain, familiar stew was nourishment, and they all needed to keep up their strength for the next struggle to survive that was sure to come. Bland food was strange down in Mexico, because the smell of onions, peppers, and spices that wafted from the *comandante*'s office and the adjoining guards' barracks made their stomachs rumble several times a day.

He and the boys figured the grub they brought to them was boiled up well before anything else was added, other than the salt needed for the prisoners to survive, providing another form of punishment for all those locked up in that hellhole. Only on Sundays were their tortillas and beans flavored with *nopales* and chilis so hot they seemed to be an added punishment instead of a treat.

Hack and the hard-eye boys with him ate every bite of whatever the Mexicans dished out and were proud to get it. They had to stay strong, because only the fit could survive in a world of bandits, murderers, and thieves.

There were two kinds of men in Purgatoria. Predators and prey. Sometimes, Hack was of the mind that only the wicked survived, while the dead were finally released from the tribulations that delivered them to dry graves outside the penitentiary with startling regularity.

The Long Gang, as they were known both inside and outside of the prison, had long ago proved capable of protecting themselves, but it was essential they continued to project a sense of menace worse than what they'd been dragged into.

That made them harder men than when they had stumbled through the gates of the Mexican prison in chains. None of them were without scars, and over half of those they shared were earned in attacks and fights that usually resulted in the deaths of the instigators.

Every day, they had only fifteen minutes to eat before going back to the copper mines, though it always seemed much shorter. On that day, Luke Fischer lowered himself to the hard ground beside the gang leader and adjusted his position to keep an eye on the other prisoners. "You feel it?"

"I do." Jaws aching, Hack shifted the tough piece of meat to the other cheek and chewed some more.

One of the newer inmates, a man with a wispy mustache, passed the American prisoners, looking with dead eyes for a safe place to eat from those wolves who stole food. Swift attacks to take the weaker men's twice-a-day allotment usually spilled more than they gained. The slender young man named Escobedo had only been there for a week, and in those few days, he'd lost half of his portions as well as his shoes.

Eyes glassy with hunger, work, and fear, he sat only a dozen feet from the Norte Americanos and wolfed down his meal. Two fresh cuts from an altercation the night before marred the smooth skin over one eyebrow and on the opposite cheekbone.

Andelacio Morales rose from where he squatted with a clot of other prisoners near the long row of cells and swaggered across the bare yard. Hack couldn't *stand* that man because he stunk so bad. That's part of why he and the boys steered clear of him whenever possible.

He was also the worst, most blackhearted human being Hack had ever seen. Morales's worn-out shoes crunched on the hard-packed gravel. Even the hot air stilled as the man towered over Escobedo, who kept his eyes lowered to the tin plate between his knees. Escobedo seemed to collapse inward as his spirit vanished. Hack sensed that he wished to sink into the ground.

Morales towered over Escobedo and spoke to him in Mexican. "Your portion."

The younger man quickly tilted the bowl to his mouth and swallowed without chewing. His Adam's apple bobbed as he swallowed, and Hack wondered how he got any of that gristle down without chewing.

Morales's face twisted. "The rest of that's mine."

Like a child, Escobedo twisted sideways to protect the bowl until he could get the last mouthful.

For the past several months, the Long Gang had stayed out of the trouble that swirled around them like a *chiindii*, the Navajo word for a dust devil. That's what those little fights in the yard reminded him of, the skinny twisters of sand that walked across the desert floor. Those kinds of fights were as common in Purgatoria as breathing.

Knowing what was coming next, Hack put down his

empty bowl and rose, using only the muscles in his stout legs. The corners of his eyes tightened, and he wondered why he was getting involved in someone else's business.

It didn't matter. That familiar tingle in his head rose with a hum. There are some things in this world the wanted outlaw wouldn't tolerate, and one of them was people who preyed on other, weaker men. The red tinge at the edges of his vision would soon narrow down to a tunnel with only Morales at the end. It had happened more times than Hack or his best friend, Luke, cared to admit.

He shifted over to make Morales see a fresh target rather than his young victim. "Go away and leave him alone."

The hulk of a man didn't take his eyes off Escobedo and the tiny bit of food left in the wooden bowl. "I'm not talking to you, *gringo*."

Across the yard, Juan Perez perked up. From the corner of his eye, Hack saw the head guard grin at the incident boiling to life in the hot sun. That evil man liked nothing better than watching a good beating, and he didn't give a whit about who was on the wrong end.

When Hack was a young man, his old daddy had always said to get the first lick in on a fight and to use anything that came to hand. The only things Hack had nearby now were his fists, and Morales was hard as the packed ground under their worn-out old boots.

"But I'm talking to you, *estupido*." Hack's right fist shot out in a blur and landed squarely against Morales's jaw, spinning him to the side. A hard left landed on the point of his nose, which exploded in a gout of blood that gushed from both nostrils. The cartilage crunched under Hack's large knuckles, and the man's expression went dull.

Morales staggered backward before regaining his balance. Pursuing his advantage, Hack followed up with two more swings that immediately split the skin over Morales's eyebrow and split his cheek. The stunned man blinked several times to clear his watering eyes. Half a dozen of his *compadres* gathered behind him like regimental troops, as if preparing for a charge, shouting and urging him on.

Still behind Hack, Luke Fischer barked a laugh and rose to square off with the others. Using his fingers to comb back a tuft of brown hair from his forehead, he set his feet in case somebody charged. "Darn, son. I think I just saw water shoot out of six holes in his head."

The other members of the incarcerated Long Gang heard Luke chuckle. Two-Horses, Gabriel Santana, and Billy Lightning put their bowls on the ground and stood as one. The boys drifted behind Hack and scattered out. Had the members of the Long Gang been armed, that action would have had the makings of a shootout, with deadly results. They were all experienced gunmen and had done their share of killing both good and bad men.

Instead, they faced Morales's lackeys and prepared to fight.

Morales was an experienced prison brawler, and a couple of hard licks and a little blood didn't faze him all that much. A large man, he'd survived innumerable fights by using his weight and power. He shouted and rushed in to get his hands on Hack, where he could use his considerable prison experience gained from years of preying on weaker men.

Hack was far from weak and had no intention of letting that happen. Planting his right boot, he cocked his arm as if ready to swing. The instant Morales ducked his head to plow a shoulder into his chest, Hack settled back to use his own motion against him.

As a former town marshal, train and bank robber, and range rider who'd fought his way across most of Texas, bustin' knuckles with someone else was nothing new to the gang leader. He'd learned long ago to let a man use his own leverage against himself and almost felt comfortable with what was about to happen.

When Morales charged, Hack swiveled and dodged, at the same time grabbing the inmate's arm, and he used the man's momentum to swing him headfirst into the prison wall. The convict's skull and shoulder hit the solid rock and brick with a crack. The impact stopped the man's charge, and his knees buckled.

Morales went down for a second, but using the wall to steady himself, he regained his feet and pushed off with both hands, addled for a second time in fifteen seconds. He shook his head to clear it and blood flew. Gritting his teeth, he growled like a furious coyote and rushed at Hack.

Those friends of his were moving in, and Hack had to finish up fast. Only men who lost their tempers wanted to continue a fight just to maim and hurt. He wanted that mad dog down for good in the eyes of those who saw him as their leader, so he wouldn't have to look over his shoulder every day for the rest of the time they were there.

Morales shook his head a second time to clear the cobwebs, and droplets of blood flew like rain once again, splashing on those nearby. His face was a mask of blood that poured from his nose and a gaping split in his forehead wide enough to look like a second mouth. The edges separated enough to show his white skull, which was soon covered in red.

Hack reluctantly gave him one thing, the Mexican prisoner was tough as a horseshoe nail and had no intention of stopping. He came in again, and Hack swung a soft left that the inmate easily blocked, but it left him open, and an uppercut that started at Hack's rope belt and aimed at the top of Morales's head finished the fight. His teeth clacked from the impact that shattered his jaw, and he dropped in his tracks like a puppet with the strings cut. He hit the ground blowing bloody bubbles mixed with broken teeth.

Breathing hard, Hack faced Morales's friends and squared off with them. "This'll be the rest of you if y'all take one more step. This is over." He pointed at Escobedo. "And you leave this man alone."

Still making eye contact to maintain their machismo, Morales's men drifted off like leaves in the wind, leaving Morales unconscious in the dust. Hack's boys stayed planted where they were in case someone whirled to charge. When all the inmates were back to their places in the shade, they relaxed and went back to their own small pieces of ground.

Escobedo nodded his thanks and pushed his back closer to the rock and mortar wall, as if ensuring no one could get in behind him. He tipped the bowl into his mouth and finished the food Hack had fought for.

Hack licked his thumb and rubbed at the now raw knuckles on his left hand. With all the roosterin' between them over with for the time being, he picked up his own wooden bowl and returned to his previous spot in the shade to suck in another mouthful of the now-cold stew.

The shirt hanging on his thick shoulders wasn't much more than a thin rag, but a new rip in the back that ran from shoulder to waist parted when he sat. "It's a good thing this storm is coming." He picked up the conversation with Luke as if they'd never been interrupted. "They won't make us work for a day or two while it passes through, and Escobedo there can rest up."

Luke scratched at his brown whiskers. "I'm surprised you stood up for that feller."

Hack chewed for a moment longer and nodded at Escobedo, who watched his tormentor's lackeys haul the unconscious man off. "He'll make it now, maybe. Did you hear what happened in his cell last night?"

Luke swallowed the last of his meal. "Escobedo's tougher'n you think. He whipped Torres one-on-one."

Two-Horses stood in the sun, picking at a callus on his thumb. His face was wide, jaw solid, with prominent, protruding cheekbones. It was his White man's blue eyes that set him apart from his Comanche roots. Round in shape and always narrowed against the light, they spoke of mixed blood that almost no one, white or red, could abide.

He seldom spoke, but he seemed surprised Hack had waded into a fight that didn't have anything to do with any of them. "So why'd you help him?"

"Because what they did wasn't right. Torres paid one of the guards, and I figure it was Perez, to open Escobedo's cell after lockup. Torres slipped in, and about five minutes later they had to carry what was left of him out. They locked the cell again, and nobody said a word. That's why I think Escobedo can handle himself, but two fights so close together can drain a man down to nothing.

"The truth is, I don't like it that Perez is playing games with everyone in here. Next time it could be me or you or any one of us who's not up to snuff at the moment and can't defend themselves."

"Why did he let Torres into Escobedo's cell in the first place?" Gabe Santana wanted to know. Besides Luke, Gabe had been with Hack longer than the others. A lithe, slender man with black hair, olive complexion, and somber eyes, he'd been a man to ride the river with from the first time Hack laid eyes on him up in Llano County.

"Because I heard there was a bet over who would win."

The youngest of their group, Billy Lightning, scratched at a red spot on his forearm where a scorpion had stung him a week earlier. Looking more like a schoolboy, Billy had only a few light whiskers along his jawline and a dusting of blond strands on his upper lip. "Torres woke up in the hotbox this morning. He's still in there as far as I know."

"I knew a guy who spent three days in the Yuma hotbox," Luke interjected. "Killed him deader'n Dick's hatband. Fell out about five minutes after they let open the door. It was a crying shame for a tough man like that."

"I bet Torres wishes he'd never tangled with Escobedo." Santana stretched his legs in the dry sunshine, studying what was left of his worn-out boots.

Billy used his thumb to rub at the knot left by what he'd grown up calling a stinging lizard, which was a local description of scorpions. "You could have let Escobedo handle himself. Now you'll have Perez thinking about you and what he can do to us."

"Don't matter. I dislike Morales, and now that's settled," Hack answered. "Sometimes you have to refresh folks' memories, too."

Taking advantage of the time out of their cells and the mine, Hack adjusted himself in the narrow shade thrown by the twelve-foot wall to keep the sun off his head. The guards allowed each man a cap, of sorts, but it fit so snug, the hot material made Hack's skull feel like it was baking all day. He'd often thought he'd give anything for one of the tall sombreros worn by the locals that provided a cushion of air on top and a wide brim to shade a man's face and shoulders.

Shoot, he'd even settle for one of the military-style caps with the leather bills the guards wore. They were a by-product of the French influence there in Mexico, but Hack really wanted a good, soft felt Stetson like he'd worn across the river. All Texans love their hats, horses, and depending on the man, their dogs or women.

Only one prisoner had a hat of any sort, and that was Torres, but it would go into the grave with him if the hotbox took his life. The guards took what they wanted when a man died, and the rest was either distributed to the peasants in the nearby community, or buried.

As the boys finished their thin stew, the Long Gang sat quietly for the last few minutes allotted for dinner until an old man with sunken cheeks stopped beside them and spoke in Spanish.

"Ah, *los terribles cinco*. Do you feel it, the air?"

"The five of us aren't so terrible, unless these boys get riled, but it seems a little hotter out here than usual," Hack said. "Of course, this place is only a couple of notches below the boiling point in Hell, anyway."

The man smiled, revealing only two bottom teeth left in his head. "The wind, it comes from the south. There is a storm on the way. *Muy malo.* This time of the year, they blow off the *baja* and bring rain and life to the desert."

The last to finish his stew was Billy Lightning. He paused with the bowl still against his mouth and swallowed. "I *thought* I felt something in my bones."

"I am an old man and have seen it once for each decade of my miserable life. If I was much younger, I would ready myself to escape from this hellhole when the storm hits."

As was his habit in the Mexican prison, Hack glanced across to the guards huddled around a water bucket in the shade of a stick-and-timber portico leading into the *comandante*'s office. They were laughing and paying more attention to a dice game than their prisoners, knowing the noonday heat would dampen any ideas of trouble.

"Have you ever seen it done, an escape from this place?"

"No, but I've heard about it. No one has broken out of here in nearly twenty years. The last time was the dark of the moon, but the one before my time was when fifteen men climbed the wall. Only five got away. The others were killed by the Apaches they used to track them. For every man killed, the one who did it received two pieces of gold."

"Apaches working with Mexicans?"

"Civilized Apaches who live that way, in the Chisos Mountains."

A tingle ran up Hack's spine and an idea formed, making him feel more alive than he had for months. "How long does it take them to get a tracker from out there?"

"It would be at least a day, unless a couple were in the village for supplies or mescal."

"There's no way to get out of the cells, though, once it starts storming."

"You can be like Torres. Bribe Perez there to let you out for a midnight fight. If it was me, I would tell him you knew Escobedo outside and needed to settle with him. Perez loves to gamble like he's doing over there right now, shooting dice, and would welcome to see a match with you and Escobedo, and he'd bet on you to win."

"Well, I've already stood up for him."

"So you could kill him yourself."

Hack forced a grin off the corners of his mouth. He'd been there for so long his mind didn't seem to work, and that idea had never occurred to him. And here it was, an old man giving them all a way out, served on a platter. "Then I could take Perez, get his keys, and let the others out."

"That is a good plan."

"Why're you telling me this? This is your plan, not mine."

"Because I am too used up to fight and run. I will die here, but the other reason is that I don't like Perez and would like to see his dead eyes open and collecting dust."

Luke drew in the dust with a forefinger. "Mighty hard talk, just because you don't like the man."

"He cheated me in a dice game when I first came here and took my shoes." The old man looked down at the worn-out *huaraches* on his feet. The pitiful sandals had been repaired so many times with strips of leather they almost looked like small mops. "My good shoes would not fit him, but he sold them in the village and used the money to entertain one of his ladies of the night."

Close enough to hear, the rest of the guys remained silent, but they were working things out in their own minds. They'd learned not long after arriving at the prison that groups involved in too much discussion brought suspicious guards. They were Hack's men but had their own minds and did what they wanted. They came and went when the

Long Gang was working north of the river. Though these were his core group, there were others from time to time.

Instead of gathering to hear, Two-Horses and Gabriel Santana were stretched out along the wall, pretending to sleep. Billy Lightning sat four feet away, sanding a callus off his hand with a rock. They were all listening, and if one were close enough to feel the rising tension and elation, it was easy to tell that the men who'd resigned themselves to incarceration were once again ready to ride.

Chapter Two

The chief guard, Juan Perez, rose from an arbor shade reserved only for him and his men and sniffed the air like a dog, filtering much of the scorching air through a mustache that sprouted thick and heavy against his nostrils. In addition to the dust and manure coming from a corral outside the walls, there was a hint of dampness.

He kicked a resting guard's foot and poked another's shoulder, prodding them from the raw wooden benches against their quarters' wall. "Get up. These men need to work and a storm is coming. The *comandante* will want one last shift back to the mine before the rain falls."

Though he and the *comandante*, Raul Mendoza, would have preferred for their prisoners to work from morning to night, they long ago discovered that a full day in the mine would kill them and that a dead prisoner couldn't make money for the *jefe*'s pockets. Instead, they dug for half a day, then returned to the prison as the second shift took up shovels and picks to worry copper from the mine, then they'd switch again.

Although he acted as if irritated, Perez was pleased with the changing weather. He heard the day before that his favorite cantina server was back at work. Juana had been taken to Mexico City by a soldier loyal to Porfirio Diaz, the country's president, but for some unknown reason, he'd sent her packing, and that was fortunate for Perez. A rainy day meant he could leave the prisoners in their cells and visit with her to spend his money.

It wasn't that they couldn't work in the mines while it rained, but Comandante Mendoza was afraid the inmates would use the weather in an attempt to escape as they were moved back and forth between the mines and the prison. Better to let them remain behind bars, and besides, everyone wanted some time off, and that went for him and his men, too.

He paused to stare in the direction of the little mining village that lay between the ancient structure that was once a mission run by friars and the entrance into the low, barren mountain that looked like an animal's burrow.

Against a backdrop of gathering storm clouds and lit by the sun, which was not yet covered, two spirals of buzzards turned lazy circles over areas of interest. Perez studied the scavengers, wondering if they were human or animal bodies that lured them to those particular portions of the sky. He loved the scavengers, and he once even had the opportunity to share a *trabajador*'s pleasures while letting her do all the work as he laid on his back and stared out of an open window to watch the carrion birds float overhead.

Maybe it would happen again sometime soon. With that pleasant thought in mind, Perez remained where he was in the shade as the guards kicked the afternoon shift upright and those who'd been in the mines that morning went to their hot cells. Spending time in those hot, airless cubicles was a different kind of punishment and wasn't considered as a pleasant gift.

Finally bestirring himself, Perez used a fingernail to pick at the dirt crusted in the corners of his eyes and followed the men past the hotbox. He paused beside the sunbaked door in the windowless structure made from hand-packed adobe. "Torres, are you still alive in there?"

The man who'd been beaten within an inch of his life by the newest inmate groaned an answer, and Perez chuckled. "It seems that you are. Feel better, my friend. We need another match between you and the boy who put you in there." He gave the hotbox a slight kick, doing nothing but dislodging crumbling sand and rocks. "You cost me a lot of money, amigo. That's why you're in there. You need to earn it back and, possibly, your life."

It was a blistering afternoon. He watched the prisoners march out the front gate and went inside *la oficina del alcaide* to cool off a little and visit with the *comandante*. Raul Mendoza always had interesting stories to tell.